THE PHARAOH'S BARBER

A Mystery On the Nile

By

Marianne Luban

Also By Marianne Luban:

The Samaritan Treasure
The Exodus Chronicles
Jane Austen's Thimble

Copyright © 2007 by Marianne Luban

ISBN: 978-0-9729524-1-5

Pacific Moon Publications
PO Box 254
Ogden, UT 84401

It is Amun-Ra who speaks, the Lord of Karnak
You have come to me rejoicing when you see my beauty,
You, my avenging son, Thutmose, who lives for eternity,
Out of love for you, I show myself in my bright rays.
My heart is filled with joy over your coming to my temple,
And my hands grant you protection and life.
A wonder have I wrought for you;
I give you victorious strength against all foreign highlands.
I let your power and fear of you spread through all lowlands,
Terror of you extends to the four pillars of the sky.
I make your reputation great among all men.
I let Your Majesty's battle cry sound among the barbarians.
The princes of all foreign lands you hold in your hand.
It is I who stretch out my arms and capture them for you.
Nubians in the south I bind together like sheaves by the
Thousands and ten thousands.
And the people of the north are taken captive by the
Hundred thousands.
I let your opponents fall beneath your sandals.
Rebels you trample under your feet.
For the earth in all its length and breadth I have delivered
Over to you,
East and West are under your dominion.
Joyously you forge ahead through nations,
In your time no one dares to attack.
For I am the one who leads you, so that you meet them.
The waters of the land of the two streams you have crossed
With the strength and force which I have given you.
They hear your roar and flee into their caves,
Of the breath of life I have deprived them,
With terror of you I have filled their hearts.

Inscription of Thutmose III at Karnak

NOTE TO TEXT

When writing a novel set in remote antiquity, the conversation of the characters can be a problem. The speech of ancient peoples seemed modern and immediate to them, therefore it is hardly fair or productive to render it in an out-dated English, using the style of the King James Bible, for example. However, even in the parlance of our own day, there are two modes of speaking, one of ordinary conversation and the one of oratory and intellectual discourse. There is such a thing as "the best English", often found in writing, itself, and one cannot doubt that this applied to ancient languages, as well. This was certainly true of the Egyptian. Regardless, in this text, there are idioms that did not exist in Egyptian or in the Semitic tongues. But to restrict oneself only to constructs found in them would make this story read in a very stilted and unnatural way. Moreover, most languages contain "curse words" and obscenities, but these are not to be found in the ancient texts. Most of these are official, literary, or of a religious nature where only the highest form of the language was employed. But, where there are young men in the company of one another, casual sexual or scatological references are common and perhaps have always been, to some extent. Nowadays, they are commonly found in writing, too, but that is a fairly recent phenomenon. In previous times, that would have been unthinkable, except for the occasional "damn and blast" of the last few centuries.

A decision was also made to use the Hellenic toponyms "Thebes" and "Memphis" instead of the older Egyptian names for those great cities due to their common usage.

PROLOGUE

Even when he got older, Prince Mehy recalled the murder of the queen as clearly as though it had happened only yesterday. It was during those hours that everything had changed for him and the newly found joy in his life had abruptly vanished. Once, Mehy had a suite of rooms all to himself, adjacent to the harem, where servants waited upon him in the same manner when he was thirteen as they had done when he was three. His clothes had been put on for him, even his shoes. He had never even had a bath without someone else being present. Now that he was a man, all Mehy wanted was for people to let him alone. And they did, mostly. The staff of the palace was frightened of him now, but not quite in the same way they were of his father, the king of Egypt, who counted on being the most terrifying man on the face of the earth. The great dragon in his river, the devouring beast, the one who stopped at nothing to achieve his aims—that was how the foreign peoples in all directions saw Mehy's father. Well, it was true, and Mehy knew that better than most, even though he, personally, was not afraid of his father at all.

These days, Mehy just stayed in Caleb's old room at Thebes. That was good enough for him and what he preferred, trying to hold onto a little bit of Caleb and happier times. Also, Levi, the only friend that remained to him, followed his profession at Thebes, so there was no reason for Mehy to go to Memphis at all when the ruler moved the court. When his father wasn't around, the prince felt like less of a disappointment. As matters stood, Mehy only saw the pharaoh and his new family four months out of the year and, by the time they left in the spring, the strain of it all seemed almost insupportable. Mehy's father no longer demanded anything of him, knew better, but he refused to let his son alone and insisted on his presence. The king lectured Mehy a lot and often got angry at his passivity. The heir couldn't explain himself, didn't even know how to start. Had he attempted to, he would have had to go back to the time of the murder and Mehy knew his father didn't want to hear anything about that, a subject locked away and sealed with seven seals.

Most of those who had known Mehy when he was a boy were uncomfortable around him now. He sensed that and could hardly blame them. The change in his demeanor had been too drastic to be accounted for. Even Mehy, himself, couldn't really account for it. In all the books of wisdom he had read, there was nothing dealing with why a person's behavior became altered— except that a demon might have settled into his heart. But what was a demon, anyway? There was no good explanation for that, either, that the prince had ever been able to ascertain.

When he had grown up enough to leave the house on his own, Mehy had taken out the team and driven to the Great Place to find out what had become of Senenmut, only to discover that the old man had died. In the tomb, the prince saw that the necropolis workers had placed the architect in his sarcophagus and put the lid on it. No one had stolen any of Senenmut's furniture and his scrolls and writing materials were still there, even though the tomb stood open and unsealed. Mehy went down and instructed the masons in the workman's village to close it up and promised to send them extra provisions for doing the labor. To his surprise, the village chief told the king's son that the pharaoh had ordered the mummification of Senenmut and dispatched embalmers to perform the task. His unfathomable father, although having allowed Mehy's former tutor to rot in life, evidently found it essential to preserve him in death.

Mehy, as long as he was there, decided to have a look at his father's own tomb. Of course, it, too, stood open as the pharaoh was still living. The large sepulchre was mostly completed by then and the quartzite sarcophagus, with its carvings, ready to receive its royal occupant. By the illumination of his torch, Mehy saw that the blue ceiling was decorated with golden stars but, amazingly, instead of normal images, the walls of the tomb displayed rows of stick-figures, gods, mortals and demonic creatures, going about their activities. Probably also the pharaoh's idea—and it seemed to Mehy another inexplicable one—making the entire tomb look like a huge papyrus scroll written on by a scribe with an undistinguished handwriting or the worst artist in Egypt.

There was a little image of the king, his legs and arms no more than lines of black paint, suckling from a sagging breast that hung from a sketchy tree. This symbolic drawing appeared so comical to the prince that he had given a little laugh there all by himself in the depths of the tomb. In fact, the entire decorative scheme of his father's intended place of burial seemed comical, whimsical, anything but somber.

It then struck Mehy that the king, having had his fill of pomp, gravity and—yes—sorrow, wished to be surrounded by these droll little figures once he was dead and had no objection to their ridiculous aspect. At that moment, the thought of his father dying caused Mehy to feel almost physically ill and he hurried out of the underground cavern fashioned by the hand of man.

In his childhood, Mehy had been remarkably healthy but that, too, had ended when he was thirteen. Many others had been stricken that same catastrophic year and many had died. Mehy had survived, but the illness—or something—had drained him of strength and purpose. He had grown to be as tall as his father but that was where the similarity stopped. The pharaoh did what he had always done, but Mehy did nothing much. He didn't attend school after he became ill or take any more lessons in the things a king's son needed to know well. He never did learn to hit the bullseye every time, as Caleb had advised him he must.

Once in awhile his father had threatened him with kicking his ass and called him an idler, a slacker, but Mehy didn't care. He knew there was no way his father could make him do anything any longer. It wasn't that the prince wished to hurt or displease the pharaoh on purpose. Not at all. He really had no energy, no interest in anything around him, and didn't know how to get it back.

The pestilence had arrived in Thebes so suddenly that there was scarcely any time for anybody to escape. One day, people had been going about their business and the next day hundreds were lying in their beds, burning with fever and covered with festering spots. The prince had been mistaken about his father not allowing them to get sick or trying to save those close to him. His words to Merymaat, his Chief Physician, who had counseled his lord to go north while he could or at least send away the heir, had been

"Shall I run before this like a coward? Or my son? We must remain and give courage to the people, though we die for it."

This had been related to the prince by Levi, who had heard the entire conversation on account of being present. Levi, still a barber in those days, seemed to spend a great deal of time with Mehy's father back then, even though the constant state of mourning did not allow for much shaving of the face of the king. Yes, his father had actually grown a beard. Even the pharaoh's Theban royal barber, the other one, had succumbed to the disease, but the king had not shown any symptoms nor had Levi. But that was how it went with every plague and nobody knew why.

Mehy, now called "Amunemhat" all the time, even by his father, had refused to take a wife and, after awhile, the pharaoh had stopped insisting. Presently, whenever his father was around to look at him, there was alternating exasperation, concern or bewilderment in his eyes, as though he could no longer understand anything about his silent, solitary eldest son at all. Only Levi continued to address the young man as "Mehy" and the prince wouldn't have wanted it any other way.

Mehy, who had begun to lust after women before the murder, seemed to have mysteriously lost his sexual appetite. Levi, now a physician trained by the great Merymaat, himself, reassured him that it would return someday, but Mehy really didn't care one way or another. Nothing depended upon him anymore, anyway, as his father seemed to be doing marvelously in the sexual department, for an old fellow, and was ensuring the succession all on his own.

The pharaoh merely pretended none of what had occurred on the night of the killing of the queen had ever transpired. He behaved as normally as any king of Egypt could ever hope to do.

Everyone else did the same when it came to the murder. No one seemed to think it mattered any longer and, as far as Mehy knew, nothing remained to prove that the dead woman had ever existed except a small, foolish portrait in his father's tomb.

Certainly, the slaying was never mentioned—not before Mehy, at least. He couldn't even talk about it to Levi, the wise man who seemed to understand nearly everything about human behavior. But no one could understand everything about it; it was too difficult, too complex. The simplest explanation seemed to be that, when the murder was committed, some sort of curse had fallen upon the royal house of Egypt and no one who was still alive there felt its effect more than Mehy, himself. But on some days, when he thought about it, the heir believed that the evil had been fermenting long before that night and that things had arranged themselves, little by little, in such a way that murder was inevitable. And it had all begun with a doomed prince, who had existed long before Mehy was ever born.

It was nothing his father did against Mehy that had caused them to become estranged. Not a single thing. Even when his little half-brothers and sisters were born, Mehy continued to be the pharaoh's obvious favorite, even though he had the basic features of his mother, including those mournful eyes. The king liked to have the little kids around him, played with them, sat them on his knees. But whenever Mehy came into the room, he put them down and gave his eldest son his full attention. But the kids always ran to Mehy; he didn't know why. They wanted *his* attention, wanted him to pick them up, talk to them. Well, he did it, made faces at them, tried to make them giggle, hugged and kissed them. He liked those children. They were the only ones who didn't seem to think there was something the matter with him. One of the small girls appeared to be in love with Mehy and always told him "You beautiful, Menhat. You so beautiful." The sickness had left barely a mark on Mehy's face, even though others had not been so fortunate. Even his father seemed to be proud of how handsome Mehy had turned out to be, but the prince had no interest in being good-looking, either. Beauty caused trouble for people, and that Mehy remembered only too well. Had Caleb not been so terribly handsome, he'd still be there with him, being his friend and not a distressingly respectful one, either. And Mehy might be able to enjoy his life.

No, his father did not neglect him or avoid him. He spoke to Mehy in the same way that any man did to his adult son, the prince imagined, one who was causing him anxiety and whom he was trying to help. Every honor was paid him as the crown prince in the land, as had always been the case. But Mehy only knew that he was tired, perpetually weary, no matter how much he slept.

He stopped wanting to be king and never planned, anymore, what he would do when that day arrived in the way he had done as a lad. Mehy was devoid of plans. Had he had his way, he would have gone to live in a house in the desert, like the prince in the story, just making drawings and doing his mathematical calculations, alone as an owl and far away from the company of others who expected something from him. Mehy would have been glad to see only Levi, who would bring him the necessities to sustain him and talk to him for an hour or two. Once in awhile, in his daydreams, Mehy thought there might be some things he would like to do but, in his position, none of them was possible—even if he could somehow summon the strength to pursue them.

For some reason Levi, who used to give him advice freely as a boy, never offered that anymore. Levi also often regarded his friend with worried eyes, but didn't make any suggestions for Mehy's general improvement. Mehy, as a full-grown young man, had to be respected now in the same way as the pharaoh. Nobody could tug on his princely sidelock any longer, tell him how he should act, or call him "pipsqueak" or "imp". His father, of course, could still dress him down and that would have been Caleb's privilege, too, had he still been there. But Levi was impeccably polite these days—and Mehy didn't ask for any help.

So Mehy had to remain in the palace, waiting to see what would become of himself. He was a prince of Egypt and could only have his way in small, unimportant matters. He was as good as a prisoner in the Residence, like one of his father's captives—and that was that. There was nowhere for him to go.

Chapter One

The Egyptians knew that their leader, the man who dressed and carried himself like a royal prince, was no prince at all, even though the quality of his linen shirt and kilt was different from those of even the highest ranking among them. It was noted that he had left his jeweled collars, rings, armlets and bracelets at home, so that he had nothing about him worth killing him for. The only thing of value that remained upon him was a chain around his neck from which hung three large flies of gold. But this nobody else would dare to wear or sell, as it was an honor bestowed by the king of Egypt, himself, upon a chosen very few. It was the military decoration known as "The Lord of the Flies", meaning its owner was someone of exceptional valor and determination, one who, like the common insect, always came buzzing back, no matter who tried to repel him.

Yet even in this wilderness, this savage place, their leader insisted upon having his writing implements with him as though he were nothing but an ordinary scribe and had not once been one of the greatest men in Egypt.

During the hottest part of the day—and the heat was fearful then—when the men rested or gambled away their few trinkets, the leader wrote or drew things on a long, papyrus scroll. Just what it was he was setting down there, nobody knew or really cared. Perhaps it was a record of their long journey, some thought, but others had laughed dryly at this notion. Nobody would be able to read the writing in these regions far beyond the borders of Egypt, and the scroll would fade and crumble, for none of this party ever hoped to be able to return to his homeland. The leader had started out from Thebes with fifty soldiers and sailors, few enough to be sure. The king had selected them, himself, the hardiest of the hardy. But there had never been a test of strength and endurance like this one.

The leader's name was Ahmose, called Mesy behind his back but never to his face. Even here, far from civilization, he retained his grandeur and did not engage in unnecessary conversation with the other men who navigated the perilous waters or carried the shallow, wooden vessels overland when the cataracts were encountered. Of these there had already been five, where the winding Nile was obstructed by rocks, and the men did not doubt there would be others for this river simply went on and on. The provisions were gone and now the men ate only what they could shoot or catch. This Ahmose looked not so vastly different from the other Egyptians but seeing him naked while bathing in the river that they followed, it was observed by the men that the skin that his clothes usually covered was very light and not the yellowish color of the rest of them. Ahmose had curling black hair, but his eyes were blue. He was a handsome man—one could not help but admit—with thin lips and a long, curved nose. He belonged to the "others" and looked like them, the strangers in the land of Egypt who had come from the east.

For a man who had been sent to his ruin, Ahmose appeared as unconcerned as though he were still at Thebes, sailing on the Nile for the mere pleasure of it. He was a not a bad fellow, never mistreated anyone, and the other Egyptians would have liked him well enough had they not been sent to perish with him in the uncharted lands of the south. The king had given Ahmose the mission of finding the source of the Nile, and none of his men could conceive of a more absurd ruse for getting someone out of Egypt. What possible reason was there for the pharaoh to need to know how far the river went on so long as it continued to water the land during the season of the flood and the crops could grow? The pharaoh always needed gold and that could be found in the lands of the south, but there was plenty in Nubia, so why proceed beyond that?

This party had already been gone for over a month and there was no end in sight. Except death from this horrific heat. So far, the group had been fortunate when it came to aggressors. Small bands of unidentified peoples had watched them from a distance but had not acted with hostility toward the strangers, figuring they could not seize the splendid armaments of this small number without getting killed, themselves, but also knowing there were not enough of the Egyptians to conquer anybody or anything.

Ahmose, for his part, was resigned to his fate, whatever that might be. He was heartily sick of Egypt and what had become of his great lord, the man he had helped to reclaim his throne. The one who had shown so much promise and keenness of intellect but had proved, in a very brief time, to have the same terrible nature as the stock from which he had sprung. Ahmose had come to realize that there was nothing his former friend could not accomplish once he set his mind to it, for good or for ill, but he had preferred the latter. The king appeared to love no man or woman. What he seemed to love was power and to instill dread of him in the hearts of all those who looked upon him. Ahmose, who had never suspected such darkness in the being of the man when they were young together, sometimes wondered if the fault had lain in his own perception or whether, even then, Thutmose had the unnatural capability of concealing all but that which he chose others to know of him.

And so Ahmose, who had once believed that Thutmose had it in him to become the most humane, temperate and learned ruler Egypt had ever known in her ancient history, had been duped and betrayed. By supporting and aiding Thutmose, Ahmose now felt he had done a great disservice to those he had persuaded to rally behind the maltreated king's son. One would have thought a man who had been so misused would know better than to misuse others and would understand only too well the pain and anger caused by treachery, but Ahmose knew better now.

After the river had continued through what seemed like endless swamps and plains, Ahmose and his men had come to a place of great islands where the Nile seemed to split into two separate streams. And so Ahmose took this as an omen that he was meant to return to Egypt if it was possible to get back alive. This was the impasse, as it was now impossible to determine which of the streams to follow. It was enough, and this is what Ahmose told his men, to their great relief.

As they went ashore to try to find food, they only found they had been watched, and were captured without incident by a substantial number of tall barbarians armed with spears and shields. The Egyptians were too dejected and weary to put up any resistance. They could endure no more. Perhaps these warrior people were not really so fierce, after all, and would allow them to stay and rest with them until they were strong enough to attempt the journey back to Egypt. If these black men decided to slay them, then there was nothing to be done about that. A waste of life added to a futile errand. Here they were and here they must stay.

Ahmose, curious by nature, didn't mind having a look at where and how these tribesmen lived. No one he had heard of had ever ventured this far into unknown territory. It might be that he had come upon an honorable population—or a nation of rogues. It made no difference to Ahmose at the time, for his own land had become unbearable to him since the duplicitous Thutmose had seized control of it. And, in truth, he was no longer useful or wanted there. He was to discover that the captors had a city, which they called Saba, and that it was a mighty island fortress, besides.

On the very first day, the Egyptians were deprived of all they owned, except their kilts or loincloths and wigs. The men of Saba made much sport of the last, trying them on their own heads and laughing at one another, but evidently did not consider them worthwhile booty and they were returned. Without much delay, the captives were brought before a wizened old man, whose ribs protruded alarmingly in a way that indicated he might be ill. Yet so much deference was shown this person that Ahmose had no doubt he was the king of the place, surrounded by his courtiers. The toothless old individual was straightaway shown the possessions of the Egyptians and there was much babble in the strange tongue over the weaponry and even the papyrus scroll of Ahmose, which caused considerable mystification. Most of all, the king seemed to admire the chain with the three golden flies, which he was not long in placing about his own neck.

In due course, there came a woman accompanied by a small boy. Both were outfitted in a superior fashion and approached the aged man without any hesitation, so that Ahmose concluded they must be his family members. The king said something to the young woman and she replied, watching the foreigners the whole while. The emaciated old fellow laughed heartily, exposing his gums, and pointed to the Egyptians, saying something more to the woman.

Carrying herself with a rather haughty attitude, this female then advanced on Ahmose and his men. She studied them in a general way, but seemed to find Ahmose particularly interesting. Coming closer, she took a pinch of his skin, murmuring something. When their eyes met, the woman leapt back in fright, shouting something to the king, who then consulted with his courtiers, some of them looking suspiciously like the awful, crafty magicians every Egyptian venturing to the southern lands was warned against.

It then occurred to Ahmose that the people of Saba had never previously encountered a person with blue eyes and the question was now being debated as to whether he might be some sort of sorcerer, himself, or even a devil. Evidently it was decided that he was one or both, because Ahmose was seized by the arms and hauled before the king, being made to kneel at his feet. The old man shrank from his gaze and then hoarsely issued some sort of command, to which the young woman immediately responded with a shriek. She ran up to the king and began, it seemed, to belabor him in their tongue. No one else moved. The old one placed his hands over his ears and shook his bald head to and fro. It struck Ahmose that, king or no, the man was discouraged by the speech of the woman, probably his domineering young wife. The little boy partially hid himself behind one of the courtiers.

All at once, the female began to wail, raising her arms to the sky as though bemoaning some terrible calamity that had overtaken her. She was not at all lacking when it came to words and motioned toward the boy a few times, Ahmose receiving the impression the child was involved in her misfortunes and might yet expect some of his own to befall him. The men around the king fell to mumbling with grave faces.

At last the old man's authority appeared to collapse entirely and he coughed harshly and long, sinking down in his chair. The woman shook him as if to bring him back from the very brink of death and, catching his breath, the king murmured something that seemed to Ahmose to indicate that he had given in. In fact, he made a gesture exhorting the Egyptian to rise up. This Ahmose did and the woman grasped him by the arm in a proprietary manner. The king weakly waved his hand at her, as if to say, "Take him away and deal with him yourself. I won't be responsible for your fate now."

However, the young woman appeared to face her lot rather cheerfully and, looking up at him, directed a partly bashful yet satisfied smile at Ahmose. At this point he realized that the lady was not the old king's wife but his daughter, who had decided that, dreadful blue eyes not withstanding, this captive was a man worthy of her and far from distasteful to her sensibilities. Ahmose understood his new duty and was glad that the woman was at least a fine looking one with admirable buttocks and breasts shaped like twin hefty pyramids. For the present, he and his men were out of danger and would likely continue to be while he performed up to expectations.

The small boy, apparently deciding to assert himself now that calm had prevailed, came forward and gave Ahmose a little shove, either from resentment or as a reminder that the Egyptian was now a man with a family. Ahmose, squatting, took the lad's face between his hands, giving him a reassuring grin.

For some reason, this simple act was viewed as an even greater omen than strangely colored eyes due to the reaction it received. One after another, the people began to yell, dance about, and beat on their drums, as though it had suddenly been established that Ahmose and his followers, with their unusual weapons and appearance, had been sent to Saba by some higher power to protect and serve the interests of the boy, a great person in his own right. And there, among these unpredictable beings, Ahmose was to remain for the next seven years.

Chapter Two

"As Ra loves me", said the pharaoh, "that is a fine captive you have got there. How'd you manage it—threaten him with your razor?"

The king emitted a short, hoarse laugh that, to the youth, sounded like the croak of a great, golden frog.

Si-Bast, personal barber to His Majesty, Thutmose the Third, screwed up one eye and made a wry face. "He resisted some, O Sovereign My Lord, but I smacked him a few times in your honor and he was soon subjugated. If it please Your Majesty, I would keep him and bring him home."

The young Canaanite was lying, face down, in a very large tent on a kind of carpet of the tapestries made in his homeland. Very close to his nose were the feet of the Egyptian pharaoh, propped up on an ornate footstool. The feet were encased in sandals of embellished leather. Never in his life had the youth seen such splendid shoes or such clean toes on a man.

King Thutmose said, "Let's have a proper look at your prize" and so Si-Bast, the barber, yanked the Canaanite to his feet. Just a few moments before, Si-Bast had pushed him to the carpet in the position called "kissing the ground", the normal posture one assumed before the pharaoh—unless one was well-known to the ruler, like Si-Bast, for whom a curt little bow sufficed. But all this the boy was only to learn later and very much more. At the time, he knew only one or two words of Egyptian and had no idea of what was in store for him. To his great surprise, the king addressed him in the same West-Semitic dialect the youth had spoken all his life.

"What's your name, lad?"

Levi told the pharaoh what he was called.

"How many years?"

"I don't know for sure," was Levi's answer. "Fifteen or sixteen maybe."

"He says his name is Levi and he's younger than he looks," the king said to the barber.

"There is a trace of a mustache there, I think," the latter observed. "Ach—perhaps just dirt."

Thutmose smiled. "Yes, he is rather dirty, but I daresay he'll clean up handsome enough."

"Oh, certainly," Si-Bast readily agreed. "To be sure he will. Very good features there, a noble countenance, one might almost say, for such a lowly person."

That caused the pharaoh to laugh again and Levi wondered

what there was about him that was so amusing. His stomach rumbled and he began to feel a bit light-headed.

"Are you needed here for some reason?" the king asked the Canaanite lad.

"No," said Levi. "I mean—no, my lord. I am an orphan. I had a mother but she died. An old aunt was left to care for me but she couldn't afford to feed me. So I ran away to find work and then this man—"

"Captured you, eh? You should have fought him off. He's not so much, as you can see."

"I am...I was very hungry and weak. I thought he might give me a piece of bread."

"What's he saying?" Si-Bast wanted to know.

"He says he's an orphan," the king informed.

"Naturally," murmured the barber. "Your Majesty has made them all orphans with his victorious hand."

Thutmose shot him an annoyed glance but said to Levi, "This man wants to make you his servant. He's what we call in Egyptian a "barber", my barber. He cuts the hair from my face. He could teach you his profession."

"But why do you do it?" Levi blurted out. "Isn't it painful?" In Canaan, no man would have thought it proper to take off his beard, the sign of his maturity and virility.

"We do this in Egypt," the pharaoh told him, "because we have a lot of lice there and try to keep one step ahead of them." To Si-Bast he said, "The lad believes shaving causes pain."

26

"The very idea!" scoffed the barber.

"That is where you must come to live—Egypt," the king said to Levi. "Perhaps, since you are an orphan, you ought to do so because I am the father of all Egypt. There I will be your father, as well, and will give to you life and prosperity."

"What's that my lord has said?" asked Si-Bast.

"I told the lad that when he comes to Egypt, you will beat him no more. Upon this I gave him my sacred word as a king of men."

"By all the gods!" exclaimed the barber. "Whoever said I planned to beat him?"

"They eat well at the house of Si-Bast," the pharaoh told Levi. "Don't go by the look of him, the skinny fellow—weighs no more than a cat soaking wet. And you, too, are very lean. Go to Egypt and partake of the fat of the land."

"Yes, gladly," answered Levi. "But I shall never shave my own beard!"

Thutmose emitted another brief laugh. "We shall see what happens when you've actually got one!" Suddenly, the pharaoh's face grew serious and he peered at Levi through narrowed eyes. "Boy, this aunt of yours, was she fond of you?"

Levi shrugged. "I wouldn't say that. She's not such a bad sort, though. Just poor."

"Well, you are lucky there, son. I had an old aunt once and she was a devil!" The king turned to Si-Bast. "This lad will journey to Egypt. Henceforth he will be called 'Amun-eywy', because the great god, Amun, has sent him to you by his grace. That is my wish."

"Let it be as the sovereign commands," replied the barber. "May your great name be praised for generations to come!"

"Feed this boy at once," ordered the king. "That will be all, Si-Bast."

At the conclusion of the campaign of King Thutmose the Third in Asia, in the 27th Year of his reign, Levi, now Amun-eywy [shortened to "Yuya", for some reason] went to live in the great city of Memphis with Si-Bast. As the pharaoh had promised, the Canaanite youth got enough to eat every day and was never beaten by his master. After he had come to know him and had learned to understand Egyptian, Levi thought the barber a decent enough person. The rest of the household was not bad, either. Si-Bast's wife was there and he had a widowed sister living with him, as well as her daughter, a rather pretty girl called Takamena—"The Blind One". The slave considered this a very insensitive appellation for a sightless person, but he soon learned that almost everything was done differently in Egypt than in the place of his birth. Indeed, it was a very strange land and Levi marveled at its ways.

For one thing, nobody had any shame there. Not only were the men without beards, they painted their eyes with something that looked like soot, the same as a woman. Some of these women —and Levi had blushed on seeing them carried on their litters—

wore outfits that did little to conceal their breasts or anything else. In Egypt, they had cloth that was so transparent it appeared to have been woven by spiders instead of humans. Those who were supposed to be fine ladies looked more depraved than any harlot in Canaan, their lips and cheeks smeared with a red substance. People reeked of perfume, both sexes. On the other hand, the family of Levi's master bathed constantly, even though none of them did anything to work up a sweat. Hauling water was a major occupation for the Canaanite and, as a result, he began pouring some over himself every day, as well. His feet, formerly always a shade of gray, began to look as clean as those of a newborn babe. When the manicurist came round to do Si-Bast's nails, even those of Levi got neatly trimmed.

Everybody wore jewelry who could afford some, especially Si-Bast, who had a lot. His was of real gold and colored stones, although some of the stones did not look natural to Levi. Just made from some kind of paste. Who could have imagined an old man would want to deck himself out like that? Yet the associates of Si-Bast, of similar antiquity, had the very same inclination, each one as dandified as his fellow, waving their fly-whisks with one hand and clutching scented handkerchiefs in the other. Their garments were always in pristine condition and so full of starch that that the material stood away from their bodies like bleached paper, another thing only to be found in Egypt.

Despite their finery, the friends of Si-Bast still had leathery faces and missing or bad teeth and complained to one another about their aching limbs or spines in the same manner as the elders of Canaan. That is, when they weren't arguing over something. The only difference was that they didn't have any long appendages on their chins to tug on when they pondered the problems involved or didn't grab one another intimately by the beard and exchange spittle when the discussions became heated. If one of them had a chopped-off little beard, it seemed more befitting a he-goat than a man. However, once in awhile the slave caught one or another of these wealthy disputants fingering a bit of stubble that might have sprouted beneath his lower lip, perhaps wishing he had more to work with there.

Once the young man had learned enough Egyptian to be useful, he was sent off on errands, on the way to which he witnessed things that amazed him. He saw men squatting in the alleys to urinate like a female. People worshipped all kinds of beasts as gods and shaved off their eyebrows if a cat of theirs died. Levi's master's own name meant "Son of the Cat-goddess", a very peculiar thing for a man to be called. The Egyptian name of Levi proclaimed his own allegiance to an idol, although the Canaanite had no idea what this god, Amun, was all about—nor did Levi believe in any deity, even those of Canaan.

As for the Egyptian language, it was nasal and atrocious, with the speakers "neying" and "meying" like flocks in a meadow. In the mouths of Si-Bast and his family it did not sound so bad, but the servants and the people in the streets mumbled and gargled their words so that Levi could barely comprehend any of their speech. When he complained of this to Si-Bast, the barber had only laughed and said that he had met persons from parts of Egypt that even he couldn't understand. His master told Levi that he was to speak only proper Egyptian, as he did, but admitted that the slave had to familiarize himself with the accent of the lower classes, too, as there was no getting around that.

Even though Si-Bast shaved only the pharaoh and his own close friends, all sorts of people came to his house and consulted the barber about many things, as though he were a healer and could assist them with their ailments. Si-Bast dispensed advice freely, lanced boils, treated infected eyes, and even performed circumcisions on young men the same age as Levi. The day came when it was time for Levi, himself, to undergo this daunting ordeal and he had no choice but to submit to the barber's flint knife. At any rate, Si-Bast was skilled and Levi, eventually, had no regrets. All men in Egypt were circumcised and Levi, now an Egyptian, could not be exempt. Due to being a royal barber, Si-Bast had a fine home with beautiful things in it, more wonderful than anything Levi had ever before seen. But to Levi's way of thinking, Si-Bast was cursed because he had no son, not even a daughter. Where the young man came from, a man's true riches were his children.

For the next two years, Levi fetched and carried in the household all day long, but the work was not very difficult and he didn't mind it—except in that much of it seemed to him women's

31

tasks. He was also entrusted with honing the barber's razors, the very ones used on the King of Egypt, himself, and grew proficient at that. But sometimes Si-Bast left Memphis to accompany the ruler on more military excursions. Then he was gone for months at a time.

Meanwhile, Levi practiced the Egyptian language with the other servants and even the two ladies of the house when he felt he was able enough to exchange words with them. They seemed to like him and Levi, by the same token, had no complaints about them, either. Takamena, the young mistress, appeared to find Levi terribly humorous and made him feel like a very clever fellow. He told her some stories about his past, exaggerating all the perils he had experienced. Even though he knew how to wield a sling and had even killed a wolf with one, the wolf became a lion for the benefit of Takamena. The blind girl was the only young woman with whom Levi had ever talked at length. Perhaps, because she was lonely and isolated, she didn't mind him being so far beneath her station.

Of course, Levi couldn't tell her everything about his background. Most of that was improper for an innocent girl to hear about, so he pretended that his mother had been a poor widow and had relied upon him to take care of her. Levi was able to make such distortions believable because he had wished things could have been that way and had envisioned them differently in his own imagination long before meeting Takamena. Regardless, it was a good thing that Levi had been forced to learn to speak all over again in a new language, as he now realized that the coarse way he had talked in his homeland wouldn't have been fit for the ears of someone like his master's niece, either. Because he couldn't offer Takamena his true former self and his new self was only just forming, Levi cut water lilies from the garden pool and offered them to the girl, instead, allowing her to smell their freshness. In this fashion he attempted to let her know of his sympathetic feelings toward her and her solitude even though he was not able to relate to her his own lonely past and what had made it so.

Life was good, in general, and the young man had little cause to miss his hard existence in Canaan. He slept on the floor in the kitchen, or on the roof, upon a clean mat of rushes and had a blanket to cover himself when it grew chilly. Levi was given two white shirts and two kilts without any holes in them, mercifully unstarched. These were regularly washed by someone else. Even though he was a slave, the Canaanite was not expected to go barefoot outdoors on account of the hookworm and was presented with a pair of sandals woven from the papyrus reed. Si-Bast did not shave his head but gave him a nice, cool haircut, even praising the beauty of his formerly long, auburn locks. Since he had no status, Levi did not have to wear a wig like Si-Bast and his cronies, something at which he felt relief, as the wigs seemed to him grotesque and ridiculous looking.

Out of gratitude for all this fair and even generous treatment, Levi decided not to protest when Si-Bast finally told him to sit down and take a shave at his master's hand. By now he actually did have considerable hair above his upper lip and on his chin. Afterward, the barber handed him a polished metal object with a handle called a "mirror" and Levi seeing his face more clearly than in a pool of water, observed that he was not a bad-looking sort and that his skin was smooth and unblemished. But he frowned, anyway, as the mirror was, to his mind, another thing reserved for females, not fitting for a proper man to bother with.

"By Ptah's holy beard, I am an ugly fellow," scoffed Levi, for by this time he knew how to swear like an Egyptian.

"That's not what the women say," remarked Si-Bast, genially.

"Look at this nose," said the youth. "Curved like the *shofar,* the ram's horn!"

"If it's good enough for the king, it's good enough for you. His nose looks just like yours." The barber placed the linen towel around his own neck and told Levi to get up from the chair. "Now it's my turn. Take up the razor, Yuya."

"What? You want me to shave you?"

"Why not? Haven't you watched me shave other men many times now? At least, you were supposed to be watching."

It was true that Levi had held the implements and assisted his master in various ways while the tonsorial artist did what he did best, but was this the way to begin—to practice on Si-Bast, himself?

"But I don't know how! I'll cut you, surely. Please, master, don't force me."

"Do you think I was born a barber?" demanded Si-Bast. "There was a first man for me, too."

"Did you cut him?"

"He survived."

"Can't I try it with one of the other servants first?"

Si-Bast shook his head. "You won't be shaving servants, but a man greater even than I am. The greatest in the land, even the entire earth. You'd better get used to it beginning right now."

"What?"

"Today I cut the face of the pharaoh," admitted the barber sadly. "For the first time ever."

"No! What did he do?"

Si-Bast looked up at the youth from his seat and made one of his ironic faces. "He bled. Like any other man."

"Perhaps he really didn't mind so much," said Levi, kindly. "He's a soldier, a man accustomed to blood. Surely he has killed many men by his own hand!"

"What are you talking about, Yuya? The ruler doesn't take part in the battles. He'll mind if he gets nicked every other day, as surely as Hathor loves cows. My hand isn't so steady any longer and my eyes aren't what they were, either. I'm an old man and no longer fit to shave the face and head of the Lord of the Two Lands. What if I cut him and the wound becomes infected? Then he may die—and who will be the one to blame?"

"The way things look at this moment, I'll be the one to get

35

the blame."

"That's right—you. Except you are not going to cut the king. You are going to shave me today and every day until I'm satisfied that you are an excellent barber."

"What about you, my master?" Levi wanted to know. "What will you do?"

"Oh, I'll still shave the men of the court. They don't matter so much. But the king will be your problem any day now. Hah! The two of you can jabber on together in the Canaanite tongue. He'd like that, I'm certain."

"Do you mean I'll have to shave and talk at the same time?"

That got a laugh out of Si-Bast. "Don't be a fool. Whoever heard of a barber who didn't talk while he worked? Such a thing has never happened since the time of the ancient gods."

In fact, Levi was informed, while he learned the profession of his master, that not to talk while shaving ones subject would be considered very rude, indeed. A man expected it and that was all there was to it. However, in the case of the pharaoh, one had to be very careful, to guard ones tongue. One began by bowing, saying "good morning" and inquiring after the health of the king. If he said he felt fine, then one could begin the work. The tools of the trade would be set out efficiently by the king's servants; that was their job and nothing for Levi to concern himself about. The handwasher of the pharaoh would be the one to fetch water of the right temperature and various oils. Except Levi had to make sure the razors were properly sharpened. That was important. Si-Bast, masterful as he had come to be, knew if the implements were well-honed or not just by looking at them and Levi, for his own good, had better develop an eye for that, too. For now, he could shave off a little patch of hair from his arms to test them out in the ruler's presence. That showed the proper respect. If any of the bronze razors proved short of keen, it would be up to the pharaoh's people to sharpen them. Levi was now allowed to consider himself above such a menial task while at the royal residence. But at home he still had to work on the razors and should try to keep them in fine shape for the good of his own reputation.

If the sovereign had some complaints about his state of being that day, then one was obliged to hear them with an expression of sympathy on ones face. The same applied to other gripes Thutmose might have on any subject. Si-Bast said that, in good time, he would teach Levi about medical matters as he knew as much about them as any physician, but the pharaoh had his own doctors and would need no advice from Levi. The king had always asked Si-Bast for a second opinion when it came to such things, but most likely he would not consult a youth like himself about anything.

As a matter of fact, Thutmose knew a good deal about practically everything and Levi would be well off to listen to his lord with open ears. Hadn't he known how to speak Canaanite as though born to it? Yes, the king had always been a quick learner —just as Si-Bast hoped Levi would be. As for reading—why, the sovereign could read anything as well as the one who had written it and could doubtless write a lovely hand, himself, were he to deign to do that. But that is what scribes were good for and a king did not need to bother getting his own fingers soiled with ink.

Did Levi know anything about plants? If not, that was too bad as King Thutmose loved everything that grew and could go on about plants and trees he was raising, had brought from foreign lands yet—eternally. Truly, this was a mighty boring topic, but Si-Bast had never let on that it failed to interest him and neither must Levi, by any means. If Thutmose asked Levi any questions about himself, Levi must stick to modest responses and refrain from boasting at all cost. By the same token, one should praise the pharaoh only sparingly. Some great men ate up flattery like honey cakes—but this one didn't like it so much. He preferred sincerity and honesty. But not too much truthfulness, of course.

Learning how much of the truth to tell a king was a fine art. Si-Bast had mastered it but Levi, the novice, could do little more than feel his own way. If he were not a barber, he would be best off to say nothing at all, but a barber could not be silent and that was simply a hazard of the profession for someone in Levi's shoes and he must deal with it as best he could. On the other hand, he could count on the sovereign to lead the conversation and that was a very good thing. Thutmose was not a taciturn sort and so Levi would not have to rack his brain for something to talk about. A tremendous blessing for a newly-made barber and Levi would come to thank the gods for that each and every day.

Since Levi had not been born an Egyptian and spoke with an accent, the ignorant palace guards might be tempted to beat or mock him, drive off his donkey or pull some similar trick, but Si-Bast would take care of that by getting a document of safe-conduct for him. Once he had that, no one would dare to molest him when he approached the great house. If any of the palace women tried to talk to Levi, he should reply as briefly as possible and move on. If it was an old woman, that was a different story, but he must not be tempted to engage in any gossip with her, nevertheless.

The younger women, whether they appeared noble or lowly, he must try to avoid, lest suspicion of any sort be cast on him. The king's wives were in the harem and it was not very likely Levi would see them, so no need to worry about how to behave toward them. Oh—on no account was Levi to eat garlic or onions before going to shave the pharaoh. Moreover, he must always be washed and his teeth well cleaned. A royal barber could not go about looking or smelling like a peasant. In fact, a royal barber was practically a gentleman and had to cultivate all the manners of such.

Therefore, long lessons in proper behavior were imparted to Levi by the old barber so that he might be fit to be near a king, something the Canaanite had never dreamed would be his lot in life. Nor did the notion particularly appeal to him even now and he expressed his doubts to his master that he could become so refined so fast.

"Oh, well," said Si-Bast, "it doesn't depend so much upon refinement. That will take a little time. You are already a gentleman, in a way, because it's in your nature to be one. That's your advantage. But there are some mistakes you cannot make."

Si-Bast, the old hand, ruefully admitted there were many times when he, himself, hardly knew where to draw a line without seeming to get above his station, high enough though it might be. The problem was mainly the pharaoh and his own habit of acting too familiar with his jokes and whatnot. But he was the king and could behave as he pleased with anyone. Levi was not to emulate him in this even to the slightest degree. No familiarity with the sovereign at all. Nor was he to start telling any jokes of his own accord, unless Thutmose specifically asked him if he knew any good ones. As he probably did not, Levi was best off merely to say that he was afraid he had none to tell but to always, yes always, laugh at those of the king—but not too loudly—whether he found the jests amusing or not. As it happened, the pharaoh knew some funny stories, which Levi had not yet heard, so he would probably be all right when it came to that for quite some time.

Levi found out that, when the pharaoh stayed in his palace at Thebes, the southern residence, he had a different barber. But the ruler had always taken Si-Bast with him when he went about the business of war in the eastern lands. So Levi, too, might get to see Canaan again. The barber hoped he wouldn't try to run off when he got there and Levi thought to himself that he had no place to go and nobody to take him in now that he looked like a silly ass of an Egyptian with cropped hair, no beard, and—yes—painted eyes. The slave of the barber had long since discovered that stibium around the eyes was quite useful when dealing with the relentless glare of the Egyptian sun.

When he had finished his work, Levi should not tarry in the palace and come straight home. There would be no errands for him to run any longer, as Si-Bast's successor. All that was beneath him now, as miraculous as it may seem. If, for some odd reason or another, the king wished to continue to engage him in conversation after the shaving was done, then that was another thing. It was permitted to remain until dismissed. Otherwise, Levi was to wish the sovereign a pleasant day and express the hope and pleasure of serving him again. And that might be very soon. Should the king wish to make love to one of his wives without marring her face with late-day growth, he might call upon Levi to come back again in the evening—and do the job all over again.

Yes, for a man to have his beard removed was a necessary thing but, that being the case, he wanted it to be a sociable and relaxing occasion, taking his mind off more weighty matters— particularly should that man happen to be a mighty ruler with responsibilities and cares too numerous to mention.

"Remember" said Si-Bast, "you are not merely a man with a service to perform. You now have an office—for that is what being the pharaoh's barber implies—an office and a station. You are very young and a foreigner, besides, but the gods smiled upon you when I was following the sovereign in Canaan. I liked the look of you and I could see that the king viewed you with favor, too. It was fated to be and no one can go against the will of the gods. If I had a son, he would be the one to take my place—but there is no son. So you must do me credit and cast no shame upon my name. If you do that, as fond as I am of you, I will have you sent far south to Elephantine where it is so hot and the cataract so loud that it drives some men mad just to be stationed there. I vow I will do it and may the gods of this city strike me dead if I swear falsely! Do we understand one another?"

"Yes, master," murmured Levi, by that time near physical and mental exhaustion from all the instructions and the perilous act of shaving without drawing blood. But he had learned to do just that, at the expense of the skin of Si-Bast, which did not become infected because the barber knew enough to treat the nicks with strong wine. The remainder he drank, to strengthen himself against the onslaughts of Levi's less than sure hand. "I will act for your praise," the young man promised in the best fancy Egyptian and was rewarded by a satisfied smile from his temporary victim.

"Oh—and one more thing" added Si-Bast. "The only time you will have a day off is if—and the gods forbid it should happen—the ruler takes very ill or leaves for the south. Someone will be sent here to tell you not to come to him. Or if someone close to the king dies. Then he will be in mourning and will leave off shaving for a while. That's how it goes. Ah, there is no sadder figure imaginable than a king of Egypt with whiskers bristling all over his face! What is perfectly acceptable in a lowly man is shocking when it comes to the pharaoh, the one with the uraeus on his brow. I hate to say it, but it makes him seem not just ordinary —but something worse. Pathetic. Pitiful. Beggarly. It sickens the heart. No—don't laugh, Yuya! You have never seen this, but I have and I know of what I speak. Ah, yes—things will go well in Egypt so long as you make that trip to the palace each day."

Chapter Three

Because he had the document, signed and witnessed by several great men of the court, Levi the Barber had no trouble entering the palace on his first morning there. Despite the warnings of Si-Bast—who had decided not to accompany him that day—no flirtatious women accosted him. Nor did anyone try to make conversation with him. A silent old servant led Levi to the pharaoh's private chambers and then left, instructing the barber to wait for another lackey of the king.

So Levi stood in the corridor and waited to be summoned. Suddenly, he saw the face of a woman peering at him from behind a doorway. Was this the sort of trouble of which his master had spoken? Levi pretended he had not seen the girl and stared up at the beautifully decorated ceiling. Not very surprisingly, the lady came out and walked toward him. Levi began to perspire, anticipating that this was to be some sort of trial of his conduct when it came to the female gender.

The woman approached him and stared at Levi rather rudely. She was so gorgeously dressed and wonderfully scented that the barber thought she must certainly be one of the pharaoh's wives—not hidden away in the harem, despite the assurances of Si-Bast. The woman, a young one, wore a dark wig made up of thin plaits that hung around her shoulders, their ends fixed with golden beads. Since he was now a barber, Levi had to take an interest in wigs and had even learned how they were made. At the top of the wig, adorning the crown of the head, an extra layer of curls had been added, the color of which looked very familiar to Levi. If he was not mistaken, something had possessed his grinning baboon of a master to give his own shorn locks to this lady, who had made use of them in this startling fashion!

The lady, upon closer inspection, was not so very young, after all. She had some fine lines around her great, dark eyes and, even though they were painted with kohl, Levi noticed faint circles like bruises beneath them.

"You must be the new barber," she said in a soft voice. "The one trained by Si-Bast, himself. He spoke to me of you."

"Yes, my lady," replied Levi. "They call me Yuya."

"It would seem the loss of your curls was my gain."

"They suit you much better," answered Levi gallantly, albeit nervously.

"You are very young. But you are tall!"

"Yes, my lady."

"I am the wife of the king. They call me Neferura."

"Ah! A very great honor, Mistress of Egypt!"

"You are a pleasant young man."

"If it pleases one to say it."

"Yes, you are quite pleasant," repeated the queen. "I pity you for having inherited your position."

"Surely it is my great and good fortune to serve His Majesty!" protested Levi.

"My husband is a monster," said the queen in the same soft tone that had never varied. "Beware of him." With those encouraging words, the exalted lady turned from Levi and walked back to the room whence she had come.

King Thutmose was seated in a beautiful chair in his private chamber. Levi had not seen him even once in the last two years and, truly, he appeared quite different from the day Levi had first set eyes on him. The ruler was dressed in a simple robe, wore no jewelry, and had nothing covering his shaved head on this day. Si-Bast had told Levi that the king was about forty years old. He wasn't exactly a handsome man but of very interesting appearance. His eyes were a light brown color, the same as those of Levi, and his skin was ruddy.

"Enter and welcome!" said His Majesty, genially enough for a monster.

Levi's mind was whirling. What was it that he was supposed to do next?

"Cat got your tongue, eh?" said Thutmose. "Put your chest

down on that table."

Making a little bow, Levi complied. As soon as he set down the small chest that contained his shaving implements, or rather those belonging to his master, a servant appeared as if by magic, opened it, and began to lay out the items on a linen cloth.

"So," continued the king, "our Canaanite has come up in the world. Good fellow! That smooth-tongued rascal of a Si-Bast was like to slit my throat any day. By the look of you, you'll finish what he just missed doing." Thutmose turned to his servant. "Put down that gear and fetch this young man a chair before he collapses. Get him a drink—some wine. We can't have him in this state. And get me a cup, too, while you're about it."

Levi had not tasted wine since he left Canaan. Some swill the Egyptians called "beer" was all he ever got at Si-Bast's. The people in this land drank the stuff like it was water. A cup was handed to Levi and he took a big swallow as his mouth felt very dry, indeed. The vessel was made of nothing less than gold.

"Don't get drunk," the ruler cautioned, grinning. "Oh, by bloody red Seth—what if you do? It's your first day and it calls for a bit of a celebration. Here's to your good health, Levi!"

"No one's called me that in two years," said the young man. "I'm amazed Your Majesty recalls my old name."

"What do you prefer—talking *lashon* Canaan or Egyptian?"

"I think I can manage in Egyptian now, Sire."

"So it would seem. Well done, lad."

"How is your health this morning, my lord?"

"Oh, stow that rubbish! Don't start in talking like that proper old dustball, Si-Bast. He's a good enough fellow but a change from him isn't exactly unwelcome, if you know what I mean. He'll get his pension so let him enjoy his cozy old age. What are you waiting for? Drink, drink! We've got prime stuff here. Nicked from all the best vineyards of the east."

Levi another took another gulp. It was very good wine, indeed.

"That's better," said Thutmose. "So how's life been with Si-Bast, anyway?"

"He's a good master. One can't complain."

"Married you off yet?"

"No!" exclaimed Levi. "Who would marry me?"

"Wait and see. I was married at the age of twelve, myself. Put in the yoke before my horns were even fully grown, so to speak."

"Weren't you frightened?" Levi couldn't resist asking. "Twelve is so young."

"The details were as follows," said the sovereign. "Ten men brought me to bed. They didn't leave but just stood there smirking at me. My aunt—surely you've heard of her, the witch—brought in her daughter, the princess, just a small girl of about five who still played with dolls, and a lot of old hens who came along for the show. The princess was crying and I was shaking like a rabbit. The last thing I wanted was to be someone's husband.

Some priests mumbled some incantations for half an eternity and finally the entire mob left me alone with my little wife, whom I had never met. I thought the wretched thing would never leave off bawling but she finally fell asleep, sucking her thumb. I had my instructions not to lay a hand on her because she wasn't grown up yet—not that I had any intention of touching her. She didn't even have breasts. When the princess quit her sobbing, I got out of bed and spent the night studying the stars—the way they'd taught me to in the temple. That's where I had been living even before the king, my father, died. In the morning, the queen, my aunt, came in with her women, woke up the princess, and inspected the sheets! I don't know what the devil she was looking for—maybe she thought someone had wet the bed!" Thutmose made a chuckling noise, but it sounded rather bitter to Levi. "So I was packed off back to the temple of Amun and didn't return to the palace at Thebes for the next ten years. I had just been made king, but I was king of the sands that blew in the wind—of no consequence whatsoever."

Levi stared at the king in amazement, not knowing what to say.

"Well, that's all in the past, eh?" said Thutmose. "Calmer now? Ready to hack away at me?"

"Yes. I mean—I think I am ready to do the shaving now." Levi noticed that the stubble on the pharaoh's face and head was bright as copper.

"There's a good lad." The king turned his head and yelled

"Bring the water for the royal barber!"

By the time Levi got back to the house of his master, Si-Bast had worked himself into quite a condition. Seeing that Levi, himself, appeared rather pale, the old barber grabbed him by the neck of his shirt. "You've been gone an age! Did you cut him?"

Levi shook his head. "No, all went well."

Si-Bast let out a great sigh of relief and sank into a chair, fanning himself.

"Merciful gods," he groaned. "It's a wonder I didn't drop dead from the worry. Sit down, Yuya. Tell me everything that happened."

Levi related that he had met the queen, omitting the part about her assessment of her lord. He told Si-Bast that the king had given him some wine and asked him to have a seat while relating the story of his wedding night.

"Ha!" said Si-Bast, looking surprised but content enough. "What do you think of that! His wedding night. Some story that must have been!"

"Master, the king sent you a message." Levi opened the barber's kit and retrieved a small papyrus scroll. It was tied with a strip of the same material and signed with the royal seal. He handed it to Si-Bast.

"Now what?" wondered the barber. "The ruler knows bloody well I can't read. Now I'll have to go out and find some scribe to tell me what this says." He slapped his black wig on his head and tugged it down over his ears. "I'll be back shortly. Tell them to make you something to eat. Take a nap—you look all done in, yourself."

But Levi could neither eat nor sleep and just waited for the return of his master. He did not know the contents of the scroll but, somehow, he had a sense of ill foreboding about it. Sure enough, when the barber came back, his wrinkled face was an astonishing shade of red. When he tore off his wig and tossed it on the table, Levi noticed the veins of his forehead were enlarged with rage.

"Yuya!" he roared. "Of all the blasted fortune! The sovereign has given the order that you are to bring your things with you tomorrow morning and come to live in the palace!"

"But, master, I don't want to live there!" said Levi in all sincerity.

"Do you think I want you to?" the old man shouted. "How can he do this to me? You belong to me—to my house. The king, himself, gave you to me. And now all he thinks of is robbing me!"

Levi helped Si-Bast into his favorite chair. "Please, master, calm yourself. You'll become ill."

"I know what this is all about," said Si-Bast. "You remind him of himself when he was young. You look like him. Now he wants to take a good boy and corrupt him, turn him into a beast like himself!"

Levi had always known that his master liked him, but he had never realized the extent of that fondness until he heard Si-

51

Bast call the sovereign, whom he had normally praised at all times, a beast.

"You can't read any more than I can," the barber went on, "so you don't know what's in that safe-conduct document I gave you. It says right there that I had the intention of marrying you to Takamena so that you could become a real citizen of Egypt. When I die, she gets a quarter of everything I own. Her mother gets the other fourth, but all that would stay right here because my sister has nowhere else to go. You would have made out pretty well—the whole lot would have been yours. Meanwhile, you'd have been my nephew—in a manner of speaking—and a slave no more. You would have been a man of substance—but now the gods only know what will become of you!"

"Master!" said Levi. "I hardly know what to say. I had no idea!"

"Of course you're grateful," scoffed Si-Bast. "What else could you possibly be? You're a fine lad. No man could ask for a better heir. So, you see, the king has robbed you, too. He'll never let you come back here now."

"Perhaps he will," said Levi, encouragingly. "After awhile, I'll ask him to let me return. I'll marry Takamena, master. I like her. She's sweet and pretty. I don't mind that she's blind. I want to be your nephew! This is the only good home I've ever known."

Si-Bast patted Levi's arm. "I believe you, son. But...I know him. He obviously wants you around. So do I. If I'm reluctant to part with you, why should it be any different with the king? You're a good boy—no, a good man. You're worth keeping. So—there's nothing to be done. You'll go on the morrow and live amid splendor and untold wealth—none of which can ever be yours."

Levi frowned. "It's a wonderful place, the Residence. But it gave me a strange feeling. There's unhappiness there, I think."

"You don't know the half of it," said Si-Bast dourly. "But I will tell you now."

The information imparted by Levi's master was both astounding and puzzling. King Thutmose's father had passed from life when the present ruler was a mere boy. There being no other son, Thutmose was the unquestioned heir to Egypt's throne, even though he lived at the great temple of Amun at Thebes, where he had been sent by his aunt, who was also the primary wife of his father, to put him out of her sight. Most of the people in the land were not even aware of the lad's existence and his mother had been a mere concubine at the harem of the Faiyum, the oasis to the south, an obscure woman of no high station.

However, young Thutmose was fished out of the temple and the crown was placed on his head. But the new pharaoh had nothing to say about anything and few supporters in the southern capital, so the widowed queen ruled the country for all practical purposes. She was, indeed, very clever for a woman but not half so clever as she thought herself to be. In fact, even this lady got confused at times as to just what the proper protocol was. She married her only daughter, Neferura, to the new king—as that was the princess's due—but then promptly sent the boy back to the temple of Amun to be cared for—or rather carefully watched—by the priests there, most of whom were afraid of the cunning, headstrong widow and did not want to run afoul of her.

After awhile, the queen, whose name was Hatshepsut, committed an act never before seen in Egypt since the time of the birth of the oldest gods. She made herself pharaoh—yes, a woman king. A few other women had taken the throne in times past, but only because there were no living male heirs. Hatshepsut's excuse for doing this was that the heir of her husband was not actually fit to rule. The High Priest of Amun, himself, had confirmed her suspicions about the defects in the boy and reported that he got worse every year. The heir was sullen, rarely talked except in grunts, and showed neither reverence for the god nor his chief servitor. He didn't perform his priestly duties and wasted all his time reading frivolous books, smuggled in by unknown persons. When the High Priest had attempted to deprive him of his scrolls in order to correct his ways, the heir had acted like a mad dog. And that was when he was only a lad.

Since he had grown older, he was perceived as positively dangerous to be around and even the High Priest couldn't trust his life around this charge of his. He had to have the youth confined to a single room whose door was kept bolted from the outside. Only Prince Ahmose, that foster son of the old queen,

Meryetamun, could safely approach him. At any rate, Ahmose was respected by his fellow priests and behaved normally. He could very well become High Priest someday if he continued on the proper path and confirmed allegiance to his royal mistress. Thus spoke Hatshepsut, who would just as soon have had the handsome Ahmose achieve that great office, being no less partial to a fine-looking man than others of her sex.

Nevertheless, statues of her were carved showing her dressed as a man although, in reality, Hatshepsut continued to wear the garb of a female—except for the kingly crowns. Sometimes she even tied on a false ceremonial beard. In this manner she reigned for many years as King Maatkara, her throne name, an enigma even to the gods, who knew everything.

In the meantime, great attention was paid to her child, Neferura, whom everyone suspected the woman king was grooming to be her successor—as though forgetting that the princess was supposed to be the mere consort of her half-brother, Thutmose.

After some years went by, certain people began to grumble that all this was against *maat*, the true and proper way of doing things. Was Egypt to be under the hand of women from now on? How was the Egyptian army supposed to go to war with any nations with a female leading it? Unless one expected the opposing forces to lie down and die of derisive laughter. A woman could not show her face on a field of battle and a pharaoh who merely stayed at home while sending his men off to fight was as good as a coward, who could never hope to command the respect of anyone. Even if he failed to do any actual fighting, the king had to be in his place so that the enemy could at least see the glory of his god-like presence.

Little by little, some influential Egyptians in all parts of the land began to recall that they had never heard about the boy-king, Thutmose, having died and that he should still be around somewhere. A few of the bolder nobles and chiefs of the nomes, the various sectors of Egypt, thought an inquisition ought to be made into the matter, to determine whether the youngster who was once crowned really had anything the matter with him at all. A scandal began to erupt and so Hatshepsut, fearing for her position, brought the true king back to the palace. By now the lad had grown up.

Thutmose, instead of raving like a lunatic, merely proved to be a rather quiet, self-contained individual. Those he encountered at the palace found him courteous enough. He read the 42 books that contained all the wisdom of Egypt from olden times and even tended plants and trees like a common gardener. At night, he observed the stars and made notations about them, as he had been trained in astronomy and enjoyed watching the heavens. Mostly, the young man kept out of his aunt's way.

Persons with eyes in their heads could see a certain something about Thutmose that told them he was far from a fool. A man has a way of impressing others even without saying too much. It was said that he had "the eye of the falcon", disquieting and inscrutable.

Hatshepsut, a very wily woman, decided the best thing to do at this juncture was to make a nominal partner of the young man for public purposes. Even though Thutmose was by now well of an age to rule alone, Hatshepsut began to show him on her monuments with his own throne name, Menkheperra, following behind her own image as a kind of copy of herself—as though that were fine with him and he was content with the entire state of things, being but half a man with half a wit. People in general, those who had never even seen the nephew in the flesh, began to believe that this was truly the case and the scandal quieted down.

Thutmose had never been instructed in the martial arts while still a prince, but whenever there was some trouble or rebellion within the lands of the empire, Hatshepsut sent the young man to deal with that, probably hoping that something might happen to him as a result. But nothing ever did, even though he was often gone for long periods of time. It seemed to Si-Bast that he was glad enough to get away from Egypt and his untrustworthy aunt. Whatever tasks were delegated him, Thutmose proved to handle efficiently and Hatshepsut began to view this as a very good thing for herself and her status. Her younger counterpart kept the peace for the land and was, himself, causing no problems. She became a builder on an impressive scale and the people of Egypt, taking this as a sign of the contentment and pleasure of the gods, became, themselves, complacent and content with the royal arrangement. They still knew next to nothing about Thutmose, even though his name continued to be on a monument here and there. The only ones who were in contact with the "junior king" were the soldiers who accompanied him on various missions and he came to win their admiration.

Whenever he was in Thebes, Thutmose and Neferura appeared together as husband and wife on certain state occasions and even started to like one another quite well, according to Si-Bast, enough to actually cohabit as a genuine couple. This happened with the consent of Hatshepsut, who by now had given up on the idea of Neferura becoming her heir and yet another woman king. So matters continued for six years, neither rival being able to get rid of the other.

Suddenly it happened that the silent partner of Hatshepsut took it into his head to flee his circumstances. One day he was there and the next he was gone. It was as though he had really disappeared for good this time. No army had gone with him. Of course, some suspected that Hatsepsut had finally done away with the young man and that his body had been thrown into the Nile to be devoured by crocodiles.

But nobody could prove that such a thing had occurred and the woman king publicly swore by the name of her august father, King Thutmose the First, that she had no knowledge of what had happened to her nephew. Since it was well known that Hatshepsut had enormous reverence for her late father, nobody believed she would swear a false oath invoking his great and heroic name. So Thutmose was temporarily forgotten yet again. In his absence his wife, Neferura, who was pregnant at the time of his flight, bore him a son. The most surprising development in the matter was that Prince Ahmose had vanished, too, leaving behind the life of privilege and royal favor he had enjoyed since his childhood.

In the twenty-first year of his reign, counting from the time he was crowned as a boy, Thutmose resurfaced in an unexpected manner. While Hatshepsut was at Thebes, the nephew came to the royal residence at Memphis and declared himself "king of the northland". Somehow, while in hiding from his aunt, he had managed to acquire many loyalists and even a considerable army, many of whom were men of foreign extraction living in the north. Nobody in the south knew exactly by what means Thutmose had amassed so many supporters.

The truth was that Hatshepsut, herself, had alienated the north by virtually ignoring it and allowing the foreign element to grow very numerous there again, especially in the eastern part of Lower Egypt, despite the fact that her predecessors had warred against these peoples and even driven them out—back into Canaan whence many of them had come. But foreigners always came back by some means or another; a ruler had to be constantly vigilant against them. It was with these people that Thutmose had somehow made common cause. Also, at Memphis, those of the court remembered something Hatshepsut had done against her dead husband and the memory of this was as a stone in their bellies—so they allowed Thutmose to enter the palace as ruler there without any resistance.

As though a northern tempest had blown southward, Thutmose marched in that direction and nobody stood in his way until he got to Per Qerhet, a place in Middle Egypt. There he met whatever forces the surprised Hatshepsut could muster and a great battle ensued. No one was declared the winner, however, and Thutmose retreated. Nor could Hatshepsut's army pursue him. Each side had incurred too many losses and it began to seem as if Egypt would be divided as in times past, with one ruler in the south and another in the north.

But, in the following year, Thutmose came back with even greater force. This time he could not be repulsed and most of the men of the army of Hatshepsut defected to him, anyway. He had shown them that he was the true grandson of a great warrior and this was a kind of revelation in the sight of the people. They had been duped for the past two decades. There was nothing lacking in this heir and he had proved to be a "lord of the flies", one who persisted and came circling back even though a woman wished to whisk him away with her mighty flail. The northerners called him *Baalzebul*, with the same meaning. Lord of the Flies, the one who would never relent.

Besides, according to *maat* he was his father's son and should have been sovereign of Egypt in his own right long before. What had been his had been taken from him unlawfully and, in the blink of an eye, all those who had once supported the woman king either from fear or greed now proclaimed that she had never had any business to usurp the kingship at all. Even the High Priest protested that he had been put in the position of a jailer by Hatshepsut against his will. Never once had he given an ill report of the true sovereign to that conniving widow. The reign of the female pharaoh, though not lacking in prosperity, was over.

Levi thought he had never heard a better tale in his entire life. The cleverest story-teller could not have invented anything nearly so full of twists and turns or a more wonderful ending.

"They called him *Ha Zerah* in Canaan, the Hornet—only it isn't meant as a compliment. But, yes, it was justice done there," Levi admitted to Si-Bast. "And what became of the woman king?"

"It was not good what happened," the old barber declared. "In fact, the like had never been seen in our land since the nation was formed."

When the new ruler of all Egypt arrived at the residence at Thebes, Hatshepsut met him before a large gathering. She had summoned everyone she was able to, so that there might be many witnesses to the bravery she intended to display before the victor, a final gesture to prevent her name from going down in total infamy. Naturally, many other people showed up of their own free will, just to see what would take place when Thutmose confronted his long-time enemy, who was his step-mother and yet of his own blood. Another woman might have thrown herself on the ground before her conqueror and begged his mercy, but Hatshepsut was the proud daughter of her father, a mighty king of Egypt.

"She couldn't bring herself to do this thing—and it may

have done her no good, in any case. I was there. I heard and saw everything. The woman king got up from the throne and stood aside. She said to her nephew, 'Take what is yours but don't forget that it was by the generosity of my heart that you lived to see this day. Let me therefore live another and show yourself no less generous or noble.' I believe Hatshepsut thought this a good speech and it was perhaps her way of asking for clemency without debasing herself. In a sort of false-hearted way, there was even truth in what she said. Indeed, the overreaching woman might have contrived to kill her nephew somehow while he was helpless, but never did this."

"Even so," said Levi, "who could blame him for taking his scimitar and cutting off her head then and there?"

"Right," agreed Si-Bast. "No one would have thought it a dishonorable act at all had he done it. All of us were prepared for it to happen—but none was prepared for what actually did occur. The ruler made no answer to his aunt's words. Unaccompanied, he walked toward her and simply stared into her face, a smile on his lips, looking rather kindly, as though he might pardon her, after all. Then, with a single gesture, he tore the covering from her breasts. With both hands, the ruler pulled the rest of the dress over the hips of Hatshepsut so that it fell to the floor and she was exposed naked for all to see. She let out a gasp and covered her lower parts with her hands, looking about her to see if anyone would come to her aid.

The only one who dared to was Neferura, who ran up to

place herself between her mother and her husband. But Thutmose threw Neferura aside as though she weighed nothing. The young queen fell to the floor, injuring her shoulder badly and crying out with pain.

Now, the great throne of Egypt is very heavy, covered with gold and gems, but the ruler seized this and overturned it easily. He took hold of Hatshepsut and pushed her down over the toppled chair so that her backside was exposed to him. He shouted 'You wanted to be a man? So now you get it in the ass like the kind of man you were!'

One of the pharaoh's friends, that same Ahmose who had fought at his side, called out to him 'Is this what we came for?' but Thutmose ordered him to leave the hall. Then he summoned some of his other men to come forward. A group of them did, eagerly enough—and the king turned on the people, saying, 'Which of you cowardly servants of this thieving woman wants to join her?' And so, starting from that day, King Thutmose began to put the fear of himself into the hearts of all mankind."

"Do you think the pharaoh actually raped this Hatshepsut?" Levi asked.

"Who knows?" replied Si-Bast. "We all left, with me carrying Neferura, who had fainted. Nobody saw what occurred except those men of the king who stayed behind, but I have no doubt the woman got raped—by somebody. To this day, Neferura believes her husband took part in it. I don't know what to think. Anyway, after that nobody saw Hatshepsut alive again. I don't even know what they did with her body."

The barber added that he, himself, had had no fondness for Hatshepsut. The royal lady had played a dangerous game and lost. But Neferura he had known since she was born and he considered her the true victim of the power struggle.

"She was a good girl," Si-Bast said. "Her tutor was a friend of mine and I know she had a decent upbringing. Neferura was taught right from wrong. But after that dreadful incident, she took her mother's place as the pharaoh's arch-foe. Not in the same way, of course, but Neferura alone does not fear this king."

"Why not?"

"There is nothing more he can do to her," said Si-Bast, but gave no further explanation about that.

Levi looked around him at all the fine things his master had acquired. "But the pharaoh has not mistreated you surely."

"No," admitted the old man, "not until today! Everything here is due to the generosity of the ruler. But, then, by his own reckoning, he owes me something. Yes, he keeps a careful tally here in this land—and the man always pays his debts. But he's changed—never stops talking now, scheming and twisting things to suit himself with his clever tongue while acting the part of a beneficent ruler. He's no different from that Hatshepsut, only worse. She fooled no one, only caused fear with a heavy hand. But the other...I thought he was well disposed toward me, would respect my desires in a matter that is none of his business and by which he has nothing to lose. The plans of an old man count for nothing, it would seem. Not when his usefulness is done."

Throughout that night Levi hardly closed his eyes for thinking about the things that Si-Bast had revealed to him. He tried to imagine what he would have done had he been treated as the young Thutmose had and concluded that, being thus wronged, he would have followed the same course—except simply beheaded the wicked woman at the end. No man worthy of his name and heritage could have done less. A female stealing a throne from a man was a crime against nature, a mad thing to do. But how could it be necessary to humiliate her so savagely?

That part Levi could simply not comprehend and also failed to reconcile such brutal behavior with the kindness the pharaoh had shown him just the previous morning. And so the new barber made up his mind not to trust in the friendly manner of the new master he was bound to serve and to tread very carefully in his presence, lest one day the king might take a notion to subject him to the same humiliation he had afforded that Hatshepsut. After all, a man who could bring himself to possibly ravish his own elderly mother-in-law—and Si-Bast had told Levi that the woman was far from young at the time—was capable of just about anything.

Chapter Four

"**W**hy so glum?" asked king Thutmose on the following morning. "Miss your old master, do you?"

"Yes, my lord," said Levi, truthfully.

"You'll be grateful to me one day for having rescued you," said the pharaoh. "Or did you really want to marry Si-Bast's niece?"

"I don't know, my lord. She's a fine lady. I never thought about marrying her."

"Of course—why should you have? Yet, had you remained with Si-Bast, you'd have had no choice. Listen, boy, is your hand going to tremble like this every day? Do I need to fill my barber up with wine each time just to get a shave?"

"No, my lord," said Levi. "It's just that everything has happened so suddenly. I only learned how to be a barber this past month!"

"How much can there be to it? Nobody's asking you to

perform alchemy! All right—sit down. Calm yourself. No need to be so pale. I won't bite you."

Levi lowered himself into a chair. He was perspiring all over.

"No more choice than I had," Thutmose went on. "You would have been stuck for life with a blind woman—just as they shackled me to a bitter, unyielding one. And there wasn't a blessed thing I could do about it. My aunt, that scheming cow, didn't allow me to have any other wives while she lived—even made it plain I wasn't good enough for her precious darling. But, since no other man in Egypt was good enough for the princess, either, that left only me. So I was chained to my half-sister, just as my father before me was shackled with his. Do you understand?"

"That is the custom of the kings of Egypt," acknowledged Levi.

"A dangerous one," pronounced the king. "No wonder Neferura, my wife, turned out as she did. I was lucky. My own mother was no relative of my father. You can just imagine how my father's chief wife, my aunt, felt when I was born. Fit to be tied she was with rage. Of course, she was still young then and might have had a son of her own. But she never did, as it turns out. All that bitch ever whelped was Neferura."

Levi's response was one that Si-Bast had warned him against, but he simply couldn't help himself. He had been the Royal Barber for a mere two days, but he was already weary of hearing about the pharaoh's lack of regard for his queen and he recalled all too well the sad eyes of Neferura. Levi couldn't change the subject, but perhaps he could lighten the mood. He was a barber now and must make conversation.

"Have you heard the one about the man who wanted to divorce his wife?" he asked his lord. The joke was an old one in Canaan, but perhaps the Egyptian king had never heard it.

Thutmose looked at him in surprise but answered, "Go ahead. I'm listening."

"There once was a man who had married a woman who was blind in one eye and had no claim to beauty. After living with her in peace and harmony for twenty years, he decided he wanted to marry a pretty young girl, instead. The man approached his wife, saying 'I must divorce you. You are old, ugly, your teeth are going and you are blind in one eye, besides.' The wife answered her husband in this manner: 'You are older than I, ugly as they come, entirely toothless—and if you couldn't see anything wrong with me for the past twenty years, then it is you who are the blind one!'"

The ruler chuckled appreciatively. "I'll remember that one. I like your manner. You're modest but not dull. Your Egyptian is excellent—you must be a very clever man! Si-Bast shall not fit you in his mold, as much as it might satisfy him."

"I think he meant me well, my lord," said Levi.

"In his fashion, yes. But perhaps I mean you better. Si-Bast does not know you, cannot know you. Forget him. I'll tell you what the situation is here, as you might as well know how matters stand. Don't listen to people's gossip. If there's something you want to know about me, don't be afraid to ask. But ask me."

The young barber stared at his new master. What caused the man to imagine that he would even think of asking him any personal, prying questions? Well, Si-Bast had warned him that the ruler affected a familiar way of talking, but Levi had to admit he found that rather reassuring. What disturbed him was the king's objection to Takamena and the proposed marriage. Why should any of that matter to him at all?

"Levi, I can't divorce my wife, even though there has been no peace and harmony between us since Horus the Ancient was but a chick in the egg. She's my father's only daughter and must remain the queen, though I don't go near her. I've found me a new wife, a real little beauty. When I was a small boy, I had a nurse who was good to me by the name of Ipu. My own mother was kept away from me, so Ipu was all I had. I hadn't seen her for quite some time, but recently I paid her and her husband a visit. To my great delight, one of her younger daughters had grown up to look like a goddess. Satiah is her name, a true child of the moon, as her name implies, with a face as fair as the Milky Way, and no more than sixteen. Now Satiah is here with me and her parents couldn't be happier."

"May she give Your Majesty many sons," said Levi, dutifully, although he couldn't comprehend how a girl of sixteen could stomach an old man of forty, king or no king.

As though reading the barber's mind, the pharaoh said, "The parents are happy and I am happy but Satiah...that's another matter. I even gave her brother a post here to please her but...now it seems I have two wives who dislike me instead of only one—no, make that five. I shouldn't omit the three women from your own land. I never asked for these, but here they are nonetheless. A king cannot send back a gift."

The sovereign sighed heavily and Levi decided he'd better play his part.

"It's a wife's duty to love her husband," he suggested, only repeating what every man knew to be the primary rule of marriage. "Surely the wife of your choice will do so, given time. She's just in awe of you now. Who wouldn't be?"

"You're not," observed the king. "Not really. You had the courage to try to make me laugh—and you're about the same age as Satiah."

"I don't have to kiss my lord, a king feared by all peoples, high and lowly, in every land. Sometimes mere shyness and modesty may be taken for dislike."

"You're a quick-tongued young devil," Thutmose said, but in an amused way. "Si-Bast's worthy successor, indeed. Two days here and you're already a diplomat—in your own fashion. Tell me this—did your mother come to love your father?"

"Truth be told, my lord, my mother loved no one man," Levi said, lapsing into Canaanite. "She was a whore and laid with many of them—for a price. I never knew my father."

70

"Do you think I really knew mine?" was the response he got. "I rarely saw him, except for the times he opened the holy shrine of Amun for the daily prayers to the god when he was at Thebes. Then he sometimes said a few words to me because I was right there in the temple. After awhile, he stopped coming at all and simply stayed at Memphis all the time. Listen, Levi, forget the past. Whoever your father was, you are at present already a greater man than he could ever have hoped to be—without any help from him. That's all you need to remember."

"Yes, my lord," said Levi, getting up to resume his shaving. For some reason, his hands now felt steady. "The lack of a father means nothing to me, I assure you."

"Nor to me," replied king Thutmose. "Not now—for I have cast a shadow over my own as though he had never even existed. And I will make that shadow bigger still. I shall be remembered when he is forgotten and that will be his reward for having forgotten about me."

Levi was shown what was going to be his quarters. It was a very nice chamber and not very small. There was a window that looked toward the river and even a bed! The room resembled Si-Bast's own bed-chamber in his fine house and had all sorts of similar luxuries. There was even a chair in an alcove under which was concealed a pot so that Levi would not have to empty his bowels out of doors. His old master had one of those, as well, but Levi, himself, had never used one. Nor had he ever slept upon a piece of furniture in his entire life. Stunned by so much magnificence, intended for his own convenience, Levi sank into a chair and simply stared about him.

Suddenly, there was a hirsute young man looking at him from the doorway in a sullen manner. He was even taller than Levi, who towered above most of the Egyptians, but the hair and eyes of the other were as black as night. The stranger was one of the most handsome and impressive men the barber had ever seen anywhere. The barber rather enviously noted that there was quite a lot of dark hair on the man's forearms. Indeed, he was the very model of virility, from head to toe.

"What?" said Levi, not knowing how else to address this individual, who was regarding him as though he thought Levi had no business to be sitting in this well-appointed room.

"You—my master," replied the stranger in a broken Egyptian. Levi guessed at once where the young man was from, as he spoke exactly the same way that Levi had done when he first arrived in Egypt.

"Well, come in then," said Levi in the Canaanite tongue. "Close the curtain behind you."

"Who or what are you supposed to be?" demanded the Canaanite. "You're no damned Egyptian, that's for sure."

"Sit your ass down over there," Levi told him, pointing to the bed. "And who are you to question who I am, brother? Didn't you just say I'm your master?"

"You're no brother of mine," retorted the young man.

"Not got up like that! And you've still got your back-water accent from home, even though you probably speak Egyptian as well as the rest of these eunuchs around here by now."

"These eunuchs, as you call them, beat the holy shit out of us. Remember? That's why we're here, or do you think you're dreaming?"

"You don't look as though you're doing so badly. The name's Caleb—in case you're wondering."

"Levi. They call me Yuya now. What do they call you?"

"Nothing. Except maybe 'Canaanite dog' or some such shit in their mumbo-jumbo. What do you do around here? You somebody's pretty boy?"

"Shut your rotten hole!" shouted Levi, reverting to his old street-urchin mode of speech as though he had never been made into an Egyptian gentleman. "I'm a barber—the king's own barber, for your information." Levi made a shaving motion across his own chin, so that the bearded Canaanite would know what he meant.

"I don't believe you. Why would the king of Egypt let one of us near him with a blade? You're up to no good here, admit it! You look too dandified to be doing any work and what about all this fancy trash in here? If this is really yours, you must be doing something to somebody."

"I'll do something to you in about a second," said Levi, jumping up and raising his fist to his countryman. "You're the pretty boy in this room—not I! Talk like a human being to me or

73

I'll shove you out this window, long eye-lashes and all—you hairy-ass queen among beauties!"

"Is that so?" said Levi's slave, though he was laughing now. "You think you're a match for me, you milksop traitor? Back home, you wouldn't have dared even look at me. I'm the son of a prince and I'll bet you didn't even know your sheep-fucking father!"

"You're a son of a bitch! Nobody cares who your father is —or was—here. Cut out your filthy talk or I'll make you sorry you ever laid eyes on me. We can't fight here! We're stuck here now —both of us. And it's fine with me, son of a prince."

"Aw—sit down," the big man grumbled. "At least I can understand you—so I suppose I could have a worse master."

"Yes, you certainly could. No question there, and if you don't become a better servant to me, you'll get one! Call me a traitor, if it makes you happy, but at least I'm working and eating here. Nobody ever gave me anything in Canaan but a kick in the behind. I had nothing and was half-dead from starvation when the Egyptians got hold of me. I've worked hard for two years in this land. I just came to live here today and I don't know why I was given all these fine things—or you."

Caleb made a kind of conciliatory face. "How did you end up in this kennel?"

It was Levi's turn to laugh. "Man, you talk like this is some kind of prison. Look around you, pal. This is the Garden of Eden."

"It's a prison as far as I'm concerned," said Caleb sourly. "All right, you're hardly more than a kid and a half-dead patriot is no good to anyone, anyway. But I'm a chariot-fighter and all I want to do is get back on my wheels."

"Chariot-fighter? You mean you're *that* Caleb?" Levi marveled, now impressed. "The great one?"

"Wounded three times in battle and still around to smell your perfume, darling."

"Went down fighting, eh?" said Levi, now too interested to take offense.

"What do you think?" replied Caleb. "That bastard pharaoh of yours—he's going to get his someday. Six years in a row he's come through our land—takes our wheat and wine and whatever else he can get hold of to feed his army—and hauls back to Egypt anything worth taking. What does he leave us to eat? Well, we highlanders didn't give in as easily as you people from the south. We gave him a few good battles. Take my word on that!"

"What do you mean 'my' bastard pharaoh? I'm spoils of war, the same as you—only I got here earlier."

"The difference is—you want to stay. And I want to go home."

Just then the drapery over the doorway was pushed aside. An Egyptian, looking every bit the figure of authority and prosperity, strode into the room.

"What's all this damned row in here?" the man demanded,

75

giving the floor a rap with his staff for emphasis. "Somebody's already complained about the noise. One doesn't raise ones voice in the house of the king—unless one happens to be that king. You —barber—what's your name?"

"Yuya," said Levi, bowing his head.

"Right," said the noble. "The ruler told me about you. It seemed to me you might be a good influence on this big fellow, but it appears I was wrong."

"Sorry, sir," said Levi. "He's a bit high-strung—not used to being a servant. I'll see to it he learns his place."

"Don't break up all this nice furniture in the process or you'll make the sovereign angry. When he loses his temper, it's not a comforting sight. You lads don't want to end up in the quarries, I take it."

"What's he saying?" Caleb asked.

"Quiet!" said Levi.

"Become friends," said the older man. "That's my suggestion. A man can always use a friend, especially if he's a stranger in a foreign land."

"Yes, sir," said Levi. "Your advice is most excellent."

"Barber, listen to me. Calm this man down, if you can. Keep him out of trouble—but don't teach him his place. His place is in his homeland, as you well know. Tell him he must keep his spirit and both of you keep your wits about you. Don't lose hope, lads. Look for the good here and make the best of the bad. Or do what you can to make it better. Stick together, help one another.

Keep to the righteous path so no one can fault you. We'll meet again soon but, when we do, it will be as strangers. We never had this conversation—hear?" The man shook his finger at Caleb in a warning gesture and then abruptly turned and left.

"What was that all about?" asked Caleb.

"The Egyptian told us not to lose hope!" replied an astonished Levi. "He said we should help each other. Was there ever a stranger place than this Egypt?"

"Was there ever a stranger Egyptian than you?"

"Maybe if I'd been a rich man's son, I'd want to go home, too. But I'm just some poor nobody, as you said. With no father that I ever knew about."

Caleb held up his sinewy hand. "No hard feelings, man. I'm sorry I brought that up. So—you really do shaving here?"

Levi told Caleb the story of how he became a slave in Egypt and the circumstances under which he had risen to his present status. The chariot-fighter shook his head, as though it was the most unbelievable tale he had ever heard in his life.

"I'll be damned. That's just crazy."

"It's the whole truth," said Levi, "and nothing else. And the best part is—I've got a genuine chariot-fighter for a servant. I used to see your kind riding by sometimes and wished I could be in your place, just to be pulled along by two big, shiny horses. As a kid, all I ever wanted was something to eat—and a horse.

"I really miss my beauties," admitted Caleb. "Now some lousy Egyptian's got them and I hope they kick him in the head.

You could be worse, I suppose, but I have to get out of here. I'll go insane in this place."

"You'd be insane to run away," commented Levi. "You saw the fortress at the gateway to Canaan. You can't get past that and, if you don't get killed, they'll drag you back and give you a worse job than you've got now. Like breaking stone in a quarry down south where it's hot as blazes. You only got to come in here in the first place because you're a good-looking monkey with big muscles and the Egyptians like to be surrounded by things that look nice. Or large. The only thing they don't like big is their women. You should know that by now! It's their greatest weakness, as far as I can tell—that they just want more—of everything. More gold, more power, and more slaves. Greed."

Levi leaned back and folded his arms across his chest, having summed up the mindset of Egypt and her master as it appeared to him. "But greed never satisfies. The lack remains."

"Eh? Oh, you're a deep one, you are! I never noticed any weakness," said Caleb bitterly.

"You will," promised his fellow Canaanite. "Just hang about for awhile. And you just witnessed some kindness, too. Meanwhile, you've got a soft duty here waiting on me. Just keep quiet around the Egyptians and act like a normal servant instead of some kind of angry wild man on two wheels. Mind what you say because there are some around here who can understand our language. The pharaoh, for one."

"That man who was here is somebody very important,"

Caleb observed. "Did you see that staff of his—ebony and gold! As it happens, I saw him before—just awhile ago. I was shoveling manure near those stables. The stable master was shouting at me, as usual—as though I could understand a word he said. I looked him in the eyes and got a couple of whacks from his stick for doing that. So I took his stick from him and broke it in two. Just then along comes the king. That man was with him—I've never seen him around before, but it seemed the pharaoh knew him well, was very friendly with him. Anyway, the pharaoh got angry and said some words. I don't know whether he was ripping into me or the stable master. Probably me. Then this other fellow—the king called him Nefer-something—spoke to the pharaoh and they moved on like nothing had happened. The stable master disappeared. The stranger and the pharaoh were inspecting the horses, but this Nefer-fellow had his eye on me. I was still shoveling away, but was in a foul mood by then and looked him in the eye, too, for good measure. It didn't seem to bother him. Next thing I know, I get a bath and here I am! I may be crazy, but now I get the feeling that man tried to help me, get me away from that snake of a stable master. Now he tells us not to lose hope. Very odd, that. You ever hear of anybody called Nefer-what's-it?"

"No. Just watch your step, that's all," said Levi, thinking he was beginning to sound like Si-Bast, himself. "Act humble. Don't look anyone in the face, if you can avoid it. Keep your head down. They like that—and you could end up doing well, yourself."

Caleb stared at him. "At home they say a Deliverer will come. To break the back of imperial Egypt. You've been here for two years. You think it's possible?"

"What Deliverer?" scoffed Levi. "If a tough asshole like you can't beat the Egyptians, who the devil can?"

"I'm not so tough now," Caleb surprised Levi by admitting. "I still get headaches from when that flying battle-axe made contact with my helmet and knocked me cold. You got anything to drink in this cushy set-up?"

"Sure," said Levi. "Water. You want some—there it is."

"Not even a beer?"

"Listen, I just got here today, myself! I'll make sure you get some beer, but not too much. This isn't going to be one of your cavalry drinking parties. You're a working sod now, just as I am. Where I go, you follow."

"That's just great," mumbled the chariot-fighter. "I—and the boy barber. For all my sins, I suppose." He picked up a curved wooden object from Levi's bed. "What in the name of seven devils is this contraption?"

"It's a head-rest. The Egyptians use them instead of pillows."

"That's absurd! What are they—gluttons for punishment? You plan to use this thing?"

"Not a chance. Where do you sleep?"

"They've got some hut set up near the stables for us."

"Well, chariot-fighters are used to the smell of horseshit.

80

But you can sleep in here if you want. On the floor."

"Promise not to molest me, sweetheart?"

"I may get me a whip—just like the one you used to have. I'll molest you with that if you don't watch your yap from now on."

"I never whipped my horses," said Caleb, pointing a finger at Levi. "Just cracked the whip over their backs and that was all it took. They knew who was boss. Say, hard-on, you want to go and talk to some girls?"

"What girls? And how are you going to be able to talk to them?"

"Easily," said Caleb. "These are girls from home. They just got here yesterday. Three nice, plump little pigeons sniffling and crying but all decked out in fine clothes and jewelry. They're not slaves but the daughters of a prince of some city, who sent them here to sleep with the old bastard, your master."

"How do you know all this?"

"They told me."

"You spoke to the king's women? You can't do that, Caleb!"

"Well, I did. I helped drag in their baggage. They were very glad to see me and I'd bet they'd be happy to see you, too. All we have to do is find a way to get to them."

"No!" cried Caleb's master. "We're staying right here until somebody calls us for lunch or something."

"That's it? We just sit in this room all day?"

"I don't know! I told you—I just got here, myself. How many times do I have to say it? I don't know what there is to do around here. Hey—look at this—a gaming board! I'll teach you how to play Hounds and Jackals. It's fun. You'll like it. No—wait! First I'm going to trim your hair and beard. I'm a barber and no servant of mine is going to look like he just walked out of some wilderness. You got lice?"

"Not yet. I haven't been in this lousy place long enough."

"Well, I'll check for those," Levi told him. "Sit down in my chair. Put this towel around your neck."

"Whatever you say, barber-boy. You're the captain here."

Chapter Five

As it happened, Caleb did like the game of Hounds and Jackals and both young men, although neither would admit as much, were glad of each other's companionship and the fact that they could talk in their native language in a familiar way. As Levi had predicted, they were summoned to the mid-day meal but, to his astonishment, he was told that he was to be a guest at the pharaoh's luncheon for, this day, the ruler was eating in the presence of his nobles on account of some Egyptian holiday.

"What about him?" asked Levi, indicating Caleb, who now looked even more splendid, thanks to his own efforts.

"Your slave may accompany you," said the king's servant. "If you wish it. But he's got to put on some clean clothes."

"I do wish it", replied Levi and whispered to Caleb in Canaanite, "We're going to eat with the ruler and if you say anything, I'll kill you!"

"Who wants to eat with him, the fucker!"

83

"Ay! You're fated for an early grave! Don't speak!"

Caleb grumbled a little more while putting on a fresh shirt and kilt belonging to Levi, but then docilely followed his master and their guide through multiple corridors. They came to a hall in which there were already a number of men, seated on cushions around a long, low table of ivory and carob-wood, probably stolen from Canaan, the pharaoh at their head. Caleb promptly confirmed the provenance of this item.

"Damn!" he exclaimed under his breath. "That's my father's dining table—the old man's pride and joy!"

"All right!" Levi muttered back at him. "Keep still for your own good!"

The king pointed to an empty spot and so Levi seated himself there, Caleb standing behind him with folded arms.

"This is the new barber, Yuya," said the pharaoh, by way of introduction.

Some of the men smiled at him and others regarded Levi in a perplexed way. Then the sovereign introduced the others by their names and ranks. Some of them were very important people, indeed. Levi nodded at them all, even though he was sure he wouldn't be able to remember their names in his bewilderment over the fact that he had been asked to take food in their company.

Thutmose said to Levi, "How do you find your slave, Royal Barber?"

"He'll do very well, thank you, my lord."

"Give him a cushion and let him be seated behind you."

"He says you may sit down," Levi murmured to Caleb, pushing a pillow toward the chariot-fighter.

"He's over there," Caleb whispered. "That Nefer-fellow."

"Neferweben," said Levi. "He's just visiting. Don't talk to me now!"

Indeed, Neferweben was a very important man, as Caleb had surmised. In fact, this Neferweben was the pharaoh's southern vizier, the highest office in Upper Egypt. Evidently, he had come north on some sort of official business and, of course, had inexplicably taken the trouble to rescue Caleb from the horse excrement detail.

"Where's your lad?" someone asked the king.

"He'll be along."

Another Egyptian raised his cup. "A toast to the health of the ruler and that of Prince Amunemhat."

"Life and health!" was the general murmur. Levi raised his cup, as well. This wasn't so bad at all! He took a sip of excellent wine, which tasted of pomegranates. Then he passed the cup to Caleb, who emptied it rapidly, his face dark as murder on account of that wretched table, probably. Well, Levi could understand his feelings. Unlike himself, Caleb had doubtless lost plenty due to Egyptian ambitions. The barber had taken a risk by allowing him to come here, but he hadn't had the heart to deny the man a decent meal and didn't know how Caleb would have been fed, otherwise. He still had everything to learn about living in the Great House.

The "lad" soon appeared. He was a thin boy of about

twelve or thirteen, beautifully attired, his little skull shaved bare except for a thick lock of braided dark hair, held together with a jeweled clip, hanging down to one side. He took his place next to his father, who patted him on his pate.

"Well, Mehy," said the pharaoh, "what have you been up to today?"

"School, as usual," answered the prince. "This afternoon I have to practice shooting and tomorrow it's horses."

"Isn't that better than reading and writing?" his father wanted to know.

"I'm good at reading and writing," the boy said, "but the rest—I..." Evidently thinking better of saying more, the prince grew silent. Then he spotted Levi and piped up, "Who's he?"

"The new barber. His name is Yuya."

"He's younger than Si-Bast by a long shot! Might he shave my head, too, father?"

Some of the men chuckled into their wine cups.

"Certainly—if you like!"

"Who's that behind him?"

"Let's ask him," proposed the king. "Mehy, say in Canaanite '*Mi atah?*'"

The boy repeated the question and, to Levi's horror, he sensed his servant rising to his feel behind him.

"Prince," he heard Caleb say in a loud voice, "I am called Caleb. I am an officer of the chariotry, with three wounds received in great battles."

"What did he say, my son?" asked the pharaoh, as though not having understood, himself.

"He says he's a chariot-fighter and has got three wounds!" said Prince Mehy, excitedly. "Could he show us the scars?"

More laughter. The pharaoh shook his head. "Not at mealtime. Perhaps another day. "

"Are you a bowman?" Amunemhat asked Caleb.

"I got a crow right through the eyes once."

"Both of them?

"As straight as you please."

"Sit down!" hissed Levi.

To his relief, Caleb obeyed.

"I'd like to see that!" said Mehy. "Father, please let him come to archery practice today."

"We'll see," said the king. "Now here come some cooked birds—not crows, I hope. Eat heartily, my good sirs—and you, too, Mehy. None of your usual nibbling. If you ate more, you might get to look like Caleb yonder."

Great platters of birds, bread, vegetables and fruit were placed on the table and, after the sovereign and Mehy helped themselves, the rest of the company did likewise. Levi waited until the others had taken their portions, remembering the caution of Si-Bast to do just that in case he ever ate with men greater than himself. He was about to seek out something for himself and Caleb when, all at once, the king's heir grabbed an entire fowl, sprang up and ran over to the chariot-fighter, offering it to him with both hands.

This time, even the officials of Egypt forgot to laugh in their astonishment. Levi turned around just in time to see his servant accept the tribute and say "Thank you very much, king's son" in the humblest possible way. Glancing at the pharaoh, Levi saw that he did not appear displeased at all. Nor did that grand person called Neferweben, who was scratching his ear under his wig in an amused kind of way.

When Mehy resumed his seat, instead of reproving him, he noted the tenderness with which the King of all Egypt regarded his boy. A lump rose into the throat of the barber and he had difficulty swallowing his lunch for sometime.

When the meal was consumed, amid much talking and general conviviality, servants passed around bowls of water and little drying cloths. It occurred to Levi that nobody had spoken of Canaan, but had restricted the political talk to other parts of the empire. So the Egyptians had good manners, after all, and were not disinclined to regard his feelings as a guest at the king's table. He was even asked a few questions and answered them in a discreet fashion that would have done Si-Bast proud, had the old man not been so irate over the whole idea of Levi being taken into the Residence.

The next thing Levi knew, Queen Neferura approached with a couple of her women, bowed to the king and his officials, and took the good little prince, Mehy, away.

"His mother," an Egyptian next to him told Levi.

And behind him, he could swear he heard Caleb murmur in Canaanite, "A goddess! How beautiful she is!"

Thanks to King Thutmose, Levi and Caleb had something to occupy them besides yet another game of Hounds and Jackals that afternoon.   They had been summoned to join Prince Amunemhat at archery practice. Even Levi, who had never pulled an actual bow, but only ones made of branches as a child, looked forward to this distraction. When they came into the courtyard where the targets were set up, the wizened old Egyptian who was the prince's shooting master regarded the young men with suspicion but Mehy ran over to greet them.

"*Shalom aleikhem*," said the prince. "This is splendid!"

"*Aleikhem shalom!*" Caleb answered, unsettling Levi by placing an arm about the boy's neck as though he was his little brother or something. But the "little brother" didn't seem to mind at all and had a big smile on his face, besides.

"How did you learn our language so well?" Levi asked Mehy.

"It was father's idea. He wants me to be just like him. Some chance of that, eh?"

"This your gear?" Caleb wanted to know.

"This is it," replied the prince.

"How old are you?"

"Going on thirteen."

"You're nearly a man!" exclaimed the chariot-fighter.

"How come all they give you is these puny bows?"

"I'm not very good," admitted Mehy matter-of-factly. "But I keep trying in order to please father."

Caleb said, "Why not ask the old fellow here if he has any real bows?"

Mehy asked his instructor to go and fetch a better bow, but the man held up his hand and shook his head in protest. Levi didn't blame him. How was he to know if these two foreigners could even be trusted around a proper weapon?

"Doesn't he obey you?" Caleb said to Mehy. "Tell him to get a wiggle on and bring us a Canaanite bow. A composite bow and nothing else."

"Perhaps he shouldn't," said Levi. "That's a dangerous thing."

But Mehy was all for it. "We need a composite bow!" he said imperiously. "At once!" Then, in a different tone, he added, "Aw, come on, Huy, it's all right. Father said they could fool around here with me today. He's watching from up there somewhere."

Mehy got his bow, a big, strong one made of wood and horn, already strung by the teacher.

Caleb tested it out. "Now that's what I call a bow for a king's son. This is what you should be pulling. How are you going to build up your arm on those other bits of kindling?" He picked up an arrow. "Give it a try."

"Could he hurt himself?" Levi wanted to know.

"With all that leather on his arm? I doubt it. Don't mind him, prince. He's just a barber. What does he know about weapons?"

"What's sharper than a razor?" Mehy asked Caleb.

"Good point," Caleb conceded. "All right, nice stance, good position. Let her fly when you're ready."

Mehy let loose but his arrow failed to reach the target. He yelped, "Holy goldfish, I could barely pull that thing!"

"That's what I mean", said Caleb. "You've got to learn to. What if someday you get to be pharaoh and you go to war—the family business. Suddenly, you find the enemy coming at you and all your guards are dead. So now you have to make a stand all by yourself. You can't turn and run because you're king of all Egypt and a god besides. The honor of your country depends on you. You have plenty of arrows in the two quivers on your chariot but...only a twig of a bow! Because that's all you're accustomed to. Some stand that will turn out to be!"

"When he's older they'll start him on a better bow," protested Levi.

"Older?" cried Caleb. "He could become the fucking pharaoh by next month if the gods willed it so!"

"What's 'fucking'?" asked Mehy.

"Ah, no," groaned Levi.

Caleb cleared his throat. "It means 'ferocious' in Canaanite. Just common speech used a lot in the army and cavalry."

Mehy punched the chariot-fighter playfully in the arm. "You're lying! I've got it now. But don't say that around father. He's not young like us—and might not like it. Come on, Caleb. You take a shot. You want to wear my wrist-guard?"

"No, keep it on, prince. Hand me that bow, please."

There was no doubt about it—Caleb was certainly a tremendous marksman. The man was in his element. He and Prince Mehy were as happy as two prancing colts in each other's company and were making quite a lot of noise. Even the old archery master was smiling now, rendered mellow by such a wonderful display of a bowman's prowess. Caleb had made a face out of arrows on a target—a human face complete with a beard. Then he split the nose in two with yet another arrow, to the great delight of the king's son.

"I hope you don't mind this interruption too much," Levi said to him. "My apologies."

"Forget it," said old Huy. "He doesn't get much fun, the lad. It's good to hear him laughing for a change."

"Caleb!" yelled Mehy. "Look up there! A bird! Let him have it!"

The marksman raised his bow and the doomed bird came plummeting to earth. Mehy ran over and knelt beside its corpse.

"You missed the eyes, Caleb!" he crowed.

"Pick it up and bring it over here. Let me see."

But Mehy stood up and didn't touch the bird. Caleb

walked over to the prince. "What's wrong?"

"The thing has got blood all over it!"

Levi, moving toward them, saw Caleb scoop up the dead bird and hold it out to Prince Mehy. He heard him say "You become the pharaoh, you get blood on your hands. Might as well get used to it."

The intelligent boy looked up at the tall foreigner with a rather shamefaced expression but manfully took the dead bird from him without shrinking back. "I shouldn't have told you to kill it," said Mehy. "It wasn't doing us any harm."

"Don't forget that part," said Caleb, gently. "This is what the bow and the arrow are really all about—not aiming at targets of straw or wood. The end result is blood. Just remember that, won't you, prince? If you think a bird looks pitiful with an arrow stuck in it, wait until you see a man in the same condition."

"I suppose it hurts a lot if one doesn't kill them right away," said Mehy. "But you never missed, did you Caleb?"

"Plenty of times," said the Canaanite. "We chariot-fighters just plowed our horses into the foot soldiers like they were nothing more than wheat in a field—and the cavalry of your father did the same to our men. We went so fast that we couldn't always pick out a target—but just let fly, one arrow after another, as quickly as we could grab them. A terrain full of wounded and dying men is an awful scene, Prince Mehy. Some of them make horrible sounds or weep and call for their mothers like they were little boys again. A lot of buzzards show up in a hurry. The sky gets dark with them and the dying men know what they've come for. Believe me, king's son, it's nothing at all like this nice place with those targets all neatly in a row."

"Don't worry," the lad told him, holding up his head. "I won't forget."

"Good," said Caleb. "You're as smart as they come. I can see it in your eyes. But, meanwhile, you've got to learn to hit the target. You've got to be able to scare people a little with what you might be able to do if you had a mind to. A king always has enemies, even the best ones. Intimidate them with the strength of your arm. That'll keep their hearts true. Let them see you hit the bullseye every time. Maybe you won't today, or even tomorrow. But there's always the day after that."

"When I'm king," said Mehy, "Yuya can be my barber. I'm sick of just old people around me. Holy cats, am I glad you two showed up! But what about you, Caleb? You'd never fight for me, I suppose. But, you see, I only mean to defend myself. Nothing more."

"I'll fight for you," said Caleb to the heir of Egypt's throne, giving the boy's sidelock a little tug. "Count on me." And somehow Levi didn't doubt that he meant it truly.

The two Canaanites, having nothing better to do, sat on a bench in order to watch Mehy continue his practicing. They heard the king's son say to his teacher "From today, I will use only this bow."

"He doesn't have the arm for it," Levi said to Caleb. "He's

not very strong. Why are you putting these notions into his head?"

"What do you know," answered Caleb derisively.

What Levi didn't tell Caleb was that Prince Amunemhat was the product of generations of incestuous unions. The chariot-fighter would have been shocked to hear of such a thing. Levi, himself, had trouble comprehending how the Egyptian royals could hope for sound progeny under such circumstances but it seemed to him that Mehy, cursed with his lineage, had turned out remarkably well despite it.

"Did you know there's a song about you?" said Levi. "I heard some girls singing it in my town."

"I'll bet they don't sing it now. They'll have to find another hero. If they can."

"You don't know people. They're still singing the song, but they've changed the ending. Now they sing about how they know you'll return. They don't want to give up hope so easily. These days in Canaan, even a song is better than nothing."

"You know—you're really not that dumb," Caleb remarked. "And not really that pretty, either. Maybe you do know a thing or two. I apologize for casting aspersions on your character —so just don't go proving me wrong for saying I'm sorry."

"I accept your regrets. But you're still pretty."

"What do you want me to do about it?" said Caleb, but in a good-humored sort of way. "So you think they're still singing about me, eh? But for how long?"

"Possibly forever."

"I haven't got forever."

"They won't care," Levi replied.

Chapter Six

"Levi," said the pharaoh, "I was observing the target practice of yesterday from a window. My lad really seems to like that Caleb of yours."

"I think they like one another," the barber told him.

"How that man can shoot! Unbelievable!"

"My lord, may I ask you a question?" Levi ventured.

"Certainly."

"My needs are not so very great," said the barber. "Therefore, I'm wondering just why I require a servant to wait upon me."

"The man was assigned to you," said the ruler, "because it seemed to me he might take a notion to kill my stable-master."

"Ah," was all Levi could think of to say to that.

"I was concerned you might be lonely here. One wouldn't like ones barber to grow melancholy. Therefore, Neferweben, the vizier, and I determined this Caleb would be a fitting companion for you—you and he speaking the same language and all.

However, that was decided before I recalled just who that man was —or is. Now it seems to me I could find a better use for this fighting man and his great skill."

Levi wiped off the razor with a deft motion of a cloth. "Forgive me, my lord," he said, "but he'll never serve you."

"Is that so?"

"However, he'll serve your son very well. I think he has given the lad a greater interest in becoming a good archer already."

Thutmose was silent for a moment. Then he asked, "Will Caleb teach him what he knows?"

"I have no doubt of it," was the answer, "but that may be the difficulty. Caleb might teach the prince too much. You see, Sire, our chariot-fighter has been known to speak in a very vulgar fashion—some words there not fit for a child."

Thutmose gave one of his little laughs. "Is that all? What of it? The boy can't be kept innocent forever. His mother and everyone else have been coddling Mehy too much. Do you imagine my own soldiers talk like grandmothers? Mehy will get an earful one day with or without Caleb. The puppy must get accustomed to rough ways—toughen up. And the sooner the better."

"The heir seems a fine lad," said the barber. "Your Majesty must be very proud of him."

"I love my son more than anything on this earth," admitted the sovereign. "But even I can't protect him from all evil. That's why it's my duty to get other sons, as well. I think you understand what I mean. But I can't do it with Neferura. I was fortunate with Mehy but I have no intention of tempting the gods in that way again. It was on account of Mehy that I decided to escape from Thebes, the city of a hundred gates—the stifling prison of my youth."

According to the king, once he came back to the southern residence to live, he scarcely knew what to do about his situation. At first he was amazed that Hatshepsut had allowed him to leave the temple but, gradually, by listening to the gossip around him, Thutmose figured out the reason for his sudden release. His aunt had been under pressure to produce him by certain factions in Egypt. So he merely decided to bide his time and see what would happen once people knew he was alive and kicking—albeit possessed by an evil spirit, as his aunt had let it be known.

Meanwhile, Thutmose had also taken a fresh look at Neferura, who had grown up to be quite lovely. His wife, whom he hadn't seen in ages, seemed to think he hadn't turned out so badly, himself. They got on well in those days and Neferura, he thought, began to love him in spite of her mother. They slept together as much as was possible and there came the day when his wife told Thutmose that she thought she might be with child. It had taken the girl five years to become pregnant, but that was only because he was scarcely ever at home, the pharaoh told Levi. He was always off somewhere policing the empire. But Neferura was frightened and even confessed to Thutmose that she couldn't be sure of how Hatshepsut would react—whether she might take her baby from her, if it was a boy, and hide him away somewhere as had happened to Thutmose, himself.

This was the first and only time the young man had ever heard Neferura express doubts about her mother. But Thutmose realized she had good reason to be fearful. A lone male heir was one thing to suppress, but an entire succession of heirs was perhaps too much for the female pharaoh to deal with.

And so it was then that a great resolve settled into the heart of Thutmose. He could wait no longer. Something must be done in order to be rid of his powerful rival once and for all. Thutmose seriously contemplated killing her with his own hand but thought better of that, knowing it was possible that one of her adherents might kill him, in turn. There were men who owed a great deal to Hatshepsut and these men, fearing they might lose their lucrative positions when Thutmose came to be sole king, may well have gotten rid of him and made Neferura the ruler, instead. Her they could handle as they pleased but him they could never trust now. And right they were—as these villains had all betrayed him. Especially one.

"And so," said the king, "I bade farewell to Neferura, told her I was going away for a long time, perhaps years, and made her promise to look after our child as best she could until the day of my return. She begged me not to leave her alone but I resisted her pleas and she understood that nothing could stop me."

"How could you trust your wife not to inform her mother of your plans?" Levi wanted to know. "She must have known that you wouldn't come back except to take your place as the one and only king."

"Neferura loved her mother," said Thutmose, his mouth twisting in a slight smile, "but in those days she loved me more. And now she was to be a mother, herself. Since my aunt despised me, Neferura thought she might hate my child, too. My wife never broke her word to me. She didn't betray my plans to her mother and did not allow our son, Mehy, to be taken from her sight—even to be handed over to a wetnurse. She fed him from her own breast —a thing very unfashionable for such a high-born lady. Neferura vowed to Hatshepsut that she would kill herself if her child was ever removed from her—and so Mehy stayed right where he was born until the day I returned in triumph. But I was a stranger to my wife, really. She knew me no better than all the rest. Because I was gentle and affectionate with her, Neferura thought I would spare her mother in the end, for her sake. But she was mistaken."

"Did you...did you ever love the queen?" Levi asked, deciding to satisfy his curiosity. "I mean, with you finding her beautiful and all."

"What you really want to know is whether a man can love his own sister in that way."

"Well, yes—I suppose so."

"I didn't grow up with Neferura," Thutmose told him. "Therefore, I didn't see her as my half-sister. When we were children, I only got to spend one day with her, which was the day after that wedding night I told you about. I was enjoying myself by sitting on my throne, thinking I really was king, and Neferura was hanging around me, still clutching that doll of hers. She asked me if I liked her new gown and I, being only twelve, said something about her and her doll looking like a couple of dressed up little monkeys. That made Neferura angry and she said to me, 'You better take that back, husband, or I'll hit you with our baby!'"

Levi laughed and the king said, "Yes, it was funny. I told her she mustn't speak that way to me and she stuck out her tongue, indicating just what she thought of my greatness. Then along came a man named Senenmut, who proceeded to tell me that I had to go back to the temple for a little while. Ha! As he led me away, Neferura followed behind, wailing, 'He can't go away now! He hasn't finished telling me the story!' Senenmut told her to be good and I took a last look at Neferura and said, "Yes, you be a good girl. I'll be back. I'll finish the story.' And damn me if I didn't finish it good and proper!"

"Hmm…yes," said Levi, thinking the tale, whatever it was, had not ended so happily for poor Neferura. "You wrote your own ending."

The pharaoh looked at him. "The tale is called The Doomed Prince—wicked stepmother and all. Ay, what one remembers from ones childhood! Love the daughter of my mortal enemy? I love those who are for me and reward them well for their loyalty. For those with divided hearts I have no time. That will do for today, Levi. Oh—I nearly forgot. Caleb may serve my son. The boy must learn to choose his own men and evidently he saw something in Caleb. That Canaanite took a stick from his master and broke it in half. I saw it with my own eyes. If Mehy emulates Caleb, that will be no bad thing at all. If the man proves loyal to him, he will be rewarded, as well. Only promise me on your honor that this man will be no danger to my boy."

"My lord," said the barber, "I would wager my life that Caleb would never harm the heir. The heart of a warrior went for the price of a roasted fowl."

Thutmose chuckled at the recollection. "In that case, I will let it be known that Caleb will be Mehy's own Master of the Horse from this day forward. You may go now."

"Yes, my lord," said Levi, bowing. When he was nearly out of the room, he heard the pharaoh call his name and so he turned around.

"You are an excellent barber," said the king, winking at him.

Levi observed that his friend, Caleb, who claimed to hate all Egyptians, made a great exception for Prince Amunemhat and, not only served the boy, but treated him in the manner of a father to a son, praising, teasing or reproving him as he saw fit. The prince, the second greatest person in Egypt, accepted it all good-naturedly. He never ordered Caleb about or Levi, either, for that matter. The imp that he could be, at times, he treated everyone well and Levi thought it a very good omen for the future of Egypt.

On the other hand, Mehy's skills in warfare and the handling of a team of horses improved considerably under Caleb's tutelage and sometimes Levi wondered whether it disturbed the Canaanite to know that he was teaching the prince to become a warrior in the manner of the pharaoh, who had proved a mighty conqueror despite only being trained as a priest. Surely there must be something of the nature of Thutmose in Mehy and the boy's great-grandfather had been a terrible aggressor against the eastern lands, as well. Yes, there was that blood there, perhaps intensified by all the inbreeding, and Mehy, albeit now only a youngster and not fully formed, hailed from a family where even the women could be ruthless, crafty, and cruel. Although Levi had been told that the name of Hatshepsut was never to be mentioned in Mehy's presence, she was his grandmother, after all.

Everything was merely a game to Prince Mehy now and his only responsibility was to absorb an education. One couldn't really predict what he might become later, when the great burden fell on his shoulders and others began to advise him.

And yet Mehy was such a cheerful and guileless little fellow at present that Levi failed to see any of the darkness inside the heart of his father there at all. In fact, the boy seemed to be a duplicate of the good-humored, tolerant and kindly aspect of the monarch. Perhaps, it occurred to the barber, the young Thutmose could have been just like him as a youth, had he not been relegated to that temple, the child of some female Hatshepsut probably despised. Although the barber had come to recognize that another side to his master existed, he, himself, had so far not been the victim of it even once. But that day might yet come. Who could say?

All Levi knew for certain was that he, too, had conceived a great liking for the king's son and spent most of his extra time, of which he had plenty, with Caleb and the lad. Evidently, it didn't trouble the king that the two closest companions of his only son were foreigners—one of whom was a prince, himself, and had even fought against the pharaoh's armies on several occasions.

Levi, for his part, had been instructed to join Mehy in his schoolroom and to try to learn to read and write. The barber thought the Egyptian writing system surely the most complicated thing ever invented by man, but little Mehy seemed to have no difficulty with it and even helped Levi learn the basic signs so that he now was able to read a simple exercise. Levi, who had never expected to become an educated man, felt most happy when he was in the schoolroom with Mehy and the scribe who was their teacher. Even Si-Bast, despite the wealth he had acquired, had not known how to read and would probably be amazed that his former slave was doing just that these days.

But the next time Levi met Si-Bast, he didn't have the heart to boast of this learning, even so it was small, to his former master. The old barber said that he had meant to look up Levi before, but had been ailing for quite some time. He was feeling better now and the two men expressed the hope they would see one another more often.

"It's nearly winter," said Si-Bast. "The pharaoh will likely be leaving for the southern residence. You must come to my house then. Takamena hasn't been the same since you left. I'm afraid the girl is pining after you."

"Tell her to be of good cheer," replied Levi. "I'll come soon."

Si-Bast scratched under his wig. Why did these people wear those things if they itched so much?

"Yes—unless the ruler has forbidden it for some reason." Then he whispered, "One never knows with him."

"I'll ask him, master," Levi said. "Why shouldn't he allow it?"

"It's Si-Bast to you. I am your master no longer. You may address me as an equal now. We are both in the same profession, after all. Except...there's something you must know. I am a free citizen of Egypt. I wanted to make the same of you, but was prevented from doing so. You might be able to visit my home, but you'll never be able to do as you please or have a house of your own or take the wife of your choice. The fact that you have nice quarters and fine garments is good and I am glad of it. But these don't make you an Egyptian in control of your own destiny. You have a great position—yet you remain a slave—perhaps forever. It is a strange business—but true. Only the pharaoh can free you now."

Following the visit of Si-Bast, Levi began to take stock of

his situation and came to see clearly that his old master had spoken the facts. Here he was and here he would remain. There would never be another life for him but this one, within the confines of the Memphite residence. Levi wondered if he would ever be able to get married or have any children of his own. Si-Bast had wanted him to, but the old barber was no longer in charge of him.

Suddenly, his comfortable chamber began to seem very small to him. There was room there only for him, not for a wife and certainly not children. Caleb, too, now had a room all his own, being a Master of the Horse, and a bed to sleep on. He had advanced his station in Egypt even more quickly than Levi had done. But Caleb was now Mehy's slave and the prince didn't even have the authority to release him, even had the boy wished to do so.

Mehy, however, wanted to please Caleb, who was a hero in his eyes, inasmuch as he was able. One day, he brought Caleb the most beautiful shirts Levi had ever seen up close. The barber didn't doubt that once Caleb had owned tunics exactly like them—in the days when he was still the son of a nobleman of Canaan and had a future of his own to look forward to.

"See, Caleb," said Mehy, "now you'll only have to dress like an Egyptian from the waist down. These you can wear over your Canaanite heart."

"They're marvelous," Caleb declared. "Mehy, however did you come by these shirts? Didn't nick them from your father, I hope."

Mehy pulled the two men closer to him. "Mother made them for you, Caleb" he said softly. "But don't tell anyone!"

"How did your mother learn to embroider Canaanite patterns?"

"She didn't do that part," murmured the prince. "The other wives did it."

"You mean the princesses from our land?" asked Levi in surprise.

"That's right," answered Mehy. "Mother asked them to."

"Does the queen speak to the girls?" Caleb wondered.

"You know she can't," said Mehy and added mysteriously "But there's someone else who can!"

"You acted as interpreter? You met these women?"

"Sure," said Mehy, with a toss of his braided sidelock. "Their names are Marta, Menukhah and Manahet. Three sister with big—you know." Mehy made an obvious gesture, cupping his hands, to indicate what he meant. "They were so happy that mother came to visit them. No one else comes. And they were glad to do the embroidery to have something to pass the time. My mother gave them all the needles, threads and other things, too. Perfume and whatever ladies like."

"What do you know about that!" exclaimed Caleb.

"Mother stayed and spoke with the sisters for a long time and I was kept mighty busy telling everybody what everybody else was saying. It was kind of fun until they all started in crying. Even mother. Whew!" Mehy blew out a breath. "Anyhow, the work got done and mother practiced how to embroider, too—but not on these shirts. She didn't want to mess them up. Now almost every other day I have to go to the harem just so mother can visit with the sisters. She likes them, but I suppose father doesn't as he never goes near them." Mehy made a sour face. "Father only likes Satiah. He's always with her."

"That's not your affair, Mehy," Caleb told him. "And you know it. One of these days you'll have wives of your own and I'll wager you won't neglect any of them. I can just see you now—dropping from exhaustion."

"I might get married any day now," Mehy speculated. "Maybe father will let me have the Canaanite girls, if he doesn't want them. I think I could handle them!"

Levi laughed. "I'll bet you could, you little demon."

The prince moved his eyebrows up and down in a comic way. "But I'm not selfish. I'll keep one and give the others to you and Caleb."

"Dream on, sonny boy," said Caleb. "Anyway, thank your mother for me. Tell her I'll think of her every time I put on one of the shirts. No—better not. That's too much."

"Oh," said the prince, "I don't think so. Mother's always watching you."

"Shhh, Mehy," hissed Levi. "You mustn't say such things!"

"Who would I tell but the two of you? We're all men here. Mother's happier than she used to be. That's all I know and all I care about. You big oxes are my best friends. The only pals I've got. You've got to learn to trust me and stop treating me like a dumb kid. When I'm king, you two will be the greatest men in Egypt—next to me, of course. Just think of the fun we'll have then! We could round up all the most beautiful girls in Egypt and —"

"We trust you, great one," said Caleb. "Forget about those girls for now and let's get cracking. We've got work to do."

"Levi, please take the shirts into the house," said Mehy, "and put them in Caleb's room. Don't let any nosy servants touch them or ask too many questions."

"You're really something, Mehy," said Levi.

"You'll find out," said the prince. "Just keep your eye on old Mehy."

Chapter Seven

"**Y**our friend, Caleb, looks very fine these days," the sovereign told his barber. "Soon he'll be better dressed than I am."

"Prince Mehy is very kind to his servant," said Levi.

"I wasn't aware that Mehy knew how to do needlework. Well—so be it. My son needs companions now that he's growing up and they might as well be you and Caleb, older and wiser heads. I had such a friend once. His name was Ahmose."

Ahmose was a man whom Thutmose had met while serving in the temple of Amun. The parents of Ahmose were lowly folk but he had become a "child of the *kap*" a kind of royal nursery into which certain boys were adopted to make them into civilized men. Some of them were sons of foreign rulers and others were Egyptian lads who showed promise and whose parents were close to the royal family, even their servants. The youngsters were educated at the palace with the idea that they would get to know the the royal family and serve it with loyalty later on.

Ahmose was taken into the *kap* under the sponsorship of a queen whose name was Meryetamun. She was the sister and wife of King Amunhotep, of blessed memory. Meryetamun had no children of her own—but liked children in general. One of the serving women in the Theban residence had a son who was clever and very nice to look at. Meryetamun actually adopted him—did more than just allow him to be a part of the *kap*. Ahmose became like her own son and people called him "prince", even though his actual father had been of no distinction. By the time Thutmose's grandfather had been designated the successor by King Amunhotep, who had no living son of his own body, Ahmose was being groomed to be a high priest in the temple where Thutmose was sent. Levi was told that neither of the first two kings who shared the present ruler's name had managed to have very long reigns, even though the grandfather, known as "Thutmose the Handsome", had made marvelously good use of his years on the throne.

The king's son and the young man became friends and Ahmose was the only one Thutmose trusted the entire time he lived at the temple. The last time that Thutmose's own father visited the house of Amun, this friend of his did an extraordinary thing. While carrying the golden image of the god, he had persuaded the other priests to stop the procession before the boy, Thutmose. This was viewed by the monarch and everyone there as a sign that Amun recognized the prince as the future king of

Egypt, even though all knew that the consort of the pharaoh, Hatshepsut, had persuaded Thutmose II to put aside this son by a lesser wife.

Thutmose never forgot this gesture on the part of his friend and when it came time for him to run away, it was to Ahmose that he came for counsel. Ahmose, by that time already a prophet of Amun, a very considerable position, left everything to accompany the prince on his journey to the north. The two of them, dressed in poor garments, had some jewelry to pay their way. They found a ship and sailed to the north far away from Thebes, recognized by nobody. Once in the northland, they lived among the Aamu, bedouin tribesmen from Canaan, while figuring out what to do about Thutmose's future. When at last he made his triumphal return to Thebes, Thutmose made Ahmose the Keeper of the Royal Seal and Chief of the Treasury. After serving in that capacity for awhile, Ahmose went to the southern lands on a mission for the pharaoh. After that, Ahmose simply disappeared as he had done the first time with his king. And now nobody knew what had become of him.

"One would think this Ahmose died in Nubia," Levi said. "Si-Bast told me the people there are very barbarous and have sorcerers that can kill a man by merely making a little wax likeness of him and sticking a pin in its heart."

Thutmose shrugged. "If that were true, my Nubian enemies would have done me in quite some time ago. But, yes, Ahmose was once my very good friend and I owe much to him. I

113

had to send him away in the end. He couldn't mind his own business. He was making enemies with his outspoken ways and had even killed a man with his bare hands."

"Why did he do that?"

"Well," said the pharaoh, "the man had a hot temper. Ahmose was interested in architecture; he had an interest in many things. One day he was watching one of my building projects go up. There was an Overseer of Works there—I forget his name— who was too handy with the rod. Ahmose saw him beating on some elderly man, some slave, and told him to let the man alone. Then the overseer and my friend had an argument and Ahmose ended up landing a punch on the other man's jaw. The overseer fell backward and cracked his head open on a stone block."

"But that was just an accident!" said Levi.

"True. However, the slave they had quarreled over was someone from your own land, whom my grandfather had captured. People began to say that Ahmose had killed an Egyptian on account of Ahmose being more interested in the welfare of the Canaanites than he ought to have been. Ahmose, from the way he looked, was suspected of being of your people, anyway, and so various types began to view him as a dangerous man who might try to influence me to go easy on the enemies of Egypt."

To that, Levi said nothing right away, but just kept rubbing some oil on the pharaoh's head. He had a large, thick cranium of an unusual shape. Everything about the king seemed slightly off-kilter, unique. It seemed to the barber that Thutmose had allowed others to influence him, instead—against a man who had done him a great service and who had only wanted to help an old man.

Levi felt the impulse to give his master a sharp rap on that skull of his but, of course, he did no such thing. It also occurred to him that he could easily kill the pharaoh with his razor and become the greatest—but deadest—hero, ever, in the eyes of the Canaanites. Yes, he would even get his own song.

But the ruler seemed to be perfectly relaxed around Levi, one of those so-called "enemies" of Egypt. Life was strange. There was no question about that. The barber felt sure that, if he made some enemies of his own, even unintentionally, the pharaoh wouldn't protect him, either. Just send him to some god-forsaken place and forget about him, too. Queen Neferura had been right. Levi had inherited a bad position being so close to this king. What if someone suspected *him*, who hadn't even been born in Egypt, like Ahmose had, of trying to exert some influence?

With the most defiance that he had ever shown since coming to this land, Levi finally said, "If I saw someone beating on an old man, I'd punch him out, too."

"You would?" said the ruler and then added, "What do you think would happen to you then?"

"Get sent south, I suppose," murmured the barber.

"Well, my lovely lad, there's where you're wrong. Hey! Look me in the eye. Come on!"

Levi looked the pharaoh in the eye. The king said, "What kind of man do you think I am? Forget it—don't answer—you don't know me so well yet." Thutmose made a fist. "See these? Five good ones, and damn it, I'd use them if I saw someone mistreating an old man. But I wouldn't have to, would I? Nobody would try anything like that around me because he'd know better. Go ahead—you can laugh. I know you want to."

He was right. A laugh sputtered out of Levi.

"You like the notion of me engaging in a fistfight, eh? Like to see somebody knock my crown off and give me a black eye? Huh? You think I'd be a better lover without my two front teeth?" The king, who had somewhat of an overbite, anyway, made a face like a hare and wriggled his nose.

"Stop!" chortled Levi. "Say no more!"

"All right," said the ruler, laughing, too. "I'll stay out of trouble. And don't worry yourself about Ahmose. He'll be back."

"But won't he be afraid to return?"

Thutmose laughed anew. "You don't know Ahmose. Hopefully, he'll have learned his lesson and leave well enough alone. He can dig up that gold he buried before he left and live a retired life. He's not so young—a few years older than I am."

"He buried a treasure? How do you know that?"

"Well, he didn't leave it with me for safekeeping; that's for certain! When I chided him for killing my overseer, Ahmose told me I'd gone too high and mighty and a blow to the head might straighten *me* out."

"He dared to say that to you?"

"Well—he was a friend of my youth. But that was the day

116

I realized I couldn't have a friend any longer— a man who treated me as an equal. Only servants. Ahmose is rich. I made him wealthy. Now I've made him wiser. Would you like to go to Thebes with me, Levi?"

Well, thought Levi, so much for my being able to visit Si-Bast and Takamena.

"It was told to me," he said, "that Your Majesty has another barber at the southern residence."

"True. But you tell better jokes—when you're in a good mood and don't feel like punching someone. So come to Thebes, anyway. Mehy can't do without you and Caleb. The lad would be unhappy if you were left behind."

This was no news to Levi. Mehy had already made it plain that he wouldn't be able to stand the sight of Thebes unless he had his friends for company. In the words of the prince, he would "shrivel up and croak" if he had to "molder in that old mummy pit" by himself. So they all went together on the river. The ruler couldn't do without Satiah and they traveled in one large ship, accompanied by her brother, Nebamun, who was the steward of her household, and some of the pharaoh's guards and other personal servants. Queen Neferura couldn't do without the Canaanite sisters, as they had all begun work on a huge tapestry, according to Mehy, and these occupied yet another vessel with their handmaidens. Mehy was supposed to go with them but swore to his father that he'd be damned if he would "piss over the side with a bunch of women around" now that he was grown up and subsequently rejoiced in the fact that he was allowed to ride in the baggage boat with Levi and Caleb. With an armed Caleb there, Mehy would need no other bodyguard, as the pharaoh had already noticed some time ago the chariot-fighter was, indeed, very loyal to his son.

Until Levi had begun to travel on the Nile, he had never truly realized how beautiful the land of Egypt could be—or how much agriculture there was. On both sides of the river, as on and on they went, there were fields newly fertilized by the inundation of the fall season that had recently receded. Farming, Levi came to see, was what Egypt was really all about. There were all kinds of trees and rushes along the river and birds of all varieties darted out among them. The peoples of Canaan would be astonished to know how peaceful it all appeared and how calmly and diligently the peasantry went about its business—unless the farmers saw the royal vessel of the king with its sails of red and green and then they waved and shouted with joy. Yes, here there was nothing but tranquility and lush scenery, with nobody being besieged, slaughtered or taken captive.

Mehy apparently knew his history and, every time they came to a larger town or some monuments, the prince was able to recite something interesting that had occurred there in the past or who had built a temple to which god. When the little fleet arrived at a place called Khimunu, Mehy announced, "This is where Kamose the Liberator began to fight for the north against the shepherd kings."

"What shepherd kings?" Caleb wanted to know.

"That's what we call them," said the prince. "They were very powerful foreigners who once ruled the northland of Egypt for ages. Nobody could oppose them until two Thebans named Kamose and Ahmose decided to have a go and started a long war with the shepherds. Finally, they were kicked out and Ahmose became king of all Egypt, even the north. He's a very famous hero. Haven't you two ever heard of him?"

Levi shook his head. "We never went to school as kids like you do."

"I've heard about some people leaving Egypt once in a great number," Caleb admitted. "But nobody said they were shepherds. Whoever heard of fighting an army of sheep tenders? Those people know how to aim a mean sling, though. I'll say that much for them. They feel like killing you—they can! A little pouch of leather and a stone is as deadly as a bow in their hands."

"Will you teach me how to use a sling?" asked Mehy.

"I'm no shepherd," said Caleb. "I never used one of those things."

Levi had, but he said nothing about it. The poor folk of Canaan had little enough to defend themselves against anything, man or beast, and he was not about to show the Egyptians any more arts than they already had when it came to bringing down their chosen enemies. Not even Mehy. Not even for fun.

Yet Levi now knew one bewildering fact. The Egyptians

of the north had once been ruled by foreigners and other Egyptians had to rebel against these aliens in order to take back their country. Could the Canaanites ever do the same? With men like Caleb stuck in Egypt as slaves, the prospect seemed hardly likely.

"When we get to Thebes," Mehy went on, "I'll show you two a big secret. Actually, I know a lot of secrets."

"Probably not for our ears," Levi told him.

"That's right," Caleb concurred. "The less people like us know, the better off we are."

"You mean because you're just servants? Ha! Who do you think is the real slave here? The two of you have plenty of free time—but I have my nose to the grindstone from morning until evening. Whoever gives old Mehy a break? It's learn this and study that and that's the way it's been ever since I could barely walk. When we get to Thebes, it starts all over again. By the time I'm as old as you two, I've got to know everything. My head is so crammed with learning I feel like it's going to bust sometimes."

"You poor little mutt," said Caleb, chuckling.

"You've got to have knowledge," Levi told the prince, "so nobody can pull the wool over your eyes when you're pharaoh."

"What's 'wool'?" Mehy wanted to know.

"That's the stuff that comes from sheep," said Levi. "We make clothes from it in Canaan."

"Oh, that stuff," said the boy. "That's unclean. The priests say so. We can't use it."

"It's nice and warm," Levi explained. "Those things you Egyptians call blankets don't keep off the chill at night like a proper spread of wool."

"Only one thing better than a woolen cover at night," said Caleb, leering at Mehy, "and you know what that is! So you've got some learning left to do yet, sonny."

"Lead me right to it," said Mehy. "I'm game. But, say, unless you two let me show you things in Thebes, you are going to be bored stiff in that town. I'm going to ask father to let us do anything we want when we get there. He will because nobody can..." Mehy stopped himself and frowned.

"Nobody can what?" asked Caleb. "Out with it, pipsqueak."

"Nobody can escape from there," muttered the boy. "It's too far south."

"I get it," said his Master of the Horse. "Clear as a little bell."

"Your father once escaped from there," Levi reminded Mehy.

"Well, he can do anything. Nobody can stop father. Everyone knows that by now."

"Too bloody right," murmured Caleb, darkly.

Mehy awarded his friend a little shove. "Aw, quit grousing. Everything will come out right one day. I'll tell you what—but don't you two dare breathe a word to another living soul. When I'm king, anybody who doesn't want to live in my land can go—someplace else. I give the two of you my solemn oath right now this minute."

"Mehy," said Levi, "you mustn't swear such oaths. You don't know what will happen when you're the pharaoh."

"Who says I don't? I'll do whatever I like and nobody will stop me, either. And here's more. When I'm king, I'm going to let my mother marry whatever man she wants to. If she isn't too old or dead or something by then. What do you think of that? I've even figured out how to keep peace on earth."

"How's that?" asked Levi.

"Nothing to it," said Mehy. "My idea is to make friends with all the rulers of the foreign lands, not fight with them. First, I'll send them some gold as a gesture of good will and then I'll ask them all to give me a daughter or sister—whatever they've got handy. I'll become the relative of the entire world and nobody will bother me."

"Mehy," replied Levi, smiling, "sometimes you're frighteningly brilliant."

"I don't know," said Caleb. "I've never come across a youngster so intent on collecting women. What if all those girls sent to you aren't pleasing in your eyes, don't attract or excite you —what will you do then?"

"My duty," answered the prince, gravely. "It'll be my duty to keep them all happy for the good of my nation."

"My boy, that's a duty you'd soon weary of. Take it from one who knows. Did it ever occur to you that you might come to love one girl above all others and desire only her?"

"Not when I'm king," said Mehy. "That isn't how it's supposed to work. I'll have to marry some Egyptian girls, too, and make one my chief queen. But, since you brought it up, I think I'm rather in love with somebody right now."

"Who would that be?" Levi wanted to know.

"Well…Marta. Whoo—she's a beauty! I find I think about her a lot. She's the eldest Canaanite sister."

"Marta is your father's wife," Caleb reminded the lad. "And she's grown-up. I met her once."

"Is it my fault I love her? It's her own fault for looking like she does and being so nice." Mehy stood up. "Can't you see I'm growing up, too? Why does everyone treat me like a child? Never mind—don't say another word. I've got my future plans and I know what I'm doing."

The prince pulled off his shirt. "It's too hot on this river. I'm going for a swim."

"That's what you think, Mehy," said Caleb. "Sit your butt back down here."

"Too many old geezers on this tub telling me what I can or can't do. I'm the captain of this vessel or I'd like to know who outranks me!"

"You're the captain," Caleb conceded. "Just sit down, please, and don't desert the ship."

"Quit worrying!" said his charge, dropping his kilt and scampering quickly over the baggage like a gleeful monkey.

123

"I'm a terrific swimmer," he called back. "I can catch up with this slow-moving old bucket anytime. I've had lessons in everything there is. Just you watch!"

With those words, the prince climbed over some piles of rope and dove into the Nile. Even Caleb had not been able to move fast enough in the crowded boat to grab him.

Chapter Eight

Thus, Mehy had escaped the "old geezers". The barber knew for certain he didn't know how to swim a lick and maybe Caleb didn't, either. Caleb said nothing reassuring about that but kept his eye trained on Mehy, who, true to his boast, seemed to be practically a fish and was not only keeping up with the progress of the vessel but had even gotten ahead of it. He was waving to his companions and smiling, keeping himself afloat with no problem whatsoever. A couple of times he dove under just to frighten them, Levi supposed. It was just when the barber was starting to have confidence in the prince that one of the sailors who was with them yelled in Egyptian "Crocodile!"

And sure enough, a great beast that had seemingly appeared from nowhere, was heading straight for Mehy. The thing stuck its snout out of the water and showed rows of horrible teeth.

"Shit!" snarled Caleb and went swiftly into action. He shoved a quiver of arrows into Levi's hands and let fly three missiles in such quick succession that Levi hardly took a breath in between. Of course, Caleb didn't miss his target but that didn't satisfy the chariot-fighter.

"The monster has got its own armor!" he said. "Maybe it's not dead."

Caleb threw down his bow and grabbed the dagger from his belt, unsheathed it, and jumped into the river fully clothed with the blade between his teeth. By this time, Mehy had, naturally, figured out what was going on and was swimming back toward the boat, looking rightfully terrified. Caleb was now nowhere to be seen and the thrashing water where Levi had last spotted him had grown red with blood.

The barber tossed away the quiver and leaned over the side, crying, "Mehy, Mehy, over here! Swim faster, damn it, boy!"

But Mehy had stopped swimming. He just bobbed up and down, staring at the bloody water. Then, to Levi's utter horror, he evidently decided to make for the source of the blood.

"Mehy, no! Come back!"

And, suddenly, there was the head of Caleb. Not only the head, but then also an arm, brandishing the knife in a victorious gesture. There was no crocodile surfacing, however.

Mehy reached Caleb and was rewarded for his bravery or foolishness—whichever it was—by being repeatedly submerged by his guardian until he looked half drowned. Only after that did Caleb tow him back to the boat and allow Levi to pull him into it.

"That'll teach you, you little fucker!" the chariot-fighter roared.

But Levi, a barber and therefore a kind of honorary physician, immediately tended his gasping patient by holding him upside down so that he could disgorge the water he had swallowed or breathed in.

As was to be expected, this incident had come to the attention of the entire flotilla. The pharaoh had evidently given the order to drop anchor and the crew of the baggage boat was signaled to row up alongside the main vessel. When this happened someone called down, "Foreigners and king's son—board ship!"

Levi climbed the rope ladder leading to the deck. Behind him was Caleb with Mehy slung over his back like a sack. Waiting for them was Thutmose, who even gave Levi a hand on board and commanded someone to take Mehy from Caleb. The boy was laid on the deck, still looking much the worse for his experience. "Let him be," the pharaoh told his men, "He'll be right enough."

"The blood of a crocodile is poisonous," someone remarked anxiously. "Perhaps the lad swallowed some of it."

Just then a wasp hovered over Mehy. The pharaoh dealt with that by clapping the creature between his palms and its little carcass fell upon the trembling youngster.

"Ay!" cried another. "An evil omen!"

This resulted in a collective gasp, for the combination of a

127

crocodile's blood and a wasp following its toxic scent was an irrefutable portent that a murder was about to occur. However, no one dared pronounce the dreadful word.

"Fools!" the king growled. "Cease yammering your nonsense. Get away from that boy! Give him some air and let him dry out. Mehy! Lift your head and show them a brave one can drink blood like a lion!"

"Yes, father," said the prince, doing as he was told. His teeth clattered like castanets. "I'm very well." Then he threw up a little more water.

Thutmose plucked the harbinger of death from Mehy and ground it beneath his sandal, showing his servants how little he cared about the thing's auspicious arrival. Paying no further attention to his heir, the king made his way to his chair under a canopy, motioning for Levi and Caleb to follow him. His face was grimly set and Levi wondered what he was about to do to his servants for allowing the prince to go into the crocodile-infested waters. The barber thought it wise at this time to kneel before the ruler and muttered to Caleb to do the same.

What the pharaoh did was unfasten the magnificent collar of gold and precious stones from about his neck and offer it to Caleb.

"Hero of the Nile," he said in a loud voice, " stand on your feet and accept my gratitude for the life of my son."

Caleb stood up but, to Levi's shock, did not take the collar from the hand of the pharaoh. In fact, he made a gesture of refusal. "I...I...have son," Caleb said in Egyptian, so that everyone present could understand. "I am father."

A murmur like a great sigh arose from the onlookers. No one within living memory had ever refused an honor from a king of Egypt. It was a sacrilege being committed, hero or no. A miracle had occurred with the rescue of the prince, but now it was one woeful sign after another.

Thutmose sat down and placed his collar on his lap. It was obvious that he was at a loss for words, for once. He merely stared at Caleb in wonderment. Just then the loveliest creature Levi had ever seen came up behind the king. This could be none other than the favorite, Satiah. Were she not, she would probably not have dared to lay her bejeweled hand on the pharaoh's shoulder, as she did.

"My lord king," she said, "do not punish this foreigner, I beg you. He doesn't know our ways. Punish, instead, your reckless son who defied the power of the crocodile god, Sobek."

There was more gasping from the people on the ship. Satiah's husband removed her hand and said to his wife, without even so much as looking at her, "Woman, do not presume to advise me. The next time you do, you will become a meal for Sobek, yourself. Take yourself to the cabin—at once! And the rest of you—have you nothing to do but stand around like moaning cattle? Get about your business!"

The chastised Satiah quickly moved away with the others, but not without stealing another appreciative glance at the drenched—but undeniably still very handsome—Caleb. It seemed to Levi that more than one lady of the royal household would be watching Caleb in the future.

"Men," said the pharaoh in Canaanite, "you may go back to your vessel. Caleb, you have done well in all respects. When that impetuous brat, Mehy, is king you will be known as 'father of the god', one of the greatest titles in the land of Egypt. This means you were as a father to him once and will be as long as you live— even when his actual father is no longer around. In the meantime, Mehy must obey you in all things until the day he succeeds me. This is my order and so it shall be decreed. That will be all—and take that soaked puppy over there with you before I beat his little ass black and blue. Tend him, Levi, and don't let him catch a fever."

Somebody wrapped Prince Amunemhat in a cloak and Caleb carried him back down to their boat. As this "tub", as Mehy had called it, waited for the other ships to pass it so that it should once again take its proper place in the order of the voyage, Levi saw the women of the second ship were calling out to them and waving some scarves or whatever they had to hand. *"Gibor! Gibor!"* the Canaanite wives were shouting ecstatically, *"Gibor gadol!"*, indicating that they, too, were impressed by the valor of their countryman. They appeared to be supporting, with their free hands, a wan-looking Queen Neferura, who must have been half in a faint from what she had witnessed. Suddenly the great lady seemed to come to herself and began tearing the bracelets from her wrists and arms, tossing them one by one to Caleb, who caught them with his usual dexterity. This tribute he did not refuse and his fine teeth were bared in a brilliant smile that elicited even more praise and compliments in Canaanite. Probably, the sisters had not known such joy since the day they arrived in Egypt, even though a tragedy had just been narrowly avoided. One of their men had shown the Egyptians that spirit and courage could not be broken by bondage and Levi, too, felt a belated surge of pride in his breast.

On the other hand, the heart of the king of Egypt, who hadn't moved from his seat, was feeling rather heavy. Once again, he had done something to alienate Satiah, even though she had brought it upon herself by behaving so outrageously—and had left him no choice but to reprimand her. Well, no one had trained her how to act around him, especially in public, but plain common sense should have dictated against her actions. Traditionally, nobody was to address the pharaoh without permission or unless spoken to first. Such customs were meant to uphold the dignity of his office as one in the company of the gods. At any rate, these conventions had succeeded well enough for more than a thousand years, even though Thutmose felt sure that the gods probably looked upon him as a very dubious relative. By the same token, he didn't have all that much confidence in them, although he mentioned their names often enough, lending the impression he and they were on intimate terms. Other than the necessity of fostering such absurdities, given his circumstances, the pharaoh believed in the power of knowledge versus that of superstition. But, as it happened, the great majority of his subjects took a different view and so it had always been. Satiah, hailing from the Faiyum, where Sobek was the chief deity, had babbled about the power of a crocodile-god when she had just only witnessed a mere mortal slaying one of Sobek's finest. But, evidently, that hadn't given her any pause.

Nevertheless, Thutmose often allowed people to address him freely when he wasn't sitting in state. Usually, they had some important information to impart, anyway, and were not merely trying to engage him in idle chatter. When he felt like just passing the time chatting, himself, he let them know that and there was seldom any difficulty with any of it. But no one had ever yet boldly laid a hand upon his body, much less tried to tell him what to do! What Satiah had done was unheard of, terrible—yes, humiliating. Certainly, his wife could touch him when there was no one else present. That he liked and would never have discouraged. But under no circumstances did he require advice from a mere chit of a girl!

Of course, a man's own wife would be the last one to appreciate his godlike qualities, knowing what she did about him —even though "beautiful god" was always written after his name on monuments. As told in tales, the divinities of Egypt were up to all kinds of fantastic tricks but, presumably, none of them ever farted, blew their noses, had to get up to take a piss in the middle of the night after too much beer or had morning breath. Thutmose didn't expect his wives to worship him, but a woman should have the wisdom to know her place and to defer to her husband in all things. Otherwise, there would be no peace in the household. Two or more masters couldn't co-exist under one roof.

Also, Satiah's own manners were far from ideal, in general. Nor were her habits. Even though she was lavish with cosmetics and used up expensive perfumery like he could simply produce that by magic and didn't have to order it from far-off places—she seemed to have an aversion to water. Finally, Thutmose had instructed Nebamun to make sure his sister got a bath at least once a week. Of course, that jumped-up villain had wondered if so much washing might not harm Satiah's health, like the peasant he really was at heart, despite his trying to ape the speech of a gentleman these days.

No, Satiah was hardly in a position to hold Thutmose to any high standards, even though his standard of behavior around women was probably better than that of a good many men. At least he was polite in private and tried to be a considerate lover. That is, he was now, although, the first time, he had been obliged to storm Satiah like a fortress due to her total lack of cooperation. Eh—one had to make a breach and now the gate opened readily enough and his young wife often attacked *him* once they were in bed. Even when he was tired, Thutmose did his best to accommodate Satiah—not that it required such a great effort on his part. Yet, by daylight, she was as stiff with him as she had expected him to be at night. Neferura hadn't acted that way, had always regarded him cheerfully in the morning and—no! He mustn't think of how Neferura used to be.

Yes, that was the root of the problem—Satiah was not well bred. In fact, she was totally ignorant, couldn't even speak the King's Egyptian with a proper accent and, worst of all, failed to fully appreciate the heights to which she had been raised. Thutmose felt that he ought to have his vizier or even that brother of hers have a talk with the girl but his own sense of pride made him abandon the thought. It was up to him and no one else to make sure that his wife showed him the proper deference. Unfortunately, he had failed to achieve that in the case of Neferura, but that one had been raised to believe she was his superior in station and breeding by her brimstone beast of a mother and, besides, had gone a bit mad somewhere along the path.

Probably, if he looked more like Caleb, there would be no problem at all in dealing with the contrary Satiah. He wouldn't have to do anything except just *be*—instead of spending the rest of the day placating his wife so that she'd be willing to at least look him in the face again. And, yet, he couldn't actually apologize to Satiah—no more than he could to anyone on earth. That would never do and he'd be damned to the tenth circle of hell and cavort with fire-belching demons before he'd lower himself to grovel before some country bumpkin who ought to be grateful and smiling instead of—well—what she was instead!

So exactly what could he do to mollify this creature who

had upset his inner balance from the very first day he had seen her? The pharaoh decided there was nothing to be done and that he had better ignore Satiah until she got tired of being disregarded or became worried about her position and did something to get his attention again. That would be the best strategy, yes—but not here. How was it possible to avoid her on the ship where they shared sleeping quarters? Could he ignore her in bed? Thutmose didn't think so. Not a chance there. Even he didn't have that much determination. However, perhaps he could forbid everyone to give his wife anything to eat until she asked him for food, put her under siege, so to speak. That would take her down a peg and force her to speak to him in a humble way. The pharaoh silently upbraided himself for harboring such odd and desperate ideas. Of course he couldn't starve Satiah into submission. He might be a lot of things, but that much of a petty jackass he was not. Well, not yet—but heaven only knew what kind of behavior that foolish creature would yet drive him to before he stopped loving her so terribly. If only that day would arrive soon!

Thutmose wiped his brow with his hand. It was growing hot even under the canopy. He needed a drink, but the wine, the beer and the best shade were in the cabin with Satiah. So, lost in gloom, the pharaoh just continued to sit there and sweat, fingering the collar on his lap in an absent way. He never noticed the lithe, snub-nosed girl observing him from behind some barrels. If he had, the ruler would have been surprised by the look in her ebony eyes. It was an expression of curiosity, even awe, as is commonly found in young females who see something in a man that strikes them as marvelous and moving, even though no one else might be experiencing the same vision or anything near.   Nor could Thutmose possibly realize how much this person longed to dip into one of the barrels and offer him a drink of water. Perhaps, had he not appeared so melancholy, so ill-tempered, she might have done him this kindness sooner but, under the circumstances, simply remained immobilized in her attitude of fearful veneration.

Then the girl recalled her father and his chair covered with the skin of a lion, one he had slain with his own spear, and what he would think could he see his high-spirited, resourceful child cowering in such a manner.   Had she really changed so much since being brought to the land of Egypt? No, it wouldn't do. That foreign hairy man hadn't lost his courage and neither must she. Not ever.

Rising, the girl lifted the cover from one of the barrels, set it down, and dipped the cup with the long handle into the water. She sipped from it slowly, waiting for the king to notice her. At last, he did, and even made a drinking motion with his fist, indicating he, too, was thirsty. The girl brought the pharaoh the wooden cup and held it out to him. Wonder of wonders, he didn't remove the vessel from her hand but, gently taking her arm, allowed her to hold it to his finely-shaped lips! She studied his boney, jutting nose, thick pale lashes and the freckles under them with fascination. He drank deeply but, of course, didn't thank her when he was done. The girl didn't even know how one said "thank you" in Egyptian or even if these people had such an expression. Certainly, no one had ever thanked her for anything in this country.

At Memphis, the king had never come to the harem when the girl was awake and so she had not been able to see him except from a distance. However, once on the ship, the impression she had received of him from her only source appeared to be not so very accurate. The pharaoh was really quite handsome for a white man and looked as strong as an ox with muscular legs and a chest as big as that of a cock pigeon. Certainly, he was on the old side and running a little to fat and yet exuded more energy and virility than many younger men. More than anything else about him, the girl liked the way he spoke to the others, his servants and sailors, in a good-humored, hearty fashion—well, when he actually was in a good humor, which was most of the time. Of course, the king had no occasion to address the girl, who didn't usually wait upon him, and didn't appear to want to now, either.

Regardless, she backed off a little and said softly, "Pharaoh?"

"Hmm?" the man murmured absently, his troubled eyes not on her but on the river.

"You want more?"

The king shook his head and then added, "Better go and see if your mistress requires anything" in a dull tone.

In the cabin, the girl was rushed upon by that very mistress, who clasped her by the wrists. "Tabubu, can you believe it? It was the same man we saw from the window! All that hair was showing right through his wet shirt. I thought I'd just fall down and die right there! Isn't he simply too splendid? Like a veritable god!"

"Yes, my lady," Tabubu replied. "I see him. He some wet white man, alright, but not fearing nothing it looks like."

"No!" exclaimed Satiah rapturously. "Have you ever seen anything so amazing in all your life? Listen, Tabubu—the king is bound to come in here at any moment. When he does, let's you and I just leave and talk some more elsewhere. I'll be damned if I'm going to sit still for any lectures from him now. What's he going to do about it—chase us around the ship? Let him yell his head off if he wants to and look a perfect monster in front of everyone. He doesn't scare me!"

"No?" wondered Tabubu.

"Of course not. What can he do except send me back home to my village? I wish he would! I can't breathe around that man when we're alone together." Satiah shuddered purposely and leaned against Tabubu, a girl near her own age to whom she often clung for comfort and, to her credit, treated more or less like a sister now that she no longer had any of her own near her.

"Eh? What you talking?" said Tabubu, making a face. The word among the servants on the ship was that Satiah's breathing was very forceful at night and even during the day, as the cedar walls of the cabin weren't particularly thick. "What you father do you get sent home? He die of shame, surely."

138

"Who cares? Someone else will marry me."

"Maybe you get a worse one," suggested the practical Tabubu. "You father not be so particular next time."

"You wouldn't understand," Satiah sighed, even though she knew Tabubu was right. "You've never had a husband, especially some old tyrant who always makes fun of you when he isn't ordering you about!"

"Pharaoh not looking for you," the slave assured Satiah in a dejected voice. "He just resting now. My sweet lady, why you not go and say something nice to him?"

"What for?" said Satiah, throwing herself down on the bed. "He'd only act all high and mighty and ask me why I left the cabin without his permission. Besides, I'd rather talk to you. Hmm…I wish we were on the second ship. Those women can do whatever they want back there."

"They just sewing," Tabubu replied.

"But think of the view they've got from the rear! We can't see anything from here. Aargh!"

"They can't look on those men!" the slave told Satiah. "They knowing better. Those men don't have such a wonderful ship as this one here. They got no little house with a hole in the bottom. They must do all their business—outside! Those ladies try watching those foreign men, they see plenty, alright."

Satiah laughed and so did Tabubu, but they had little more time to enjoy the notion of the men on the baggage boat exposing themselves, for the door opened. In the view of Tabubu, the pharaoh loomed in the doorway like a giant come to tear down everything around him. She gazed at him with widened eyes, but her mistress merely turned her face and looked away.

"Get out of here, girls," the king said in a normal if not exactly jolly tone. "I want to take a nap."

"Yes, pharaoh," said Tabubu, rising immediately. Satiah, for her part, took her time in getting up. She smoothed her dress and did a bit of rearranging of the plaits of her wig. To Tabubu's great discomfort, her mistress actually took up a mirror and added a little paint to what was already on her eyelids. Then she changed her earrings, studying their effect in the mirror, as well. Tabubu stole a glance at the ruler, who had folded his arms and was watching all this impassively. The slave scarcely knew whether to flee the cabin and leave the royal pair to themselves—or keep on attending Satiah, as she was accustomed to doing until dismissed.

Tabubu remained, transfixed by this scene of her lady calmly defying the great man and the expression on the face of the latter. There was even a moment when the pharaoh looked at Tabubu with a kind of cool appraisal, causing the girl to blush. Tabubu, although rather on the thin side, knew she was not wholly lacking in attractiveness to the opposite gender. She was wearing a skirt, but was naked from the waist up with the exception of a string of beads about her neck. Her skin was a warm, brown shade and her breasts were firm and pointed like those of all the girls of her village before they had any babies to nurse. In her home, Tabubu had been considered a beauty, but she didn't suppose anyone in Egypt found her very remarkable. Especially not compared with someone like her mistress. Oddly enough, the only person who had ever praised her looks in Egypt was the incomparable Satiah, herself. In fact, she sometimes amused herself by painting the face of her slave, covering her with ornaments and admiring the exotic result. Normally, however, Tabubu wore no cosmetics and had no desire to. In her village, it had been the men who were the painted ones, on certain occasions, and not the women.

Yes, the king was only a man, too, and he couldn't help but look at a girl's breasts, even if bared ones was hardly a rare sight. At any rate, he had observed those of Tabubu and she wondered if he found them or anything else about her appealing. Since she suspected he probably did not, that made Tabubu feel even worse, more wretched still.

Finally, Satiah was ready to get out. She marched right past her husband without a word and he didn't say anything, either. Tabubu gladly followed but gave a polite little bob of her head in the king's direction. The maidservant simply couldn't fathom her mistress. Tabubu had been taught at an early age that one didn't snap at the offering hand, lest it become a fist. And someday that fist would come down on Satiah with the savagery of a man who had been tested to his limit. The slave, although not knowing the pharaoh at all, instinctively knew more about him than did her mistress, for she had grown up with a man just like him—her own father. Tabubu could never have explained how

141

she realized these men were alike, it was just something communicated to her in some mysterious fashion. If Satiah continued down the path she was treading, something worse was going to happen to her than just being sent home, but even Tabubu couldn't be sure in what way that would occur. All she knew was that her father was an indulgent person, in some ways, and knew the meaning of patience, but if he turned irrevocably against someone who had done him wrong, he showed no mercy and the offending party was doomed.

A similar destiny was in store for Satiah if she failed to alter her ways. Of this Tabubu felt certain. But the girl was fond of her lady and didn't relish the thought of harm befalling her, while also knowing there was nothing she could do to prevent it. Once events were in motion, there was seldom any way of turning them back. Even Tabubu's father had found that out after the pharaoh's army had come in his direction. However, if one encountered a mightier opponent, one had to give way to him. That was the order of things and so it had always been. Tabubu, although lamenting the dispersion of her people and missing her loved ones, basically believed that everything happened for a reason, although the exact purpose of it might be obscure at the time. One couldn't avoid ones fate, but one shouldn't unnecessarily pursue a bad one, either, in the way that Satiah seemed to be doing.

Tabubu knew of another thing, too, something she had learned from her grandmother, a witch-woman of great renown.

Once evil arrived in a place and could not be driven off, it stayed put in one form or another. This had nothing to do with warring, for that was part of the nature of men and they had been engaging in that since time immemorial. Yet, if a human life was taken for private reasons without sufficient cause, senselessly, or for the mere pleasure of it, the ill consequences of that act could perpetuate themselves for as long as the stars hung in the heavens. It engendered a curse that lingered long after the initial grief of one family and the shame of the other and the retribution for the murder did nothing to dispel it. One never knew exactly what shape this affliction, this blood curse, could take from generation to generation. Yet it would inevitably be passed on until both the families of the victim and the perpetrator were no more. Not a one could wholly escape its effects.

Hesitating outside the ship's cabin, the little slave thought how good it would be if she could impart this secret knowledge of her grandmother to the pharaoh. Perhaps, being a learned Egyptian, the man would be able to understand what it was all about. Tabubu had never known her father to have any regrets about anything *he* had done, but her father's wives had appreciated their duties and him. They understood his limits and just how far he could be provoked. Things were quite lively at times but a balance had been maintained. Something different was brewing here, something that might affect the pharaoh as badly as it would her mistress. For the servant had now seen, with her own eyes, that Satiah exerted a power over her royal husband that none of her father's women had been able to do. She could make him sad as well as angry and that was an ominous combination. Jealousy, that destructive, gnawing beast always lurked near those unhappy in love. Tabubu would have liked to turn around and tell the king to give up on Satiah and send her home to whatever awaited her there. Before it was too late and *someone* died merely on account of the lack of sound judgment and started up the curse. Perhaps, sometimes, one should attempt to change the course of things that could only get worse, otherwise. But it was impossible for the slave to even try, much less hope to succeed.

Chapter Nine

Back in the baggage boat, Mehy, still a little blue in the face, if not the behind, was shivering under a piece of old sail-cloth, as though hiding from the wrath of Caleb. The latter appeared more downcast than angry, however, staring at something in the darkening distance.

In an effort to cheer up the valiant man, Levi said, "You were wonderful. I won't forget this day as long as I live. Even the pharaoh was in awe of you."

Caleb merely grunted.

"You never told me you had a boy," Levi persisted. "You never even mentioned being married."

"Maybe I'm not," mumbled the crocodile slayer. "Who knows now? Who knows what's happened to my wife—or my son. He was only three the last time I saw him. Now I'll probably never see him again."

"I told you that you can go home someday," said a quavering voice from under the canvas. You just don't believe me, that's all."

"Shut up you," said Caleb, albeit not very wrathfully.

"Don't speak to him like that," said Levi. "He's still the king's son."

"Who now has got to obey me ALL OF THE TIME!" replied Caleb loudly, for the benefit of the unhappy youngster. "By royal fucking decree!"

Nobody knew what else to say until Mehy broke the silence. "You know something, men? I wish I had a nice wool blanket right this minute. When I'm king, I'll tell everybody that wool is fine. I'll wear it myself, even. I'll show 'em all. Nobody will ever be able to tell me what to do anymore—except you, Caleb. I'd still listen to you. But you won't be here. You'll be back in Canaan." The boy began to sob at the very idea.

"What are you sitting way over there for?" Caleb wanted to know. "Get your ass over here! I don't want to take any more chances of you falling overboard or something. Move it!"

The prince crawled out from under his stiff covering and tightened the cloak about him. He nestled close to Caleb, putting his head on the man's big chest as though he were no more than three years old, himself, and not a young man who "might get married any day now". Caleb put his arm around Mehy and the lad soon fell asleep, comforted by the warmth of his savior's body.

"Caleb," whispered Levi, "the boy swam right over to you with all that blood in the water. He had no way of knowing whether you'd killed the beast or if it had done for you. He just did it. And he had no knife."

"Sure he did it!" Caleb muttered back, pulling an indifferent sort of face. "I'm not raising any cowards around here. Every day I tell him how important it is for him to act brave, even if he feels afraid. See...I love the lad. I'd never let any harm come to him, but I'm going to make damned certain he keeps his promise about letting our people go free. If he keeps out of mischief and lets me live that long. Anyway, the monster was already dying. One of my arrows got it deep in the neck. I jumped on its back and slit its belly. But it was amazingly strong and kept rolling me over and over as I held my arm about its neck before I was sure it was dead. I'm lucky it didn't break every bone in my body and I hope never to encounter another."

"Do you think the king behaved well today?" asked Levi, feeling rather mischievous, himself.

"Well," said Caleb, "the king told that woman of his not to speak to him unless spoken to. Even I could tell that. That's what I would have done. I know that much."

"That was Satiah, the new wife. He loves the girl, I think."

"Too bad for him," replied Caleb, chuckling softly.

Prior to docking at Thebes, a little papyrus craft had pulled up alongside the cargo vessel and Levi was told to get aboard. The barber figured that the pharaoh wanted a shave so as not to appear "beggarly" when he entered his southern capital. Nobody had shaved at all in the past week. Traveling, even by luxurious crafts as the first and second of this little fleet, was not the same as being at home. The king, in allowing Levi to stay with his son as a companion, had forgone this particular daily ritual. Levi, himself, had considerable stubble on his face, and he felt he must look a wonderful specimen of a barber, indeed.

When Levi knocked on the door of the king's cabin, he heard the ruler tell him to enter. However, the king was not alone. He was fully awake and in his chair but Satiah was still in bed, yawning and rubbing her eyes.

"Satiah, my pet," said Thutmose, "time to get up and get dressed. I need a shave."

"I'm tired," protested the woman. "Must I get up so early?"

"Go rouse that maid of yours and take a wash. That'll wake you up. The sooner I get shaved, the more room you'll have in here to get prepared. Don't you want to look beautiful when we dock? The Thebans are going to see you for the very first time."

"Almighty gods," groaned Satiah, but she pulled the covers off herself and Levi, to his alarm, saw that the girl had nothing on whatsoever. Being an Egyptian woman was the reason, Levi surmised, that she had no modesty and didn't seem to care that a strange man was standing right there in the cabin. Levi was unable to avert his gaze, however. Satiah was simply too glorious. Her skin was as white as milk and her nipples rosy, not the brownish color of those of some Egyptian females, as Levi hadn't been able to help but notice. The hair of her head and the thatch between her legs were black but the eyes of the beautiful one were green. Satiah's fair face, however, was reddened about the lips and chin—no doubt due to her husband not having availed himself of the services of his barber lately. The king's wife smelled of perfumed ointment and something else Levi recalled from having lived with his mother years ago. Levi felt hot blood suffuse his face—and elsewhere, too.

"Which one are you again?" Satiah asked.

"Uh...Yuya...great mistress." So this was the "shy and modest girl" he had imagined being overwhelmed by the embrace of the ruler. She looked at the king's servant with the bold eyes of a wanton creature and, suddenly, Levi longed for the respectable house of Si-Bast, in which all the women were adequately covered and behaved with decorum. In fact, had Si-Bast been here in his place, the old barber might certainly have fallen down with a stoppage of the heart. Thutmose, who had prevented Levi from marrying or even being able to visit a good girl like Takamena, had taken to himself a woman who was not cursed with blindness —but, on the other hand, didn't even have the decency to lower her gaze before a stranger who had been forced to view her nudity against his will, much less try to hide anything from him. In fact, it seemed to Levi that Satiah wanted to stay right where she was in her naked splendor and watch him practice his craft.

The barber believed the pharaoh when he said his new wife was merely sixteen—for no man of substance would have considered marrying a girl much older than that and most were already married by then, anyway—but Satiah didn't look all that young, somehow. Something about that face struck Levi as mature, even cynical, although there was nary a wrinkle to be seen, of course. Well, the girl had said she was tired and perhaps that was the reason she appeared older. But her figure! It made Levi feel weak in the knees.

"Satiah, farewell," said the ruler. "We don't have all day."

The girl gave him a bored look but got up and received a playful slap on her snowy backside as she passed her lord and master. Without further comment, Satiah exited the cabin, doubtless to give numerous others the benefit of a look at her awesome charms.

"Anytime your hard-on goes down," Thutmose said to Levi, "you can start. Aw, quit blushing. A woman is a thing of beauty. No shame in looking upon it."

"If you say so, my lord," said the barber, spying some razors already laid out on a little table.

"Satiah doesn't have much use for me," the king went on, "but there's one thing about me she's gotten to like. So both of us are happy right there."

The king made a motion of his head toward the bed. Levi remembered Si-Bast having said the ruler was reputed to be well-endowed and doubtless his new wife had come to appreciate that aspect of her imperious husband, whether he humiliated her in public or not. Some people around here have all the fun, Levi thought. Old men fucked girls young enough to be their daughters and the young men...well, they could just go whistle. Something not right there.

"So that's what passes for love around here these days," said Thutmose, rather dismally. "Something not right there."

"What?" said Levi, looking up in surprise.

"You heard me, boy. Well, never mind. How's the heir doing?"

"Back to normal. All's well with Prince Mehy. Lively as a cricket."

"Levi," said the pharaoh, "the other day I saw something that gladdened my heart. I saw my son was not a coward. He did his duty toward his friend like a man of courage and now, if I die tomorrow, I can go the West knowing that Egypt will be in good hands."

"May the king avoid the West and enjoy many more years. True...Mehy was brave...in an amazingly foolish kind of way. He didn't want Caleb to die—but how could he prevent it? The lad had nothing with which to fight the crocodile."

"Foolish, yes, but...the cub of the lion. Mehy gave the people to know his fearless heart. That's all that counts when there are so many enemies."

"Mehy has enemies?"

The pharaoh made a deprecating face. "Not now...but later on he might. How happy I am that the lad has shown the stuff he is made of. Soon the story will be all over Thebes and Mehy, though not yet feared, will be respected at least."

151

The barber wondered what the sovereign would say if he knew this son of his had sworn to free all the captives the father had brought to Egypt.

"He has turned out well because he knows he has a father who loves him," said Levi, the words just tumbling from his mouth. "It makes him feel worthy and capable of anything."

The king nodded. He looked up at his barber and asked, "Why didn't my father love me? In my heart, there is always that question. But there's never an answer. Why didn't my father protect me, his only son? I'd do anything for Mehy. What kind of man puts his son in a gloomy temple to be raised by somber priests without a woman's gentle voice or touch—ever—when he is ill or lonely?"

Levi pondered this for a moment. "Did anyone ever try to harm you in the temple of Amun?"

"No. Nobody. I might have died of boredom there, though."

"See? Out of harm's way," said the barber. "That much your father did for you. No one to love you—but no one around to hate you, either. So you didn't have to deal with that. What little boy can?"

"What is it that makes you so wise?" wondered the king of Egypt. "Si-Bast, for all his years and experience, never answered me so well as you do. Yes, my father spared me from Hatshepsut while my heart was tender—but he deprived me of my own mother, as well! That's why I let Neferura come to Thebes—so

Mehy can have his mother near him. If it weren't for him, she could just bloody well live away from me the year round. That harem in the Faiyum still stands. My father and his father liked the place and used to keep some women there. That's where I'd like to send Neferura—and building a high wall around her would be best. I always have the feeling that woman is biding her time, waiting for the day when she can get revenge on me."

"Did you ever see your mother again after you were grown?"

"No—too late. Her name was Isis and that's all I know. She died there in the Faiyum."

"Some men, like your father, are easily influenced by their wives," Levi observed. "They give them too much power and no one knows why."

"Well, you won't see that happening around here! No woman is going to manage me, be she as beautiful as the Seven Hathors combined. And that includes Satiah. She's young and willful and I indulge her plenty—but when she gets above herself, I put her in her place, as you saw. A wife doesn't grow to love a husband she doesn't respect."

"Yes, my lord, very true."

"Well," said the pharaoh, after a slight pause, "I don't want to scare her, either. You know—be too harsh."

"Certainly not," said Levi.

"I realize this sounds very odd but...I would like to get to know my wife. I would like to know what she thinks...even about me. If Satiah were to tell me what's in her heart, we might have a conversation about that and then I could reassure her that all will be well in the end. Tell her just to be patient. I could explain myself to her, as well, so that she might understand me. Meanwhile, all I do is tease her like a patronizing uncle—because there's nothing else to talk about. And she becomes offended."

"You could explain yourself," said Levi. "You can do anything you like! Why wait for her to open her heart first?"

The ruler shook his head. "I can't do it."

It then occurred to Levi that, in his own way, it was the pharaoh who feared his young wife and was even intimidated by her youth, good looks, and what appeared to be an irritable disposition—although nothing on earth could ever move him to admit as much. He said, "Perhaps Your Majesty could allow me to rub some sweet-smelling essence of lilies on his cheeks next time. Si-Bast told me ladies like that. I believe he said it 'stirs them up'."

"Eh? How would Si-Bast know? Must have a long memory, that one. Bah! That stuff is for you young dandies and you're welcome to it. I can't smell too good or people will think I'm getting delicate or something—you know."

Levi rather thought he did.

"Essence of lilies," Thutmose muttered scornfully. "Damn it all, I *am* getting soft! What's the point of talking to women, anyway? What do they know—especially the young ones? They can't read or do mathematics—much less know anything about politics or foreign lands and where they lie. One might as well converse with a cat or a dog as with them."

"Some of them have innocent hearts and there is something comforting about that." Levi was thinking of Takamena, but the pharaoh did not seem to take any solace from the notion of feminine guilelessness. Perhaps he was a stranger to that, anyway. He just grimaced in a skeptical manner.

Then he said, "Years ago, I could talk to Neferura. She's different from most women because she had an education. Yes, she was taught things so she could be the ruler of this land one day —can you imagine?"

"If Your Majesty had a daughter, would she be educated, as well?"

The pharaoh stroked one of his eyebrows with a finger, seemingly thinking that over. "I suppose so," he finally answered. "If a daughter of mine showed keenness and a curiosity about things, it would not be in me to deny her an education. I love learning too much, myself...By the gods, I couldn't have saved the life of my own son!" Thutmose said suddenly, as though the thought had just hit him. "I never learned how to swim in that bloody temple. All I ever did was study. I never even learned how to shoot an arrow until I was twenty years old."

"I assume my lord became a fine marksman," said the barber.

"I had no choice," was the answer he received. "It was the only way to gain respect. What does one know of the former rulers of Egypt except their monuments and deeds in war? Of which of them is said 'He knew all there was to know' or even that he knew a thing or two? Not a one, I can assure you."

"Mehy is a great one for mathematics. It's amazing what he does, drawing little shapes and angles and making calculations. Our teacher says he has the gift of an architect."

"Wouldn't surprise me if he did," said the pharaoh. "Not a bit."

Levi moved the face of the sovereign to the left and the right to make certain he hadn't missed any hairs. "Will Your Majesty perhaps be building a pyramid? Those have lasted a long time, according to Mehy."

"A thousand years, at least, but those are things of the distant past. To build a giant pyramid, one needs twenty years of peace. I can't spare the manpower." Thutmose smiled. "Yes, there stands the great pyramid of King Khufu and every time someone looks at it, he thinks 'This was built by a reprobate.' So is remembered Khufu and probably the same will apply to me. Not much point in erecting a huge pile of stones just to be called a degenerate, is there?"

Chapter Ten

Thebes, as Levi expected, was a large city, just as sprawling as Memphis. The king's house, on the west bank of the river, was no less impressive than his other one. Perhaps even more so, because behind this palace, at a distance, was a wonderful mountain that glowed with a reddish gold hue in the sunlight. The main difference from the residence at Memphis was unfamiliar people coming and going, none of whom appeared to be slaves from Canaan, as far as Levi could tell. There were black persons, though, perhaps taken from the territories to the south of Egypt's border. Levi had never before been around such people but Caleb had something to say about them.

"There were lots of black men in the pharaoh's army," informed Caleb. "They were the fiercest ones, if you ask me. Tall, too—not like some of these puny Egyptians. They were put at the head of the infantry and, when they beat on their shields and cried out in their deep voices in a kind of a rhythmic chant, it made my blood run cold. I don't know where the pharaoh gets them or why they fight for him, but they're brave. No question there."

"If they're such fierce warriors, why is the pharaoh able to subjugate the southern lands?"

Caleb shrugged. "Our men are brave, too. But we're subjugated. The pharaoh is a great general."

"You think so?" asked Levi, surprised at this compliment coming from his friend.

"I know so. I was there. A lot of tricks up that one's fancy sleeve."

Then Levi related to Caleb what had occurred when he had gone to shave the ruler on his ship. Caleb shook his head and spat contemptuously on the ground.

"Some brothel they've got going here," he said. "I'd have killed any man who tried to look at my wife's bare tits. Incredible. I'm surprised he didn't invite you to give that Satiah woman a good shag. Ach—probably wanted you to envy him, that's all."

"I don't think so," was Levi's opinion. "The pharaoh finds her beautiful and wanted me to admire her. He thought nothing shameful in it and said so."

"Egypt—the land of no shame," said Caleb. "I'd heard about it, but never really believed the tales until I came here and saw it all with my own eyes. How a place can be so depraved and yet so mighty is beyond me. Did you see that god of theirs—the one with the big hard-on? Gave me a laugh, anyway."

"That's Min. I suppose the ladies pray to him. I don't know. I don't get what goes on here any more than you and look

158

how long I've been around now."

"Don't the Egyptians have any decent, useful gods—like for thunder and lightning or rain?"

"You ever notice it rain since you got here?"

"No," said Caleb, "come to think on it. Not once."

"The Egyptians don't have such gods because they don't need rain. They have the Nile and that's all the water they want."

"Bah! What I'd give to smell the air after a nice shower and to see the streams running down off the mountains, clean and clear without vicious monsters lurking in them. Or to see some proper trees, like an oak, and wild flowers growing in the valleys. I'd love a bite of an apple—or a leg of lamb, for sure. I'm tired of eating goose and stuff that I don't even recognize."

"They feed us well," Levi reminded him. "I know what it's like to starve. Anything's better than that as far as I'm concerned. We can eat the bread of Egypt without losing our own way of thinking. We don't need to become depraved."

"Well, they can just pray to my hard-on, all of these strange fuckers here. Mehy is never going to become like them while I'm in charge of him. I'll make sure he treats women with the proper respect. That Satiah is beautiful—sure—but I'd like to know what's wrong with the other one, Mehy's mother. To me she looks more beautiful. A man should honor the mother of his son, not behave like she doesn't even exist."

"Some say the pharaoh fucked his wife's mother—you know, raped her with a bunch of other men."

"Eh? What the devil for?"

"I don't know," said Levi. "But I don't believe it—not anymore."

"Let me tell you something—I heard the Egyptians stuck it to some of our own men after some battle. Perverted assholes! Maybe that's one of their customs, too—humiliate the enemy as much as possible. Don't bend over in this place. Might be kind of dangerous."

"We'd better quit this talk," said Levi. "Watch out—here comes the little man."

Mehy was running toward them with an excited look on his face.

"I just spoke to father," he announced breathlessly. "It's all set. We can go anywhere we like. So long as you're armed, Caleb, he won't worry. I don't even have to go to school for a few days. Isn't that grand?"

"How about that?" said Caleb, smiling fondly. "Where would you like to go?"

"Well, father says I should take you men to the temples at Karnak. A lot of nice buildings there. But they can wait. I've got other plans."

"Mehy," said Levi, "why do I smell trouble?"

"Yeah," Caleb added, "probably he wants to visit a whorehouse or some beer joint."

"You know I do!" the prince confirmed. "But father would flay me alive if he found out I was hanging around such places. So that's out. Didn't I tell you men before that I know a big secret? That's what I want to show you!"

Levi regarded him with one eye closed. "Mehy...would the ruler approve of you doing that?"

"No...but his exact words were that we can go wherever we want to. And this place I want to go to isn't bad. In fact, it's damned holy!"

"No booze and no whores there, I take it," was Caleb's response.

"Naw! This place is a kind of a...how do you say 'place where they bury people' in Canaanite, Levi?"

"*Bet olam*," Levi told him.

"*Bet olam*?" said Caleb. "Some kind of spooks there or something?"

"You got it!" replied Mehy. "We're going. But we have to venture—to the WEST!" he added with great gravity. "The abode of the dead. You two aren't afraid of ghosts, are you?"

"I could be," admitted Levi. "Well...when do we leave?"

"No time like the present. The horses are all hitched up. Let me drive, Caleb, please!"

"Sure, why not? But don't try anything wild. Don't set them off running, hear?"

"Thanks!" said the prince and ran off to tell the groom to bring out the team. And so Levi got into the car, behind Mehy and Caleb, for his first chariot ride ever. He held onto some straps, as he was told to do, and was advised to keep his balance at the rear, no matter what. Then Mehy took the reins and gave the command for the horses to begin their trot. When they came to a road, Mehy said, "Let's go a little faster, eh?"

"Fine," said his governor, "but not too fast. Change places with me, Levi. I don't want you falling out backwards."

Levi cautiously moved up in the crowded car and Caleb took hold of the straps, instead.

"Gallop!" yelled Mehy and the well-trained team plunged forward, the chariot bumping up and down on the unpaved road.

The whole thing was rather unsettling but fun, thought Levi. He wouldn't mind doing this every day. Caleb, too, apparently enjoyed the freedom of being on two wheels again outside of the palace training grounds and said, "Let 'em go, Mehy!"

"Yeehaw!" shouted the boy, and the team flew down the path to the desert until, at last, Caleb shouted, "Halt the car!"

Mehy obeyed, pulling back on the reins. The two young men, happy and laughing, shoved the exhilarated king's son around a little bit, showing they were proud of his handling of the animals.

"All right, you men, get out," Caleb told them. "I'm going to show you something, but, Mehy, don't ever let me catch you trying this yourself!"

When Levi and Mehy had jumped clear of the chariot, Caleb took the reins and vaulted up onto the back of one of animals. He gave the order to run and so they did, whereas Caleb stood up first on one horse and then straddled them, one foot upon each. In this fashion, he made them charge around in a wide circle in the sand, the empty car rattling behind. Never for a moment did Caleb threaten to lose his balance and Mehy jumped up and down with glee, waving his fists in the air. Levi just shook his head, smiling.

When Caleb finally brought the team back, he leapt down from his perch and Mehy hugged him enthusiastically.

"See?" said the Canaanite, putting a choke-hold on the prince, his white teeth flashing in a grin. "That's the true meaning of 'Master of the Horse'—and don't you forget it, lad!"

The great necropolis on the west bank of Thebes was one of the most desolate, yet eerily splendid, sites Levi had ever seen. It was an arid spot at the base of those cliffs and mountains that surrounded it. After Mehy got some guards to let them past a gate where the hills formed a narrow entrance, Levi saw that there were even a few man-made structures in this barren environment and very grand ones, at that.

"They're the Temples of A Million Years," the heir explained. "Each one honors a dead pharaoh. Father says he's going to start building his own pretty soon, but his tomb here has already got started. When I'm king, I'm going to build me a nice big temple, too, so that the priests can make offerings to my soul and nobody can ever forget me. But I don't think mine can be nicer than the one over there—unless I can get the man who designed it to draw up the plans."

The temple that Mehy was pointing to seemed to be built right into the mountain, only it was as magnificent as any palace, absolutely huge. Levi was certain there could be no more wonderful building in the entire world. It wasn't as large as the pyramids near Memphis, of course. Mehy had told him they were the biggest things on earth and had even drawn a picture of them for his friend. However, being Mehy, he had put crossed eyes and a silly grin on the face of the pharaoh with the body of a lion that rested near them. Yes, those other things might be impressive, but surely nothing could be as gracefully beautiful as the temple of the "holy mountain", as Mehy called it.

"Yes, kings are buried here," announced Mehy, grandly, "with heaps of treasure. A few other people, too. The rich and famous."

"You sure are the little historian," said Caleb. "Where's the treasure?"

"We can't see that!" said Mehy, rolling his eyes. "It's all underground where nobody can touch it. And there are guards here all the time to make sure people don't try to find it."

"It's a wonderful cemetery," said Levi. "But it doesn't look so haunted to me. Can we go inside the beautiful building?"

"That's the mortuary temple of Hatshepsut," Mehy informed. "Right beside the one of old King Montuhotep, who's probably rolling right there in his grave on account of an upstart woman encroaching on his sacred territory. We'd better not go there. Just in case."

164

"In case of what?" Caleb inquired.

"I...I don't like her," said Mehy. "She was mean. If her spirit is there, it might be an evil one."

"Mehy," said Levi, "do you know all about her?"

"Sure! Nobody can keep anything from me. I just don't want to go in there, that's all."

"So that's the secret—the temple of a wicked woman?" asked Caleb.

"No, that's not it! Uh oh...here come the Medjai, the guards! Let me handle this, men."

A couple of dark-skinned men approached. When they noticed the princely side-lock of Mehy, they gave him the salute.

"What brings you here, king's son?" one of them asked.

"I've come to venerate the goddess of the mountain peak," Mehy answered coolly. "And to show my friends the Great Place of my ancestors. They don't have anything like this where they come from."

"I'll just bet," said one of the Medjai. "Look around, if you want to, but don't get hurt or anything. Don't get us into any trouble, if you know what I mean. There are scorpions and snakes about."

"Sure there are!" Mehy told him. "But my big friend here can kill anything that moves as fast as you can say 'phooey'. He's the man who slew the crocodile that wanted to eat me in the river, in case you haven't heard."

"No fooling—that's him?" said the guard. " We did hear

165

about it. All honor to you, great man!"

"He doesn't understand Egyptian so well," said Mehy. "But I'm teaching him little by little. So let us pass on and don't worry about a thing."

"Good to see you, king's son. Take care!" The Medjai saluted again and went off somewhere.

"That settles them," said Mehy. "Now all we have to do is climb that big hill over there. The one with the statue of the man sitting at the top."

"What about the snakes and scorpions?" Levi wondered.

"There aren't that many," Mehy scoffed. "People actually live here. That's their village over there. They dig out and decorate tombs for whoever wants one. But tomorrow is a holiday and they'll be celebrating early because they just got their allotment of beer for the next month. Nobody working here today."

"Why do we need to go way up there?" said Caleb. "Looks pretty high to me."

"The secret is up there. Let's go!"

It was, indeed, a long, dirty climb to the summit of the hill and Levi and Caleb glanced at one another wearily from time to time. But Mehy, like a little mountain goat, didn't seem to mind the effort or how filthy he was getting.

"There's the tomb!" he announced, pointing upward. "Doesn't it look great?"

"That's a tomb?" said Levi. "It could be somebody's villa.

It looks just like the house of my old master from the outside."

"It is someone's house! Just come and see! Wait. Hold on. First you have to swear an oath you'll never tell anyone you've been here."

"Ay! Didn't I say I smelled trouble?"

"All right, we swear," said Caleb. "Is it a tomb or not? What's in there?"

"A ghost," said Mehy, looking very pleased with himself. "A real live ghost."

"Bullshit!" said Caleb. "Mehy, there had better be something up there worth coming all this way. Go, go, let's get it over with."

When they reached the grandiose tomb, Mehy took a deep breath and yelled, "Come out and show yourself, my lord! It is the king's son, himself, who wishes a word with you!"

"Here goes nothing," murmured Caleb. But he was wrong. After a moment or two, a figure did appear. It seemed to be a man dressed in nothing but rags, with long, unkempt hair and a beard in the same condition.

"Some ghost!" Levi said, giving Mehy a little push. "That's nothing but a hermit. We've got plenty of those in Canaan. You dragged us way up here for him?"

"Not so loud," said Mehy. "He's no hermit. He's the greatest prisoner in all of Egypt—that's who he is! And we're going to visit him."

"Is it really you, Amunemhat?" the old fellow called out

hoarsely.

"Nobody else!" Mehy replied. "May we come up?"

"Come and be welcome," said the man. "Be careful of the stones."

The tomb—or house—didn't smell too nicely but its walls and ceiling were decorated and there were a few pieces of fine furniture in there. There was also a big stone vat with carvings on it, filled nearly to be brim with straw.

"Sit wherever you can," their host invited.   Mehy decided to seat himself on the edge of the stone bathtub and Caleb joined him there.   Levi, having the idea there might be considerable vermin amid all that straw, opted for a chair. The old man took another.

"This is Senenmut," Mehy said in Canaanite. "But you can call him Seni if you want to. Or maybe '*adon*' would be better. He's a very important person."

"Does he speak our language?" wondered Caleb.

"Sure! He knows everything, don't you Seni?"

Senenmut cleared his throat. "Canaanite? Yes...I will remember it in a moment. It's been so long."

"He hasn't seen me since I was a kid," Mehy volunteered. "Not since my father came home in victory. It was father who made him stay here—in the very tomb he had prepared for himself."

"Why is his bathtub full of straw?" asked Levi. "Nobody wants to haul that much water way up here, I suppose."

168

Senenmut emitted a kind of rusty sound that Levi supposed was a laugh. "That's a sarcophagus—mine. I was supposed to be buried in it. I will be one of these days, perhaps. But for now it serves as a bed."

"Levi never saw a sarcophagus in his life," said Mehy. "He's from Canaan and he shaves my father because Si-Bast's hand got shaky. Beside me is Caleb, a very famous crocodile killer—also from Canaan. Say something to Seni, Caleb. He'll understand you."

"I am also a prisoner, sir. Taken in battle."

"I've heard of you," said Senenmut. "You have all my gratitude."

"You've heard of me?" Caleb wondered. "Well, what do you know about that!"

"Aw," Mehy protested. "he's not a real prisoner anymore. Father's made him my governor—just like you used to be to mother."

"How fares it with your mother?" Senenmut inquired.

"Not so badly," said Mehy. "She's well. I know she'd come to see you if she could."

"How did you get permission to do so, Mehy?" wondered the old man. "I never thought I would see you again."

"He didn't get permission," said Levi. "But here we are, anyway!"

"These are my best friends," Mehy said. "They'll never tell. Men, that big old temple you saw down below—Seni built that. He designed it. That's why he's still alive. Father wants him to look at it every day for the rest of his life. You see, Seni was...well, Hatshepsut depended upon him because he's so intelligent. He was my mother's tutor when she was little and mine, too...for awhile."

"And now," continued the architect, "I'm a reviled traitor and a dead man for all practical purposes...as you see. All that's missing is the mummy wrappings."

"I don't believe you're a traitor," said Mehy. "You just did your duty. You couldn't help it if the woman decided to make herself king in my father's place. You couldn't stop her."

"Mehy," said Senenmut, "forgive me, but I didn't try to stop her. Not at all. I was nothing but a son of servants who had the good fortune—if you want to call it that—to be educated in the palace. It was Hatshepsut who elevated me until there was no greater servant in all of Egypt. Yes, I served much too well."

"I know all about it," said Mehy. "I may look young, but I know everything. When I'm pharaoh, I'll pardon you and set you free."

"Will you, Mehy?" asked the old man with a little smile. "I'll try to hold on until then."

Mehy wiped away a tear and Caleb said to him softly, "No crying, Mehy. Never in public—remember?"

The prince nodded. "Even I'm a traitor just for saying those words—but I don't care," he said with a little hiccough. "I'm tired of people suffering...my mother, everybody. Why can't he let people be happy—live the way they want to? Why is my father so angry at the whole world? Why can't he forgive people anything?"

Senenmut leaned his emaciated frame forward. From his profile, under his scraggly hair, Levi could see that he had once been a good-looking man.

"Mehy, listen to me," the architect said. "It's not his fault. All the trouble began before he was even born and fell upon him like an evil sickness. I'm not innocent, lad. I belong here. I betrayed your father and his birthright. He was already the king and I should have been on his side. But I didn't help him. I helped the woman, instead, because I didn't want to be poor again. I did some bad things. None of what took place in those days was right—and I was part of the wrongdoing. Very much so. But, Mehy, my heart rejoices at seeing you. You are a man now! I appreciate you and your friends coming to visit me, but I think you must go back. I don't want you to get these men into difficulty on my account. Give my best regards to your mother and tell her I love her as always."

"Yes, Seni," said Mehy, rising from the sarcophagus. "I will. Do the people from the village bring you enough to eat and everything?"

The old prisoner nodded. "I have enough."

"Pardon me, sir, for asking," said Caleb, "but what do you do up here to keep from going mad?"

"I have books and lamps and—and things to write with.

The craftsmen of the cemetery are good to me because my reputation with them, at least, remains sound. They give me food and beer and oil because I once supplied them well. On my last day as a free man, the king said to me 'Go up to that great tomb, which you built for yourself at my expense, and write the story of your misguided life, learned man'—and so I do as he suggested, when the arthritis isn't too bad and my fingers can move."

Caleb just shook his head but Levi said, "Farewell, then, Senenmut. As you have repented, I wish you well."

"Goodbye, Seni," said Mehy. "Just remember what I told you."

"Goodbye, lad. You are very good. You have the eyes of your sweet mother."

On their way down the slope, Levi said to Mehy "You made it seem like a joke, at first, but now you're sad. What's the matter with you? This was a dangerous errand."

"I made it seem like a joke—an adventure—so I wouldn't have to come here alone. I can't go anywhere alone—you know that. If I had said 'Come with me to see an old man', you wouldn't have wanted to do it."

"So we're all traitors now," Caleb said, glowering. "Your father will find out about this visit somehow. Maybe they've got some empty tombs up there for me and Levi."

"What's more, you've got to stop telling people you plan to change all that your father has done when you're the king!" Levi warned. "Perhaps your intentions are good and just—but please keep them in your heart. Say nothing more about them until the day the crowns of Egypt are upon your head. Be true to your father while he wears them."

"All right," Mehy promised. "I know how to take advice."

"The old man looks ill. He'll be dead soon. You won't be able to do anything for him."

"Don't be so hard on the lad," Caleb surprised Levi by saying, gruffly. "Can't you see he just wants people not to lose hope? Maybe you're not the best one to advise him, Levi. You don't seem to hope for anything."

With those words the chariot-fighter went on ahead as though he were in a big hurry to get out of the valley of the kings, the domain of the dead.

"You're the prudent man," Mehy told Levi. "The one the old sages whose writings I have to read always praise. But I'm not so foolish as you think. Father likes you very much. I think he's got plans for you."

"Plans?"

"Sure!" said Mehy. "He put you in school, didn't he? Once I asked him if he could find another boy to study with me and his answer was that I get up to enough mischief on my own and don't need any distractions. But you're in school with me and a barber doesn't need to know reading and writing. So maybe father doesn't intend for you to just do shaving all your life. I'll tell you what—learn as much as I know and I'll make you my chief advisor someday. But you've got some catching up to do there, pal."

"I'll do my best," said Levi.

"So you're not in danger and neither is Caleb. He wouldn't punish you—even if he found out we came here. Have you ever noticed how clever my father is? I'll never be half as clever, but I know one thing he doesn't know. That old man we just visited—he's my mother's father. Even Seni doesn't realize I know about that."

"Does anybody else suspect this?" Levi asked, completely taken aback.

"Probably only half of Egypt," the boy replied. "Everybody knows Hatshepsut couldn't stand her brother, the father of my father. But Seni...with him it was a different story. The woman-king adored him. Anyway, my father's father was a leper."

"A leper? Mehy, are you making all this up?"

"Why would I? I'm sick of all these secrets. Sometimes I even wish I didn't have to be king and could have been born into a nice, quiet family somewhere. At least I used to wish that. I didn't have any friends, no boys my own age to play with—nothing but work to do. But now I feel better. There are people I can talk to. When I get married, I'm going to be good to my wife —whoever they find for me. Even if it kills me, I'm not going to make her mad or feel sad. When my wife has babies, I'm going to hold her hand and try to comfort her, make sure my kids are born properly."

"That's nice of you, Mehy," said Levi, "but men shouldn't be around when babies are being born. That's women's work."

"You think so?" said the prince. "Who do you think delivered me?"

"Who?"

"Si-Bast—that's who. A barber, just like you. He was the only one my mother trusted to do the job. Not one single other person."

"Wasn't he a servant of her mother?"

"Not really. Even a woman-king doesn't need a barber. Si-Bast shaved that man up on the hill. Don't you get it—a man's barber has got to be his friend. If he doesn't like the barber, he has to get rid of him. You can't have a suspected enemy holding a sharp blade to your throat every day."

"I get it," said Levi.

"That's why Si-Bast got to be father's barber until he became too old. That was his reward. For doing a good job with me and making sure I was born alive."

Levi shivered. "Brrr...it's getting rather cold out here."

"Well, it's winter," said Mehy. "We'd better get home."

Levi took hold of the prince's arm. "Listen, little man—just one more thing before we go. I think you're forgetting that, for you to become king, your father will need to die. If I had a father who loved me as much as yours loves you, I think the day I lost him would be the worst day of my life—nothing to look forward to at all."

"But it's father who told me to think about being king a lot —so that I won't be overwhelmed by so much responsibility when it happens!"

"Mehy, you're going to be overwhelmed, anyway. And the one person you'll most want to turn to for help and support won't be there. He'll be here, in this place."

"I know that," said Mehy, "but it's not going to happen for a long time. My father's a strong man. It'll be ages before he ends up here."

"Well…he lives a dangerous life, going off to war every spring. It only takes one enemy arrow."

"Aw, Levi—you never saw all the stuff father's got. You should see his body armor—nothing could pierce that, I'll bet. Besides, who'd dare to kill my father? People get scared just looking at him. They run away and hide in their walled cities or some caves or something when they see him coming. He hardly even has to fight with them all that much anymore, that's how terrifying his reputation is now. That's what he told me and he ought to know!"

"Yes, you're right," said the barber, putting his hand on the heir's shoulder. "I forgot about all that. Of course nobody could kill your father. I'm a fool even to imagine that anyone might try something so daft. Come on, let's go."

"Yeah," said Mehy, "I'll have to be scary someday, too. You know something, Levi —and don't tell this to Caleb because he'd only laugh—there are certain people who scare me right now."

"You? The man who faced the crocodile without a weapon?"

"I can't believe I did that," replied the prince, a modest person at heart. "I'm frightened of girls—well, not all of them. Only the ones who are so beautiful that their faces freeze a person right in his tracks! Does that make me weird?"

"I'll tell *you* a little secret—most men are scared of such women."

"But not my old man! He even yells at them and everything. You think Caleb is scared of those awfully beautiful girls?"

"Not he!" answered Levi. "Because he knows he's just as pretty as they are."

"Hey!" said the boy, quickening his pace. "I think I'll tell him you said that!"

"No you won't, you little beast!" said the barber, hastening after the prince and losing his footing. "Mehy! I'll settle you, do you hear me?"

"How?" the prince called out over his shoulder.

"How? What about that picture you drew in class of the teacher doing something to a woman? The one you made me hide in my shirt when he came back into the room!"

Mehy stopped and turned around, his jaw having dropped.

"I've still got that picture—keeping it in a safe place for the day it ever snows in southern Egypt!"

"Aw, calm down, can't you? I was only joking! I'm no telltale."

Levi got up and tried, unsuccessfully, to brush the dirt from his clothes. "Artist!" he called after Mehy in an irritable tone.

Chapter Eleven

That evening, Levi received a note from Mehy, asking him to come to see him. The lad, bathed and safely tucked into bed, wanted to say goodnight and murmured some apologies for his "childish behavior". Mehy asked if Levi couldn't see his way to burning that drawing. The barber promised to get rid of it and said, "Mehy, do you know a story called The Doomed Prince?"

"Sure," said the boy, "it's famous now because my father wrote it when he was young. It's amazing, what there is of it, and has been copied about a hundred times. A dog even talks in it! I've got a copy."

"Does it end well?"

"There is no ending," said Mehy. "The prince meets a demon and that's about it—stops right at the best part."

"Why would anyone want to copy a story missing a conclusion?"

"Because it's the work of my father! It shows his genius, even as a boy, and what a shame it is that no one knew that about him then and that he was treated so badly, besides. I asked him how the rest was supposed to go on and he said he didn't know. The prince makes friends with the demon is all, makes a pact with him. Father told me the story was about him, in a way, and that no one can really imagine his own fate—or doesn't really want to. He believes people will just keep on copying the tale until, one day, a clever man will like it enough to think of a way to make an end. That's what father wants to happen. But you know something, when I was able to read it on my own, it seemed like the tale was about me!"

"Why was that?"

"Well, the prince grew up in a house in the desert with just a few servants and could never go anywhere or have any fun on account of the Seven Hathors having predicted a bad fate for him when he was born. That he was going to die by a crocodile, a snake, or a dog. He couldn't even have a dog because the hound might bite him or something. I felt like that boy. Well, you can imagine."

Mehy laid down his head and Levi pulled the covers up to his neck. "You had a dog, Mehy! You told me you didn't want another because you were too sad when it died."

"Did you have a dog when you were a boy?"

"No, I didn't have anything that was any good."

"You'll be rich someday, you know. If you'll just stay here and keep me company."

"I will, Mehy. Trust me, the Seven Hathors, those good

enchantresses, blessed you in your cradle. They gave you everything you need for a good life. You're already past the worst part, aren't you? You're grown now and don't believe in fanciful tales anymore."

"That's right," said Mehy. "But I just wish my father had written a different story and not something creepy about a doomed prince waiting for the thing that kills. They say writing is magical and anything written can come true—like a prophecy. You believe that?"

"No, I certainly don't—and I'm sorry I even mentioned that story. Things don't come to pass because someone puts ink on paper. Your father wrote the tale because he was unhappy. In his mind, he was a doomed prince—but look at him now! On top of the world."

"Levi, I think it was father who was waiting for the thing that kills."

"Perhaps," said Levi. "Probably. But you mustn't dwell on that now, Mehy. It was all so long ago. Nothing happened to him."

"Well, goodnight, Levi, and say goodnight to Caleb for me."

"Sleep well, Mehy. Your destiny is for no man ever to dislike you. That's what I predict—all I know for sure."

Levi went out into the spacious courtyard of the palace to get a breath of air. The thought of that man in the tomb,

181

Senenmut, had made his mind restless. Indeed, he was a traitor but, at the same time, he seemed hardly a villain and Mehy obviously recalled him with fondness. Why not, as he was the boy's own grandfather. Levi wondered if the pharaoh, himself, knew of this. If he did, then what was the reason he referred to his queen as his half-sister? But Neferura was no sister to the king at all, but merely some sort of relative. Now Levi the barber was privy to a secret that he could not tell his master on account of Mehy and the whole idea of that made him feel ill at ease. If Thutmose disdained Neferura while believing she was the daughter of one of his enemies, how would he feel about her if he knew she was born of two? Certainly, the situation of the queen was pitiful enough as matters stood, her beauty wasted while she languished as the wife of a man who had no use for her. The same applied to the Canaanite sisters. No wonder all these ladies had decided to forge a sort of alliance in their neglected state.

But Levi, as soon as he got outside, was shown by the light of the moon that Neferura was not so ignored as he had thought. For there, in the courtyard, stood Caleb, staring up at a window of a dimly lit room. Gazing back at him was none other than the chief wife of the pharaoh. From somewhere in the house there was the distant sound of music and a male singer chanted a plaintive melody of love in a strong voice that could still be heard outdoors in a muted fashion—doubtless for the entertainment of Thutmose and Satiah.

Levi gave a low whistle and got the attention of his friend.

"Caleb, over here!"

When Caleb joined him, Levi frowned and said, "Isn't there trouble enough? What is it you think you're doing now?"

"I'm only a man, aren't I?"

"Come over this way," urged Levi. "Let's sit down."

Caleb followed him, glancing backward over his shoulder. But the lady at the window had gone.

"She's too fond of you," whispered the barber. "Don't you know that? A lonely wife can cause problems—particularly this one!"

"What if I'm fond of her? I'm lonely, as well—aren't you?"

"No!" Levi told him. "At least not so much I'm willing to risk my life over it."

"I came to this land full of hatred," said the chariot-fighter, "but fate decreed for me that I should love first a boy and then his mother. The family of my enemy."

"You can't love her," Levi protested. "It's just the moonlight and that blasted singing. What about your wife in Canaan?"

"I'll never see her again. I can feel it in my bones. This is where I'll die—right here in Egypt. I know that, too. So while I still live, let me feel something besides anger and grief. I'm tired of only evil things inside me." Caleb bent forward and put his head in his hands. "I wish I could kill him so that Mehy could be the king. Maybe I should."

"Mehy the Deliverer, eh?" said Levi. "You're talking nonsense—and the same old evil. Mehy's just a boy who doesn't know what he's saying half the time. He loves his father, besides. Do you suppose he'd thank you for getting rid of him?"

"I'm not so sure Mehy thinks his father is so wonderful," Caleb replied. "You're the one who loves that son of a bitch."

"I don't love the pharaoh. But I know him. He's...."

"What?" asked Caleb, derisively.

"Just a man. A man like you—except not so young and not so good-looking that he's got half the women here in heat over him."

"He's got what he wants, hasn't he?"

"No," said the barber. "I don't think so. That's the problem."

"I wish I could go up there," said his friend, staring at the empty window again. "I'd like to take her in my arms and make love to her all night long."

"What? You're crazy. You're twenty-six years old and she's maybe..."

"I don't care what she is. Her lovely, sad eyes have bewitched me. She's beautiful but her husband doesn't want her. I want her! She looks at me like I'm not just some servant but the equal of the king. She hardly ever smiles, Mehy told me. But I've seen her smile at me from her window. Haven't you ever wanted a woman?"

Levi decided against telling Caleb about his fantasies of

Satiah. Besides, he didn't think the older man's longing for Neferura was quite on the same order. He understood that much now, as Caleb had not used his favorite word in reference to what he wanted to do with the pharaoh's chief wife.

"Forget it," was all he said. "It's useless talk."

Suddenly, there was someone else in the courtyard. It was the ruler, himself. The blood rushed to Levi's head. But he couldn't have overheard their conversation—much less be able to read their minds. This must be something having to do with Mehy and the valley of the dead kings.

"Beautiful evening," said Thutmose in Canaanite. "But a bit chilly, don't you think? Why don't you men come inside and have a drink? Come on, follow me."

Having little other choice, Levi and Caleb wandered after the king. He led them to a room in which were the favorite, Satiah, and the musicians, who were still playing. Satiah seemed to visibly brighten when she saw the young men. At least she was dressed, this time, and adorned with every kind of wonderful jewelry, besides, glittering like a little piece of the firmament in the light of the lamps.

"Have a seat," invited their master. "Hey—you musicians —do you know any Canaanite songs?"

The music stopped. The singer, evidently a blind fellow, said, "Certainly, my lord. Their music is rather wild, however."

"Well, good—then make it something lively. And you others over there—bring these men something to drink!"

185

Levi began to enjoy himself and clapped his hands to the rhythm of a familiar tune. In this, the pharaoh joined him. He seemed in a merry mood and evidently didn't care if the entire household was kept awake by all the noise. In fact, Thutmose appeared a bit drunk already, which was a good thing in Levi's estimation. Otherwise he might have noticed Satiah ogling Caleb, who was proceeding to get inebriated, himself.

After this had continued for a while, suddenly the pharaoh called out "That's enough playing! You musicians can go to bed. Satiah, we have availed ourselves of your beauteous company long enough. Good night, darling."

The girl didn't look very happy about being dismissed, but knew better than to argue. She got up and swept out of the chamber, a cloud of scent in her wake. The musicians gathered up their instruments and went their way. The pharaoh also rose, a bit unsteadily, motioned to Levi and Caleb to remain where they were and walked over to say something to one of his servants. When he came back Thutmose said, "Not tired, are you? Mehy didn't wear you out today, I hope."

"No, my lord," Levi answered. "We're fine."

"That's good," said the king, "because we're about to get a visitor."

To Levi's immense relief, the ruler asked no questions regarding where they had been that day and what they had done. He just said something about how much he liked the music of Canaan and some dancing girls he had seen there who had hips that could move faster than a dog could shake water from its fur. The pharaoh's conversation was easy and unstrained. He asked how Mehy was progressing with the Canaanite language and seemed very content when Levi told him he now spoke it as well as Caleb and himself.

"Does he say the curse words?" the ruler wondered.

"Well," said Levi, "he *could* say them, but Caleb here won't allow it. He's very strict with the lad, wants to make sure he grows up to be as dignified as possible, considering his future expectations. Still, my lord can well believe Mehy could talk like a soldier any time he liked. He could swear worse than a sailor, come to that, if he took the notion. He's the best educated boy in the world."

Thutmose laughed and slapped Levi on the back. Before very much longer, a girl appeared, quite a good-looking one, dressed in nothing more than a wig, some trinkets, and a thin girdle about her own naked hips.

"Here's one of our own dancers come to entertain," explained the pharaoh.

"Doesn't she need music?" the barber wanted to know. By now he had drunk too much wine to be shocked by anything.

"Oh, I don't think so," the king told him. "Well—good night, men. Enjoy the rest of your evening. Do me the favor of putting out the lights when you're through." With those words, he took his leave.

The dancer smiled and, spying the pharaoh's half-full

goblet, drank the wine that remained. She seemed to feel right at home in her surroundings.

Levi looked at Caleb, who said "Help me up, pal."

"Caleb, we can't just..."

"I can't—that's for sure. Give me a hand."

Levi helped the chariot-fighter from his cushions on the floor and Caleb, shaking his head a little as though to clear it, staggered out through the door.

So that leaves only me, the barber thought to himself. Well, why not? One wouldn't like to offend the master by refusing his gift.

Caleb, for his part, wasn't all that drunk. He had been, after all, a cavalry officer and had swallowed a lot more wine in the company of his comrades than he had this evening with no ill effects. Caleb could hold his drink well, he knew that—but he also knew that Levi was too shy and inexperienced to have intercourse with a woman with anyone else around. So he had left his friend to learn what that was all about and decided just to go to bed. It wasn't that he didn't need a woman. In fact, he needed one badly. But it wasn't some little trollop of a dancing girl that he lusted after.

It was late and the palace was dark and still with only a few lamps on stands burning in the halls here and there. In the best condition, it wasn't that easy to find ones way about the big house and Caleb, being new there, certainly didn't know the place and his condition could have been much better. He became confused. Where were his quarters? To the right or to the left? Caleb turned to the right and come to a hallway that he thought looked familiar. He entered a room beyond a curtain that had only one small light burning in it. That couldn't be his room. Nobody ever left a light in there. Besides, this chamber was much larger and there were three beds in it and not merely one. Caleb smiled. So that's where they were kept.

The Canaanite entered the room and cleared his throat noisily. One of the sleeping figures bolted upright and gasped "The pharaoh!"

"No!" came the response from the next bed. "Too tall!"

"It's the *gibor gadol*!" said yet another voice. "And he's in our room!"

"*Shalom*, my little beauties," said the "big hero". "I seem to be lost."

"You're lying," somebody said with a giggle.

"Upon my honor—I really have lost my way."

The girls crept forward on their beds to get a better look at him. From what Caleb could see, they don't look too frightened or displeased.

"We should boot you out," said one of the princesses.

"Aha!" replied Caleb. "So you think the three of you can take me on, eh?" More giggling. "I think I'll sleep right here. Who's got room for me?"

"You're a very bad man."

"I'm a very good man. Who wants to put me to the test?"

"Just listen to him. He must be drunk!"

"Sure, I'm best when I'm drunk," said Caleb. "I'm used to four at once but I suppose I could make do with only three."

"Such a boastful fellow. Thinks he's so great."

"You don't like me? Too ugly for you pretty little doves?"

"No!"

"Don't tell him that! Don't encourage the big fool!"

Caleb laughed. "Fool am I, then? There's a bigger fool here than I am because he isn't in here right now!"

"Ah, shame on you for such talk!"

"Better go before you get caught!"

"Oh, well," said Caleb. "I know when I'm not wanted."

"Maybe you can stay just a little while..."

"No he can't! What's the matter with you, sister?"

"You girls liked me on the river, but it seems you've changed your minds."

"We like you! We just want you to keep your big, swollen head."

"Do I need it for something?" Caleb asked. "All right, you ladies are too grand for me. I know my place. But I'd heard so much about your great beauty that I couldn't resist having a look for myself. See—I'm wearing one of your works of art—never had anything finer in my life. Nice talking to you, sweethearts. Sleep well."

"Good night, Caleb. We won't tell anybody you were

here."

"You just got lost, that's all."

"I wish you could come during the day."

"Hush! Don't tell him that. He just might do it. He's not scared of anything."

"Especially lovely women," Caleb agreed. "Farewell, little kittens."

"Farewell...beautiful man."

When Caleb left the room, there were tears in his eyes. What had those sisters ever done to deserve this helpless existence? Come to that, what had he? The chariot-fighter thought he'd better not drink so much in the future, for tonight he felt as though his heart might burst. Meanwhile, his bladder felt the same way and he urinated out of a window. Somehow, he found his way back to his own room, although it took him awhile to do it. Caleb undressed in the dark and got into bed, pulling the sheepskin cover, that Mehy had provided, over himself, grateful for something at least. He had just begun to drift off when he heard a slight noise, as though someone had brushed up against something. Caleb had become a very light sleeper as he trusted no one since he had come to Egypt—except Levi and Mehy, who were decent fellows. He opened his eyes to see a white figure moving toward him. A woman! Caleb sat up. This was becoming a very strange night, indeed.

For a brief moment the Canaanite thought it might be Neferura, but that was only a hopeful illusion. Then he recognized the strong perfume. It was Satiah! The woman unexpectedly flung herself on top of him and Caleb fell backward onto his pillow.

"No!" he whispered in Egyptian. "You—go!"

"Let me be with you," insisted Satiah in a breathless way. "I'm sick of sleeping with the old man. I'm young!"

Caleb had understood hardly a word the girl said, but her actions were clear enough. The gown covering her body was as thin as gossamer and he could feel her large breasts pressing against his bare chest. Satiah began to kiss his mouth and when Caleb turned his head, started on his ear. This was too much for Caleb. He was a young man, to be sure, and his body began to respond rapidly, even though every bit of sense in his head told him he must pry this girl from him and push her out of the room. But, instead, he almost instinctively began to caress her left breast and move his mouth onto hers. Before long, Satiah pulled the cover down and lowered herself onto Caleb's erection, moving up and down in an expert fashion. Caleb, who had not lain with a woman for a long time, would have climaxed very soon except that he had imbibed plenty of wine and so he lasted long enough for Satiah to gratify herself. She collapsed on his chest with a sigh.

"Go, go!" Caleb rasped. "Go now!"

And, to his great relief, the king's wife did just that, recovering enough to slip out of his quarters as silently as a phantom.

Caleb put his arms under his head and stared up at the ceiling, engulfed in a mixture of remorse, sadness and loneliness. He had always considered himself a man of strength and action, casting aside fear when put to the test, but he had just been vanquished by a mere woman and now he was really up against the wall. Caleb knew that Satiah, who was just as guilty as he, would never say anything about what they had done together—but what if somebody had chanced to see her coming or going? And what if this audacious female, having developed a taste for him, decided to make a habit of coming to him in this way? It seemed to Caleb that he was a marked man for certain. Well, thought Caleb, if I'm to die then at least I've cuckolded my enemy, shamed him worse than he has done me by dragging me here in handcuffs as a dishonored, defeated warrior.

Yet, somehow, this notion gave Caleb very little satisfaction. No man, even the king of Egypt, deserved to be brought that low—having his own wife sneaking into the bed of another. And this very night, the pharaoh had even offered him a woman so that he and Levi needn't feel too deprived. In his own strange way, this king seemed to care about his servants, grateful, no doubt, for their loyalty to his son.

Mehy! Caleb felt that he had wronged the boy, as well— wasn't it he who was teaching him to be a man of courage and honor? And Neferura, too! The queen, whom he loved, and whom he was almost certain loved him, would never have crept into his room like a dissolute piece, no matter how much she might have liked to be near him. And Levi—if he knew—would probably never want to speak to him again. Levi, although having come from the lowest level of society, seemed to have as much sense of what was right and honorable as had he been raised in a noble house. Yes, thought Caleb, like I was—the prince without any honor left at all.

Chapter Twelve

The next day, a weary Caleb was reminded by Levi that it was a big holiday. The barber, as reticent as usual, offered no information to his friend about his adventure with the dancing girl of the previous evening. Levi, for his part, found it very odd that the chariot-fighter asked him no questions or made any teasing remarks. In fact, Caleb looked in a bad way. Probably, the man was suffering from the effects of the wine.

"You sick?" Levi asked. "You look awful."

"I feel like shit. Where's Mehy?"

"Getting ready for the big day, I suppose. Today the pharaoh sits in great state, outside where anybody can see him. I hear that any man in Egypt, no matter how lowly, who has a petition or some grievance can present it to him. It's a custom. It happens this afternoon."

"You think I could petition him to drop dead?" grumbled Caleb.

"You're not a citizen of Egypt—and stop being so grumpy. You want some hair of the dog? I can get it for you."

Caleb shook his head. "I don't want anything—except to get out of here. I'm at the end of my rope. I can't take it anymore."

"I think you should go back to sleep," Levi said. "Better try to get some rest because you're expected this afternoon. That's the word I got. The pharaoh has requested we both show up. We're to be honored."

"What?" Caleb looked aghast.

"Why is that so surprising—especially in your case? Listen, Caleb, you can't refuse any more honors. You got away with that once, but don't push your luck. You can't embarrass the king twice. Are you listening to me?"

Caleb heaved up a great moan. "I wish I were dead."

"Well, you look half-way there already. I'll tell you what —lie down. I'll get you something for your headache. I've met one of the ruler's physicians here, not a bad fellow at all. He was summoned because one of the pharaoh's personal servants took sick. He's got some medicine that will help you, I'm sure. I'll ask him. After that, I'll trim your hair and beard a little to make sure you look nice as you can."

Levi was surprised to note that the expression of Caleb had changed. Instead of appearing gloomy, he was regarding Levi in a way that he had never done before.

"Whatever happens," began Caleb, "I want you to know

that your friendship has meant a great deal to me. Maybe I don't always show it—but that's the truth."

"Aw...what kind of talk is this? Nothing's going to happen. But just don't refuse that honor—that's all. As a friend, I'm asking you. No, begging you."

"I'm not refusing much of anything these days," Caleb told him. "Don't spoil your day by worrying about me. I don't need any medicine. You can cut my hair, if you want to. It's fine with me. I'll make it through the ceremony."

The occasion of the pharaoh showing himself to the people, even allowing them to speak to him in person, happened only once a year on the last day of the month before the second season of the Egyptian civil calendar, winter, began. The event took place in a field outside of the temple of Amun. The king's throne had been brought there and also a number of other beautifully wrought chairs. Most people had to stand, of course, including the sovereign's two Canaanite servants. Hundreds of persons were present.

Levi had discovered that it was not exactly true that just anyone could talk to the pharaoh. There was not enough time for that. Only a certain number of petitioners had been selected by the highest official of the king—his vizier, Neferweben. This great man was the first to emerge from the temple and he was followed by the high priest. Neferweben held a long, golden pole in his hand, topped with a big white feather. The High Priest had the pelt of a leopard draped over his upper body. The exalted pontiff of the chief god of Thebes, Amun-Ra, took a seat, but the vizier intoned, in a loud voice, all the names and titles of King Thutmose.

Then the king, himself, appeared amid much cheering, whistling and the clapping of hands. That was something new to the barber, this clapping of hands when there was not even any music to keep time to. Another strange Egyptian custom, apparently. The pharaoh sat down in his place. On his head was a high crown of red leather with the cobra attached to it and on top of the red crown was an even higher white object, tapering off into a rounded tip. Levi thought that some men could look mighty silly wearing this odd headgear but on Thutmose, with his strong features, it appeared absolutely regal and magnificent. In fact, he looked magnificent in every sense, his body covered in white, pleated linen, his belt and apron heavily encrusted with gleaming threads, beadwork and studs—even his sandals being works of art. In each of his fists the pharaoh held an object of gold and some blue material, one resembling a shepherd's crook and the other being a kind of stick with strands of beads of various colors hanging from it. These were crossed over his chest.

Next to come out was Mehy, also carrying a pole with a white plume. The prince stood next to his father. For him there was tremendous cheering and clapping, as well. Unlike the pharaoh, who had shown no sign of emotion, Mehy smiled at the people and even waved to them before he bowed to the king. This acknowledgment of their presence caused such a roar from the onlookers as Levi had never heard in all his days. The boy has a lot of style, thought Levi, and looked at Caleb, who was smiling, himself, now with pride. Mehy sat himself down on a stool at the feet of his father, who gave him a little tap on his head with one of his royal implements. This gesture caused much laughter and more whistling and applause. The king put his royal scepters down on his lap.

Then the vizier announced the name and titles of Queen Neferura. Evidently it was not considered polite to whistle and cheer at a lady, but her appearance aroused murmurs of admiration, nonetheless. She wore a kind of tight-fitting white dress, with two straps that failed to conceal her breasts entirely, but did well enough in that respect. A scarlet cloak decorated with glittering sequins hung about her shoulders.

"Look at that," said Caleb. "She's got a vulture on her head!"

Surely enough, the crown of Neferura consisted of a golden vulture, head, wings, claws, tail-feathers and all. However, the presence of this ugly bird atop her wig did nothing to detract from the beauty of the queen and even enhanced it in a way. In her left hand, the king's chief wife held a very ornate thing that resembled a drooping flower. The great lady bowed to her husband and offered him her right hand, which, to Levi's amazement, the pharaoh held to his lips. Then Neferura took her chair at the king's right. After that followed the other wives of Thutmose—all four of them! More murmuring, very much more. Satiah had on the same dress as Neferura but her cloak was blue. On her head she wore a different type of crown of a very complicated design. She held the same object as Neferura and her hand was also kissed by the pharaoh, but Levi noted that he lingered a bit longer upon the hand of Satiah. The queen did not watch this but looked impassively straight ahead, as though nothing about Satiah was worth her attention at all.

The Canaanite wives wore their colorful, embroidered dresses they had brought from home but they also had some beautiful golden things upon their heads and all kinds of jewelry on their necks, wrists and ankles. Each one had a little ring in her nostril. Their eyes were painted like the Egyptian wives, but not so much, and they were lacking reddened lips and cheeks. But their own blood in their cheeks gave them the blush of roses. Instead of sandals, the sisters wore on their feet small shoes of yellow leather. Levi was glad to see that the scorned sisters confronted the pharaoh, whom they did not know at all, bravely, and held their thin, arched noses proudly before them. Having been told what to do, each sister offered her hand to the king and he duly pressed his lips to all of them. They were pretty girls and Thutmose regarded them in a very friendly manner, even speaking a few words to the last one. Hah—thought Levi. Now he knows what he's been missing. It was quite a revelation to the barber that his brusque master could behave with so much grace and gallantry toward women in public and it also occurred to him that perhaps the man was more charming to them in private than anyone suspected. Well, not to Neferura, surely, but at least he showed her public respect.

To the Canaanite girls, the queen made a point of paying every attention and even smiled at them, giving all the people to know that she was on good terms with these lesser wives and held them in no contempt whatsoever. She even put out her hand and pressed the arm of the last and youngest sister, as though to say with this gesture, "Take courage. I am here with you."

"How kind she is," murmured Caleb. "How noble!"

"Yes," said Levi, agreeing wholly with the sentiments of his friend.

"I would die for her now," Caleb whispered. "If only I could kiss her hand!"

When the ladies were seated, Neferweben called out "The Master of the Horse of king's son, Amunemhat, and the barber of Menkheperra, the Good God, appear before his most august majesty!"

"He means us," said Levi and he and Caleb approached the ruler. Levi had instructed Caleb that, on this particular day, they must "smell the earth" at the feet of the king, even though he had never required this of them in their time in Egypt. This they did.

"Arise, men!" the vizier commanded. One of his assistants came forward, holding a pillow upon which were some golden objects. The pharaoh handed his staves of office to Neferweben, who just tucked them under his own arm, and stood up.

"Master of the Horse, Caleb of Canaan," he shouted, "be thus honored for saving the life of the heir to the throne, Amunemhat! Bow your head, you who will be called Father of the God!"

Even without any prompting from Levi, Caleb lowered his head. There was no defiance whatsoever in him this day and he said nothing. Levi swallowed hard with relief.

Then the vizier handed the king a sort of necklace of many golden discs strung together and he fastened them about the neck of Caleb. The common people made a lot of noise and the Canaanite sisters stood up and ululated in the way of the women of their homeland. Mehy stood up, too. And, to the amazement of everyone, Queen Neferura also rose from her chair and bowed her vulture-bedecked head to the hero. The crowd nearly went mad with excitement. Never in the long memory of the Thebans had a king's wife done such a thing—bow to a mere servant and a foreign one, besides. And this was the daughter of the haughty woman-king, Hatshepsut! To Levi, it all seemed like a wedding back home, when people gave free rein to all their emotions, carried away by the joy of the occasion. Thutmose gave his queen a cynical look but then composed his face and cleared his throat.

It was Levi's turn next.

"Amun-eywy, also called Levi of Canaan, Chief Barber to my majesty, be thus honored for good and faithful service to your lord. Henceforth shall you be called Sole Friend of the King and Smoother of the Way before my majesty and a noble among nobles! When you go forth, men shall bow before you and know that you have the wisdom of the great god, Thoth, in your heart. Amun-eywy, three times great, lower your head!"

Levi thought he would faint from shock. He could scarcely believe what he had heard. Chief Barber? Three times great? Only Thoth, the god of wisdom and learning, was ever referred to that way in Egypt. And how was a mere slave to be counted as a noble? But he lowered his head and the honor was tied about his neck. The women ululated once again and the people also expressed their approbation. It was the greatest moment in the life of Levi so far and, not having the hardened nature of Caleb, tears began to stream down his cheeks.

"Great king," he managed to say, "we thank you and honor you all of our days."

"Well said, well said!" Mehy piped up in his yet high voice.

"Yes, indeed," said the pharaoh and the two men walked away, each overwhelmed in his own fashion, according to his private thoughts.

"Now, then," cried the king, still standing, "which of you here wishes to come before me with a petition or an injustice that must be rectified?" Then he sat down.

No sooner had Thutmose uttered these words, than the voice of a man rang out, "I do!"

The man came forward. He was dressed in what had once been fine clothes but they seemed rather shabby now. Around his neck was some sort of necklace consisting of three golden flies. This is no Egyptian, thought Levi. This one wore no wig and his hair was long and untended. He also had a beard. In his hand was a plain staff of wood like that of a wanderer.

The vizier, Neferweben, consulted the papyrus scroll in his hands. He seemed puzzled.

"You won't find me on that list, Neferweben," the man told him. "You know me by name, if not by sight. I am Ahmose, who has returned from the southern lands, from a place no man of Egypt has ever seen."

"Ahmose!" cried the pharaoh. "Is it really you?"

Neferweben rolled up his list and it seemed to Levi the vizier's lips had turned up ever so slightly in something that resembled a smile.

"Yes, I am alive," said this Ahmose. "Though it might disappoint you, mighty king of Egypt!"

At these words, uttered in such an insolent tone, people spoke to one another in a hushed murmur. The king's face darkened and Queen Neferura held a hand to her lips in a stunned gesture. Some of the king's guards advanced on the man as if to arrest him, but their master shouted, "Stand your ground! Let him have his say, since he's come so far to say it." Then the ruler added in Canaanite, "Caleb, come and get the boy!"

The guards halted, but did not retreat. Caleb, who didn't really understand what was transpiring, rushed over to Mehy and carried him away.

"Put me down!" Levi heard the prince, saying. "People will think I'm a baby!"

His governor set him on his feet but said, "Get behind me this instant. There's trouble here."

"I'll say there is," was Mehy's response, but he refused to get behind and so Caleb had no choice but to just hold him close to him.

An incredulous Levi had no idea why this upstart had arrived to ruin this wonderful day, but the man was not long in explaining.

"Yes," said Ahmose, "an injustice has surely been done. Did you not, Thutmose, send me to find the source of the Nile? I tell you, it cannot be found. The river does not end but we got to the far place where two rivers join it and there your men became lost. Some of those who survive now live among the black people there and will not return to Egypt. The rest came back with me and have gone home."

Great gods, thought Levi, this is the same man the ruler spoke of, the one who had vanished. And he had actually called the pharaoh by his private name!

"What did you do there by those two streams for seven years?" the sovereign wanted to know.

"I was made the husband of the daughter of the king of the city of Saba. When her father died, I was their king."

"Why, then, have you left your kingdom?" asked the pharaoh. "Did you realize the hardships of rule and have come back to commiserate with me?"

"The woman had a son—not mine—and I put him in his rightful place when he was grown. Justice was done to him—as it was to you once."

"Did you manage to make a civilized man of *him*?" wondered Thutmose, with a hint of amusement.

"Not entirely," was Ahmose's sardonic reply, "but his eye is now toward Egypt, appreciating her refinements and your greatness. If he still lives. I suggest that you never try to go anywhere near Saba as its situation is impenetrable and you would only come to grief. Especially now. I don't know what will happen with the kingdom of my wife's son, but I know now what has happened with your own! The foreigners in the northland fought for you. You lived among them and learned their language. It was they who made you pharaoh and you promised them peace!"

"They have it," said Thutmose. "No one is disturbing them."

"True enough," Ahmose replied, "but now they feel betrayed because you have slaughtered and besieged their brothers in Canaan. You have enslaved them, the kindred of the same men who laid down their lives for you. Now, I have heard, the northerners wonder how long they, themselves, will remain free. Yes, you have betrayed them and me, the man who vouched for you. I assured those tribesmen you would be a just king to all people, one who merely wanted to reclaim what was his by right—

but you have made a liar out of me! I, the son of Canaanite servants, have been fooled by the son of a Canaanite harem girl!"

"There you are," said Mehy. "Another secret out of the sack."

This was too much for Levi. His legs grew so weak that he had to sit on the ground. Mehy patted him on the head.

The pharaoh rose from his seat. "Yes, I am the son of such a woman. I honor my mother. Does anyone here object to her, my Canaanite mother?" he roared.

Of course, no one did. The people had been stunned into immobility. They dared scarcely breathe.

"Just as I expected," the king continued. "Well, Ahmose, my old friend, did you not see the condition of my Canaanite slaves? Have you not witnessed how I have raised and honored them? Men of Canaan, do you wish to leave my house and go back to your land?"

Levi the barber looked up at Caleb, fully expecting him to say that he did. But Caleb remained silent.

"There, you see," Thutmose said to Ahmose, "they are content. Content with their positions and honors, the best of the men of the eastern lands."

"And what of the least of those men?" Ahmose inquired angrily. "What of their women and children? What of those who remain in Canaan and must fight against you year after year lest they become either your subjects or your chattels? All those people who had the courage to stand against you have no more

207

land and every time you go east yet more peoples lose their lands, their property and their lives! What gives you the right to violate the land of my fathers—and of your own? Because you are Pharaoh of Egypt—you—who are royal in only one of your little fingers? Now you call yourself a god. Are you the same kind of god as Amun, who could be made to move by the will of men and do their bidding in that temple? Yes, there is yet another false god in Egypt as holy as his crimes! When will you be done with siege by starvation and bloodshed? When the Nile, itself, flows pure blood right before your door? You great devouring crocodile in your river—someday all those you brought here will become too many and too mighty even for you. You have emptied Canaan but you will make a Canaan here in Egypt!"

Thutmose sat down. "Is that all you have come to say, Ahmose? If Canaan is the land of my fathers, all of them, by inheritance and conquest—then it surely belongs to me without question. All in Egypt are my servants, Egyptians and foreigners alike. I care for them as a father cares for his children. They serve me and I see to it they are well-served, in turn. No one is starving in my land, nor is short of occupation. I rule it as I see fit according to the plans of my heart. I dispense justice here and make certain that the borders of Egypt will be secure while I live and even after I am gone. My legacy from my grand-father was an empire and I honor him by preserving what he gained. That is my duty and I will continue as I have begun."

"I have no doubt of it," said Ahmose contemptuously.

"But I have yet more to tell you, Thutmose. There is pestilence in the south and it will come here. There is death everywhere upstream. The winds are carrying the plague here even as I speak. Perhaps it is a message to you from the gods, eh? Perhaps they wish you to make a different plan in your heart."

The pharaoh rubbed his jaw. It was apparent that he believed his former friend and ally and did not mistrust his information.

"Let the people go, Thutmose. Let them return to their lands and leave them in peace from now on. Then the wrath of heaven may be turned away from you. Meanwhile, go to Memphis or as far north as you can. Take your son, your women and your Canaanites with you, as the foreigners will have no defense against any of the plagues that come to Egypt from the south, let alone one so terrible as this. Let anyone who can hear my voice escape from this crowded city of Thebes and go elsewhere!"

"What is the meaning of this—striking terror into the hearts of the people?" was the heated reply the petitioner received. "All cannot escape! Listen to me, all you subjects—I will remain here and make daily offerings to the great goddess, Sekhmet, for your protection. Go about your business calmly and don't spend your strength through useless anxiety. There is no wind blowing from the south except from the mouth of this man! Ahmose, you, yourself, have leave to go. Go anywhere you like. Depart from Egypt unharmed, but I will see your face no more. Do not return until you have learned that I am dead."

"Your heart has become a stone in your breast," said Ahmose. "Farewell, then, you whom I once called friend. But return I will. Let us see who is the greater Lord of the Flies—you or I!" With that, the man ripped the chain from his neck and hurled it at the feet of the ruler.

Thus went the brief but astonishing exchange between two men, both learned and knowing how to speak well in the most superior form of Egyptian. And so Ahmose, who dared to raise his voice to the pharaoh and even accuse him, went back into the crowd from which he had appeared. In fact, the people shrank from him as though he carried the plague he had warned of, himself. Soon Levi lost sight of him completely.

The pharaoh got up from his throne and went inside the temple. Evidently, he was now in no mood to hear any more petitioners. Neferweben motioned to the shaken women to follow their lord. He also beckoned to Mehy, but Mehy stayed where he was and the vizier did nothing more to persuade him to come away. The vizier said some other calming words to the people and they dispersed.

"Let's stay away from father just now," Mehy said to his companions. "Let's just find our own way back home.

"Who was that man shouting at the king?" Caleb asked him.

"A friend. The one who had helped my father reclaim his throne from the woman-king. But they aren't friends anymore."

"He had a lot of courage, that one," said Caleb. "Or maybe he's just weary of life."

Mehy frowned. "I think my father has made him tired. He won't let Ahmose stay in Egypt because he's not afraid of my father. Well, you saw that. Wait a moment!"

The prince ran off and returned with the broken gold chain and the flies, which he showed to Levi and Caleb.

"This is for great bravery in battle. Hardly anyone ever gets this award. Ahmose deserved it or my father wouldn't have given it to him. If he returns when I'm pharaoh, I'll give it back to him. He'll be surprised that I kept it."

The two Canaanites glanced at one another.

"Mehy," said Caleb, "when you're king, you can't allow people to shout at you or insult you. Someone gets so crazy as to do that, you've got to make an example of him. You can't be too lenient and you can't have men like that around you."

"So you think father was right to banish Ahmose from Egypt? Even though he told him to stop making war on your people?"

"Is that what he said?" Caleb examined one of the golden flies in Mehy's hand. "The man remains valiant, but he deserves to be banished. He got off easy, if you ask me. I'm not saying this Ahmose is wrong to have his feelings. I agree with him. But, as your governor, I'm telling you—let no man speak to you in that way when you're king. So much will depend on people respecting you—yes, even fearing you. Don't let anyone take advantage of

211

your good nature."

Levi said to Mehy, "What did this Ahmose mean by 'pestilence'? What sort of illness could it be?"

"Aw, don't worry about that," the prince said. "There's always some fever coming out of the southern lands, usually at the time of the flood. If something comes here now, we can go back to Memphis. Father won't allow us to get sick. That man, Ahmose, will go away somewhere and there won't be any more trouble."

Chapter Thirteen

But Mehy was wrong. There was much more trouble and, for Caleb, it began that very same night. As he had feared, Satiah came to his bed again, but this time Caleb was not about to repeat his error.

"No!" he told her fiercely. "Go!"

"Let me stay with you," Satiah pleaded, holding onto him. "The old one is in a foul mood and he's shut himself up in his rooms. He's sent me away tonight and no one will know I'm here. Didn't you hear what that man said today? We're all going to die. What's the difference what happens now? Why shouldn't we live while we can?"

Caleb had barely understood any of this speech, but he sensed that the woman was more upset than lustful. What was she pleading with him for? Something told Caleb that the Egyptian wanted him to comfort her, but that sort of comfort she was not going to get.

"Please," he said in his own language, now begging, himself. "Please let me alone and never come here again. You'll kill us both—don't you understand that? Get out of here and don't let anyone see you!"

Satiah didn't know Canaanite but she got the message, anyway. She gazed into Caleb's eyes and the man saw they were full of sorrow.

"You don't know what it's like. I had no more choice to come here than you did. I'm a prisoner, the prisoner of the pharaoh. I wanted a husband my own age, someone I could love. Someone like you. Because I'm beautiful and have white skin, my father was waiting for a rich man to claim me. Well, one did. The wealthiest of them all."

Caleb only knew a few words in the Egyptian language, but the term for love was one of them. Was this girl telling him she loved him?

"Stop talking to me," he hissed. "Stop tempting me! And don't cry, for pity's sake...no, don't do that."

But Satiah had begun to sob, trying to choke back her tears. Her lovely breasts heaved up and down. Caleb put his hand over her mouth.

"Stop! Be still. Calm down."

Satiah nodded her head like a little child. All anger dissipated in the heart of Caleb and he took away his hand. Satiah's own fingers reached up into his hair and then pulled his head toward her face. He both wanted to kiss her and didn't want to, but kiss her he did. Before long, she was under the cover with him and they were practically devouring one another. After it was all over and Caleb lay panting on top of Satiah, he thought to himself that he would never be able to resist her. Twice he had tried and twice he had failed. Everything about her was simply too much for a man of flesh and blood. Even the most scrupulous individual on earth, who still had any life left in him, would want to make love to this girl and Caleb was no holy man and never had been. And Satiah was very responsive in bed—more than any woman Caleb had ever known. His own wife had never shown him the passion of Satiah. This one had no inhibitions or modesty and such abandoned behavior could become an addiction for a man—like drink. Although Caleb had not been faithful to his wife, he was rather fond of her and treated her with kindness. So the situation would have continued had it not been for Satiah's own husband, who had put Caleb into his house and under the eye of his wife. This time, at least, he had managed to pull out and spend his seed on her belly.

But what about next time? Satiah, if she really loved him or even merely desired him so much as she obviously did, would never stop coming back. He might get her with child—if he hadn't already done so previously. If the child looked like Caleb, the pharaoh would know the truth, if not long before that. The only way for Caleb to get rid of Satiah now, he thought, was if he actually killed her.

Sometime the following morning, Levi was shaken from a deep sleep by an agitated Mehy.

"Mehy," he groaned, "what are you doing? Surely it's too soon for school."

"Forget about school," the prince told him. "There won't be any. You've got to go and see father!"

"What's happened to his other barber?"

"Nothing. Just get up. Father needs you."

"Has he sent for me?"

"No—but he needs you anyway. Come on, Levi. Put on your clothes."

"All right, hand them to me, will you?"

Mehy, who had never dressed himself in all his life, helped Levi put on his shirt and kilt and even his sandals. He dipped a towel into a bowl of water and wiped the barber's face with it. "There, you look good enough. Let's get going."

Taking Levi by the hand, as though he might escape, Mehy led him to the quarters of the pharaoh. Nobody tried to prevent them from going in, of course, although two of the king's guards were standing near the doorway, frowning and talking to one another in low voices.

Thutmose was sitting in his chair, his chin sunken onto his breast. He looked very ill, as though the plague that Ahmose had predicted had already struck him. No one had shaved him—that was apparent. But there were no physicians there, either, nobody attending the man who appeared in a state in which Levi had never before seen him. The ruler's face was the color of ashes. He didn't even look up at Mehy and Levi.

The prince pulled at the pharaoh's sleeve. "See, father, here is a friend of your heart. Won't you speak to him? You always like to. You told me so, yourself."

"Mehy," said the ruler, "get me a drink."

"You've got one, father. It's right here in front of you." Mehy picked up the cup and held it to his father's lips. The pharaoh took a sip and then spat the liquid back into the goblet in disgust.

Is it possible he's only drunk? Levi thought. But so early in the morning?

"All right, Mehy," Thutmose murmured. "You may go, lad—but Levi may stay."

Mehy left promptly, as though knowing full well he had no business in that chamber, but not before giving Levi a look that seemed to say, "Do something."

"What is it, my lord? Are you ill? Shall I send for your doctors?"

"They've already been here," the pharaoh told him. "My wife is dead, Levi."

The barber knew which wife it had to be. "What—Queen Satiah?"

"Yes," said the ruler, the life seemingly gone from his own eyes.

"What's happened to her?"

Stiffly, the king heaved himself to his feet. "Follow me."

In the next room, on the king's own bed, lay the body of Satiah. She was a bluish color. Levi was not afraid to view a dead person; he had seen others in his younger days, including his own mother. But Satiah was a horrible sight. On her long neck was a big purple gash, still caked with blood, even though someone had taken the trouble to wipe most of the blood from the girl's corpse. Levi's gorge rose. He gagged a few times but nothing came up. Tears rose to his eyes from the effort and the king said "Go ahead and vomit. It doesn't matter."

But Levi was able to get control of himself. "This is murder!" he said in Canaanite. "Who'd want to kill Satiah? She was so beautiful!"

The pharaoh took him by the arm and led him back into the other room. Thutmose, also, seemed to have come to himself a bit more. At least he was on his feet.

"Take a drink," he told Levi, indicating his own cup. "No —wait! Don't touch it. It's full of a drug that makes one feel numb, horrible. It's no good."

Levi took the cup and emptied it out the window. He washed it in a bowl of water and threw the water out of the window, as well. The king had found a wine-jar and was drinking straight from it. He poured some wine into the golden goblet and indicated to Levi that he should use that. The barber certainly needed a drink, but wondered if the ruler, in his present condition, should be imbibing too much, but there seemed no stopping him. The men sat down.

"Satiah was found lying in her own bed in her quarters," said the ruler in a hoarse tone. "One of her maids got up early and heard her...well, we won't go into that. Then the maid started screaming and woke up half the house."

"I didn't hear anything," said Levi. "Mehy woke me up."

"I heard it, but I sleep nearer to the harem than you do. And then I came and saw my wife in that state. I told my men to bring her in here so her maid would quiet down. And I took the instrument of murder with me."

"What was it?" Levi asked.

"This." The pharaoh shook out a cloth on the table and a bloodied razor was revealed. "You ever see it before?"

"I...I don't know," was all Levi could say. "It's just an ordinary razor."

"None of mine are missing," informed the king. "What about yours?"

Levi raked his fingers through his hair. "I didn't look at them. I didn't have time."

"You can look soon enough," the ruler told him. "But, don't worry, I don't suspect you. You haven't the stomach for killing. You just proved that to me. I know it wasn't you."

"Of course I didn't do it," Levi said. "I had no reason whatsoever!"

"I'll tell you something, as it will have to come out,

219

anyway. The physicians came and examined Satiah. They cleaned her up. But, before they did, I saw something...well, how else can I say it? There was dried white stuff all over her belly. A lot of it—and I think I can recognize that when I see it. Semen. It wasn't mine, Levi. That I know for certain. The doctors noticed it, too, I'm sure—but they didn't say anything. I know they think it was my doing."

Levi swallowed hard, trying to think. Finally, he said, "No. They know you wouldn't spill your seed because you want more children." Levi didn't say this to his master, but he rather thought that, had someone taken Satiah by force, he wouldn't have spilled his seed, either, but sowed it where he threshed it, as they used to say in Canaan.

"Therefore, my wife had a lover," the pharaoh said.

"And yet who would have dared to be that one?" Levi asked.

"There are a hundred men within these walls, surely. Satiah, as you say, was a very beautiful woman. And she was with child. That much I do know. Or think I know. She told me, herself, that she suspected it only yesterday morning. I was happy, of course, but instructed her to say nothing to anybody until she was sure it was true."

"I'm terribly sorry, Your Majesty," Levi said. "What a dreadful thing to have happened! But...if Satiah had a lover and she was not yet completely certain that she was with child...I don't think she would have been so quick to tell you of her suspicions.

220

She would probably have waited to inform you until there was no more doubt in her mind. A woman with both a husband and a lover doesn't look forward to a baby in the manner of an innocent wife. I can't believe she would betray you. Perhaps it was rape."

The pharaoh smiled bleakly. "Three times great. I always knew you had it in you. Even though you're still young, somehow you've been given the gift of understanding the hearts of people. Perhaps, then, Satiah had no lover and was set upon by a man who shot his arrow before he found the target. Ah—last night I was in such a troubled mood. You know why. Satiah came in the evening and wanted to ask me some questions. She was worried about a plague coming. But I told her not to plague me and to let me alone. I didn't want to talk to her. I never really could—the way I can talk to you. She wasn't three times great. She had no wisdom at all."

The king leaned back. Any other man would have wept with such a look on his face, but Levi knew this one had forgotten how to weep a long time ago.

"But I loved her," said the grieving man. "I love her now. Perhaps it was only her beauty. I don't know. Satiah didn't understand my jokes or ever tried to make me laugh. She did nothing to make me happy...but I loved her nonetheless. Perhaps I somehow believed I could win her, make her appreciate how I felt about her. But one can't conquer the heart of a woman. It must be freely given or not at all."

Levi was perplexed. What man could have possibly

ventured into the harem and done all those things to Satiah without waking up her household? Who could have been that bold or stupid? So far, none of it had made any sense to him.

The barber asked, "What will happen now?"

"Tomorrow there must be an inquest." The pharaoh rubbed his eyes with his palm. "That can't wait because I can't have a murderer running loose. Satiah will be taken away and, in a few days, she'll be given over to the embalmers."

"In a few days?" said Levi. "In Canaan, we buried people the next day. How will you be able to preserve the body of poor Satiah in this manner?"

"There is no way to preserve Satiah. I can't give her to the embalmers yet, even though her great station demands that she be mummified. Even with her throat cut from ear to ear, she's still too beautiful."

"Ay!" breathed Levi, comprehending what his lord was trying to say. He just shook his head. Then he said, "Don't feel betrayed, master, on top of your other grief. In your own words, you satisfied your wife at night and often, I'm sure. Why would she need another man? Your wife may have not had the wisdom to understand you, or even the wit to entertain you, but how could she possibly disdain you or see another as being more worthy of her? You are the greatest man on earth!"

"And you are possibly the kindest," the pharaoh told him. "I want to believe you!"

"By your leave, my lord, I'll go and see if any of my razors are missing. But even if one should happen to be, I swear on my mother—whom I loved despite her way of living—that I did not kill your wife. Even if I hated her, which I didn't, I wouldn't have done that to you."

The pharaoh looked at him. "What do you mean, Levi? That you don't hate me, either, despite what I've done to your people?"

"I should hate you, probably, but I can't. I was fond of Si-Bast. I am fond of him. But you..."

"What can I possibly mean to you?" said Thutmose in a bitter tone. "Why would you want to spare me grief even now? Because I have elevated you in the eyes of men?"

"No, that's not the reason. I'm not so elevated that I can't still feel the dust on my feet." Levi hesitated. How could he explain this to the pharaoh without seeming to get too familiar? But he said, anyway, "I never tried to understand Si-Bast. Perhaps there wasn't so much to understand there. But you I can understand."

"Well, that makes one of us at least," said the king. "But I will remember you. Even on the darkest day in Egypt, whether that be now or some future day, I won't forget the first person who ever tried to comfort me since I became invincible."

This last word Thutmose uttered in such a way as if to indicate he knew it did not apply to himself at all. At least not any longer.

Before long, Levi was back at the king's chambers. The

223

ruler was leaning out of the window, vomiting in the way that Levi had not been able to do. When Thutmose sat down again, his face covered with sweat, the barber went into action. He wiped the ruler's face with a wet cloth, just as Mehy had done to him that morning. After that, he rolled up the little towel and held it to his master's forehead. This was repeated the next time the pharaoh heaved up some more wine. The man groaned, but said nothing, only breathing heavily. Levi continued to wet the cloth so that it could remain cool. At last, the king said that he felt better and asked for a mere drink of water. This Levi gave to him.

"You may take a chair," Thutmose told him. "No need to stand. From this day forward, you may sit in my presence without asking leave to do so."

"The razor is mine," said Levi, remaining upright. "I had two and now there is only one. That's all I know—except that someone is trying to make me out a murderer."

"The only one you need worry about is the man right here. And I'm not pointing a finger at you. They've taken Satiah away to an empty room. I can't keep her with me forever. I shall never see her again."

"Very wise," said Levi. "The sight is too much to bear. Why not lie down in her place? My lord is ill. He should rest."

"I can't rest. I don't know that I can ever sleep in that bed again. Let it be burned."

"Then I offer you my own bed."

"Levi, do me the kindness of covering up that damned

razor and talk to me. Tell me anything you like. My own thoughts are driving me mad."

"All I know about is my life as a boy in Canaan."

"That will do. Tell me everything that happened since the day you were born."

Levi began to narrate the story of his life, as much as he could recall. He and his mother hadn't been exactly destitute because she was a woman of some reputation as a harlot and good to look upon. When Levi was a child, he used to go to the market place to buy food because his mother didn't like to show herself there. People felt sorry for him and didn't cheat him too often. Some even treated him with kindness. His mother did, too, mostly —except that every time there was a man in the house with her, he had to wait outdoors, day or night, until that man was gone. No matter how cold it was, and sometimes Levi thought he would freeze to death. Frequently he got sick, but he survived all the fevers, and then never became ill as he got older, his hardened body having become used to any kind of weather. But the noises of the animals frightened him in the dark and so Levi made up his mind to be ready if any ever decided to attack him. An older boy he knew taught him how to use a sling and even made one for him for a price. The price was Levi's own mother, but that was nothing unusual in those days. So Levi practiced constantly with that sling. Stones were plentiful. Levi aimed them all at a single tree and after awhile there was hardly any bark left on it—because Levi had learned to use the weapon very well. He took the sling outside with him at all times. Once he had killed a hungry wolf that had wandered too close to where his house was. Sometimes Levi had killed birds of the kind that could be eaten so that his mother could cook them. But that was about all. Levi could have killed just about any smaller animal had he wanted to, but he never had much inclination for sport.

The pharaoh listened to this with an expression on his face that indicated he found it not uninteresting.

Finally he said, "Did you ever use the weapon to defend yourself against a human enemy?"

"Once I killed a man, but not in my own defense. There was someone who used to visit my mother. Sometimes, this man had had too much to drink by the time he got to our house and when he couldn't perform with my mother, he'd get angry and beat her. She told me this, herself, but said she didn't mind too much. When he was sober, he was generous, and never hit her so hard as to do any real harm. But I got tired of this man striking my mother. It troubled me very deeply. I would have fought him, but he was too large for me. I was just—perhaps thirteen. One night, when the moon was full and I could see fairly well, I followed behind this man at a distance. He had to walk quite a long way to get back to his own house. I took aim and hit him in the skull. Then I went home. I had killed him, but nobody much seemed to care. If they suspected me, I was never questioned about it. But, my lord, that was enough killing to last me for the rest of my life. The thought of what I had done troubled me more than the reason for having done it and I didn't know why. And, besides, the year after that my mother died and there weren't any more drunken men."

"You had a lot of resolve for a lad of thirteen," the pharaoh remarked.

"Well...my life hadn't exactly been an ordinary one. I was thirteen in one sense but far older in another. I was so angry in those days but, after my mother died, something changed in me. There didn't seem to be anything to be angry about any longer."

"Not even when we came?"

"No," Levi told him. "By that time I was living with my aunt and starving. She had very little and was too old to sell herself any longer. All I cared about was finding something to eat. I never thought about joining the rebels against Egyptian rule, even though I was tall enough to pass for someone older. But I left this town where my aunt lived. One day I saw your encampment and hung around Si-Bast until he captured me. I pretended to resist a little so he wouldn't think I was a complete dolt." Levi smiled wanly at the recollection.

"But you could have killed Si-Bast had you followed him like that other man."

"What good would that have done? I couldn't bring down all of you. I'm no fighter."

"I never used to think I was, either," said Thutmose. "Yes, a man can change."

But the pharaoh, evidently, didn't want to talk about any of his own distant past beyond that observation. He embarked, once again, on the subject of Satiah. A servant brought some food and Levi ate, but the king didn't want to. Levi told him he'd better try because he was bound to start in drinking again. So Thutmose ate a little and relived the day he had first laid eyes on the beauty and made up his mind to marry her at once. He spoke of things he might have done to make her happier and things he shouldn't have said to her. It was hard for Levi to tell which was troubling him the most—what he hadn't done or what he had. Ahmose, the angry accuser, had been wrong about one thing at least. The pharaoh's heart was not made of stone. Whatever it was made of, it seemed quite broken now, and the man was beside himself. Levi remained with him until nightfall, when the pharaoh ordered that his bed be taken away and a different one brought in. Then he changed his mind and demanded the old one back because he had slept in it with Satiah and had enjoyed some happiness with her there, as he reminded Levi. Thutmose told Levi about how he used to carry his young wife from that bed in his arms, back to her own, as he was in the habit of rising early and Satiah didn't like to.

"She was always half asleep and I carried her like a child," the pharaoh said. "I was her servant at those moments and surely she knew I loved her to do that. Only then, between sleeping and waking, was she content to be in my arms in a wholly innocent way. But I never said those words to her—that I loved her. I don't know why. It's too late now. I can't believe Satiah is gone. My beautiful girl!"

And, of course, the king sent for more wine and wanted Levi to join him in that. The barber couldn't refuse but drank as sparingly as possible. The pharaoh, being a man and a powerful king, besides, was doing his best to behave with courage but he drank plenty and, at last, fell asleep in his armchair.

That same night, it was Levi who received a visitor. At first, he thought he was dreaming that a giant of a man was looming over him, ready to attack him, but it was only Caleb, trying to get him to wake up.

"Aw," moaned the barber, "I'm beat. Can't I get any sleep around here? I've been up since nearly dawn."

"Where have you been all day?" Caleb demanded, shoving Levi aside so he could sit down on the bed. "I've been looking for you."

"I was with the pharaoh. He's in pretty poor shape. I suppose you heard what happened."

"Everybody knows," said Caleb. He pushed back his hair with his hands and blew out a big breath. Even by the light of the moon, Levi could tell that Caleb didn't look in such great shape, himself—for Caleb. "I've got to tell you something. I shouldn't, but I've got to. I slept with Satiah."

"No fooling?" Levi didn't sound very surprised.

But, if Caleb noticed that, he gave no indication of it. In a low and hollow tone, the chariotry officer narrated the story of the two times the dead queen had come to his room. He left out many of the details, but admitted to his friend that the woman had worn him down. He couldn't stop himself from giving her what she wanted. He had been too weak.

Levi scratched his neck and then said, "She never came in here, but, if she had, I don't know what I'd have done. I suspect I would have been scared soft."

"You'd have screwed her," said Caleb with conviction. "Same as I did."

"Did you kill her?"

"What—are you crazy? I couldn't kill a woman, especially one who looked like her. That would be like destroying..." But Caleb couldn't find the words. He pushed back his long hair again like it was really bothering him that he even had hair. "You know something—I think it was the pharaoh who did it. He can kill anybody. No conscience there."

"I'm telling you," said Levi, "he loved that girl. I was with him all day. He's taking it hard, drinking like there was no tomorrow."

"I'd be drinking, too, if I'd just cut some girl's throat. Listen, if my wife had betrayed me like that, I'd have killed her with my bare hands."

"I thought you just said you couldn't kill a woman!"

"I'd make an exception there. So that's what happened. The pharaoh found out about Satiah coming to my room and— goodbye little darling. He'll get me next. Some way."

"How come you're still sitting here right now?" Levi

230

wanted to know. "Don't you think the ruler has enough men here to arrest you if he knew the truth? Even you couldn't fight them all off. Shit, you couldn't even fight off a woman."

"You don't have to rub it in! I'm still alive because the king is too ashamed to admit that he couldn't satisfy his wife. Why in the devil would she come to me if he could?"

"Well," said Levi dryly, "maybe you're just too handsome for all these gals here. They don't have too many men like you in Egypt."

"I can't help that!" Caleb growled. "Who told them to bring me here so that their women would go berserk? They should have thought of that possibility, eh? Eh?"

"I wouldn't let you near any woman of mine," said Levi. "But it so happens that Satiah was murdered with my razor."

"Shit!" Caleb exclaimed but then held up his hand and shook his head. "No...no...you couldn't have done it. Not a chance. Listen—does anyone know it was your razor that did the job?"

"Yes, the pharaoh," said Levi. "He knows because I told him."

"Then you really are crazy—and I give up."

"He doesn't suspect me. He said so, himself."

"I believe that," Caleb answered, "because *he's* the murderer. Look—anybody could come in here while you're gone and steal your razor. Even when you're asleep. You don't wake up easily."

"The king has his own razors. If he wanted to kill someone with a razor, why would he need mine?"

"That's simple—so he can put the blame on you!"

"Well, why hasn't he done it? Why am I still here?"

"He's waiting until tomorrow," Caleb told Levi. "That's when the investigation into the matter takes place. Mehy told me that. The lad's very upset, seems worried. About us, I'm sure. One of us is going to get the finger, for certain, can't you see? Probably you, because of nobody wanting to admit that I fucked the pharaoh's wife. Don't you get it? We can't wait until tomorrow. We've got to get out of here. Tonight!"

"Caleb, why didn't you tell the pharaoh you wanted to leave Egypt when he asked the question at the ceremony? And don't tell me you didn't understand what he said. Perhaps, if you had said you wanted to go, you would have been sent off with that man, Ahmose."

"I understood the question," admitted Caleb. "I couldn't say anything. Damn and blast and bugger—but my heart is here now. I couldn't leave the woman and her son."

"You have a woman—and a son—of your own!"

"I know," sighed the chariot-fighter. "If they're still alive, they've got my old man or my brothers to look after them. Look —I don't know why I didn't say anything. Except that I don't love my wife. Don't get me wrong. She's a good woman. But I didn't choose her. My father did, and if you knew my old man you'd know that nobody could go against him. The only woman I

232

ever loved is here and I've never even touched her! I don't know how it happened. It just did. But, listen—all that was yesterday. Nobody was murdered yet. Now we've got to leave!"

"Yeah—maybe we should," said Levi. "But just how far do you think we could get? Caleb, we're not going. I don't think either of us is going to get the finger."

"What makes you so sure?"

"Oh...something up here." Levi tapped his skull. "The Egyptians believe people think with the heart—but I don't. I don't believe anybody does, but I know for sure I don't. My guess is the ruler doesn't want either of us to be guilty of the murder. In fact, I don't think he—"

Caleb didn't give him a chance to finish. "What are you talking about? Why should he care what happens to us? I know I was a fool to do what I did with Satiah, but you're a fool to trust that man. He's not your protector and not your friend. Men like him are only kind when it's convenient. If you weren't so young, you'd understand that. The pharaoh can replace you in the blink of an eye—and the same goes for me, of course, crocodile-slayer or not. The ones who seek power look upon everyone as expendable. You think when that bastard stands there in his golden chariot, directing his battles, he worries about how many of his own men he has to sacrifice to satisfy his ambitions? The truth is—*you* don't want *him* to be the killer—and I'll be damned if I know why!"

Levi wanted to tell Caleb about what Thutmose had said to

him about carrying Satiah like a child, but he simply couldn't divulge this confidence. He silently cursed the dead girl and his own friend for not being able to send her away.

"What I want doesn't matter," he said. "I know that. It just doesn't make sense to me that he would have done it. The pharaoh's grief is genuine. He couldn't fool me about that. When you see him, you'll realize it, too."

"Then who killed Satiah?"

"The one with the most reason to kill her, that's who."

Caleb rolled his eyes. "Well—shit—that could be just about anybody. I had a reason to kill her. She was driving me mad and trying to get *me* killed!"

"And yet I'm the prime suspect in the eyes of the law. My razor—remember? That's the one established fact of the matter so far."

"What kind of killer are you? You couldn't kill anybody if your life depended on it."

"You never know," said Levi. "People don't have 'murderer' written on their foreheads...Caleb, if someone murdered your wife, what would you feel like doing?"

"What would I do? Not just sit there grieving, that's for sure. I'd hunt down the coward and annihilate him. After that, I'd feel free to mourn. But not before I spent my rage on that man who committed the act."

"I can well believe it," said Levi. "But...this isn't Canaan. They have a legal system here and even the king is bound by it, so they say. Maybe it's true and he has to leave everything up to the court."

What Levi didn't say was that it bothered him somewhat that the king hadn't shown any of the rage that the chariot-fighter had mentioned as being his first reaction in a like situation. But Caleb, obviously, was a man of impulse, hot-blooded and not very much in control of his passions. He and the pharaoh weren't the same kind of man at all. Thutmose would grieve first and act later, but exact retribution all the same. In cold blood, regarding the murderer with eyes of ice, while pronouncing the sentence upon him. The question was—would he doom the right man, the one who really deserved to die?

"Better go to bed, Caleb," Levi advised. "You've got to have your wits about you tomorrow. And I'll certainly need mine. I've got to get some sleep."

"How in the devil can you sleep? How can you be so calm? It's unnatural—the way you're acting. You're scaring even me right now."

"Please," said Levi, "get out of my bed! I'm exhausted! But I'm telling you to trust me just this one time. Go and rest and put any thoughts of escaping from here from your mind. Don't point the finger at yourself by any rash action. Goodnight!"

However, Levi did not go to sleep. He knew now that he couldn't. Not yet. He got up and dressed himself and, with great stealth, made his way through the dim corridors to the harem. Levi tried to calculate where the chambers of Queen Neferura might be in relation to the position of her window as he had seen it from the courtyard some days ago. Judging distance was something at which Levi was good. He didn't dare rap upon her door, make any noise, so he simply opened it. Then he crept inside the chambers of the queen to see if that great lady might still be awake. She was, and only one of her maids remained with her, removing her jewels, presumably to prepare her for bed. The barber had no choice but to advance on them and say, softly, "My lady, I must speak with you."

Both women regarded Levi with shocked faces, but Neferura quickly regained her composure.

"You may speak with me," she replied and then said to her maid, "If you ever tell anyone you saw this young man here, you will surely die."

The maid nodded and quickly took herself off.

"What is it you want of me, Amun-eywy?" asked the queen.

"I...I want to know something. Suppose I were to tell you that a certain man loved you with all his heart. But, as you surely already know, men are not so strong as they appear and some appear very strong, indeed. If this man who loved you had made an error, even a grievous one, could you find it in your own heart to forgive him?"

Neferura stared at Levi. Her dark eyes were not sad any longer but Levi could read nothing in them.

"Yes," she finally said, "if that man loved me, and I loved

him, I could forgive him that weakness in this instance."

"If that man were in great danger, would you help him? Possibly even save his life?"

"I would," replied the noble lady. "Particularly if it was the man who had saved the life of my son."

"That's all I have come to say, great queen. Now I must go."

"Go, then, very carefully, and sleep without fear, Royal Barber. *Leila tov*," said Neferura, telling Levi goodnight in his native language.

"*Leila tov*," repeated the barber, smiling, and then went away.

Chapter Fourteen

The inquest into the matter of the murder of Queen Satiah took place in the great audience hall of the Theban residence, the Honorable Neferweben presiding. Not only was Neferweben the king's vizier, he was also the Chief Justice of the South. In Memphis, there was yet another vizier with all of the same duties. Neferweben, in his present capacity, wore a little gold statue of the goddess of truth, call Maat, suspended on a chain around his neck and he carried his staff of office. With him was his assistant, Rahotep, who had the task of interrogating the witnesses. In Egypt, no one who was accused of a crime could have an advocate on his behalf because justice might be confounded by the glib tongue of an able orator. Each person in an Egyptian court of law was required to answer for himself or offer his own defense. Most of the time, Neferweben had other judges hearing the cases with him, but in this very delicate situation, which involved members of the royal family, whose secrets might be revealed, the fewer there to hear them the better. So only the Chief Justice would be there, accompanied by the Chief Interrogator.

Of course, Neferweben did not have sole control over this particular hearing. The pharaoh also had the right to intervene if he wished for the very reason that there was no one to prevent Menkheperra Thutmose from doing so. Before coming to the palace, the Chief Justice had told his wife that it troubled him that the king should be involved in this matter in which he could not be impartial. After all, it was the pharaoh's own beloved wife who had been killed. He could not be emotionally detached from the case, as a judge like Neferweben was expected to be.

But Neferweben, even though occupying the highest dual office in Upper Egypt, was still a servant of the pharaoh, who owned everything and everyone in the entire land, in a kind of general way, and could order or disorder things as he pleased. In theory, the Egyptian king was not above the law, himself, and was not supposed to countermand the caselaw, the decisions that had been set down for many centuries.

In fact, few pharaohs had ever been known to meddle in such matters. As a result of this caselaw, many disputes were easy to decide, as the manner in which they should be handled was already well known, especially to the Chief Justice, who had studied them. If there happened to be some question regarding the proper decision, Neferweben had scribes who would look them up, even if it took days. In the experience of the judge, these always found some applicable situation from the long history of Egyptian jurisprudence. However, most trials consisted of one litigant against another. Those were civil matters.

Even felons were handed out prescribed punishments and they also had trials. In years past, some of these trials had not been so fair and confessions had been obtained by torture. But Neferweben prided himself on being a fair-minded man and he'd be damned if anything untoward was going to happen during his term of office. Yet who could really prevent someone like King Thutmose from interfering in the legal process? Not Neferweben. If the pharaoh chose to indict someone, he had to be tried.

Regardless, today there would be no actual trial but only an inquest in order to determine exactly what had happened and who the suspect or suspects might actually be. No one would be judged or sentenced. Not yet.

The hall was packed full of the king's family and servants of all types. Rahotep, the Chief Interrogator, held a scroll in his hand and stood next to his seated superior. The pharaoh was on his throne, wearing the striped *nemes* headdress and Prince Amunemhat was with him, perched on the steps of the dais. Below the dais, on which rested the great throne of Egypt, and at a small distance from it, were some chairs arranged in a sort of semi-circle. Queen Neferura and the Canaanites sat there, men and women. The women were present because they lived in the harem and might have seen or heard something. The men were there for the reason that the murder weapon had belonged to one of them—and both knew where it was normally kept.

Opposite these were seated one Tabubu, handmaiden to the deceased, the primary witness, in the opinion of Neferweben, and her master, Nebamun, the dead queen's brother. Nobody sat especially close together, except the three Canaanite wives, and Tabubu and Nebamun had made sure their chairs were far apart. Neferweben sat apart from all of them, his chair being nearest the king. The Chief Justice nodded to Rahotep, who addressed the throng of standing servants.

"Listen you people, this is not difficult. These persons seated before you will remain in this room. As for the rest of you, if anyone here has any information as to anything that happened on the night of the murder of Queen Satiah that might be connected to that great crime, that person must remain to give testimony! All others are given leave to go about their duties."

As Neferweben had expected, no one who was not already seated stayed behind. If any of the other servants of the pharaoh knew anything, they would not want to get involved. Neferweben didn't really blame them. All were frightened of the idea of somehow being implicated in the murder. Some of them barely knew Neferweben and those who did and were aware of his scrupulous ways, were still afraid. Mainly of the pharaoh. All people, high and lowly, thought they had reason to fear this king. And the Chief Justice could not actually blame them for that, either. His reputation had been established years before. Just two days ago, Thutmose had spared a man who had opposed and tried to humiliate him before many, but that man had once been his close friend from his youth. Even so, this Ahmose had been banished and told never to return to Egypt within the lifetime of the pharaoh. Friendship had its limits in that case, no question there, and doubtless this king would not hesitate to deal harshly with anyone else who had acquired his disapprobation by some means.

The Chief Justice waited for the servants to clear out and that happened in a very short time. He turned to the king and said, "Do we have Your Majesty's permission to proceed?"

"You do," said the pharaoh, who, it seemed to Neferweben, looked quite ill and a strange version of himself with his unshaven face. "But remember, Neferweben, there are some here who don't understand the Egyptian language."

"Is there someone who can interpret?" asked the Chief Justice.

"That duty I will give to Amun-eywy, also called Levi, my Chief Barber, on this day."

Neferweben didn't exactly need a translator. His own parents had been foreigners and a West-Semitic dialect had been spoken in the home when the vizier was young. Neferweben's father had risen to the highest office in the land, regardless. While still a slave, he had been given the rather ironic name of Ahmose, after the pharaoh who had battled the "foreigners", but Efficiency was the name that suited him best. The joke had been made regarding Neferweben's father that the moment he had come to Egypt he began to consider ways to organize the nation. And that was what he had ended up doing. Everything his hand had touched had prospered. There was no number so large that the old vizier couldn't add, multiply or divide it with lightning speed. He could immediately figure the cubic space of any granary or storeroom and seemed to instinctively know how much something weighed without benefit of scales. No sooner did the Nile flood its banks, than Neferweben's father calculated the price of all commodities that year and the rate of taxation. Nobody had argued with him when it came to anything to do with the economy or commerce as old Ahmose had never been wrong in his estimates.

His eldest son, Useramun, had succeeded him in his office in the usual manner. Useramun, who had also been a very intelligent man, passed from life in Year 28 of the reign. The present king had interrogated him, when he reclaimed his throne, on many subjects and had not found him wanting, even though Useramun, Neferweben's brother, had carried out his duties under the supremacy of Maatkara Hatshepsut, the woman-king. When Thutmose had asked the Chief Justice how he could have served an illegal king, Useramun had pointed out to him that, under the law, Thutmose was the king from the day the crown was put upon head and, legally speaking, there was no other sovereign beside himself, no matter who claimed differently. At this response the pharaoh had laughed and said, "Very well, you're a clever fellow. I have heard no ill report of you and so you may continue in your position."

When it was Neferweben's turn to take over as vizier, he had very big shoes to fill. He had not proved a disappointment, evidently, as the pharaoh praised him highly. And yet, each morning, when Neferweben arose to take his place at the helm of Theban affairs, he could never rid himself of the nagging feeling that, although he virtually ran the south, he was still a stranger in the land, despite having been born there. Even his father, Ahmose, had told his sons that the prominence of their family when it came to serving the royal house was only temporary and was bound to end someday. But not while the man behind me sits in his place, thought Neferweben. He knows how much the cleverness of the men of the east can benefit Egypt. As long as they are willing to play the game his way.

"Very well, my lord," said Neferweben. "You may question those assembled, Rahotep."

The assistant cleared his throat and consulted his list. "The first person I wish to interrogate is the servant, Tabubu."

Tabubu was a pretty, thin, dark-skinned girl from the southern lands, which one Neferweben had no idea. Something about the long-lashed eyes of this Tabubu told the Chief Justice that she was no fool. Whether this expression was one of intelligence or mere cunning, Neferweben would have to wait to find out.

Rahotep said, "Tabubu, can you understand Egyptian well?"

"I can", replied the girl.

"She had better," said the pharaoh, "because there is no one present here who knows her native tongue except herself."

"Tabubu, did you serve your late mistress, Queen Satiah, every day?"

"Yes, every day."

"Was she was a good mistress to you?"

"Yes," replied Tabubu.

"Did she ever beat you or have you beaten?"

"No. That lady never did that."

"Did she speak to you in a friendly way?"

"She talk to me all the time. I do everything for her. She give me some dresses. This one I wear now."

"Then the royal lady must have been content with you, Tabubu."

"I think so," said Tabubu. "She doesn't complain. About some others she complain—but not Tabubu."

"What sorts of things did you talk about with your mistress?"

This time Tabubu did not answer so readily. Finally, she said "Woman things."

"And what is it that women talk about?"

"Umm...what she like to wear, her jewelry, which she has very much...her hair...you know. Woman things."

"All right. Tabubu, did your mistress ever say that she was afraid of someone?"

"No!" said Tabubu. "Why she be afraid? She wife of

pharaoh, the great one."

"Was there someone that your mistress disliked?"

"No," answered the girl firmly.

"Tell the truth, Tabubu," said the pharaoh, wearily. "If you lie, I will know it."

"How you know, king?" Tabubu asked, and at this even Neferweben had to laugh.

"That will do, young woman," he said, however. "Just answer this man's questions and don't leave out anything. You have nothing to fear. We only want the truth."

"Well...eh...my lady doesn't like anybody. Maybe just Tabubu."

"Only you? No one else?" said Rahotep.

"She say, my lady, 'Tabubu, you good girl. You much amusing.' But she never say she like any other people."

"Now, Tabubu, did your mistress ever talk about men with you? And by that I don't mean His Majesty, the king. Only other men."

"My lady...sometime she ask me, 'Tabubu, you think that man looks good?' when we see him from the window. Sometime I say yes and sometime I say no."

"I see. Can you remember the names of the men she asked you about?"

"Those men," said the servant, pointing at the Chief Barber and the other Canaanite, a heroic figure known to practically everyone by reputation. "She calling them something, some stranger word. But I forget the name she call them."

"So your mistress asked you if those men over there looked good to you?"

"Yes. And I say to her, "My sweet lady, what so good about white men what have big sticking-out noses like those ones?"

This observation even got a laugh out of the exhausted appearing pharaoh, who surely had the most prominent nose in the room. Rahotep, who didn't have much of a sense of humor, was able to go on without so much as a smile.

"Let us return to the matter of the 'woman things'. Did your mistress tell you that she might be with child?"

Tabubu hesitated. "She say nothing of this to me, but I hear her say so to Nebamun, the brother of my lady."

"When did she say this—how long ago?"

"Not long. Only on the same day before she die."

"And what did Nebamun say?"

"He say 'Well, sister, do not tell the king now. Wait.'"

"And what did your mistress answer?"

"She say 'Why? It his child. I cannot wait.'"

"What did Nebamun say then?"

"He say no more," replied Tabubu.

"Did anyone else hear this talk between Nebamun and Satiah, deceased?"

"I don't know."

"You're sure, then, that no one else did?"

"Well, that great lady there with her sewing. Maybe she hear."

Neferweben noticed that Queen Neferura, who was working on a bit of embroidery, looked up briefly. But then went back to her needlework, with no expression on her face.

"I take it you mean the Great Royal Wife, Neferura. Where was she that she might have heard this talking?"

"She pass by the door."

"So it was open?"

"Yes. And I am by the wall. This great lady stop. My other lady—she and Nebamun talking loud. Then this great lady go away."

"Tabubu, now I must come to the most unpleasant part. Tell us what happened on the night that your mistress was killed. Why did you wake up?"

"I...I wake up because I hear a noise."

"What sort of noise?"

"Eh...um...like somebody cannot breathe so good."

"Do you mean to say you heard a choking sound, Tabubu?"

"What that mean, 'choking'? Strange word."

"Well! You heard a choking noise. What else?"

"Nothing," said Tabubu.

"So this noise woke you out of your sleep?"

"Yes. Then I get up to make water, and pass by the room of my lady. From there was the ch...choking and I smell blood. I look for this bad smell and I see my lady."

"You saw that your mistress was dead."

"No," said Tabubu. "She not dead. She making the choking and she looking at me. And she take her hand and catch me like this." Tabubu placed one of her hands over her wrist. "Then I shout."

"Do you mean you began to scream?"

"Yes. What you say."

"And who came to you then?"

"Nebamun come, the brother to my lady. He look on my lady and say 'She dead. Somebody kill her.' Then he go away and come back with pharaoh."

"Was your mistress dead before Nebamun left to summon the king?"

"No. She still making the choking. Then she dead. Before pharaoh come."

"In that case, why did Nebamun say his sister was dead?"

Tabubu shrugged. "I don't know. He just say she dead."

"Is it possible that Nebamun might have said 'She's dying'?"

"If she not dead, why Nebamun say somebody kill her?"

"Well...this may all be a question of your understanding of the Egyptian language, so we will leave that alone. Did any women come?"

"Two women come after Nebamun. They some more servants to my lady in this house of the south, some witches. I don't know them so well. They just talk some in their language."

"Didn't they scream, too?"

"Those? Hah! Nothing too terrible for them. I am doing all screaming and crying. They just 'mumble, mumble, mumble' like always. But I stop screaming and touch the face of my poor lady like this." Tabubu caressed her own cheek. "Then she stop making the noise and die. Too bad my lady cannot talk before she die or somebody be in much great trouble."

"What about the other ladies in the harem? Did they appear?"

"No," said the slave, "they staying away."

"Tabubu, is that absolutely all you heard the entire night?"

"I am hearing nothing. I am sleeping because I am tired. Tabubu has much work."

"Was Nebamun, the head of your mistress's household, always there at night? Nebamun has his own house in the city."

"Sometime...he go to his house and sometime he stay here."

"All right. Now, Tabubu, do you know any of the other ladies in this room?"

"I see them," replied the girl. "Those ladies from a strange land, they live close by my lady. I don't talk to them. Nobody can."

"And your lady also never spoke to them?"

"No. Only the very great lady there." Tabubu indicated Queen Neferura.

"So you heard the Great Royal Wife speaking with the Canaanite ladies?"

"Yes, with the son of the king. He some very smart boy with doing talking. Ah...one night I hear pharaoh speak to those ladies. They are laughing."

"Neferweben," said the king, "Tabubu is mistaken. I never came to see those women. By day or by night."

"You heard what His Majesty said, Tabubu," Neferweben told her. "It must have been another man."

"Yes," said the girl. "Another man, then. Who knows the other strange language."

"On what night did you hear this talk in the strange language?"

"I don't know," said Tabubu. "Um...maybe two, three nights pass. I tell you Tabubu very tired in the nights."

"Can it have been the night your mistress was killed?"

"No. I hear nothing. No talking this night."

"Well, Tabubu, if you are so tired at night, how can you have heard the Canaanite ladies talking to a man down the hall when you heard absolutely nothing on the night your mistress was murdered practically under your nose?"

Neferweben sensed that Tabubu had found herself trapped. Finally, she said, "On account Nebamun. He there on the other night, too."

"Did Nebamun wake you up for some reason?"

"He always wake me up for the same reason."

"I see. And what reason was that?"

"What you think?"

"Are you saying Nebamun woke you up in order to do to you what men do to women at night?"

"Yes. In the day, Nebamun don't like Tabubu. In the night, he like her plenty. Nothing to like about him, even if somebody drown him in gold."

Neferweben could certainly see why the deceased, Satiah, had found Tabubu amusing. He said, "You mean even if Nebamun were dipped in gold, he wouldn't appeal to you?"

"Not even if he have a solid gold prick."

"That may be," said the Chief Justice. "But you must keep a civil tongue, Tabubu." He glanced over his shoulder at the king, whose chest seemed to be moving with contained mirth.

"Even I don't have one of those," the sovereign admitted.

Rahotep raised a skeptical eyebrow at his witness. "So you had sexual intercourse with Nebamun on the night you heard the talking in the room of the Canaanite ladies. Did he do the same to you on the night that his sister was murdered?"

"No."

"Did Nebamun say anything to you, on that other night, about hearing something going on down the hall?"

"No, he too busy."

Even the Chief Interrogator was having a difficult time keeping a straight face now.

"Did anything else happen after that—when he was done

being busy?" he said to Tabubu, holding out his arms as if to add, 'Here I am, Tabubu, your helpless victim.'

"Umm...yes. Nebamun just worn out and he lying there by me like he don't want to get up—and then my lady come in."

"Your mistress saw her brother lying next to you. Did she say anything?"

Tabubu shook her head.

"Question Neferura next," said the pharaoh. "Let's hear what she knows. Wife, do you think you can favor us with your attention for a moment?"

Neferura did not answer her husband, but her hand stopped working the cloth and she looked at Rahotep.

"My lady," said the latter, "do you have anything to add to the testimony of Tabubu?"

"No," said Neferura.

"Did you hear or see something unusual on the night of the murder of Queen Satiah, deceased?"

"It would have been unusual for any woman in Egypt to be 'queen' while I still live," was the response. "Satiah was a mere concubine of low birth."

"It is I who makes a queen," said Thutmose, not bothering to conceal his displeasure, "and that's not for you to pronounce upon. Do not try my patience today, Neferura. Answer the question Rahotep put to you."

"Very well," said Neferura. "I heard or saw nothing having

to do with any murder. Except the screaming of that Tabubu and all the commotion that followed."

"And you didn't venture forth to see what that was all about?"

"I? Whatever for? Noise issuing from that apartment was hardly an exceptional occurrence."

"What do you mean by that?" asked the interrogator.

"I mean," said Neferura, "that it's hardly a quiet place. People were shrieking and shouting in there constantly. At best, women were screeching with laughter. It sounded like what it seems to have been--a den of iniquity, inhabited by contemptible creatures and savages."

"When was your last visit to a den of iniquity, Neferura?" said the pharaoh, his tone heavy with sarcasm, but he received no reply.

"Mistress of Egypt," said Rahotep, quite gently, "did you hate the Lady Satiah?"

"Hate?" asked Neferura. "I had no hatred to spare for that girl. As for envy—the love of some men is not to be depended upon, much less missed. A mountain of sand may be there one day and gone the next, being at the mercy of an unexpected wind. A woman is nothing but a helpless creature. Even Satiah—no more no less. Now she is out of her misery, no doubt."

"That will do," said Neferweben curtly. "Rahotep, interrogate the men from Canaan. Begin with the Chief Barber."

To Levi's surprise, the Chief Interrogator bowed to him,

but then he recalled that the pharaoh had decreed that all men must. Hard to believe, but there it was.

"Amun-eywy," Rahotep began. "I'll put it to you plainly. Have you ever been in the rooms of the Canaanite wives of His Majesty at night?"

"I might have been," said Levi.

"You might have been?"

"Yes. You see, sir, the other night I got rather drunk. I had trouble finding my way back to my own room. On this night, I may have wandered into the harem corridor."

"Are you in the habit of getting drunk?"

"Only when I supply the wine," called out the pharaoh. "Probably, he is referring to three nights ago."

"I see, my lord."

"And if he spoke with my Canaanite wives, I pardon him for that now."

"As you wish, my lord." The interrogator bowed to the king.

"Amun-eywy, did you come back to the harem after that night when you were intoxicated?"

"No. That was the only night I drank too much and I wouldn't have gone there while sober."

"Amun-eywy, did you hear or see anything on the night of the murder of Queen Satiah that might be of importance?"

"No, sir, I did not."

"Did you hear any screaming? Any shouting?"

"No, sir. I am a very sound sleeper, I'm afraid."

"Did you find the next day, as you told His Majesty, that one of your razors had gone missing?"

"Yes."

"Do you know who might have taken the razor?"

"No."

"Have you ever spoken to Satiah, the deceased?"

"Yes, once. In the presence of His Majesty."

"At no other time?"

"No."

"Did you feel desire toward this lady?"

"Well, yes. Her beauty was beyond compare."

"Have you ever attempted to force yourself upon Satiah, the deceased?"

"No!"

"Did you ever have the opportunity to do that?"

"Never."

"Have you ever killed anyone, Chief Barber?"

"Yes."

Neferweben saw, by Rahotep's expression, that the interrogator had expected an answer in the negative. Well, so had he. Rahotep gazed at his witness with widened eyes.

"When?" Rahotep wanted to know.

"Years ago. I killed a man who had assaulted my mother."

"Years ago?" was Rahotep's astonished response. "You must have been a child!"

"Even so," said Amun-eywy.

"But not with a razor, I assume. You people don't shave in your own land."

"No," agreed the barber, "we don't. I hit this man with a stone hurled from a piece of leather."

"Did you devise this...er...weapon yourself?"

"No. It's a common thing in my homeland. Many use it."

"But I don't suppose you ever killed a woman in those days of your uncivilized youth."

"No," replied the Chief Barber, looking at the floor, "I didn't have the courage to do what was necessary when it was required of me."

Behind him, Neferweben heard Prince Mehy utter a kind of gasping sound.

"What do you mean 'necessary'?" wondered Rahotep in an appalled fashion. "What sort of place do you come from, then?"

"It was an ordinary place. Or so it seemed to me once. My mother...a dreadful sickness had come upon her. There was a lot of pain and she suffered greatly. At the end, she was screaming in agony and there was no one who could help her. It was night and we two were alone in the house. My mother said to me that she couldn't bear the pain any longer. Her words were 'I'm dying, Levi. Take the knife and kill me.' I refused, but she kept begging me to stop this horrible pain. But I, who didn't hesitate to slay that man without looking in his eyes, couldn't bring myself to end the suffering of my mother. However, in the morning, my aunt came

257

to us. She saw the condition of her sister and went away for awhile. When she returned, she had something with her and made a drink from it, giving that to my mother. Then my mother died peacefully. A woman was able to do what I couldn't. Therefore, I suppose I am a coward. Wouldn't you say so?"

To Neferweben, it seemed that the barber was actually soliciting the opinion of Rahotep, as though to confirm something the young man had been wondering about for a long time.

"So which is it?" replied the Chief Interrogator, rather stonily. "What do you want the court to believe—that you are a killer or a coward? Why have you told us that you slew that man?"

"You asked me," said Levi.

"Perhaps you only imagined that you were capable of avenging your mother as a mere boy. Could that be so, Chief Barber?"

"Well!" the pharaoh intervened. "We can find that out here and now. Mehy, take off your belt and give it to me."

The prince unwound the leather sash from around his waist. With a bewildered look, he placed it in his father's outstretched hand. The pharaoh held up the girdle, which consisted of an oval shape for the center with much thinner long straps hanging from each side and studied it briefly. The ruler then placed the oval part on the floor and dug his toe into it, pulling upon the straps. Hanging the belt over the arm of his throne, he took the ceremonial dagger from its holder at his own waist and rapped it sharply a few times on the stone steps of the dais. The ball of rock crystal that served as a knob on the hilt broke off and rolled down toward Rahotep and the witnesses.

"There is the pebble," said Thutmose. "Bring it up here, please, Levi."

When the barber complied, the pharaoh asked him, "Can this belt do for a sling?"

"Well, perhaps—but I haven't done this for a long time!" Levi objected.

"Aim for the Eye of Horus on one of those doors yonder."

"Those beautiful doors?"

"Decorate them a bit more. Get out of the way, Mehy."

Mehy, looking quite stunned, backed off. The pharaoh did the same. The barber, having no other choice, put the crystal orb into the depression the king had created in the leather and swung the belt above his head in a quick, swishing motion. A loud, thudding sound came from one of the big doors and the Eye of Horus was seen by all to have been provided with a new, gleaming pupil.

"Holy goldfish!" yelled Mehy.

"Shit!" Caleb exhaled.

"Hee!" cried Tabubu.

"Great fornicating gods!" Neferweben added in a murmur.

Only the Canaanite wives didn't look surprised. They, evidently, had seen this kind of skill before. However, they appeared quite pleased by what they had just witnessed. So did the ruler, who hadn't minded ruining a superbly crafted knife in order to vindicate the word of his barber. The vizier had never exactly disliked his sovereign previously but, in that moment, he actually conceived a liking for the king. Although the man looked worse than Neferweben had ever seen him, recent events had evidently wrought some positive change there, too. This pharaoh had the reputation of rewarding those who served him well in order, it was supposed, to buy and ensure their loyalty. Yet it was never suspected that the ruler was fond of any of his servants or viewed them as anything except the means to his own ends. As for that pampered creature, the late Queen Satiah, it seemed she, too, had been valued as more than a beautiful prize. In public, the king had not demonstrated any unusual affection toward this girl—only Prince Amunemhat was the recipient of that—until today. Indeed, the man had been careful to hide any weaknesses ever since Neferweben had known him. Except a little in the case of Ahmose, but everybody knew what the ruler owed that astonishing individual. Now the pharaoh's sick face gave away his feelings for his wife and his actions indicated a love for his barber. Neferweben's suspicions about that were soon confirmed.

"Now we know for certain," said the pharaoh. "This man could, indeed, be a formidable enemy, if he so chose. But he does not choose that here. Levi, you may resume your place. Well done, my Chief Barber!"

When Levi came back to join Rahotep, the Chief Interrogator bowed to him once more.

"Amun-eywy," continued Rahotep, but his tone was not an accusing one, "did you murder Queen Satiah with your razor?"

"I will reply for him," said Thutmose. "The answer shall be that he could not and did not. Let no man say otherwise today or on any other day while I live."

"Yes, my lord," Rahotep acquiesced. "Let the witness be excused."

"Listen, all you here who can understand my speech," said the king. "Until I met this man, I wrongly imagined that no one had been subjected to a more dismal upbringing than myself. Amun-eywy is not a son of my body, but he is a child of my heart. For I know him well. You did no wrong, Levi. It was too much to ask of a son—all that which was asked of you."

At these words, even Queen Neferura looked up at her husband, regarding him with something akin to benevolence. Then she raised one eyebrow and gave the linen material on her lap a quick stab with the needle. Yes, thought Neferweben, men can understand each other's hearts, but would they not be well off to try to comprehend those of women? If they did that, there might be far less trouble here and everywhere. A woman was not, after all, a creature from whom a man could assume loyalty and obedience like he did of his pet hound. Since the time of the oldest gods, males had taken mastery over females for granted, as though it was their due. Yet the pharaoh should have already learned long ago that women could not be depended upon to be docile or even loyal and could prove treacherous, besides.

"Chief Barber," said Neferweben, "are you able at this time to assist Rahotep in questioning the others?"

"Yes. I can do it."

"Sure he can!" said Mehy. "Those Canaanites are as tough as they come!"

"All right, Mehy," said his father, gently. "Neferweben, who's next?"

"Interrogate the other Canaanite, Rahotep" instructed the Chief Justice. "With the help of Amun-eywy."

"Master of the Horse, Caleb, can you understand any of our language?"

"Yes. A little."

"Were you not once an officer of the chariotry in your own land?"

"Yes."

"Were you not taken captive after your last battle?"

"Yes. I was knocked unconscious at the time."

"And then you were brought to Egypt. Well...you are here in Egypt. So my question must be, how do you feel about being in this land?"

"It could be worse," said Caleb.

"What is your attitude toward His Majesty?"

"He could be worse."

"His Majesty has given you a great honor. Isn't that somewhat better than 'could be worse'?"

"True. But I was honored in Canaan, as well. I am considered a hero there."

"You are quite the hero everywhere, it would seem."

"I do my bit," said Caleb.

"Are you a hero with the women, too?"

"I used to be."

"So you like the company of beautiful women."

"Who doesn't?"

"What would you do if a woman ever spurned your advances?"

"Just try my luck elsewhere, I suppose. That is—in the past I would have."

"And now you've changed?"

"Everything about my life has changed."

"Would you consider yourself a handsome man?"

"How do I look to you?"

"Amun-eywy," Neferweben said, "advise the witness to just answer the questions and not ask any of his own."

Levi relayed the message to Caleb.

"Did you find the deceased, Queen Satiah, beautiful?"

"Who wouldn't?"

"He means 'yes'," said Levi.

"Did you ever 'try your luck' with that great lady?"

"I don't have that much courage," was Caleb's reply.

"What of any of the other women in His Majesty's household?"

"No. I can't talk to them. There is the problem of language."

"But you can speak to the Canaanite ladies."

"I could."

"Did you ever do this?"

"Yes," said Caleb, "I spoke to them the day they arrived."

"It seems you aren't so short of courage, after all. Didn't you know they were the wives of the pharaoh?"

"I guessed as much."

"But you spoke to them anyway."

"Yes. I've already said I did."

"What about the Great Royal Wife, Neferura? Have you ever spoken to her?"

"No. That wouldn't be possible."

"Have you ever spoken to the king's wife, Satiah, deceased?"

"I can't speak Egyptian. I can understand some—but I can't say much. So how am I supposed to speak to these women?"

"Did you hear or see anything on the night of the murder of Queen Satiah?"

"Such as what?"

"Such as anything."

"Nothing out of the ordinary—no."

"You didn't hear any screaming? Any shouting?"

"Well—yes. I heard those things."

"Ah! So you weren't sleeping at this early hour?"

"No."

"Why not?"

"I don't sleep as well in Egypt as I used to in Canaan."

"Did you take the razor of Amun-eywy, the Chief Barber?"

"No! The man is my friend!"

"Do you consider our lord the king your enemy?"

Caleb paused.

"Why do you not answer?"

"It's not that simple."

"Either a man is your enemy—or he is not!"

"He's right," said the pharaoh. "It's not that simple. Do not ask him that question, Rahotep."

"But my lord!"

"Let us have the next question."

"May I say something?" Caleb asked.

Before Levi could translate this request, the Chief Justice had a momentary lapse in concentration and said in perfect, unaccented Canaanite, "Very well, but keep it short."

To his left, Neferweben heard the foreign wives murmur among themselves. Caleb, also, appeared a bit startled. Rahotep coughed discreetly behind his handkerchief.

"The witness has leave to speak," pronounced Neferweben, this time in Egyptian.

"I never thought I'd be in servitude to another man," the chariot-fighter began, "but the service I do here isn't distasteful to me by any means. If one can even call it work, it's the most

265

pleasant work I've ever done, training that lad there, as fine a little man as ever lived. I know I'm instructing him in things connected with warring, which is what I know best, but I've come to find out that teaching a youngster is a lot more satisfying than killing men. That's all I have to say."

Rahotep sighed and Neferweben understood why. The Canaanite had interrupted his line of questioning by making an unexpected speech that placed the man in a sympathetic light. Of course, he, Neferweben, had let him do it, but even Neferweben hadn't counted on Caleb admitting he enjoyed being the tutor of the prince. The judge had merely figured the slave intended to make some further denials regarding his lack of meaningful contact with any females since arriving in Egypt. It was beginning to seem to Neferweben that the people in the Great House liked one another better these days than he had previously imagined they might. Maids chatted with their mistresses like girls at the grindstone, royal masters and captives had created a bond, and great, gloomy queens sought the company of their inferiors. But which of them had disliked Satiah enough to put her to death?

"So men have died by your hand?" Rahotep inquired of Caleb, forging steadfastly ahead.

"Yes, many," was the fed up response. "Why even ask?"

"Have you ever killed a woman?"

"No!" said Caleb, glaring at his interrogator. "What for?"

"Would you slay the wife of a man you considered your enemy?"

"No. No women. No children. Not I."

"Would you ravish the wife of your enemy?"

"Rape? I never did that. Never once."

"Did you murder the royal lady, Satiah, deceased?"

"No."

"Did you commit rape upon her body?"

"No."

"Did you desire that lady?"

"Yes. I admit that I desired that lady. Anybody would."

"Do you also admit that you could overpower any woman whom you desired?"

"With what? My charm?"

"No. By main force."

"Any man can overpower a female," said Caleb, disdainfully. "Even you could."

"But I wasn't in the Residence on the night of the murder. You were, Master of the Horse."

"Right. But that doesn't make me a killer, does it?"

"You already admitted that you *are* a killer."

"But not of women. No woman ever tried to shoot me, lance me, or throw an axe in my direction."

"I'm through with this witness," said Rahotep, shaking his head. "May I go on to question the Canaanite ladies?"

"Only the eldest," Neferweben told him. "That should be sufficient. Please do the honors again, Chief Barber. Which of them is the eldest?"

267

"This one," said the barber, indicating yet another lovely girl, of which there seemed to be many in the house of the king, but one had to expect that. This foreign girl was dressed in her modest but ornate costume and eastern jewelry. She had a slender, fair face and a long, very thin nose with flaring nostrils. In one of these was a small ring and Neferweben found that it looked very beguiling in its setting. Beautiful lips and startling blue eyes completed this picture and the Chief Justice, knowing that the ruler did not go near these women, certainly thought he would had he the chance. This particular girl seemed to him to look neither shy nor bold. Just shrewd, thought Neferweben, as her luminous eyes were alert in the manner of those of Tabubu. Her sisters, whose appearance was somewhat like the eldest Canaanite, merely seemed subdued. In the opinion of Neferweben, there were two calm, self-possessed Canaanites in the room but one of them was not the hero, Caleb. Splendid figure of a man that he was, his face looked no less tired than that of the pharaoh and this Caleb's black eyes had a haunted quality such as the Chief Justice had seen many times before in the cases of criminals who knew they were doomed.

"What is your name, young lady?" asked Rahotep and Amun-eywy translated his words.

"Marta."

"A very nice name. Are you aware, Marta, that the night before last, a wife of the pharaoh was murdered in her bed?"

"Yes...I know this."

"Do you also know that in the king's court you must tell the truth?"

"Yes."

"Did one of these men here of your land ever come into your room at night?"

"Yes."

"Which one?"

"This one. The one who speaks Egyptian."

"What did he do there in your room?"

"Behaved like a fool."

"In what way did he behave like a fool?"

"He was very drunk. He said some foolish things to me and my sisters and we laughed at him. He had lost his way."

"Did he try to do anything improper to any of you?"

"No. After a short time we threw him out. We don't know what became of him after that."

"What night was this?"

"Hmm...perhaps three nights ago. I'm not sure. There's been a lot of excitement here. But this man was not in our room on the night of the murder of the lady."

"Did you hear or see anything unusual that night?"

"Yes. I couldn't go to sleep this night. It was on account of the man who made trouble at the king's ceremony. I couldn't stop thinking about him."

"Did he frighten you?"

"No. I just couldn't get him from my head."

"Well...you couldn't sleep. Did you hear or see anything?"

"I saw the beautiful lady. The one who was killed."

"You mean before she died?" Rahotep, the digger, had finally struck gold.

"Yes. She spoke to me."

"She spoke to you? In what language?"

"In the Egyptian."

"Can you understand Egyptian?"

"Only the few words the great, kind lady there has taught to me and my sisters."

"And your sisters? Were they awake?"

"No. Both sleeping. I don't know what the beautiful young lady said but I think it was that she was afraid. She pointed to my bed and it seemed she wanted to come in there with me. So I let her do it. She pulled the covers up over her head and lay very still, very near me, so that we appeared in the dark as not two persons but one."

"And then?"

"I did not put my head under the covers. I kept watch to see who it was that the young lady feared."

"Did you see anyone?"

"Yes," said Marta. "That black one, Tabubu. She came and she looked at me and I looked at her. Then she was gone without having spoken a word."

"She lying, that foreign land white girl!" Tabubu yelled.

"I never see her!"

"Silence!" shouted Neferweben. "Keep still now, Tabubu. Not another word unless you're spoken to!"

"Satiah had three serving women from the southern lands," said the pharaoh. "Levi, ask Marta if she is certain that it was Tabubu whom she saw."

The barber translated the question and Marta said, "I know there are three black women, but all do not wear their hair in the same way. It was Tabubu's hair arrangement that I recognized and not her face."

"Marta," contined Rahotep, "you claim that Satiah, deceased, came into your bed. How long did she remain there with you?"

"It was a long time. She came quite early in the evening. I wanted to ask her why she was so frightened but I couldn't, of course. I didn't know the words. Finally, after Tabubu had gone and no one else appeared, I fell asleep. When I woke up there was much screaming. But the beautiful young lady was no longer in my bed."

"Could someone have removed Satiah from your bed while you were asleep?"

"I don't think so. Unless she went with that person of her own accord. Anyway, I never noticed that she had left."

"Rahotep," said Neferweben, "you may question Tabubu again now."

"Tabubu," said the king in a warning tone, "tell the truth!

You needn't fear anyone while I sit on this throne. No one in this place is greater than I am. And I don't believe that you did nothing but sleep all night! Speak the truth!"

"Ask him!" said Tabubu, pointing to Nebamun, Satiah's brother. "Find out from that one the reason Tabubu can't go to sleep!"

"Yes, why not ask him?" said Neferweben.

"Nebamun," said the Chief Interrogator, "what do you say to the words of Tabubu?"

"She's lying," said Satiah's brother. "I know nothing of what Tabubu does during the night. She's nothing but a wild, ungovernable creature and I have no desire toward her whatsoever. All three of them who were part of my sister's household did little else but steal and find ways to waste time. I complained to Satiah constantly about them, but she didn't seem to mind what they did. 'They amuse me,' were her words, 'and they don't steal anything of any consequence. Whatever they take I can easily replace. Let them be.' So I did as the queen, my sister, told me."

"Is that true, Tabubu? Were you stealing from your mistress?" Rahotep demanded.

"Not Tabubu! I don't know what those other black women do. They not from my people. Why Tabubu has to steal when her lady give her all things?"

"One could certainly understand your mistress giving you an old dress," said the interrogator, " but one can't help notice that you're wearing a remarkably costly pair of gold earrings. Did your lady give those to you, as well?"

"No, but they mine!"

"They can only have been made by the royal jeweler," Rahotep rightly observed," and are of the finest Egyptian workmanship. You didn't bring them with you from your own land. You took them from your dead mistress—isn't that so?"

"No! Never!"

"Did your lover here make you a present of them?"

"I got no lover!" said Tabubu fiercely. "What I got is a son of a dog who give me nothing except what I don't want!"

"Rahotep," said the king, "let her alone about those damned earbobs. I gave them to her, myself, and the reason is my own business."

This was the truth. On the ship, after Satiah had taken her time vacating the cabin, followed by her slave, the pharaoh had called to Tabubu to come back inside. He had told her to hold out her hands and placed the earrings that her mistress had just removed on her palms.

"As of this moment," the king had said, "these belong to you."

"But, pharaoh," Tabubu had objected, "those my mistress liking especially much!"

"Are you, too, going to refuse a gift from me? So much the better if your mistress likes them especially. If she tries to take them back, you can tell her all her other jewels go right into the river. Understand?"

273

But Satiah had made no effort to take back the earrings. When she saw her maid's tearful expression, all she had done was cry out, "Oh, no! He hasn't taken you away from me, has he? Please don't tell me he's done that!"

When Tabubu had assured her mistress that they weren't going to be separated, the relieved Satiah had put the objects into the earlobes of her maid, herself, and told her they looked becoming. "He'll give me others," she had said. "Just you wait and see." And that had come to pass. Within the week, Satiah had received three more pairs.

At any rate, Rahotep certainly respected the ruler's private business and quickly dropped the matter of the suspicious earrings. Neferweben wondered why the pharaoh had given the maid the jewels. Was he, too, sleeping with Tabubu? Or was this the price he had paid for her silence on some matter? The judge sincerely hoped it wasn't the latter. If so, he and Rahotep were wasting their time and effort. But Neferweben had plenty of experience with witnesses and the black girl, having claimed to loathe Satiah's brother, seemed to him to be telling the truth there. But why would a girl who got golden ornaments from a king need to accept the unwanted attentions of a mere steward? So perhaps Tabubu had been bribed, after all. For what reason, then? It seemed to Neferweben that one word from the sovereign should suffice to silence a defenseless creature like Tabubu, if that was his intention. What a strange case this was!

"That Nebamun, pharaoh, he the lazy one," Tabubu fumed, evidently emboldened by the ruler's defense of her honesty. "He never do nothing and probably the biggest stealer. And liar, too. My lady not afraid of me. She like me best as I can talk Egyptian and the other women—I don't know what they talk. Nobody know, only them. Pharaoh, the great one, listen please to me. The foreign land girl lie. Nebamun, he been hitting everybody with his stick, mostly Tabubu, when my lady not there. He shouting and we yelling from pain. The great lady there right about that. Nebamun drinking plenty, sometime too much, and then he get worse. The night he been having sexual whatever with me, he see my lady and go to her room with her. Then they argue. He angry and she angry."

"Tabubu," Neferweben remonstrated, "you must not speak to His Majesty here!"

"Speak only to me," said Rahotep. "Why was Nebamun angry?"

The girl said, "He angry a lot, but not at my lady. Not before."

"Do you think your mistress was angry at her brother because of what he was doing with you? Perhaps the two of you had awakened her."

"That never happen."

"Had you ever told your mistress what Nebamun was doing to you?"

"No! I was afraid of Nebamun and his stick."

"All right. Then why do you think Nebamun was angry with your mistress?"

"She say to him 'Keep you hands away from my women!' Then Nebamun say, 'What you care what I do to such women?' My lady say 'She will get a baby and then there be trouble for me as I must keep it here!' Nebamun say 'Why you not with pharaoh, Satiah?' My lady say, 'He send me away.' Then Nebamun say, 'You say that before. Why you go back in your nightdress and he send you away another time?' My lady say 'That not you affair. I am queen and you my servant now.' Then Nebamun say, 'You fool creature, you better not make king angry or you not be queen anymore!' My lady say, "I not making nobody angry, but you making me plenty angry. Go away from me, Nebamun, and don't stay here at night no more.'"

"But Nebamun was in the harem before dawn when your mistress was found with her throat cut. Did he stay overnight there again?"

"Yes," said Tabubu, "he there because he not listening to what my mistress tell him. My lady come back from see pharaoh. He send her away again, it seem to me, and so she say 'Tabubu, take off my things. I tired and want to go to bed.' So I put my poor lady in her bed. After that come Nebamun. He say to me, 'Where you mistress? She stay with pharaoh?' I say 'No, she in her bed.' Nebamun make a strange face and then he say to me, 'Tabubu, do not go to sleep. Watch the door that lady my sister. She doing something. Find out what that is she doing, or I beat you good.' I say, 'Yes, Nebamun, if she go I follow her and she never see me.' In my land, we follow people they never see us, not all day and all night. Then Nebamun leave me alone and go someplace. By and by my lady get up and leave her room. So I follow my poor lady on account her bad, lazy brother and his stick, the only thing he not lazy with. Well, two things he not lazy with. But the stick the bigger one."

Neferweben could hear the muffled whelping of Prince Mehy over his own chuckling.

"She's mad!" shouted Nebamun. "I wouldn't even send her on the simplest errand, much less to follow my sister about."

"Order!" Neferweben tried to sound irritated. "This is an official inquiry. Nobody can say anything unless Rahotep asks. We can't have all this talking out of turn."

"Listen to him," said the pharaoh, "or the next one who talks out of turn gets the whip. And the whip doesn't care whom it bites."

Rahotep wiped his brow with his handkerchief. From the effort of having to think so fast on his feet all the time, thought Neferweben. And that Rahotep could do very well. That was why he was the ruler's Chief Interrogator. Rahotep said, "Tabubu, you may continue. You followed your mistress, Satiah, deceased?"

"I say I do and I do! But only on account Nebamun, the one he doesn't let me sleep. I follow her and does she see me? No!"

"Satiah must have seen you—or why would she have

277

hidden in Marta's bed?"

"That foreign white lady—I don't know what she talking about. She say my lady come to her bed early in the night, but that not true. And why my lady hide from me if she do see me? Why she fear her own Tabubu? I am no witching-woman!"

"Eh? What do you mean by that?"

"I mean I never make magic like those other black women who with us! I got no power to harm nobody, especially my lady."

"What?"

"They witch-womans, I told you! I see them do that magic. I say to them 'What you do that for?' They know I am asking and they say 'Evil come here!' I can understand what is 'evil' in their language."

"Are you saying, Tabubu, that the serving women of Satiah were trying to bring, by sorcery, evil to the house of the king?"

"No! I never say this. They want to make it go—not come. You think they stupid? Evil comes to a place, it comes to everybody. Nobody safe. They witch-woman ones and can smell evil. Well, it coming, don't it? They smelling pretty good!"

"Humph! Tabubu, witch or no witch, you know perfectly well that if your mistress saw you following her, she'd want to hide from you. Because you are the ally of her brother and sleep with him, perhaps even willingly. You have just told the court that you never complained about that to your lady and promised her brother, Nebamun, you would inform him of where your mistress went. What kind of loyal servant to your mistress is that?"

"That what you think!" Tabubu told Rahotep. "I tell Nebamun I follow my mistress but I never tell him where she go. Like my lady say to him, it not his affair. Tabubu not servant to Nebamun, but to my sweet lady!"

"Did you see anybody in Marta's bed other than Marta?"

"I never see this Marta. I never go in that room!"

Chapter Fifteen

At that very moment, Neferweben saw Merymaat, the pharaoh's Chief Physician, come through the big double doors. It was a good job he hadn't appeared earlier or he might have found himself felled by a precious gem! The vizier knew that the doctor was scheduled to be a witness, but had been detained on account of tending the king's steward, who had fallen ill with a stroke recently.

"Hold on, Rahotep," Neferweben said. "Allow Merymaat to take a seat."

"How goes it with my steward?" the ruler wanted to know.

"He is in the hands of the gods," replied the doctor. "I fear his time has come."

"Now that's a pity," said the king morosely. "Rahotep, interrogate Merymaat now so that he can return to his patient."

"Merymaat," Rahotep started in, "why not simply tell the court what you saw on the morning after the king's wife was found murdered?"

"Well," said the witness, "my assistant and I were summoned. The Lady Satiah was on her bed. I took her pulse and looked at her eyes. She was dead—no question. Her wound was terrible and there was no chance of survival as one of the main arteries in her neck had been severed. Much loss of blood there and very quickly. Also, the trachea was damaged by the action of the razor."

"Even so, do you think it possible Satiah can have spoken before she expired?"

"It's difficult to say—but I can't entirely rule out the possibility."

"Did you further examine the deceased?"

"Yes. After she was taken to the quarters of His Majesty."

"And?"

The doctor rubbed the back of his neck. To Neferweben, Merymaat also appeared weary.

"I examined the lady but could see no other signs of violence. No bruises—nothing like that. Just some irritation about the face. She had long fingernails and there was blood on and under them, probably from clutching at her own throat in her panic before expiring."

"Her maid said Satiah seized her wrist."

"A young, strong individual can't be killed instantly," was the physician's opinion. "Not very often, anyway. Queen Satiah was cut while she slept, but then she would have awakened immediately."

"And seen her killer?"

"Yes, of course."

"Did you, Merymaat, notice anything else upon the body of Satiah, the deceased?"

"Yes. Seminal fluid. Dried. And menstrual blood."

"Are you certain that it was menstrual blood?"

"Reasonably certain. There wasn't much, so the lady's time of month had just come upon her."

"Is it possible," said Rahotep, "that this bleeding down below can have been the result of forcible sexual entry?"

"I'm thinking," said the physician, "that perhaps it isn't proper for Prince Amunemhat to hear all this."

"He can take it," was the pharaoh's reply. "Let it be part of his education. You will have heard, of course, Merymaat, that Mehy was not deterred by the sight of blood in the river."

"I heard," said the king's Chief Physician. "Brave lad."

"Therefore continue."

"From what I know," said Merymaat, "my opinion must be that rape is difficult to explain in this case."

"No one claimed to have heard anything," Rahotep informed Merymaat, "even though the murder was committed in the rooms of Satiah with four persons present. If you were a woman and someone came in intent on raping you, would you have made a sound when threatened with a sharp instrument?"

"Rahotep," said the doctor, "there was time for the victim of rape to utter a cry for help. One can't commit such a deed and threaten the victim throughout the act and then simply cut her throat when it is over without giving the woman the opportunity to cry out even once. At the end, if the murderer held the razor in his right hand, he couldn't hold it over the woman's mouth to stifle her cries. If he did the stifling with his left hand, that would have been in the way of the slashing, in the case of this long wound. All this applies to a left-handed individual, as well. The ravisher would have had to remove one hand. A wife of the king would have known that anyone who violated her would have to kill her— or face the consequences. Is she going to let him get away with that without uttering a sound in order to save herself or at least make his presence known? Since the young woman was surely killed in her bed, all the blood being confined to that area, rape, immediately followed by murder, is not a likelihood. Not in total silence. She was murdered in her sleep. If Queen Satiah had been violated at some earlier time, I am unable to account for her going to sleep without telling anyone what had happened to her."

"Even if she hid from her assailant in fear most of the night?"

Merymaat seemed to think that over. Finally, he said, "I am only a physician, but I was trained to view matters in a way that makes sense. There is no sense in what you propose, I'm afraid. One doesn't hide from an assailant in terror somewhere and then just go to bed in a place where there are only sleeping people without asking anyone for protection from the same assailant. I didn't see what occurred, of course, but it seems to me that this female caused her own death by perfidious and wholly unwise actions. Our lord king is well rid of such a wife."

This declaration on the part of the Chief Physician, a man bound to preserve and respect human life, appeared to have rendered Rahotep speechless. Evidently everyone else who could comprehend Egyptian was likewise struck, as Neferweben could hear not a single word or sound of protest. Nebamun glowered, but kept silent. Even the grieving pharaoh held his tongue. Perhaps he, too, had grown to see the lack of logic in the theory of rape.

"Er...that will be sufficient, Chief Physician," said Neferweben. "We will require no more of your time."

"Yes, you are excused," added the pharaoh, simply.

Merymaat rose and bowed to his lord. He was not at all slow in making his exit from the chamber, Neferweben couldn't help but notice. He also wondered whether Merymaat recalled, as he did, that the last known act of rape in the Theban residence had been instigated by none other than the sovereign, himself. Of course, the Chief Justice, too, had found it very odd that the deceased had not remained with the foreign girls until daylight and then reported what had happened to her, if she had been raped. Why should Satiah have gone back to her own chamber and directly to sleep without having complained to anyone that she had been assaulted? If Nebamun had been there, it seemed to Neferweben that Satiah should have awakened him and told him everything that had occurred.

Neferweben had the idea that, probably, the astute Rahotep also did not give much credit to this "taken by force" business, either, but had merely kept suggesting it out of respect for the dead woman's honor and the bereavement of the pharaoh. This was correct procedure in the estimation of the vizier, for the innocence of the deceased should be presumed by the court in the case of a victim of foul play until if and when the balance tilted to the opposite side. Knowing Rahotep, Neferweben was certain the interrogator would soon have found a way to raise the possibility of Satiah not having been the loyal spouse he had thus far seemed to take for granted she was—and make it appear he had stumbled upon the information purely by accident. However, now that was no longer necessary. Merymaat had done his work for him. Well, Neferweben would have to wait and see what had yet to come out. Whatever it was, it might not be the whole truth. Not here in this place. Neferweben realized he could probably count on that. But, as he was not his father's son for nothing, he also knew he would be able to organize something out of it, anyway.

"All right," Neferweben said. "Tabubu's turn again."

"Well, Tabubu," said Rahotep, "it appears to me that you must have lost sight of Satiah. Perhaps you're not so good at following people as you claim. She saw you and you lost her."

Tabubu was thoughtful, but only momentarily. "Why I look for her in the strange women room? What I can say to that foreign white girl? How I can ask her where my lady now? In which language? I know my lady never see me. But maybe she hear me."

"Why would she hear you? Did you have shoes on your feet?"

"What? Tabubu? Shoes? Hah! I never have shoes in my land and not in Egypt land. But...I forget something. These!"

Tabubu held out her arms, both of which were covered with numerous bangles. She shook her arms and the ornaments made a rattling sound.

"See?" said the girl. "These I do get from my lady. They just from copper with blue paste and not stolen! My mistress wearing them in her village home and don't need them. Maybe Tabubu not follow people for long time. She forget how be very quiet."

"Hmm. Does anyone besides you wear those bracelets that might have alerted your mistress to the fact that someone was following her?"

"You blind? You never look on women? See there! All have them. The very great lady and the foreign land girls—and even that boy who is son of the king! Even he have some. But they gold and silver, you notice. Some even from glass, but that breaking easy, it seem to me, and better for perfume bottles and such. Egyptian magicians make this glass but it still breaking. Something wrong there." Tabubu dismissed the conjurors of Egypt with a shrug.

Rahotep blew out a long, exasperated breath. "All right, Tabubu. After you lost sight of your mistress, what happened then?"

"I go back. Nebamun waiting for me. He ask me where is my lady and I say 'She with pharaoh.' Nebamun grab my hair and say, 'You lying, you black bitch! I hide near the door of pharaoh and never see Satiah go there. You better tell me where she go or I flay you hide!' I say to Nebamun, 'You Egyptian son of pig, beat me if you want! Then I tell my lady you make me follow her. Then you not head of this place no more!'"

"Did Nebamun beat you then?"

"You see my hide flay?" Tabubu asked the Chief Interrogator, archly. "Nebamun do nothing. Just say some more bad words to me and let me go to sleep. That Merymaat man, he seem to be knowing something about Nebamun. When Nebamun coming to me in the night, he put his hand over my mouth the whole time. I just lucky he don't bring his razor with him, eh? Then maybe I be the dead one!"

"Young woman," said Neferweben sternly, "you are out of order. Kindly keep your remarks to the point and don't talk so much. We have noted your complaint about Nebamun. You belong to the king, not to Nebamun. The brother of Satiah will be your master no more. There will be nothing more happening between you."

"You sure?" asked Tabubu.

"Yes," said the vizier. "Totally certain."

"Now I must ask you, Tabubu," said Rahotep, "where was she going, your mistress, Satiah, deceased? That is, before she escaped you."

Tabubu folded her arms. "I no remember."

"That whip is waiting, Tabubu," said the pharaoh, menacingly.

"Oh, pharaoh, the great one, why you bring Tabubu to this Egypt land? In my home, if people say they don't remember, other people think maybe something there better to forget! You say 'Tabubu, talk or you feel the whip', but if Tabubu remember, it is pharaoh, the great one, who will feel the bite. Let me go away from this place, pharaoh. Please—do not allow them ask Tabubu any more! Just let me go."

"Give Tabubu some more time," Neferweben said. "Give her a chance to think over the importance of speaking the truth and allow Nebamun the opportunity to answer her previous statements. I can see he is very angry. You can return to her in a moment."

The elder brother of Satiah, being of her blood, had good features but was not handsome in the extraordinary way that the dead queen had been. The man was the same age as the pharaoh. Neferweben felt that the best way to describe Nebamun was "unremarkable" and, were it not for his fine clothes, the man could probably pass unnoticed by most people. At any rate, the Chief Justice had noticed that Nebamun spoke in the accent of the Faiyum, even though he had cultivated a good manner of address, somehow, despite not being a highborn person. Well, if the Chief Barber, who had been in Egypt for only a few years, had been able to accomplish that—why not Nebamun, who had lived there all his life? Satiah's brother had obviously decided long ago that the royal connections of his mother gave him some status and, therefore, had adopted a superior manner. Regardless, he had not been able to rid his speech of the rather comical way in which the Faiyum people pronounced their "r"s, and Neferweben recalled a time when the pharaoh had good-naturedly teased Satiah about her own accent and the girl had taken great offence at that, giving her husband the cold treatment for as long as Neferweben had been in the same room with them. Even when the ruler had admitted to the girl that he had spoken the same way in the beginning, having been nursed by Satiah's own mother, the favorite had not been mollified. Truly, this lovely wife of the pharaoh had seldom worn anything but a glum expression on the occasions that the vizier had seen her, and now her brother appeared even more sullen. Well, that was only to be expected, as Tabubu had accused the man of much.

"Very well." Rahotep turned to Nebamun again. "You heard all that Tabubu has said. Is she still lying or not?"

"Of course she's lying," said Nebamun. "What do you expect? That's all these people do. Either steal or lie. Both come as natural to them as breathing. First off, I never quarreled with my little sister. We've always been on good terms. If it were otherwise, why would she have asked the ruler to make me her steward? I went about my duties efficiently and did the best I could, considering the kind of help I had about me."

"Did you ever beat those black women?"

"Yes," admitted Nebamun. "I had to have a switch about or nothing would ever have gotten accomplished in that household. But I never beat any of them severely at all. Mostly just brandishing my switch at them was enough to get them going. They're lazy, but they're not stupid. Cunning is what I call them. Most Egyptians would be surprised at how clever they can be if they want to. "

"Were you aware, Nebamun, that some of your sister's women were practicing magic?"

"They didn't when I was around! But if I had to pick out one witch among them, Tabubu would be my choice. Nobody's more devious or clever than that creature. You may not find her Egyptian very good, but she picked up what she knows very fast. It wouldn't surprise me if Tabubu even knows Canaanite. As for the language of the other black women, whatever it is, you can well believe Tabubu knows that by now, too."

"You've already denied that you ordered Tabubu to follow your sister, Satiah, deceased. Do you deny it again?"

"I'd deny it a hundred times! As for my lurking about the area of the pharaoh's quarters, that's absurd, as well."

"So your sister never told you that you could no longer stay in the harem at night?"

"Of course she didn't! It made no difference to Satiah one way or another."

"And that's why you were present when your sister was found murdered. Because your sister allowed you to stay at night."

"Yes."

"Tabubu said that on a certain night before the lady Satiah, deceased, was killed, your sister was sent away by His Majesty twice. Wait. May I have leave to ask His Majesty whether he can recall if he sent his wife away twice in one evening recently?"

"You may," said the king, "and I recall no such thing. If Satiah had come to me in her nightdress, it would be because I had sent for her. Once she was there, she would stay with me until morning. I did send her away on the night that she died, but she was dressed in her regular garments at the time. If only I hadn't done it!"

"Thank you, my lord," said Rahotep. "So Nebamun, you did not inquire of your sister why she had been sent away by our king more than once on any particular night?"

"No, I didn't. It really wasn't any of my affair, in any case."

"What about your sister having told you that she might be with child? Is that one of Tabubu's lies, as well?"

"That part, at least, is true. Of course Satiah would have told me if she suspected such a thing."

Rahotep turned to the pharaoh. "By your leave, Sovereign —can you tell me when Satiah, deceased, told you about possibly being with child?"

"It was on the morning of my appearance before the people. She came to me early and said that she had something to tell me. That was her news, her suspicion about being with child."

The interrogator bowed yet again. "Very good, my lord. Nebamun," Rahotep said, changing his tone, "what was there for you to do in that harem household after dark when the serving maids had already gone to bed and Satiah, the deceased, was usually with the ruler? A bit of dishwashing, a little sewing, some sweeping, perhaps? A bit of reading by the light of a lamp? Do you know how to read, Nebamun?"

"No."

"Do you not like the house that His Majesty has given you in the city?"

"It's a fine house. Of course I like it!"

"Is your wife there with you?"

"No," said Nebamun. "My wife is in the Faiyum just now. I had very little time to spend with her on account of coming to Thebes and having to be present in my sister's household."

"Don't you require the company of your wife at night?" Rahotep asked him. "You're still a young man, Nebamun. Don't you need a woman?"

"Yes," replied Nebamun, his masculine pride scarcely allowing him to respond otherwise.

"Why didn't you go home while it was still light and you could catch a ferry across the river? What was the reason you needed to sleep in the harem at all? That's no place for a man at night, unless he's a eunuch. Wasn't it because of Tabubu? It seems odd to me that this slave would admit that your sister caught the two of you together, unless that was true. After all, there was no murder committed on that particular night and Tabubu was not under any great duress to account for her actions that evening. Were you together with Tabubu or not, Nebamun?"

"All right!" barked the witness. "I was lying with Tabubu. I was ashamed to admit as much. But I never forced her. She liked it well enough—and that's why she never complained to my sister. Tabubu would have been happy if I'd done it to her every night, all night. What other man was there about to satisfy that wild thing's insatiable desire?"

"That had better be the last falsehood we hear out of you today, Nebamun," the ruler advised. "Did you think you'd be hung or impaled for sleeping with a servant girl?"

"Well, she's black," said Nebamun, sheepishly. "I beg your pardon, my lord."

"You're a bloody fool, Nebamun," Thutmose told him. "Black! But not between the legs, eh? Speak the truth from now on or, as Ra loves me, I'll make you see black and every other color all at once, do you hear me? Do you comprehend?"

"Yes, my lord," Nebamun answered. "I hear His Majesty."

"Proceed, Rahotep," said the king between his teeth.

The Chief Interrogator began anew. "Nebamun, did you advise your sister not to tell the ruler about being with child?"

"I did. But only because she didn't seem sure of it. It seemed to me that she shouldn't give him any false hope that a child might be born to him."

"Why would that be any of your affair—the things a wife tells her husband?"

"I suppose it wasn't, really, but the pharaoh hasn't had any children for a long time. I assumed he would like more and didn't want His Majesty to be disappointed in the event Satiah was mistaken. So that was my advice—correct, it now appears. My sister was young and impetuous. She hadn't had time to learn to think matters over carefully."

"Do you believe, Nebamun, that your sister might have been so impetuous as to betray His Majesty the king?"

"No, I can't believe that! His Majesty has done our family a great honor by marrying Satiah. We never dreamed such a thing was possible—but it happened and all of us were very grateful to him. Our family isn't wealthy or important. We come from the country, from a village in the Faiyum. The only reason we have anything is that my mother was chosen by someone from the Faiyum Harem to be His Majesty's nurse when he was born. When the king came back in triumph, he rewarded my mother by building us a good house in the village and giving us many things, but Satiah certainly didn't have the kinds of things she received from the pharaoh after he chose her. She was very happy with all of her nice things here and beautiful jewels. Why would my sister do anything that might take all that from her and put her life in jeopardy, besides?"

"Nebamun, must I remind you there were signs on her body that your sister had, indeed, been with a man? What if I told you that His Majesty, himself, had confirmed the signs, the nature of which are not necessary to mention again?"

"In that case, I don't presume to argue. My family has been dishonored and we will never be able to hold up our heads again. That's all I can say, except to apologize to His Majesty and to assure him that Satiah will be to our family as though she had never existed. We will not attend her burial or ever mention her name again."

"Well, Nebamun," said the Chief Interrogator in a sarcastic tone, "you certainly don't go to any great length to defend the reputation of your sister. I never told you we had any proof that Queen Satiah had betrayed the king. All I told you was that there were signs upon her body that showed she had been with a man, as you heard Merymaat testify. His Majesty denied responsibility for those signs, but even the king cannot know whether or not your sister was taken by force. Don't you allow that might have occurred?"

"How in the devil would I know?" Nebamun demanded loudly. "I didn't examine the body of my dead sister as closely as some evidently have. I don't know anything about the findings of Merymaat!"

"That will do, Rahotep," said the Chief Justice. "Say no more to Nebamun. Continue with Tabubu."

"I am tired," complained the servant girl. "How I can remember things when I am so tired? I say one thing, others say different. So what use for me to say anything more? Egyptian man says what Tabubu say is lies. Who is going to believe this black Tabubu now? So let me go from here, please, pharaoh. Let me go back to my home where I am born and far away from this Nebamun!"

"Tabubu," said the king, sounding much more tired than she, "you cannot go anywhere. You must finish here."

"So—pharaoh has order it!" cried Tabubu. "Ayee! What kind place is this Egypt land? Why people want to know everything here? In my land people say, 'There is much wisdom in that Egypt'. If so much wisdom, why still so much asking? Ahh...I follow my lady. She go to the place where lives those white men there."

"How do you know where those men live? Do you follow them about, as well?"

"No! Tabubu just know."

"You just know, eh?" said Rahotep. "Could you share with us how you know?"

The slave looked at the king for a moment and, with a sigh, reiterated, "I just know. One day I with my lady, like always, in Memphis. I am looking out from the window across the...what you call that empty place...um...the courtyard! I see another window and there is a man standing there. I say to my lady, 'Oh, my lady, come and look! There is a white man there what is cover with hair!' He not wearing a shirt and has black hair, very much, here." Tabubu pointed to her chest. "In my land, I never see a man with so much hair there, thick like a monkey fur! So my lady look and she very amaze, too. We both laughing, but my lady cannot stop looking at that man. She say, 'Oh, Tabubu, he some very beautiful man! Where do he come from?' I say, "Pharaoh bring him here—what else? He a slave, for sure, and not wanting to be in this place. He just some poor foreign white man what been brought to Egypt from his home, where he belong.'"

Rahotep made a disapproving face. "So that's how you spent your time, girl—keeping watch for naked men to point out to the wife of the king? And why did you follow your mistress in the first place? Why were you so interested to know where she was going?"

"I tell you why before! That father of all liars, Nebamun, tell me do it! I wait until my lady come out from that room and then I follow her back. I lose her. I can't follow her so close or she see me! But when I go back to that harem place she not there! Maybe she do go in that foreign land white girl bed, but I don't look for her there. If my lady go there, it not early at night but much late! You think Tabubu not knows early from late? You think Tabubu not know the night better than that white girl?"

"I think you know all there is to know," Rahotep told her. "And you are not going to get out of telling it. Once more—where did your mistress go? I want the precise details this time and, if I suspect you're leaving out anything at all, I'll make certain you find out the meaning of 'obstruction of justice'!"

"She go to the last room and she stay in there for long time. That all I can say, and if I know more, I hope something strike me dead! But listen this—I am the daughter of a great chief of my land. Now I become a slave and you can do to me what you want, but my heart is the heart of my father!" Tabubu stood on her feet. "Up there is the great one, what beat my father because he more powerful. So now he my master and a very great king, wise and knowing what is true and what is false better than you or even that judge there with his big wig. I put myself on his mercy. I am finish here and that mean done!"

Tabubu scowled at Rahotep, as though daring him to ask her one more thing because, if he did, he was going to get nothing but silence for his trouble. Either that, or he just might find out whether or not she was a fierce-faced "witching- woman", after all.

"Just a moment, Tabubu." Rahotep took off his wig, as he was perspiring too much now. The assistant looked at the Chief Justice for guidance. Neferweben beckoned the interrogator to approach him and the two men whispered together.

"I'll solve your problem for you," the king called out to them. "The last room belongs to the Master of the Horse, Caleb! So now we have the truth, finally."

"What truth would that be?" Queen Neferura asked her husband, putting down the embroidery she had been doing the entire time of the interrogation of the others, as though she had no interest in any of what had been asked or answered. "Am I to get the whip, as well, for speaking unless spoken to? Or perhaps what happened to my mother would be a punishment more to your taste, my lord! I don't know what your precious Satiah was doing in Caleb's room—but I know he wasn't in it on the night she was killed. Satiah may have been waiting for him, but she waited in vain. Caleb was with me, in my own chambers!"

"Your chambers?" asked the pharaoh. "And doing what there, pray tell? Showing you his hairy chest?"

"What nonsense—he was talking with me. From early in the evening until nearly dawn. There was much to talk about, all that which had happened during the day."

"What's this? Are you saying, Neferura, that you invited Caleb to come to your rooms in the evening? You dared to do that?"

"Well, husband," Neferura retorted, "all cannot be judged by you according to your own desires. Not all of us think of nothing else but wanting to engage in carnal pleasures with beautiful young people. Some of us are left alone and need conversation. Our lives are dreary and the hours very long. Nothing but endless days and empty nights. I have conversed with your wives here, those flowers of Canaan whom you have allowed to wither in absolute solitude. So why should I not talk with that great hero, Caleb, the man who saved the life of my only child?"

"Talking! In what language?"

"Tell your father which language, my son," Neferura said to Prince Mehy.

"Egyptian for mother and Canaanite for Caleb," said Mehy, standing up. "Of course I had to be there to act as interpreter.

Without me, the whole thing would have been a total wash-out."

"Mehy," said his father, "didn't you hear Caleb say before that he had never spoken to your mother?"

"I heard him. He didn't speak to her because he doesn't know Egyptian, just as he told the court. It was me that he spoke to and I spoke for them both."

Chapter Sixteen

"This court is now dissolved," announced the king abruptly. "All may leave except the judge, the interrogator—and my barber. Tabubu, go back with the women. Nebamun, report immediately to the captain of the palace guard and tell him that you are to be locked in the guardhouse until further orders from me! Go nowhere near the harem and nowhere near Tabubu. Is that clear, Nebamun?"

"Yes, my lord," said Nebamun, bowing his head.

"Hah!" said Tabubu, triumphantly.

"You may all go," Levi said to the Canaanites. "The pharaoh says there will be no more questions."

"You mean never?" Caleb wanted to know.

Levi shrugged. "Not today, anyway."

When the others had gone, Thutmose left his throne and came down to sit with the three remaining men.

"I have never heard such a pack of bold-faced liars in my

life," he said, folding his arms across his chest. "Well, Neferweben, what do you think we should do now?"

"I think," said the Chief Justice, "that we should take a lesson from Tabubu and choose wisdom over further questions."

"And let a murderer go free?" said the pharaoh, incredulously. "My wife had her throat cut. She's dead and gone forever! Where is her justice? You—Levi—what do you think about all this nonsense here today? I know you must have an opinion."

"My lord," responded Levi, "I know you're grieving and are not yourself, otherwise you would have seen immediately that justice has already been done. Do you believe Tabubu when she said that Queen Satiah had gone to Caleb's room?"

"Yes, I believe her," said the king gloomily. "I believe her only because she didn't want to tell it. For showing concern about my feelings and the reputation of her mistress, I am protecting her from Nebamun until we can investigate the matter further. Just in case she's right about him and he's not so virtuous with that stick of his as he claims."

"And what should, in your own opinion, have been Satiah's punishment for going into Caleb's room?" Levi asked his master.

"It was treason!" Then the king muttered, "Punishable by death. For what other reason would she have gone there at night if not to betray me?"

"Would you have been able to carry out that sentence?"

302

"Yes!" replied the pharaoh and then, "I don't know..."

"In any case," said the barber, "someone saved you the trouble of having to decide what to do about Satiah." Levi turned to the astonished vizier. "Neferweben, sir, in the land of Egypt, in an ordinary village, if a girl behaved in such a manner as Satiah had done, or would have liked to do, what would happen to her?"

"If she was found out, her husband would kill her. And if she had no husband, then it would fall to...her brother to kill her. By the gods—yes! And nothing would happen to him as a result. The people of the village would see that as a man upholding the honor of his family."

"In that case, why wouldn't Nebamun simply admit he had done it?" demanded the ruler.

"For fear of you, my lord, the man whom he knew loved his sister so much," was Levi's reply.

"Now I suppose you'll tell me that Nebamun had intercourse with his own sister before he killed her!"

"No...someone else did that. But, since Caleb wasn't there in his room, in what way will these men here ever be able to learn which man it was? Satiah was a woman wandering about the house in the dark. Even Tabubu had lost her. Anything at all might have happened to her between that time and the time she came into Marta's bed. Obviously, Satiah was fleeing from her attacker. I can't agree with Merymaat that the lady couldn't possibly have been raped at some point. Probably, she didn't report that to her brother because she didn't know he was there!

303

She had forbidden him to stay the night, after all. Yet Nebamun *was* there—and believed that his sister was up to no good or he wouldn't have ordered Tabubu to spy on her."

"Well, I wasn't far away, either," said the ruler. "What would have prevented Satiah from telling me what had happened to her instead of her brother?"

"Perhaps she was more afraid of you than the other man, the attacker," replied the barber, evenly. "You had already sent her away earlier because you were in no mood for her company. It seems to me that the one person a wife who had been sexually violated would be most hesitant to tell about it would be her own husband."

"Why do you say that?" asked Rahotep, himself curious now.

"Because she might worry that he would believe she had provoked this assault in some way. Or question that she was telling him the truth at all. Or even want her again after another man had used her."

"By the gods, young man," said Neferweben with no small degree of admiration, "how do you manage to think of all these things?"

"Three times great," the pharaoh told him. "Didn't I say so? He thinks of everything just at the right time. A very useful man to have for a friend. Oh, yes! If I weren't so certain that he honors me, he'd give me a bit of a worry, I can tell you—for I'd rather have all the princes of Asia come against me with full force than face this barber of mine armed only with his wits!"

Truly, it was a good thing no advocates were allowed in the Egyptian judicial system, thought Neferweben, because this Amun-eywy had the potential to be the most glib-tongued one that ever confounded any court. Or was this young man merely adjusting matters to suit the one with the "eye of the falcon"—somehow sensing how the pharaoh preferred everything could end? Neferweben would have given one of his sardonic little smiles, only he knew this was no time to look amused and so kept a straight face.

"My lord," he heard the barber say, "when you entered the harem quarters after Nebamun had come to fetch you, was it already dawn?"

The pharaoh considered. "No, it was still dark. I asked Nebamun for a light when I entered Satiah's room. He had none with him and I hadn't thought to bring one."

"Nebamun had no light? Could he find your chambers in the dark?"

"Certainly. It's not that far. And I know my way to the harem. I could find it in the dark even without a light. In fact, I've done it more than once."

"Tabubu never said Nebamun had a light, either. She just said she screamed and then he came and said somebody had murdered Satiah and left immediately, without ever taking a good look at his sister with a light."

"All true," said Rahotep. "He must have already known

305

she'd been slashed. And was only waiting for Tabubu to find her."

"All right," said the king, "maybe Nebamun killed Satiah. But I don't believe Neferura and her Caleb story—because she hates me. I don't believe Mehy, either, because he loves his mother and would want to protect her. I think we should go and ask Mehy's servants if he was gone all that night."

"I'd say it's a bit late for that," submitted the Chief Justice. "The answer will now be that he was, whether that be true or false. Everyone here in this great house is loyal to someone...out of love...out of fear...or would lie simply on account of self-interest. It's the same with every trial or inquest, Your Majesty. All one can do is to wait and see if the witnesses trip over their own tongues or whether someone else can offer a greater proof against their words. All the witnesses today are clever people. Not one convicted himself by the words of his own mouth. Nebamun, himself, only admitted to having lied about his interest in Tabubu. Yes, the truth can be as elusive as a fleeing gazelle and here, beside me, is the hunter, Rahotep, who can only pursue it with words. Rahotep is a skillful interrogator but no one can be forced to tell the truth, not even by torture. Your Majesty does not approve of torture and neither do I. It only makes people lie more and accuse innocent others. My opinion is we should assume that Nebamun did the deed and let him go about his business. We can't convict him. If we do, we make murderers out of too many men in Egypt and no one will think he has the right to protect the honor of his family. Then what becomes of the chastity of the women? But I think Nebamun will know better than to try to do any harm to Tabubu now. Putting him in the guardhouse has sent him the message. Once you let him out, he will never come back here again. Your Majesty, I have watched many witnesses tell their stories. I believe that Tabubu is no liar—but merely hesitated to tell the truth, at first, for fear of Nebamun. And why would Tabubu want to risk her comfortable position as a queen's handmaid and the presents she got as a result of that—by getting with child by the likes of Nebamun, from sleeping with him of her own free will?"

"Well, yes, I grant you that. But what if Nebamun, despite lusting after Tabubu and being a rascal in general, happens to be innocent of murder?" asked the ruler. "What if he can see well in the dark and needs no light? There's still an unknown killer in that case."

"Then who is there left to suspect?" Levi asked. "Nebamun, according to Tabubu, didn't have much interest in his dying sister. He just left her to her maid and ran off to inform you. Very cold-blooded—and very suspicious. Yes, the murder was committed with my razor. That was a rotten thing to do, but killing is a rotten business. This murder was planned with care—at least that much care—to put the blame on someone else. Who stood to gain the most by the murder of your wife? The man who ravished her? Would he have gone to all the trouble of getting a razor from my room? Does every man in this entire residence know just where it is I stay or where I keep my things? I think we can safely rule out the rapist being the murderer."

Neferweben peered at Levi with narrowed eyes as if he were the greatest curiosity the judge had ever seen. Then he nodded in agreement. "The barber has asked the right question. Who stood to benefit? What do you say, my lord?"

Thutmose said, "Well...there's Neferura. She may well have learned that Satiah was with child—or thought she might be. Knowing I preferred Satiah over her, she may have believed I might have ultimately preferred a son of Satiah over Mehy. That may have been her motive for the killing. But...if I allow you to indict Queen Neferura, my son will hate me all his life. There's even Mehy, himself—as horrible and incredible as the idea may be. He didn't have much liking for Satiah to begin with—and it's not difficult to understand why. But, if he thought Satiah might get a son by me, well... Mehy is the cub of the lion. I have said so myself. If he could face a crocodile without a knife, he could face a sleeping woman with a razor in his hand."

"No, surely not Mehy!" said Levi. "He's only thirteen years old! And he's a good, kind boy."

"You killed a man when you were that age," the pharaoh reminded him. "And for far less reason than a kingdom. As you are a good man, surely you were once a good boy."

The king passed a hand over the growth of stubble on his jaw. Levi thought to himself that Si-Bast had been correct. The pharaoh, the one who wore the cobra on his brow, only looked right and mighty when he was shaved and things in Egypt were good only when the barber came to the ruler every day. Yes, his old master had spoken truly. The king appeared nothing less than pitiful.

"By all the gods, how shall I view my house and my family now—as a nest of vipers?"

"What was it when you were born?" Neferweben asked him. "What was it but that? Give us your leave to go, my lord king. There is nothing more to do here for us."

"And what about me?" the pharaoh added. "I could have murdered Satiah. Is there someone in this land who would indict me for having killed my faithless wife?"

"Great one, let it suffice," Neferweben said in a pleading tone. "A man does not kill his wife if it means killing his own heart. In a moment of anger, perhaps, but not by careful planning. Even in a village, a man who loves his wife would have thought of a hundred reasons why she should be allowed to live and be forgiven before his plans were fixed. This was not a crime of passion—not that sort, anyway. Allow us to go. Rahotep and I have heard enough to satisfy us. Let the killer be Nebamun and let all go."

"Yes, you may both go with my praise," the pharaoh told a relieved Chief Justice. "But not you, Levi."

"Very sharp, that Neferweben," the king said to Levi when they were alone. "No doubt he goes home to a wife whom he trusts, loyal sons, and a cheerful household under the hand of a beloved master, thankful that his private life differs from mine in every way."

Levi said nothing and just waited to hear why the pharaoh had kept him behind.

"My heart told me not to trust Satiah," said Thutmose. "Everything about her warned me that she wasn't true to me. But I paid no attention. It never occurred to me that she would dare to betray me. You know, Levi, I once knew a man who loved honesty so much that he never hesitated to tell the truth. It was Ahmose. We disagreed about many things. I was tired of Ahmose and he was tired of me. I asked him if he would go to look for the source of the Nile and his words were 'Gladly. Perhaps I can find some innocent people there.' You wouldn't know it to look at him now, but Ahmose was once like your friend, Caleb, the most beautiful man in Egypt. Wherever there was a woman to save him, he would be saved. Can you imagine—he managed to marry the daughter of a king and a kingdom was given to him—just on account of a pair of blue eyes."

"My lord should rest," said Levi, "or he will become ill. And then, after a time, he should find another wife."

"Perhaps I should marry that girl, Tabubu," said Thutmose, in an ironic manner. "She could make me laugh without even trying. We could have the witches around to help me ward off evil. It seems a good plan to me right now."

"Why not keep Tabubu nearby?" suggested Levi. "A man could hardly be sad around her for very long. And what about

Marta? A real beauty."

"I agree! But too loyal to Neferura now, I suspect. My own fault. I should have gotten to this Marta before Neferura did. But I was too obsessed with Satiah. Well...those women are all I have left now. I haven't the time to search throughout Egypt for a woman who might love me. Perhaps there is no such woman and I will find the same fate as my father."

It was then that Levi learned what had become of the pharaoh's father. Thutmose had obtained the truth from the people at Memphis. One day, while at dinner, Hatshepsut had pointed to a sore spot on her husband's arm and asked "What have you there?" King Thutmose the Second had told his queen that it was nothing and that it would soon go away. However, before long, more of the same sort of spots appeared on his body, and the physicians were called upon to examine him. They did not know what to tell their master except that only time would tell whether these sores would go away or become worse. But Hatshepsut would no longer dine with the pharaoh or go near him again. She declared the king a leper and left for the southern residence, never returning to see whether the condition of her husband and half-brother had improved or not.

"My father was a small, slight man," Thutmose told Levi. "He never did have a very strong constitution. Yes, some disease had gotten hold of him but Si-Bast told me that he knew of other men who suffered badly from unknown conditions of the skin but did not develop the later signs of leprosy. My father didn't get

311

these signs. Perhaps he never would have...anyway, he didn't have time. He became convinced that he was, indeed, a leper and shut himself away. For all her evil ways, Hatshepsut was a good-looking woman and my father had a feeling for her. I don't know whether it was because she was his wife or his sister...perhaps some of both. At any rate, he suffered greatly from his fears and her abandonment and refused to take much of any nourishment. So my father grew very weak, his hair began to fall out from starving himself, and then a fever set into his lungs and he died. He was no more than thirty years old. I knew nothing of this when I was a boy. I thought my father had come to dislike me, too, and that's why he never came back to see me. But he was my father and I..." The king could not go on.

"You loved him," finished Levi. "Why not just say it and be done."

"Yes, I did love him—despite all. If only my father had sent for me! I wouldn't have abandoned him. But I suppose it wasn't my comfort that he wanted."

"My lord, if you thought you had contracted leprosy, would you keep Mehy close to you for company? Of course not. Your father was not like you in some ways, but you have succeeded him, as he would have wished. Do you doubt that much, at least?"

"No," admitted Thutmose, "I don't doubt he wished it. If my father suspected the woman might try to take my throne, probably he couldn't believe the Egyptians would allow that.

Well, they did allow it, but my father couldn't be blamed for that. I don't know why I blame him!"

"I'm glad I never saw my father," Levi told the king. "One less person to blame, I suppose. And have you forgotten Neferura? She loved you once, you said."

"As a boy I was given only two things—a crown and Neferura. I lost both, but placed the higher value on the one most difficult to regain. And paid the price—as you can see. Neferura is her mother's daughter in every way but one. Neferura had a heart. I was the one who broke it and now she has broken mine. The question is…what will I do about it?"

Levi knew better than to ask how Queen Neferura had managed to break the heart of the man who had never loved her. Was the pharaoh telling him that he, indeed, suspected his first wife of being a murderess? It seemed to the barber there was only one reason Neferura would have wanted Satiah dead. On account of Caleb—and not any future son of Satiah—for only an imbecile would think that anyone could supercede Mehy in the heart of his father. And that was only assuming Neferura had known all along what had transpired between his friend and the young beauty. Levi wondered about that possibility. He also recalled the statement of Si-Bast about Neferura knowing right from wrong. Could Si-Bast, who had known the woman all her life, have been so mistaken about the queen's character? Also, if Neferura was the pharaoh's chief suspect, why did he not show more anger toward her now? In fact, he changed the subject, evidently not wishing to discuss his wife any further.

"Levi," the pharaoh went on, "I want you to understand something. The first time I went to Canaan with a very large army was in the 22nd year of my reign. My grandfather had conquered your land and I went there to battle those who had become rebellious to Egypt while a woman sat on my throne. They were many, these princes of Canaan, and they had mighty allies to their north, as well. I subjugated those princes but I must keep going north and cannot get there without passing through your land. Whenever I do, someone attempts to rebel again. Your people are not cowards. But I must keep the borders of Egypt secure or what happened in the time of the shepherd kings may occur again. Mehy...Mehy has a generous heart. Perhaps too much so. He wants people to be happy and probably he'll sit here with you one day, telling you that he never could understand me. He would be a beloved king, but Egypt can't survive on love. Therefore, I'm leaving him nothing to do. Meanwhile, I am the one who has to be the great devouring crocodile in his river, as Ahmose put it. I am the one who must make it possible for my son to be a happy ruler in a land that is free from fear of invasion as all those who could be feared will have already been broken."

"Can one break them forever?"

"Perhaps not," said Thutmose, "but for a long time to come. Mehy may have a son who is like me or my grandfather, so that forever may not be necessary. When I am dead and if Ahmose still lives, he can return to Egypt and be happy with

Mehy. As for myself, I prefer men around me who are clever enough to know that the truth shouldn't always be told. Like Neferweben—and like you. I couldn't say this to the others—but I will say it to you now. A falsehood is not necessarily a wicked thing. I think there are times when it serves justice better than the truth."

"Yes, my lord," replied the barber. His gaze met that of the sovereign and the latter grimaced in a knowing but resigned sort of way.

"What now?" the king asked, gently. "Why do you appear so sad?"

Levi didn't answer. It was too difficult even for him to put into words.

"Don't care to unburden your heart to me, then? Am I nothing to you, after all? Have you no faith in me even to this day? Levi, it's not often in this life that a man sees his double in a stranger—or at least someone who puts him in mind of himself at a certain age. That's why you were rather a shock to me when I first saw you in Canaan. I couldn't improve my own lot when I was that age, but I had the capability of improving your own. When I told you that I would be as a father to you, that was no idle remark. Has it come to pass or not?"

"Yes," Levi had to admit. "My lord has only done me good."

"Then what is troubling you?"

"I am thinking, I suppose, of the misfortunes of women

315

and how their lot in life can affect both us and them."

"Eh? Well—doubtless there is some female that troubles you most. Not Satiah, as you barely knew her—so which one is it?"

"Truth be told, Si-Bast's niece. Everything that's happened here has somehow caused me great concern for her, although I can't tell you exactly why. Suddenly, she weighs very heavily upon my heart."

"And?"

"You don't know Takamena, my lord, but I do. She was so kind to me when I was less than nothing. She's gentle, an innocent, and…"

"Vulnerable," said the pharaoh. "Do you love this girl?"

"I don't know," Levi replied. "But I think perhaps she loves me—without ever having seen my face at all. Takamena must marry and I worry that someone will take her for Si-Bast's property and then not value her because she's blind, perhaps treat her cruelly."

"Ah! So you would be the man who'd never misuse this Takamena, eh? But I tell you that you would. The day will come when you'll want a woman who can see your face, who will look into your eyes and you'll want to drown in that gaze—ach, you've never been in love. What becomes of Si-Bast's niece when you come across that other girl who steals your heart? Will she be content to become a neglected or pitied wife when she expected something else? Anyway, you have nothing to offer Takamena now. When you're a bit older, I'll build you a house and you'll become a man of worth—and have your choice among the girls of Egypt. Now you're too young to make a wise decision, clever as you are otherwise."

It seemed to Levi that the pharaoh was hardly the model of wisdom when it came to the business of choosing a suitable mate.

"What are the expectations of women in this land?" he asked. "Don't the men of Egypt have more than one wife?"

"Most don't," the pharaoh told him. "It isn't thought proper these days. You mustn't judge by this household. No woman here ever expected to be the only wife. I'm not like the common men of this nation. If I had only one wife, people would think there was something wrong with me—yes, that I was without the proper virility or stingy with my wealth and favor. People expect me to marry their daughters because they're great men and think it's their due. Plenty are already grumbling because I haven't done it. But—don't you see—I haven't time for so many women. I'm not even in Egypt for months out of the year. At my present age, one wife is plenty for me now. I didn't really even want anyone but Satiah. I still don't and damn me for that! But, I'll have to take more wives. I can't get out of it and my personal feelings are of no importance, really. They never have been. Just as Egypt belongs to me, I now belong to Egypt and my every move has a meaning greater than myself. Who I am is of no significance. Only what I do matters. Levi, trust me on this. Takamena is better off taking her chances with the one Si-Bast

317

finds for her. That old barber won't choose a bad man—probably one of his elderly widowed friends who will be glad to have a gentle, sweet young wife."

"Oh, no!" groaned Levi. "How dreadful!"

"You'd be surprised," said the king. "Some of those old men are still up to plenty. Besides, Si-Bast's niece won't be able to see her husband. His wrinkles and missing teeth won't mean much if he's kind to her, appreciates her. She could even come to love him. I've seen it happen in like cases—although not to me. I want you to be happy in the way I never have been. If I have any say in the matter, you will be, and Si-Bast's girl is not for you. I know you better than you know yourself. You're a man of imagination and such a man becomes a passionate one. If you want a favor of me, ask for another."

"Very well, my lord," said Levi promptly. "Can you not improve the lot of the Canaanite women? I know such girls were raised to be dutiful and respectful wives and wouldn't dream of—"

"For the sake of your tender heart, I will do it," promised the pharaoh. "When I am more myself and done mourning, I will take up with Marta, try to give her children, and end her shame. Neferura or no, I am wrong to neglect her and stand corrected by you there. Yes, I find this Marta a most intriguing girl. Her sisters are very young and I'd only frighten them. In a year or two, I'll turn them over to Mehy. He'll be a better-looking man than I ever was and I'm sure there'll be no complaints. Anything else?"

"No," said Levi. "I'm very pleased at your words and bow

to your wisdom."

"All right. Do an errand for me, Levi. I'm at the end of my strength just now. Go to the guardhouse and, in your grandest manner, tell them to release Nebamun in my name."

"Will anybody listen to me?" Levi wondered aloud.

"Make them listen. Make them bow to you as is your due. Escort Nebamun from these walls, yourself. And should you happen to learn anything interesting from him, I leave it to you to choose how much of it to tell me—or anyone. Three times great or a brimstone devil of a barber—whichever one you really are—I trust you will decide well."

Levi managed to persuade the guards to free Satiah's brother. Although he hadn't been locked up for very long, Nebamun's face was as pale as though he had been in prison for years.

"Nebamun," said Levi, "you're free to go. Walk this way with me."

While the two men crossed the short distance to the palace gates, Nebamun said, "Then they don't think I did it?"

"Why ask me what they think? I'm only a barber."

"I'm telling you, barber," Nebamun insisted, "I didn't kill my sister! I curse Satiah for a slut, but I loved her. What do I have now without her?"

"I'll tell you what some think, Nebamun," said Levi. "Some think you're a village man who killed for honor."

"Honor!" sneered the other. "I prefer wealth. I did not kill my sister!"

"I know you didn't," Levi told him. "If I were you, I'd pack up and go back to the Faiyum."

"Wait!" said Nebamun. "If you know I didn't murder Satiah, then that makes four people who know it. That inquest was nothing but a sham. Rape—hah! I saw who it was that did the killing. Tabubu was asleep by then, but I wasn't. At least I thought she was sleeping—but with that southern shrew, who knows? Anyway, how could I sleep when I felt sure my sister was looking for trouble at night? I felt it my responsibility as her brother to find out what she was doing and make sure she didn't do it again! But Tabubu was right; my sister had told me not to stay the night. So what could I do? I had to hide from my sister. Satiah didn't come back until nearly dawn. She entered into her own bedchamber in the usual way and I just decided to get away from the harem for a few hours. She never saw me. No one did, and I thought all was well for the time being. I even considered that I might have been mistaken about Satiah's actions. But I was thirsty and went to get some water before leaving, and the next thing I knew, someone ran out, dropped the razor, and Satiah started making noises. Tabubu slept very near her mistress, but I was close to the doorway. Tabubu just got to Satiah first, that's all. But there's nothing to be done now, is there? There never was."

"I'm sure you're right," said Levi. "I don't doubt that at

all. Don't tell me who the killer is, Nebamun. You can leave here, but I can't. You know I can't, perhaps not ever. I will have to live with that murderer. Say nothing to anyone. Plead ignorance in every respect in the matter of Satiah's murder, or the day may come when you, like Ahmose, are a man without a country for knowing and saying too much."

"Right," said Nebamun. "As you please, then, and I'm not such a fool as to open my mouth once I leave here. I'm a true man of Egypt, a servant of the Crown, who fed at one breast while the king fed at the other. See how I'm repaid for my loyalty? Driven from these gates like a dog! Farewell, Royal Barber, and good luck in this bloody place of secrets!"

Then, Satiah's brother, remembering something, smiled ironically and made a little bow to the Chief Barber of the king. Without another word, he waited until the portal was opened and then passed through.

Chapter Seventeen

That night, Caleb and Levi were standing together on the roof of the palace. Overhead, the stars shone with a pitiless clarity, as though the entire universe had grown cold and cheerless. A wind had suddenly blown up and the two men shivered in their thin clothing. The Master of the Horse seemed to have aged by a decade. Nevertheless, he gazed at the heavens and said, "Home— if only I were there," as though he were a small, homesick boy and not a man of intimidating size and strength and a king among women on account of his wonderful appearance. For the first time in his life, Levi recognized that beauty was not the advantage that it seemed to be and the people who owned it could find it a dangerous possession.

"I've got to get out of here," the handsome man said. "I hate this place, this Egypt. It's evil. I can't even breathe here."

"I'm not breathing so well, myself," Levi admitted. "Anyway, just so you know, Neferura and Mehy saved your neck.

They claimed you were with them in the queen's chambers all night long. So that must be your story, too, if you're ever asked again."

"They did that for me? And the pharaoh believed them?"

Levi shook his head. "No. But he's got to accept their word. He won't bother you, I think. Now that Satiah's gone, he knows he can trust you. He knows her for what she was now."

"You say it, but I don't believe it. How can I look upon his face or he mine?"

"Brazen it out," said Levi. "The real test of your courage comes now."

"Such tests aren't for me. I'm a fool but an honest one—mostly. I can't play the double-faced deceiver. I have to go."

"Caleb—unfortunately you can't understand Egyptian. If you could, you would have been surprised at what went on today. Regardless, you're here—no one has arrested you. I think the matter is closed and won't be re-opened. The great general has found himself trapped in his own residence. He fears no man in any land—but of the truth he is now afraid. You must stay. If you run away, that's as good as an admission of guilt."

"I can't understand all this! Marta said Satiah had spent most of the night with her," said Caleb. "If the girl was scared of someone, why did she go back to her own room before dawn? I heard that screaming and I know it was still dark then. It doesn't make sense to me."

"Why would it? Marta was lying. She never saw Satiah.

She just said that to give you—or me—no way of having had access to Satiah all evening. You don't really think those girls want anything to happen to us, do you, Caleb? Marta figured we were suspects because Rahotep was interrogating us. So she helped us in the only way she could think of. She even placed me in the room of herself and her sisters on the other night when we got drunk, because she was intelligent enough to sense that the king had already pardoned me for being there."

"By all that's holy," exclaimed the chariot-fighter, "I do remember now that Marta said Satiah came to her bed early in the evening. I don't recall exactly when she came into my room, but she didn't stay there all that long. She was gone long before dawn. I should know. I certainly didn't close my eyes after she left! Well, then—where was she—just in her own bed, sleeping, until the murderer came in?"

"Oh, I don't think so," said Levi. "Tabubu would have known if Satiah had come back to her bed after she left your room. But Tabubu said she wasn't there. The girl didn't lie about that."

"Then where did Satiah go?"

"To the one she knew would protect her," replied Levi, "her husband, the king. That's my guess."

"What?"

"I don't think Nebamun really meant it when he told Tabubu he was watching the pharaoh's quarters to see if his sister had gone in there. He was just testing Tabubu, trying to get the truth out of her. Satiah did, I think, hear or see somebody following her and then ran as fast as she could. If anyone knew how to find the king easily, it was Satiah. So she crawled into his bed with him to make a liar out of anyone who might inform on her. I imagine he was sorry that he had sent her away so abruptly earlier in the evening. In fact, the king admitted as much to me. He wouldn't have objected to her coming to him later. Probably, the pharaoh believed Satiah was just scared of the plague. That's what he told me."

"Then I was right," said Caleb. "The pharaoh did murder Satiah! He was the last one to see her alive!"

"No. The king doesn't do his own killing. He never actually gets blood on his own hands. I was summoned to shave him many times quite early in the morning. But there was never any Satiah there with him. The only time she was there was on the ship and I could tell she didn't like to get up early. I know that the pharaoh usually just carried her back to her own quarters in his arms, even while she was asleep or half-asleep, so she could stay in her own bed as long as she liked, undisturbed. He loved her, Caleb, as little as you may believe that, and he's a strongly built man. He could easily have carried Satiah. The pharaoh always had many things to attend to, but Satiah had nothing but the beautification of herself. I would say that on the terrible night, the pharaoh simply wasn't sleeping so well, himself, so decided just to get up and carry back Satiah earlier than usual. And while in her husband's arms, Satiah knew she had nothing to fear from anyone. Very likely, she had already stopped being afraid at all. So the king put her in her bed. He said he could find his way to the harem in the dark and I believe him. But he didn't see the other person hiding there somewhere, waiting for the return of Satiah. And then, once that person knew the pharaoh was well away, Satiah was murdered."

"Was it Nebamun?" wondered Caleb. "Mehy told me he got sent to the guardhouse."

"Not Nebamun. He had everything to lose if he killed Satiah and nothing to gain. He's already been set free."

"But if Satiah had been with the pharaoh, why didn't he just say so?"

"She was with you, too. Did you just say so? Is there some reason the pharaoh would want to be a suspect in the murder of his wife, anymore than you do? He wants to be feared by people, but not in that way—not as the sort of man who could slice the throat of a female in her bed!"

"How can you be so sure the pharaoh isn't the murderer? How do you really know?"

"Because I know him," said Levi. "I know his heart."

Caleb made a disbelieving face but said, "Who was the killer, then? Do you know that, too?"

"No," said Levi. "Nor do I want to. The less people like us know the better off we are. Your own words. Caleb, we're strangers in the land of Egypt. No matter how long we stay here, they'll never see us as one of them. No matter if we have grand titles or people bow before us. In the end, it won't make any difference.   Ahmose was right. If we grow to be too many here, we'll become the enemy in the eyes of the Egyptians—only right here in this very land.   But, meanwhile, I'm going to serve the pharaoh as I have done so far and you're going to serve Mehy. We have no other choice. Our lives are in the hand of our master, subject to his whim. And yet this king knows how to be merciful as well as cruel. We have to trust him. Show him some good faith and stay clear of his women from now on. Your love for Neferura is useless. You know it's so."

"Yes, I know it," said Caleb. He was silent for a moment and then his expression turned hard and resolute. "I can't walk around here with my head bowed in shame. This land is not for me. If I must die in Egypt, I'll go down fighting to get out. I didn't murder Satiah, but she's as good as killed me. I'm going, my friend. Thanks for everything—Master of the Sling. It's been good knowing you but, after tonight, you won't see me again."

Levi put a hand on his friend's arm. "Don't do it, Caleb. You won't make it out. There's no need to die!"

"Why in the devil can't he make it out?" said a voice from the stairway that led to the roof. "I did it. So can he."

The stunned Canaanites regarded the figure of their master, the king of Egypt. The haggard, unshaven ruler came toward them. He, too, was not warmly dressed and the wind seemed to shrivel him. But he drew himself up like a proud man, trying not to shiver and not altogether succeeding. The pharaoh looked up at the night sky.

"I was taught to read omens in the heavenly bodies," he said. "Tonight, they predicted for me that no one is going to die on account of Satiah and that her murderer will never be found. The killer will be punished at the hands of the gods only and it is written above that his penalty will be harsh, indeed. As the stars are older than I am, they are surely wiser, and I would be a fool to go against them. Caleb of Canaan, I've already decided to set you free. You may go home. As for you, Levi—do you want to go with him? Tell me the truth."

"I'll sorely miss his company—but Egypt is my home," Levi said to the pharaoh. "There is no other. I'm content to serve Your Majesty—and that is the whole truth."

"Good. Remain, then, as a free citizen of Egypt. Caleb, I think it's best you do go tonight so Mehy can't see you. Don't worry, he knows you love him and I'll make him understand that you have a son of your own who needs you." Thutmose handed Caleb a leather bag. "Here is gold and a safe-conduct document, written in my own hand and signed with my seal. The gates will be open to you—all the gates of Egypt. My own men will take you to the harbormaster of Thebes, who will put you on a ship for the north. Bring your weapons with you in case of any trouble and put on all your shirts at once against the chill. When you reach the north, find a wandering people called the Aamu. They'll show you the way out of this land. Thank you for the life of my son. Goodbye and good luck."

"Thank you, great king," replied Caleb. "Thank you for

giving me back my life and my honor."

"Well, that's it, then," said Thutmose. "The next time we meet, do me a favor and don't shoot me through the eyes. Goodnight, men."

The king had one more visit to pay—to his harem—that place of so-called "relaxation" that he, himself, had largely avoided frequenting. Was it not true that more than one ruler of Egypt had discovered the harem to be the origin of plots against him? Pleasure and poison, a concoction that could deceive even the wariest of men due to his one great weakness.

The lights were still burning in Neferura's chambers. The pharaoh had noticed, from a distance, that the woman always avoided going to bed early. Probably, she slept no better than he did but, unlike himself, didn't resort to drink to make her drowsy. Or perhaps she did. Who knew what Neferura did in the night?

Thutmose hadn't given any thought to what went on in the heart of his chief wife for a long time. In fact, he hadn't imagined her thinking or feeling at all—just stolidly accepting her fate, content to be the mother of the future king with all the status that implied. Neferura was seven years younger than himself, but the pharaoh had seen her as being old for years, feeling he had known her practically forever. Yet, today, she hadn't appeared old at all, even full of uncharacteristic fire, her eyes as bright as those of a woman in love. Well, it seemed he hadn't really known Neferura at all.

Thutmose found his queen seated in a chair, fully adorned, with her golden vulture crown upon her head, as though she were waiting to be summoned to a state occasion. On Neferura's lap lay a dagger.

"At last you've come, Thutmose," she said to him, "as I knew you would. And yet...I know you haven't come to slay me. You couldn't kill a woman. Years ago, you left it to others to murder even your greatest enemy."

The pharaoh lunged at his wife, seizing her by the shoulders.

"Did your mother deserve to die or not? Answer me!"

Neferura shut her eyes. "Yes," she replied. "Yes! But she was a king's daughter. My mother should have been allowed to die by her own hand, as befitted her station!"

Thutmose released the queen and snatched the weapon from the hollow between her legs in a sudden motion.

"What's this for?" he asked. "Are you cutting linen for another shirt for Caleb? Are you a king's daughter, Neferura? Some say no. You will not die by your own hand—not for any reason. You will do nothing to cause my son to suffer. You will continue to wear that thing on your head at my pleasure, as you have always done. That is your reward—for the great service you did me once."

"Just don't harm Caleb," Neferura said, her voice shaking. "If you do that, then it will be you who will cause your son to suffer—doubly—as I won't be here to see it, I swear to you! I once warned my mother that if she ever did any harm to you or took Mehy from me I would kill myself. In those days I still thought I had something to live for but, if my mother believed me even then, you had best believe me now that I have nothing left to live for at all! Make an enemy of Mehy and who will love you, then, Thutmose? No one—just as you deserve. My mother always knew you weren't of our blood—not really. You were different, weak. By heaven, how could you let a woman sit on your throne for all those years? You didn't feel worthy to sit there yourself, that's why! You don't feel worthy even now or you wouldn't try so hard to make a great name for yourself. Meanwhile, you're nothing but the efficient steward of this land, looking after your gain, going about the business of war for profit.

You're just like Neferweben and his family—only worse. Neferweben is a kind man who goes out of his way to make certain ordinary folk aren't trampled upon, deprived of their rights as human beings. You're no hero. You're not saving Egypt—just collecting more loot and workers that cost you nothing but a piece of bread and an onion twice a day. When did you last shoot an arrow or wield a sword? Send Caleb away where I can never see him again. That should be victory enough for you. For if you fought him man to man, you would certainly lose. I know you think I killed Satiah and you can wonder about how you'll ever be able to prove that for the rest of your life. It suits me well enough! I hate you and despise you!" Neferura began to cry, her entire body shaking now. She put her face in her hand, half whimpering, half groaning.

"Yes," said the pharaoh, "I think I will send Caleb away. I really believe that should be sufficient. That will do very well, indeed, as your punishment for forcing my son to lie to me in public. Caleb has great courage, but not enough wisdom, and seems to inspire all sorts of foolishness in others, besides. By the gods—are you really so besotted with his beauty? You, with all your great pride?"

"No," was the sobbing response. "Not that. It was his voice that I heard from my window, the gentle and patient way that he spoke to Mehy, even when correcting him. It reminded me so much of a voice from long ago. Your own!"

The queen was weeping so hard now that it unsettled the pharaoh in a way that her harsh words had not been able to do. The last time he had seen her cry was before their child was born, when he told her he was leaving for the north. Tears or no, Neferura had a will like granite. Even Hatshepsut had been in awe of it. Neferura, it was said, was her grandfather, Thutmose the Handsome, re-incarnated in female form, with all of his beauty and stubbornness. And Hatshepsut had feared only one man in her entire life—her father.

"Neferura," said her husband, "I regret that I've caused you to hate me. I began wrong and nothing has been right since. I'm on the chosen path now and it seems I have no choice but to keep following it. I wanted vengeance, but now the whole world seeks revenge against me and if I stop, it will get it. And yet,

Neferura, I loved you once. I never said those words to you—nor to anyone in my life. I never could. But I waited a long time for you to forgive me before there ever was a Satiah. I loved that girl in a foolish way. And now...I'm tired. How tired you can't know. I haven't come to accuse you. I'm here to ask you, for the last time, to be a proper wife to me. My heart tells me that, despite all, it would be best for us both and for our boy, as well. We can make peace between us. Believe me when I tell you that Mehy needs this now! From this day, I will do all I can to make you happy, if you'll only consent."

"Your heart?" said the queen, her tone becoming cold again. "But, you see, there are some things that cannot be forgiven or forgotten. Now you know it surely. Once and for all."

"Very well. Have it your way," said Thutmose. "Live out your days in hatred of me, but never make Mehy choose between us again—or I'll take such measures against you as you never imagined a weakling like myself capable of carrying out."

"What makes you so certain Mehy wasn't telling the truth?" wondered Neferura. "Do you wander about the house by night, spying on everyone? It wouldn't surprise me if you did. You don't trust anyone because you know no one can trust you! You've lost your Satiah and now you want me again. You still love that girl. I can see it in your empty eyes. Do you expect me to nurse you through it? I can't love you now anymore than she could. Yet I'm a faithful wife, unlike some others. I've brought you no shame. What more can one ask?"

"Nothing," said the pharaoh. "Evidently nothing."

"Now get out of here. Don't look at me anymore. Don't talk to me and don't tempt me with your sweet words. You've had all from me you're ever going to get. Go and terrify those people who fear for their lives. I'm not one of them. Get out!"

"Order me about in my own house?" shouted Thutmose. "Damn your bloody obstinate hide! Throw me out? Me? If I wanted to, I could remain here for the rest of the night, throw *you* on that bed and do whatever I liked with you!"

"More rape, then, eh?" said Neferura disdainfully.

"You've reached the end—you're queen here no more! Your mouth has undone you, vinegar of the scorpion, and I don't care now what Mehy thinks about it! Rape! As though I would touch your filthy whore of a mother! Look at you, arrogant fool of a woman—covered with gold from head to toe. The maintenance of you has cost me a great deal more than a piece of bread and an onion twice a day—and where is my profit from that? You're willing to die for the Canaanite? Go with him, then—Queen of Canaan! See if anyone bows to you there, you spoiled creature, to whom everything was given since the day you were born. How dare you, who never put your hand in cold water, belittle my accomplishments! I, who had to fight for even what was rightfully my own!"

The pharaoh, his face now a dark red, reached out and pulled both the crown and wig from Neferura's head, dashing them to the floor.

The queen clutched her face with both hands and inhaled sharply, expecting a blow. But it never came, nor any other kind of assault.

Thutmose stared at Neferura's real hair, cropped short like that of a boy. The black locks were liberally streaked with silver.

"Oh, no," he groaned. "Oh, Neferura, not so soon!" Then everything went dark before his eyes. The king had eaten nothing all day and scarcely anything the day before. All he had done was drink.

Neferura looked at her husband of nearly thirty years, sprawled on the floor. The dagger was lying next to him and it occurred to her that she could easily plunge it into his heart—but that was actually the last thing Neferura really wanted to do. The woman knew, in her own heart, she didn't despise the pharaoh as much as she wanted him to believe. She used to hate him, but that was only while she still loved him.

When Thutmose had returned to the palace from the temple of Amun, she hadn't seen him for ten years and had been much impressed with what a nice-looking young man her absent husband had become. He wasn't short, had fine, intelligent eyes, and Neferura had thought the shape of his nose extremely handsome, quite noble. And there was something she had remembered about that night when she had to go to bed with him as a very little girl. Neferura had been terrified but the boy-king had taken pity on her, even told her some story he knew about a prince of Egypt who had wooed a maiden in a tower in a far-off land and had all kinds of other adventures. The next time she saw Thutmose, when Neferura was fifteen, he seemed to her like that prince in the tale, come back to woo *her*. And so he had, as though they had never met previously at all and were simply two young people who had been brought together by chance, looked in each other's eyes, and had fallen in love.

But then the terrible things had happened and Neferura had felt so hideously betrayed. Thutmose had still wanted her, made it plain he desired her as much as before, but Neferura had never been able to allow him to touch her again—and he had soon given up trying to sleep with her or even engage her in private conversation. Neferura knew that her husband assuaged his appetite with dancing girls and the gods only knew what other base creatures. He was always out of Egypt for many months of the year on his wars and probably found more harlots in the foreign lands, but had not taken another wife until he came upon Satiah. By then, Neferura had no longer cared.

Even so, Neferura hadn't really stopped loving Thutmose in one day, yet hated him at the same time. How she had suffered while in the throes of those mixed emotions! But loving and forgiving were two different matters and Neferura had merely gotten accustomed to addressing her husband in an insolent way over the years, whenever she had the opportunity. Why had she done it now? What was the point any longer? Perhaps because Thutmose had seemed, for so long, the one obstacle barring any future happiness for Neferura anywhere.

Neferura began to pace about in a circle, seized by a kind of panic. Thutmose wasn't dead; his chest was still moving. But Caleb—Caleb! He was really going now and, if Neferura knew anything about her husband and his ways, the man she now loved might be gone by sunrise. Caleb would leave without even a single word from her, without ever knowing that, for months, she had lived only for him, to hear his voice, to look at him.

The royal lady hadn't lied. She really wasn't afraid to die and knew someday she would. But she didn't want to die without ever having spoken to Caleb. She must go to him before he disappeared from her sight forever! Thutmose was right. Her mother hadn't been a faithful wife and hadn't loved her brother, Thutmose's father. She had been devoted to Senenmut. Why should she, Neferura, remain a faithful spouse now? No one had been faithful to her; that was for certain! No man had loved her enough to make certain she wasn't hurt by his actions and she recalled only too well how Thutmose had salivated over that Satiah. Even if she had continued to love Thutmose up to this very day, that wouldn't have prevented him from wanting and having Satiah—or any other girl—no matter what he said. No king of Egypt was ever monogamous that anybody could recall. Even Caleb had slept with Satiah, evidently—but the barber had told her that it was her, Neferura, whom Caleb really loved! Could the barber have lied? Neferura had to know the truth once and for all. She simply felt she couldn't go on with her life, dreary as it was, without finding it out.

Perhaps Thutmose wouldn't come to for awhile. That would give her time. Without even picking up her wig, much less her crown, Neferura raced out the door.

A lamp was burning in Caleb's room and, panting before the curtain, Neferura could hear the one she adored talking to the barber in their Canaanite tongue. Neferura thought perhaps she might not be able to speak, after all, her heart was pounding so hard, but then his name came forth, "Caleb!" in an anguished sort of way. But the former queen didn't care. She had no pride now, not a shred.

The curtain was ripped aside in an instant. The big man, who towered above Neferura, gaped at her in a kind of happy astonishment and then showed her that enchanting smile. He had on the shirts she had made for him and a couple of others, as well. Almighty gods, how handsome he was!

"I think she wants to come in," said Levi.

Caleb backed up and allowed Neferura access. That wonderful barber slipped by her and left the room.

The chariot fighter had never seen the queen look so pathetic—or so marvelous. He wanted more than anything just to grab hold of her, but she was no Satiah and he couldn't be sure what she had come about. Caleb didn't need to wonder long.

Neferura threw her arms around him and he lifted up her little body so that he could put his face next to hers. He never even noticed the silver strands in her hair.

"Then it's true—you do love me!" she whispered.

Caleb understood every word. "Yes, yes!" he said in Egyptian and then added in Canaanite, "You don't know how much. But I have to go!"

Neferura knew exactly what he meant. "I love you, I love you," she said, planting kisses all over his face. "*Lo yeeshkakh!*" Neferura hoped that was the right way to say "don't forget" in Caleb's language.

"*Lo, lo,*" he replied, assuring Neferura he never would and returned the kisses.

"I want to go with you!" sobbed Neferura. "I'm no longer the wife of the king. But I can't leave my son. I can't do that to Mehy!"

It passed through Caleb's mind that, now he was quitting Egypt, he was starting to understand Egyptian amazingly well.

"Don't cry, my darling," he said in Canaanite. "You don't know how happy you've made me!" But he must say more, something Neferura could comprehend. "Um...Mehy pharaoh...I come back."

"Yes!" said Neferura, clinging to him tighter. "You must come back! I'll live only for that day."

Caleb gave her a deep, devouring kiss and, though neither of the pair wanted to stop, this time it was Caleb who called a halt. He wouldn't be able to make love to Neferura now and, even had there been time, nothing on earth could have possessed him to do anything to place this woman in such jeopardy. Nothing. He said,

339

"Neferura, you beautiful, beautiful. You stay in here!" The chariot fighter pointed to his heart. "You...oh!...you go now. No more trouble."

But Neferura couldn't let go of him.

"Levi!" Caleb called out.

The barber came in. He hadn't gone very far and had merely been standing watch.

"Levi, tell her to go back to the harem. Tell her to watch for me from her window. Tell her that her face is the last thing I want to see when I leave here."

Levi did as instructed. Tears streaming down her cheeks, Neferura released her hold. Caleb set her on her feet but grasped one of her hands.

"I love you," he said in perfect Egyptian. "Forever. I love Mehy. You say to him that." Caleb lifted Neferura's bracelets from his bed and handed them to her. "You take."

The woman shook her head. Then she said, "Chief Barber, tell Caleb they are his. He'll need them. He has nothing."

"The ruler gave him plenty of gold," said Levi.

"In that case, he must give the bracelets to his wife—for all her trouble, her sorrow. I fear I won't see him again, for we may all die here soon. I'd sooner have him go than see any harm befall him. Goodbye, Caleb," said Neferura, awarding him a last, brief kiss. She pulled away her hand and began running again.

"Neferura!" she heard Caleb call after her and the tone of his voice when he said her name was nearly too much to bear. But

Neferura, accustomed to suffering, kept going, although she seemed to have no air in her lungs at all.

Once in her chambers, Neferura saw her maid standing over the pharaoh, giving him some water. But she ignored them and, deliberately kicking her weighty, gold crown aside, positioned herself by the window, her back to the others. So that nobody but Caleb could see her face.

While she waited for the one she loved with all of her aching heart to appear in the courtyard, Neferura cursed her useless sense of propriety. Why hadn't she done what Satiah had and gone to Caleb at night while the chance was there? Even her mother had had a lover, but that very same man had taught Neferura that her dignity would always stand her in good stead— no matter what. She was born to be a queen, Senenmut had told her, and must appear, at all times, to be above everything and anything that happened around her. But how could one remain detached from life, things that transpired in ones vicinity, never stooping to become involved, content merely to wear a crown? Neferura had been able to maintain her aloofness—until the Canaanites came to Memphis. Three friendless young girls and a man whose direct but kindly speech, that she couldn't even understand, who had surprised her with his ardent gaze, had caused her to feel alive again. What a fool she had been! A woman was only a queen while she had a man to love her, one whose feelings she returned. She should have gone down on her knees and begged Thutmose to let her go, to divorce her. As she was no king's daughter at all, there was no reason for Neferura to remain his wife or ever to have been married to him in the first place. While Satiah still lived, he might well have consented and allowed her to be with Caleb. But it was too late now. Satiah was dead, Caleb was leaving, and there was nothing to be done. Nothing at all.

Thutmose got to his feet. "Stay far from me, woman," he warned. "You may live here, but I will see your face no more."

Then he left. He couldn't go far enough away to suit Neferura.

In his own quarters, the pharaoh collapsed into his most comfortable chair, his limbs trembling with fatigue. In a dark corner, he spied the seated form of Tabubu, her arms about her knees.

"Why aren't you asleep, girl?" he said to her. "In my household you have nothing to fear from anyone."

"Where Nebamun now?"

"He went home. Forget him. I just hope that scoundrel didn't get you with child."

"It don't happen. The witches don't allow it. They are helping Tabubu. Plenty tricks they know, those clever ones. Let them stay in that harem place, pharaoh. They doing no harm and saying nothing to nobody."

"Did you learn their language?"

"Nothing so difficult there. More easy than Egyptian."

"Well, so be it. Let the witches remain where they are. Let them serve Neferura and cast some spells on her. Anything they accomplish would be an improvement there."

"I think that Neferura scaring even the witches," Tabubu observed. "She like some woman made from stone. How you get a baby with her? How you breaking that rock?"

The pharaoh couldn't help but laugh. "With a hard chisel. Listen, Tabubu, I've sent for you, as I want you here with me. Don't worry—my name isn't Nebamun. You can sleep here without fear."

"Tabubu not tired in the night," the servant answered, approaching. "I not sleeping so good since my lady die."

"I haven't slept well for years. Well, sit down, then. In a chair. Let's have a drink."

"Too much drinking strong potions in this Egypt land," observed Tabubu, remaining where she was at the pharaoh's feet. "In my home we drink milk—very good for people."

"Milk!" The king shook his head, chuckling.

"What so funny, pharaoh? A little warm milk and you go to sleep."

"Perhaps another time, Tabubu. I don't keep any milk here."

"We can get a cow," said the girl, hopefully. "Tabubu knows how to take care of cows."

"I'll order one for you to milk," the pharaoh said, smiling indulgently. "Anything else?"

"A little pair of shoes, maybe? But not Egypt ones. Shoes like those foreign land girls got what can keep feet warm."

"Very well. What else?"

"Um…a wig? Long hair very nice!"

"Yes, why not? Should I get some paper and make a list?" The ruler winked at Tabubu and was rewarded with a show of her beautiful teeth.

"You much amusing, king. But you not looking so good. No shaving, no sleeping, no eating—just sitting in the night making a bad face and watching the wall, I think. Good thing nobody making a statue from you now. People say, 'What pharaoh of Egypt is this? We not know this man!' Hah! You want look at that wall? Tabubu show you something there. Wait!"

The girl positioned a lamp on a table and, using her hands and arms in an astonishingly clever fashion, caused the shadows of the various beasts and birds of her native land to cavort before the smiling king.

After awhile, the pharaoh said, "Come here, Tabubu. You really are a very good girl. Come and sit on my knee."

The slave obediently obliged.

"Do I frighten you?" the sovereign wanted to know. "Do I really appear so ugly with my big, sticking-out nose?"

"From far away you scare Tabubu. Close by, you not too terrible."

"That's good to hear."

"Tabubu not too heavy?"

"You weigh no more than a feather. And I'm not that old!"

"You love that lady my mistress so much?"

"Yes, Tabubu. But we need speak of her no more. She didn't like me."

"Pharaoh," said Tabubu, "you know my mistress and I always talking about woman things. But she never say she don't like you."

"Is that so?" replied Thutmose doubtfully.

"Yes, that so. She say, my lady, you very good man in bed. Strong like a bull. Yes! But my sweet lady say she cannot be happy with you. You make her feeling stupid."

"Oh, Tabubu, that wasn't my intention! I didn't mean..."

"No, no," said the girl. "She don't complain on what you do—only on her lazy brother who want to be king in the harem. She say, my lady, 'That pharaoh, I looking in his eyes and see much knowledge there. Also, he talking so smart to all people. When I with him, I just feel stupid.' I say to her, 'My lady, you so beautiful! Pharaoh not worry what you know and don't know.' But she say, 'I cannot be at ease. I know he think I am stupid. I not feel beautiful with him, only dumb.'"

The air rushed from the king's chest. "Ahhh...."

"Listen to me more, king," Tabubu said. "What my lady do is very wrong. She prove she feeling dumb for some good reason. She sweet in some ways, but sometime one bite on a sweet and die from poison there. If my mistress was wife to my father and he know what she do, he kill her sure, and my father very smart man, great chief. He got many wives. You hearing this now?"

"Girl," said the sovereign, "I have taken people from their homes, their lands, and yet they give me something I surely don't deserve."

"Why you do that, king—capture so many people? You just bringing them to this place to be kind to them so they will love you?"

"Perhaps," said Thutmose. "Yes, that may be the reason. Who are you, child? Tell me about yourself and where you come from."

"Well, king, that some long story. Before I finish, you go to sleep."

"I'm very tired. Will you be offended if I do?"

"No," said the girl, "that no bad thing. I plan leave out all the scaring parts." Tabubu placed her head on the king's shoulder. "Listen, pharaoh, this my village. Houses from sticks and grass, no bricks, no stones. Much dust and very much flies. We always moving, looking for more grass. In the morning, the cows go out. Comes evening, we bring them back. Next day, same thing happen again."

"Go on. What happened on the fortunate day you were born?"

"How I know, pharaoh? Nothing special that day. Just cows go out and come back in."

"Cows coming and going," said Thutmose, "mooing and lowing. Very consistent. Very comforting."

"I worth many cows," said Tabubu. "That what my father say. Too many, maybe. That why nobody can afford to marry poor Tabubu."

"I own thousands of head of cattle," volunteered the king. "So they tell me."

"Well," said the girl, "don't believe nobody unless you counting those cattle yourself. Some people lying to king in this Egypt land, it seem to me."

"True," murmured Thutmose. "Any more advice for me?"

"Yes. Close you eyes. You not so old, but no young bull. You need rest. But listen, king, do not give up. The sister my mother, she marry some man from about one hundred. They have maybe ten children."

"So there's hope for me, eh?" said the ruler, but his eyes were shut.

"Why not? You pharaoh, the great one. And wise, too, like my father. That how I know I can love you."

"Me? You surely can't mean that."

"Yes! This girl Tabubu never feeling stupid. Oh, I wish I had some perfume ointment!"

The pharaoh opened one eye and peered at Tabubu. The girl just giggled and nestled her face into his neck.

"Perfumed ointment, eh? Well, Tabubu, tomorrow you may go to your mistress's quarters, collect all her things—and keep them."

The slave sat upright. "Oh, pharaoh—that be too much! What I do with so much things?"

"Whatever you please. It's all yours."

"What Tabubu has done to deserve such a big reward?"

"It's not a reward," was the reply. "I simply want you to be happy. Someone here ought to be happy. Let it be you."

"Ay! You making this Tabubu lose her speech! How I can do work here cover with heavy gold? How I can clean the floor and wash the dishes in beautiful dresses?"

"I don't suppose you can. So your working days are over, it seems. Just don't lose your speech. That's all I ask. I'll tell you what—you can live in your lady's apartment and keep the witches for yourself."

"What? No! I want stay here with you! I don't love you because you wise and got so much presents to give. I love you on that ship because you looking so sad. Please, king, don't send Tabubu away from you!"

"Bless you for saying that, you dear creature," said Thutmose, brushing his hand over Tabubu's braids. "But look around you. I haven't nearly so many nice things here as in that harem place. I get up early and do a lot of work, myself. No fun here for a young woman. I'll come to see you every day or as much as I can. I give you my word on that."

"Well, king's word is holy," said Tabubu, somewhat mollified.

"Absolutely. Give us a smile, then. Ah, very pretty! Tell me this, Tabubu—did your father manage to keep peace among his wives?"

"Sure!" said the girl. "Of course, he like the young ones best, but he keeping the old ones, too. He say to his women, 'No fighting! No showing you claws, hear?' So they must listen and each one do some work. No lazy ones allow there!"

"And they didn't dare to quarrel with your father?"

"Oh, yes, plenty! My father never say no fighting with him. He some fighting man and love quarrel with women."

"Really?"

"Why not? He get the last word, anyway. What can a man do for fun in a place where only cows are going out and coming in?"

"Hmm," said the pharaoh. "Well! Tabubu, do you know the meaning of the concept 'civilization'?"

"No! What that?"

"Civilization is a place where people control their passions."

"Phooey!" was Tabubu's reaction. "There no such place."

"In Egypt there is the pretense of civilization. You'd never expect me to be a civilized man, would you? Never judge me."

"What? Tabubu?"

"Just as I thought. You know, Tabubu, I think I am weary of sleeping in this chair. Perhaps I ought to lie down on my bed."

"Yes, much better," Tabubu agreed.

"Will you—could you—rest there with me?"

"You fearing ghosts, king?"

"Ghosts? One might say that—yes. More than that, I fear nothing can ever be the same here again."

"Listen, pharaoh," said Tabubu, "you have this girl now what knows how to drive spirits away. Nothing too terrible for Tabubu!"

"I feel sure of that, " said Thutmose, "and only one thing more. I feel sure that Ahmose will return."

"Who that?"

"A better man than I. Someone whose friendship I miss."

The slave got off the king's knee and held out her arms to him, helping him up. "Come, you sleep now. You snoring, pharaoh?"

On his feet and swaying slightly, Thutmose held onto Tabubu. "I...I don't know," was the chuckling response. "Nobody ever dared to tell me the truth about that, either. I might make some noises—but don't expect any hard chisels this night. Or perhaps for a long time to come."

"Oh, you some amusing man," the girl said. "Tabubu not expect one thing since she coming to this Egypt land. But now she happy and rich again—even without cows. How it happen? Must be will of some gods somewhere. Oh, yes!"

Lying in the dark, listening to the breathing of the girl sleeping beside him, the pharaoh tried to stop thinking about Satiah—to no avail. Perhaps he would never be able to drive away her face as he had last seen it, even though he now depended upon Tabubu to keep him from going mad altogether. Tabubu, it seemed, was the only person in Egypt who was perfectly at ease with him, expected him to be nothing but himself, and didn't object to whatever that might include. In his heart, Thutmose knew that even had she lived, Satiah would have felt no more alive than Neferura, his first victim. He would have destroyed the girl's life with his love for her, anyway, a love she had never asked for or wanted. Perhaps it wasn't wise or safe for him to love anyone. One never knew what damage might come of it. But love, it seemed, had a power all its own. No one could control it. Even the king of mighty Egypt was at its mercy now and always.

Chapter Eighteen

Young Prince Mehy was staying up late, as well. There were no lamps burning in his room and the boy was lying on his bed in the dark, a painful knot in his stomach making it impossible for him to sleep. He had heard his parents yelling at each other but didn't even have any curiosity as to what that was all about. Mehy wondered when he would ever be able to sleep again. Everything was changed now. All he could think about was the night he had decided he must kill Satiah and how badly he wished time could be pushed back beyond those horrible hours with him being wise enough to say to himself "I'm only a kid. It isn't my place to meddle in the problems of grownups" and to just leave everything in the hands of his matchlessly clever father.

During the inquest, Mehy had laughed at the funny things that Tabubu had said as though some sort of hysteria were building up inside him. His father had been threatening everybody with punishment, kept urging the witnesses to tell the truth, acting like he really wanted them to. Playing his usual part as the scary king of Egypt—and that had made Mehy feel very nervous. But his father had frightened no one into telling the truth for some reason. Maybe it was because the pharaoh no longer looked scary but like a sick, broken-down old man with a grubby, unshaved face and bloodshot eyes. Mehy couldn't be sure of the reason, although he certainly knew why his father hadn't punished anyone for lying. Including Nebamun, who was released and sent on his way. Even at the very end, when he had told that big falsehood about spending the night interpreting for Caleb and his mother, the pharaoh hadn't done anything about it. Well, Mehy had had enough presence of mind at the time to know he wouldn't.

Anyhow, nobody had given him away. No one claimed to have seen him, not even the amusing Tabubu, one of the most honest witnesses, as far as Mehy could tell. Well, Tabubu had been honestly funny, but why had he laughed? The thought of it shamed the prince deeply now. A young woman had died on account of his foolishness and there was nothing funny about that at all. Well, others had laughed a little, too, those who could understand Tabubu, but they had been people innocent of the murder and Mehy could not be included among them.

On that most dreadful of nights, the decision Mehy had made regarding Satiah had seemed necessary to him. Now the only comfort he was left with was that, when he became king, he would never have to be tempted to shed blood again. Anyone who deserved to die in his land would be taken care of by a court of law and punished according to its dictates—with no involvement on Mehy's part whatsoever. It would always be someone else's job to do the killing and never his own. But perhaps he was wrong even there. Probably, the pharaoh, Mehy's father, had once believed the same thing. The prince had never imagined the day would come when he felt sorry for his father. But even that had changed.

Mehy had sensed what his father's new wife had been all about the first time he had met her. Yet Mehy was not the sort to begrudge anybody anything and, if his father had seemed happy, then that was fine with him. He hadn't liked Satiah at any point, but he didn't have it in him to hate her. It had seemed to him that the king would soon grow tired of this glum, boring girl who, in her own way, had appeared just as unenthusiastic about his father as his mother was. Mehy had not even hated Satiah when he had caught her making her way to Caleb's chamber. He had done what he did out of love. Only thirteen, Mehy failed to realize just how much a man could grow to dislike himself.

Years passed, life went on—for some. Since his mother had died of the mysterious plague, after nursing the Canaanite sisters, who had been among the first to become ill, Mehy avoided the harem. However, his father began to spend more time there than he had ever done before because, no sooner had Satiah died, the king had taken up with her maid! People couldn't believe it, but that is exactly what had happened. It was whispered that the black girl was a powerful sorceress and had bewitched him, had him under a kind of spell. Some said she was just trying to get back the gold the Egyptians had taken from the southern lands by her witchcraft. If that was the case, then Tabubu was succeeding very nicely. But she hadn't been able to bewitch the pharaoh out of his grief with a snap of her fingers. Although his father tried to hide it from others, he couldn't fool Mehy, who observed the king's eyes more closely than others dared to—or even wanted to do.

Whatever the truth was about him and Tabubu, the pharaoh had evidently decided to trust women again very quickly. Unexpectedly, he conceived a desire for Marta and lost all interest in stupid women for the time being. Well, Mehy couldn't blame him for finally wanting Marta, whom he thought the most beautiful girl in the world, and even his mother appeared to believe the pharaoh had finally come to his senses. Still, she cautioned the girl not to fall in love with the unpredictable king, but the beauteous Canaanite confessed she was already jealous of Tabubu, her only rival at the time, and wished "that black one" at the bottom of the sea. Mehy, however, wasn't envious of his father for, by then, the prince felt, knew, that he was undeserving of any woman's love. He was nothing but an ugly, clumsy wretch whose voice broke when he tried to speak, one who would have stayed in his room all day if it weren't for his parents constantly summoning him into their separate lives, trying to include him. But Mehy felt part of nothing.

Once, Mehy had watched his father pick a crumb of bread

from Marta's lips, gazing into her blue eyes in somewhat the same way he used to look into Satiah's green ones. And Marta had smiled at his father, had actually put her hand on his cheek and kissed him on the lips. Instead of rebuking his wife for taking that liberty before Mehy and the servants, the pharaoh had removed Marta's hand from his face and kissed the palm of it in a humble sort of way. And he hadn't even been drunk at the time.

That situation didn't last long, of course. The newly pregnant Marta had lost her baby when she fell so sick. When she, her sisters, and Mehy's mother passed on, the king became terribly dejected all over again and even Tabubu had a difficult time with him in his constant state of worry over what was happening in his land. Word of all that had spread to the east and so the beleaguered pharaoh had to go there again to prove that he was alive and just as frightening as ever.

But Mehy's father had not given up on trying to get more children. Once the plague was done, he had even gone so far as to marry one of Satiah's sisters, Nebetto, so that his beloved old nurse, Ipu, could have her status back as the mother-in-law of a king. Nebetto had neither the beauty nor the temperament of her sister and caused no problems. Nebamun came with her, as part of the arrangement and, as far as Mehy could tell, had learned all his lessons and was getting richer by the day. No one heard a word about him mistreating anymore slaves in the palace and he practically groveled before Tabubu now that her position had far exceeded his own. For that very reason, the pharaoh's black wife evidently no longer minded having Nebamun around and behaved very haughtily toward the man whenever possible. Mehy's father, it was reported, always got a lot of enjoyment from seeing those two in the same room together and his son suspected he sometimes even arranged this on purpose. Well, his father could be odd.

The next great beauty that his father married was a girl named Meryetra, from a noble family, who took Mehy's mother's place as Chief Queen. Meryetra did not stir up any difficulties, either, except that she was always pregnant and always feeling poorly on account of it. Of course, there was Tabubu, the concubine who kept the pharaoh in a good humor and, of all his wives, appeared to Mehy to be the one who loved and cared for his father the best and knew how to manage him, no matter what. The king, who previously would have been outraged at being advised by a female, evidently found the bossy ways of Tabubu very amusing. Well, Tabubu had wisdom—that couldn't be denied—and Mehy felt sure that, while laughing, his father by no means disregarded her suggestions. Yes, the pharaoh was particularly kind to Tabubu, but he never looked at any of these other wives the way he had done at Satiah or Marta when they were alive.

During the worst hours of Mehy's whole life—the ones that had tainted all the hours of his subsequent days—he had happened to notice Satiah walk past his open door in her nightdress. However, as he knew his father's quarters were in the opposite direction, that had seemed very odd to him. After thinking about it, it had dawned on Mehy that there was someone in the residence whose very presence there may have attracted Satiah. He remembered how the young queen had pleaded on Caleb's behalf on the voyage to Thebes and how she had looked at his friend prior to retiring to the cabin at the pharaoh's order.

So Mehy made up his mind to go to where Caleb slept and see what was going on—if his hunch about Satiah's intentions was correct. If only he had minded his own business!

When the prince approached Caleb's doorway, covered by a heavy, closed drapery, he heard Caleb tell someone in Canaanite to go away and let him alone. Before Mehy had the chance to hear too much more, someone had grabbed him by the arm and pulled him away. It was Tabubu, Satiah's slave. Tabubu had said nothing to Mehy, had merely put a finger to her lips and then gently shoved him off in the same direction from which he had come. So Mehy had taken the hint and gone back to his own rooms.

Of course, he had realized that Tabubu knew exactly what her mistress was up to but, Tabubu, not knowing Canaanite, would never have been able to understand Caleb's desperate plea to Satiah. Well, judging from what Mehy had heard at the inquest, his father's wife had apparently been able to overcome Caleb's reluctance. But, at the time, he had distinctly heard the chariot fighter say "you'll kill us both" and the prince had known that was no idle remark or unlikely outcome. Therefore, Mehy had resolved that there was no way he was going to allow Satiah to bring down Caleb just because he was such a handsome fellow who appealed to the ladies—even his mother. Sure, Mehy's mother seemed to have been much taken with his friend, but the boy knew Neferura would never have done something so dangerous or vulgar as to try to get into bed with Caleb.

So Mehy saw that he had no choice but to get rid of Satiah. Even Tabubu already knew what was going on and, while the prince suspected the servant would keep silent about it, he couldn't be certain about Tabubu's discretion. He didn't even know the girl at the time! Besides, somehow Mehy's father seemed to be able to find out about everything and anything happening in his house. Satiah probably hadn't realized that, but Satiah hadn't lived with the pharaoh as long as Mehy had.

The boy concocted a plan. A little later, he stole into Levi's room and took one of his razors. He knew exactly where everything was in that room, as he had spent plenty of time in there, just hanging around. The barber, snoring peacefully, never heard a thing. Mehy knew as certainly as he knew the sun would rise in the morning that there were two people in the palace that the king would never allow to be indicted for murder. One was himself—and the other was Levi, the young man who resembled the king far more than even Mehy did. Yes, a razor was the best thing to do the job—very sharp, very quick. Levi shaved Mehy's head every couple of days or so, but the boy did not yet have any razors of his own.

359

As soon as he left the barber's chamber, he had the shock of practically colliding with Satiah, now apparently done with Caleb. They looked at one another. Mehy didn't think the girl saw the razor in his hand but he supposed there was something about him, perhaps the expression on his face, that frightened her, because Satiah started running. At any rate, it was fairly clear that she had never expected Mehy to be there or any other wakeful person. The prince, of course, hadn't chased her. That stupid he wasn't. Later on, he learned that Tabubu should have been somewhere nearby, too, and had probably seen him once again. But Tabubu didn't show herself to Mehy this time. However, it had occurred to him, once he heard her story, that he was the reason she had lost sight of her mistress. Mehy had been in the way of Tabubu's pursuit. Either that, or the slave was no longer interested in where Satiah was off to, already knowing all that was needed about the young queen's nocturnal adventures. Mehy, himself, had assumed that Satiah had merely returned to her own apartment but, in due course, discovered that had not been so.

Even though he had gone so far as to swipe Levi's razor, it was far from easy for Mehy, knowing what he had to do. The very idea of it scared him even more than that crocodile in the river had done. He had spent most of the night lying miserably on his bed. But Caleb he loved and Caleb had saved his life. If Mehy let something bad happen to Caleb on account of Satiah, then he was nothing but an ungrateful, rat-faced coward and never deserved to be king of Egypt at all. That is what the frightened and heartsick boy had told himself over and over again while he waited for the hours to pass until he was certain that everyone in the palace would be fast asleep. Mehy realized his father would probably be very upset when Satiah was dead. But his father had made his mother plenty unhappy and that didn't seem to bother the pharaoh at all—so perhaps he didn't really care all that much about women except just to have someone to fuck. Mehy sometimes used that word, himself, in those days—when he felt daring—and while Caleb didn't approve of him saying swear words, he was hardly in a position to protest too much as he was the one Mehy had learned the bad language from in the first place.

When he was merely thirteen, Mehy was convinced that his father would just go out and find himself some other stupid and pretty young woman to replace Satiah, never mind that he already had all kinds of beautiful wives. All right—his mother was getting kind of old—and the gods only knew how old she really was—and she hated his father, besides. But what in the world was wrong with those Canaanite girls? Nothing, as far as Mehy could tell. They were young and nice and certainly good-looking and didn't cause Mehy to feel uncomfortable around them like Satiah had always done. Well, his plans had included marrying the sisters someday to make up to them for his father's rude neglect. Or maybe he would marry just Marta, whom he loved, and let Caleb and Levi marry the other ones, if they felt like it. Or Caleb could have married his mother. That would have set a precedent in Egypt, but Mehy would have made it possible just to allow his mother to be happy for once in her life. Outside of all the foreign women Mehy would have to take on according to his political designs, it seemed to the boy a good idea for a man to have wives that he actually liked and who wouldn't scare him too much when he had to do "the thing" with them.

Satiah had seemed scary to Mehy in a weird kind of way and he had supposed that only the toughest kinds of men, like the pharaoh and Caleb, could summon the nerve to sleep with such an intimidating creature. Well, even Caleb hadn't really wanted to sleep with her and that certainly said a lot about Satiah and her hard, scary face that was supposed to be so beautiful. People said so all the time, but Mehy had never been able to see what was so great there.

Finally, and wearily, the boy had decided he had better get going on that fateful night. He was grateful that there was darkness all around him and, the nearer he got to his destination, the more he wished that the darkness would somehow swallow him up whole and relieve him of his horrible obligation. But, then, he noticed someone approaching and quickly ducked behind the nearest curtain. This proved to conceal the room of the Canaanite princesses. One of them sat up in bed and looked at Mehy. It was Marta.

"Mehy?" she said in a quiet way.

"Shh!" was his answer and the girl said no more but simply sat there watching him as he peeked around the edge of the hanging material to see who it was that was coming. And so his father passed by him, carrying Satiah to her apartment. Something about this sight caused the prince to feel even sicker at heart than before. That rotten girl had spent the night with two men, putting one of them in terrible danger, and now his father was holding her in his arms like she was just a dear, harmless baby! Mehy waited for the pharaoh to come back in his direction and that didn't take long. But, then, to Mehy's great alarm, his father stopped before the curtain.

For a moment, it had seemed to the boy that his father could actually smell his fear and that was why he had paused—to get a better sniff. And then something quite incredible happened. The pharaoh pushed back the cloth and stuck his head inside the room. Swiftly, Mehy had flattened himself against the wall. Marta was still sitting there and his father said to her in Canaanite, "Is anything the matter? I thought I saw someone's ugly little feet beneath the curtain and couldn't believe those belonged to some beautiful girl here."

"No, my lord," Marta had replied very steadily. "Nothing is wrong. I simply couldn't sleep."

"Something disturbing you?" Mehy's father said then.

"No, my lord," Marta repeated. "Nothing is amiss."

"Very well. Goodnight, sweetheart," said the king and pulled back his head.

Mehy stood motionless for awhile but then decided to hazard another peek to make certain his father had gone. Not seeing anyone, he glanced back at Marta, mouthed the word

"Thanks!" and eased his way out of the girls' room.

Satiah, being who she was, had actual doors leading to her chambers and one of them stood open. All was still inside and Mehy began to look for Satiah. It was strange how his eyes had become accustomed to the gloom, as though he had turned into some predator of the night, some beast. Mehy hadn't liked the thought of this and shook it off. He was just a man doing his duty, hateful though it seemed to him. When one became a man, one had to do repulsive things. That the prince had learned from Caleb, himself, who hadn't liked to elaborate on the repugnant things he had done in his own battling career, even though Mehy often did his best to wheedle the details out of him. Nevertheless, Mehy felt sure that his governor would approve of the decisive action he was taking now on his own behalf.

Satiah was lying on her back and Mehy could hear her soft breathing. He had never seen the favorite asleep before. Somehow, she didn't look the same as she usually appeared to him. Satiah had looked actually innocent, like a girl no older than Mehy, himself. With a trembling hand, the boy pushed the razor upward from his belt by its handle and, with the other hand, pulled it out, trying not to cut himself. Those stupid bracelets of his, which he had neglected to remove, made a little jingling noise, but nothing loud enough to awaken Satiah.

Then the oddest thought came to Mehy. It was as though someone had spoken the words into his ear "I am lost forever". And then the prince realized that if he did what he had come to do, he would not be able to live with himself on account of saving Caleb. He would never be able to forget the sleeping face before him. Not if he lived to be a hundred years old like King Pepi of times long past. It was his duty to kill Satiah but, somehow, the hand holding the razor couldn't move.

Standing there, frozen, Mehy felt a weight fall on his shoulder. His entire body jerked but, before he could cry out, a hand was clapped over his mouth. Turning his head as best he could, the prince stared into the eyes of his father. What an idiot he had been to think he could escape *him*, the man who had already been on his trail on account of probably sensing him to be in the room of the Canaanite girls, even seeing his feet. How the pharaoh could have managed to recognize his feet in the dark, Mehy never did figure out, no more than he was able to figure out how his father accomplished most of what he did or had done. However, it later occurred to Mehy that the king had only suspected him of wanting to try out his blossoming sexual urges with Marta and had hung around to see the outcome of that. Probably, he was just waiting merrily in the dark for Mehy to get ejected from the room and then planned on nabbing him to add to his humiliation.

Anyway, it had seemed to Mehy in that awful moment that he had never really taken a proper look at his father. Or maybe his father had just suddenly changed. His mother's eyes had always been sad. That Mehy was used to, although he hadn't liked the look of them. But when had his father's eyes ever regarded him like that, so full of sorrow? Never, ever before, as far as Mehy could recall. And yet, along with the sadness, there was a kind of understanding there, as though the father comprehended why his son, who had never harmed anyone since the day he was born, would be standing over a sleeping woman with a deadly weapon in his hand. No, the pharaoh had not seemed angry at all.

For the rest of his days, the prince felt sure that, had Satiah just remained in her slumber, he and his father would have walked away, very quietly and unobserved, and things would have remained about the same for Mehy, even though he would have had considerable explaining to do. But Mehy's father loved him and would have forgiven him in time for his rash scheme, one he hadn't had the heart to carry out, anyhow. Just a dumb kid, after all. Caleb would have been all right, too, as subsequent events had proved. But Mehy—and Satiah, of course—had never been the same again. The pharaoh and Mehy hadn't walked away. They had run away and, once out of Satiah's rooms, had ultimately gone in opposite directions. His father hadn't asked Mehy to explain anything, not then, not ever.

The pharaoh had shoved his boy ahead of him—not that Mehy needed much urging to get out of there. On his heels was his father. The instrument fell to the stone floor but, of course, nobody heard it, although it made a loud enough sound in Mehy's memory.

At the inquest, Tabubu had said that she had found a dying Satiah, begun screaming, and that Nebamun had come and then left to tell the pharaoh immediately. But Mehy knew that wasn't quite true. Satiah's brother would have had to pass by Mehy's rooms on his way to where the king lived and it had taken the man some time to do this after Tabubu had begun the uproar. In fact, when Mehy finally did see Nebamun, he was walking very slowly for a man who had just learned that his sister's throat had been slashed. Oh, well.

After things had quieted down some, the boy had gone to see his father. He *had* to see him, talk to him, just be with him. At the time, a distraught Mehy had wanted no one to comfort him but his father, who was always strong and always knew what to do. He never lacked advice and Mehy was the "jewel of his heart". Hadn't he said so many times? The boy needed, more than he had ever needed in his young life, for his father to tell him that everything was going to be all right, that nothing would change. He would see to that because he was the mighty sovereign of Egypt and could arrange anything to suit himself.

Now the prince couldn't imagine why he had expected the pharaoh to be sitting there in his quarters, calmly and unemotionally handling the situation, just as he had always done when something unusual came up. But Mehy never got past his father's doorway. The man he saw inside was nobody that he recognized. His father looked aged, shattered, and seemed to have no strength left in him at all. The pharaoh was seated, all right, with Merymaat standing over him. He held a hand to his breast and was telling the physician that he couldn't breathe, that his lungs weren't working properly, and he felt dizzy, about to faint.

Mehy was absolutely astounded that his father could even utter the word "faint" with reference to himself, but Merymaat didn't seem shocked or disgusted at the ruler's show of weakness. The physician was murmuring something encouraging and urging his father to take a drink from a cup. But, meanwhile, Mehy saw that the doctor had his eye on the king's blood-spattered shirt and seemed to be studying that. Then he said in his usual polite, professional voice, "You had best change your shirt, my lord, before Hori comes back." Hori, Mehy knew, was Merymaat's assistant.

Then his father looked down at his shirt with the little pattern of spots on it and seemed to grasp was Merymaat was telling him. Mehy, himself, didn't get it at the time, but later on he, too, realized that a man who hadn't been present at a murder would not have received such a splattering of blood on his clothing. Incredibly, the pharaoh had not changed his garment, or hadn't been aware of what was on it, and had gone with Nebamun to view Satiah's corpse like that! How many people had looked at that shirt before Merymaat mentioned it, Mehy had no idea but, in the end, nobody dared recall it, anyway. So Merymaat helped his father to take off his shirt and neither man noticed Mehy peering through the partly open door.

While the garment was coming off, other men arrived with the covered body of Satiah. They, also, paid no attention to the prince, pushed the door open farther, and carried her through, toward the pharaoh and Merymaat.

"Put her on the bed," the physician told them.

Mehy's father placed his face in his hands, his elbows resting on the table, until the men had left but, once they were gone, he began to choke and sputter like he was either going to weep or vomit. He still couldn't seem to breathe properly. Merymaat took his father's shirt of fine gauze, ripped it to pieces with a scalpel, and stuck the shreds inside his physician's chest. Then Merymaat just keep urging the pharaoh to swallow some draught he had mixed for him, with some success. That was enough for Mehy. He had the idea that his father might actually start crying, even with Merymaat there, and he certainly didn't want to see that.

The next time he came back to check on his father, it was some hours after dawn. The prince figured Merymaat, a renowned doctor, had probably been able to bring the pharaoh back to normal and he would be able to visit him now. Merymaat was no longer there but the pharaoh looked like he hadn't moved at all. True, he had on a clean garment but, in general, looked even worse in the light of day, older still. His father's face seemed leeched of color. His eyes were open but staring in a vacant sort of way, as though some magician had put him into a trance. Mehy wasn't hiding, but the king gave no sign of having recognized him or even wanting to. His father was looking at something on the table before him, it seemed, but there was nothing there but a golden goblet and a towel. The prince then realized that the pharaoh was just staring at his own reflection in the shining vessel and might keep on doing that all day if someone didn't intervene. So Mehy ran off to fetch Levi.

It was only some years later that it occurred to the prince that his father's bloody, telltale shirt had been "forgotten" and destroyed not because all people were afraid of the king but because he was a hero in the eyes of most Egyptians and they could forgive him plenty. Probably, Merymaat was one of those people. At thirteen, Mehy had not viewed his father as a heroic figure but later he came to realize that, outside of his own household, the pharaoh was considered a very great man who could do no wrong. Egypt's blazing star who had restored her grandeur and made her more glorious among the nations than she had ever been before.

Despite all the glory, the unhappiness in the royal residence had only intensified, even though the young prince had once believed it was the worst home in all of Egypt for a boy to grow up in even prior to the murder. Mehy's parents never spoke to one another again, not even in anger. Caleb had left abruptly and Mehy had a hard time getting over that, in addition to missing his mother terribly. Curiously, when his mother had passed on, the king had committed a previously unknown act. He had actually wept then, sobbed uncontrollably. Levi had witnessed it with his own eyes and, much later, related that to an incredulous Mehy. "He wept for the last of his youth, perhaps," the then barber had commented. At the time, Mehy had the idea it was also the last of his own.

Yes, there remained only Levi, who had proved his salvation, allowing him to stay sane by virtue of his companionship. Once he had even asked Levi if he thought Mehy *was* mad because it seemed to him he had a lot of crazy thoughts. The barber had been a little surprised at the question and then had offered the opinion that truly crazy folk didn't worry about being insane. They just went their merry way, thinking they were fine. Well, that description didn't fit Mehy. He knew he wasn't fine.

The heir's father had not ceased to love him—Mehy could tell that—but never treated him like a child again after the inquest where he had lied in the pharaoh's face in defense of his mother and Caleb. Never teased him, never patted him on the head as he had liked to do, none of those things, and, for a long time, Mehy missed all that more than he had ever imagined he could. The prince was never sure why this falsehood of his had made such a difference, or even how the pharaoh had known it was a lie. After all, his father hadn't spotted him until nearly dawn and had no real idea what he had been up to the rest of the night. But Mehy hadn't lied just to give himself an alibi; the pharaoh knew that, too.

Perhaps it had seemed to his father that Mehy had loved his mother and Caleb more than he loved him. But that wasn't true. It never had been. The boy hadn't understood his father but had loved him with all his being, regardless. Yet he couldn't make a liar out of his mother, who knew nothing about the murder or who had been where, in public. Could he? Surely his father understood that!

Sometimes, on the other hand, the prince thought maybe he had no longer seemed like a child to his father after that on account of having proved himself, for the first time, to be a wily, dissembling, quick-thinking individual—just like his sire. Perhaps, in his father's eyes, that had put the two of them on a more equal footing. That could be. But it really didn't matter now.

Yes, there was one secret Mehy could never divulge even to his only friend, Levi. Had he been able to do so, Mehy thought he might feel better. But it was out of the question. Mehy could not get past what he had done to his father. Unlike the king, he couldn't even *pretend* that the killing of Satiah was a matter best forgotten and never mentioned. Every single day Mehy felt the weight of it like a stone in his belly, which even time could not erode. He was even afraid to tell his father how sorry he was for what he had done for fear of reawakening the dreadful grief that the pharaoh had gradually been able to put behind him. Perhaps, if his father had found another woman he loved as much as Satiah, Mehy might have found the courage to do it when he grew up. But that hadn't happened and probably never would now.

For quite some time, Mehy had still been able to accompany his father here and there, whenever it was required of him, even after his near-fatal illness. He tolerated the public appearances, but no longer waved to the people or acknowledged them. The Egyptians, the populace, seemed as glad to see the heir as ever, especially now that he was a "beautiful man", an opinion many were not too shy to verbalize. The heir got hold of a mirror for the first time since his illness just to see for himself what the fuss was all about and was shocked at his reflection. There was no callow youth there with a marred complexion, as Mehy felt he must appear, but a somber stranger with chiseled features, lean cheeks shadowed by a shaved beard and eyes of a startling, grave beauty. The eyes of his mother, indeed, with the same melancholy expression, but those of Mehy seemed older than his years, even had little lines around them. How—when—had he come to appear so mature, even noble? How did someone like him manage to get a face that looked so different from the person behind it? If this was the man the people saw, no wonder they were so easily deceived.

So, Mehy, knowing the truth about himself, did not bask in anyone's admiration. He felt hollow, stiff, and refrained from looking directly at anyone. Mehy believed that anyone gazing into his eyes would cause that person to realize he was not what he ought to be—if only one troubled to take a really good look.

However, for the past two years, no one outside the Theban palace had seen him and Mehy knew all kinds of rumors were circulating as to why that was. It happened on the day before the months of winter on which the pharaoh usually showed himself to the common people at Thebes, the day of the petitioning. The prince made ready to go with the royal party, as usual, but, as soon as they had passed through the gates of the Residence, Mehy suddenly felt he couldn't get his breath, even though the weather was relatively mild. He began to perspire and his legs seemed unable to support his weight. The pharaoh was carried on a litter, but Mehy was walking, with Levi beside him.

Mehy couldn't take another step forward. It was as though some invisible barrier had suddenly been laid between him and the outside world. So he turned back, causing a delaying incident, with some expressing worry over his condition and Levi taking his racing pulse. Mehy's father had, at first, demanded that he get hold of himself. Then he actually pleaded with him, offering to send him on in a litter, too. But Mehy would not, could not go. The retinue left without him and only Levi stayed behind to watch over him. As soon as the king was out of sight, Mehy immediately felt better. On the following day, he and Levi attempted to go for a walk, but Mehy got no farther than he had before. After that, he stopped trying to go beyond the gates and only took the air in the courtyard. His courage had deserted him and he didn't know how to get that back, either.

Why did that girl, his father's wife, have to wake up? Why did she have to open her eyes and say "Mehy?" in much the same way that Marta had done earlier on that unforgettable night? Why did Satiah have to notice the razor in his hand and gasp out "No!" as if she knew he had come there to kill her and exactly what for? And why, oh why, did his father feel the need to protect him and his reputation to the point where he seized that razor from his hand and did what Mehy couldn't bring himself to do to a woman he loved so much? It was only after Satiah's death that the prince came to understand that his father had actually loved her, mourned her, and hadn't considered her so easily replaceable, after all. But his father had made the choice against her. Why? Was he, Mehy, the impetuous, foolhardy brat, worth a murder? Mehy certainly didn't think so. Especially not anymore.

At that same time he had lost the ability to face the world beyond the gates, Mehy began to think about death a great deal, more than ever. It began to become clear to him that death and his father could never be separated in his thoughts. Just what was the tally of human lives that could be laid at his father's feet? By now the number was probably incalculable, although the sovereign never gave the least sign that he considered himself a murderer, had anything so terrible to answer for. Not since the night of the killing of Satiah had he ever appeared contrite again. Slaughtering people, if not exactly by his own hand, was perhaps something his father considered a part of his kingship, even his duty to which he had accustomed himself.

What had made the pharaoh, who, as a boy, had waited for the thing that killed become the thing that killed in one way or another? What had happened to that boy who had written the tale that betrayed his own fear of death to harden his heart against the same fear in others? That was something Mehy certainly couldn't comprehend—nor why he still loved his father so much in spite of it all. Perhaps it was that doomed young prince that he really loved, the one who surfaced from time to time to do unexpected kindness, show some mercy, just to prove that he hadn't lost himself completely.

It was Mehy who couldn't accustom himself to killing and wondered why that was. Since his father was so greatly admired, considered the supreme monarch among all who had ever ruled Egypt before, the fault must surely lie within himself. Mehy, knowing he could never equal his sire in anything, fervently hoped never to become king. Now that he had brothers, he wouldn't have to, could be passed by. However, for some strange reason, his father still wanted him to succeed, spoke of it as a certainty, and that was the most perplexing factor in all of it. Why?

Sometimes, Mehy dreamt about Satiah. The dreams were always more or less the same. She came into his chamber, white and luminous as the moon, looking quite perfect, her neck being just as it was before she was killed. There was nothing frightening about Satiah any longer. She sat at the foot of Mehy's bed and smiled at him like they knew each other very well and were good friends. Satiah didn't want to sleep with him, nor Mehy with her. Although he could never remember any of the things they talked about, Satiah was always cheerful and gay in Mehy's dreams, chatting with him in a lively way that she had never been seen to do with the pharaoh, insofar as Mehy could recall. They were just two young people, Satiah and Mehy, who had that much in common and could enjoy each other's company, without one being critical of the lack of wisdom in the other.

Then his father would come into the room, looking angry, as though he suspected something improper was happening between Satiah and his son. Mehy's father held a razor in his hand and advanced upon his wife, but Mehy sprang up and stood between Satiah and his father. In his dreams, the prince was muscular and powerful and the pharaoh old and weakened. His father shrank from his menacing form and didn't even try to fight back much when Mehy wrested the weapon from his hand. Regardless, the razor cut Mehy and he began to bleed. But he didn't mind being wounded, thought nothing of it. It was the least he could do for a defenseless girl as a man of honor. When he threw the weapon to the floor, it made the clanging noise that always woke Mehy up.

When he gained consciousness, Mehy believed, for a moment, that he had saved the life of Satiah and that she would still be sitting there, looking at him gratefully, thankful that he had vanquished the enemy of youth.

But, of course, there was never anyone on the bed except Mehy, weak and impotent in every way, gasping for air. The same thought always came to him then. How could he do that in front of a boy—his own boy? At thirteen, Mehy had believed he was a man but, from the perspective of his present age, he knew he had been nothing but a child. Like the sound of rodents scratching in the dark, Mehy couldn't ignore his thoughts. Did his father really know how to love anyone in a proper sense, even him? Was it possible that it was his father who had ruined his life instead of the other way around?

Mehy refused to entertain such ideas for very long, deliberately banishing them by thinking about something else, anything. He was twenty-one years old, a grown man without doubt, but he was no more willing to believe, now, that his father didn't love him in a perfect and holy way than he could when he was thirteen. Yes, the pharaoh loved Mehy even more than he loved his country and was determined to put him on the throne even though surely recognizing his grievous shortcomings. Was it possible that his father saw something in him that justified his hopes for his son as his successor? If so—what was it he saw? Mehy couldn't imagine—and concluded his brilliant father was a fool only when it came to himself these days. Just as he had once been a fool when it came to Satiah. That was the greatest pity of all—that his father had never taken the trouble to understand that poor, beautiful, unhappy girl.

The prince, who once had planned to marry hundreds of women, couldn't now envision himself keeping anyone captive against her will. Not for peace or for love. Women were human beings, not possessions. They were important—so much so that one of them could change a man's life forever, even destroy him. It had taken a murder for Mehy to realize that once and for all.

In the final analysis, it seemed to Mehy that there was one

person against whom the pharaoh had never erred and that was his barber, Levi. Hadn't he set Levi free and insisted on his friend pursuing a vocation better suited to his capabilities, even if it meant losing one he enjoyed having close to him every day? In fact, Levi's future seemed so important to his father that everyone marveled that he took such pains to make certain the young man was set on the right path for a good and worthy life. Well, Levi deserved nothing less, in Mehy's own estimation. He was glad that Levi, who had never known a father, never had anything good as a boy, found a man who could love him in a blameless way so that he had nothing to doubt about him in the restless and lonely hours of the night.

Then, one day, for some reason, Mehy took it into his head to find his copy of "The Doomed Prince", that tale his father had started so many years ago. Having dug it out of a chest, the prince read what there was of it. He turned over the papyrus scroll and anchored its corners to the table with four heavy objects. Getting his palette of cakes of ink and reed pens and some water, Mehy began to write. He was surprised at how easily it went. Once one knew the beginning of a story, became familiar with the characters, one could make them do anything one liked. At least on paper, one had the choice to please oneself, make things come out right. Mehy had no idea how long he sat there, forming the cursive characters, but he was done before the light began to fade. In the end, the doomed prince lived happily ever after as a gentle ruler and a son was born to him for whom only good things were prophesied by the Fates.

Somehow, Mehy felt better, his heart lighter, even though his right hand was cramped. The true magical power of words, the young man decided, was that they had a life of their own, a different kind of reality. Perhaps tomorrow he would attempt yet another tale completely his own. Mehy found himself looking forward to it, thinking he might get up early to make a start.

The prince took sand from a little pot and sprinkled a light film of it over the rows of ink. A servant came in with a pan of embers and lit Mehy's lamps for him. Mehy had not slept without lights for a long time. After the man had gone, the heir carefully picked up the scroll and brought it to the window. Mehy blew the sand away with his breath. Specks of it, or perhaps flakes of old papyrus, seemed to him to float out into the dark blue, enchanted twilight of the land of Egypt.

EPILOGUE

King Thutmose III sat on the throne for several more decades. His rule lasted 54 years in all, including the time when Hatshepsut had overshadowed him. His wives bore him numerous other children. The pharaoh did not cease his successful military endeavors until after the 42nd year of his reign, when he apparently felt content enough to call a halt. The eldest son, Amunemhat, did not manage to succeed his father. No one knows exactly what became of him or of Queen Neferura and the Canaanite wives.

Satiah, it is clear, predeceased her royal husband and is shown following behind his figure in his tomb, along with other spouses and a daughter, some of them marked "dead". But Neferura is nowhere to be seen there, nor is a tomb for her certainly known, and this last can be said of Satiah, also. The burial of the Canaanite wives was found in 1916 at Thebes. All three were interred together, surrounded by splendid jewelry, headdresses, and funerary articles. The discoverer, Herbert Winlock, wrote *"Such a burial could well have followed [the ladies'] simultaneous deaths from an epidemic. Or,...they may have all been the victims of an execution for some palace conspiracy."* Given the richness of their accoutrements, the epidemic is the more likely explanation, as these women would not have had the same immunity to the various "plagues of Egypt" that the Egyptians, themselves, had acquired over time.

Si-Bast, the old barber, his niece, and his Canaanite slave, Amun-eywy, were actual living persons, attested in that safe conduct document.

The prince who succeeded Thutmose III was Amunhotep II. This son had inherited the fierce blood of his forebears but not the intellectual leanings of his father. However, Amunhotep took up the same bellicose career and brought thousands more captives back to Egypt. He became the most dreaded man in the sphere of the ancient Near East in his own time.

www.ingramcontent.com/pod-product-compliance
Lightning Source LLC
Chambersburg PA
CBHW020819180626
46814CB00001B/25